PRAISE FOR JUDGES

"Each story is quickly devoured, packed with twists and brutal political analogy... it's the rise of fascism, eerily familiar and terrifyingly plausible. This is the Justice Department as *The Wire*, and it really works."

Starburst Magazine

"There were times I had to put this books down to process what had happened and what I thought about it. It's fast-paced and uncompromising, keeping true to the essence of the Judges."

British Fantasy Society

"Some of the stories gave me the shivers; how quickly freedom can be lost is a scary thought."

Adventures With Peps

"A compelling must-read, layered with some complex morality, multiple mirrors to our own very troubled times and a nicely diverse cast of characters. I look forward to more in the series."

Down the Tubes

"Brilliantly written, moving at breakneck speed. You'll definitely want to continue your journey into the beginnings of the Judges, even if we may well be heading in that general direction in the real world."

Mid-Life Gamer Geek

"A real rollercoaster... Excitingly ambitious."

Nerds of a Feather

"By the end of the book I was left wanting more: more of this world, more of the political and social changes surrounding the Judge system, more of what was going on outside of this one little town."

Set the Tape

"This is mature storytelling, both in terms of narrative structure and themes, and pulls out twists that are both shockingly brutal and grin-inducingly effective."

Pop Culture Bandit

"A story that gets a lot done. Strong characterisations, and a gradual reveal of the history of Dredd's world."

James Green

JUDGES

A Rebellion™ publication
www.rebellionpublishing.com

First published in 2021 by Rebellion™,
This edition published 2022,
Rebellion Publishing Limited, Riverside House,
Osney Mead, Oxford, OX2 0ES, UK.

10 9 8 7 6 5 4 3 2 1

Creative Director and CEO: Jason Kingsley
Chief Technical Officer: Chris Kingsley
Head of Publishing: Beth Lewis
Editors: David Thomas Moore, Michael Rowley,
Jim Killen and Amy Borsuk
Series Editor: Michael Carroll
Marketing and PR: Jess Gofton
Social Media: Rosie Peat
Design: Sam Gretton, Oz Osborne and Gemma Sheldrake
Cover: Neil Roberts

Based on characters created by John Wagner and Carlos Ezquerra.

ISBN: 978-1-78108-927-9

Printed in Denmark

JUDGES

VOLUME THREE

MICHAEL CARROLL • C. E. MURPHY • ZINA HUTTON

EDITED BY MICHAEL CARROLL

REBELLION

Dedicated with love
to the memory of

Dave Evans,
AKA Bolt-01,

(because a dedication is easier and
cheaper than building the 500-metre tall
solid gold statue that he deserves).

INTRODUCTION

NOW, I'VE NEVER harboured a desire for power (as far as you know), but if I *did* have the inclination to become a dictator—I mean, a Glorious Benevolent Leader—I know how I'd do it. First, I'd create the concept of the herd and repeatedly tell all the people how lucky they are to be part of that herd. The best herd in the *world*, in fact. No other herd even comes close. Then I'd start pointing to the people I've decided are outside the herd and make a big deal about how they want to take what we have. They're jealous, you see. And dangerous, for they are *savages!* How do we know they're savages? Well, if they weren't, they'd be part of our herd already, right? And those savages are willing to butcher every one of us if we're not on our guard. If we drop our defences for just one minute, we are *toast.* And I don't mean enticingly crisp toast fresh out of the toaster: it'll be cold, limp toast that's just landed butter-side down on top of the dog's fluffy blanket.

And that's it, the formula for seizing power: Make people scared, then offer them protection in exchange for their unquestioning loyalty. It works equally well for nations, businesses, sports teams, and religions.

There are those who will resist, but it's easy enough to silence the Voice of the Resistance if you're the one in charge of the radio. Or if you can persuade everyone else that those who resist are lying or crazy. And the best way to do *that* is to seed the population with plenty of other loud, crazy people peddling their conspiracy theories and 'fake news'; it's not easy to tell the wheat from the chaff if you've never been given the chance to learn what chaff is or what it looks like.

That's a situation that should be familiar to readers of the legendary *Judge Dredd* strip that's been running in the British comic *2000 AD* for the past forty-five years. In the strip, the Judges are hard-line, highly-trained, brutally efficient police officers with the power to dispense instant justice. They're answerable to no one: if a Judge concludes that you're guilty, they'll sentence you on the spot. You don't get a lawyer to fight your case, there's no appeals process, no leniency, no parole.

It's a drastic solution to the problem of rampant crime, and the casual reader might be forgiven for thinking that the world of Judge Dredd, set more than a century ahead of the present day, is pretty far removed from our own.

The thing is, chums, dictatorships almost never spring up overnight. They're cultivated over time, nurtured on a balanced diet of hate and lies and fear. Sometimes the new rulers are wolves in sheep-mode holosuits, sneaking their way into power, but just as often they're motivated by some of those good intentions that will later be repurposed as flagstones on the highway to Hell.

The Judges believe that they are a force for good, but then, they're the ones defining what 'good' means. Power corrupts... and the Judges have so *much* power.

But how do we get to Dredd's world from the present day? That's where the *Judges* series comes in (and—cheeky plug—its companion comic-book series *Dreadnoughts*). Taking the classic Dredd saga *Origins* as its seed, the first *Judges* omnibus is set in the 2030s where the United States has been collapsing under the weight of crime, corruption, incompetence and a legal system choking on red tape. A drastic solution is required, and that comes in the form of the Judges.

They present themselves as the answer to the nation's problems, but the truth is that at best the Judges are a band-aid slapped over an open wound... and most of the citizens can't see that because, they're constantly being told by the Judges that the Judges are doing a great job.

The second *Judges* omnibus takes us a decade further on, to the 2040s. As the new Department of Justice continues to wheedle power away from the police and the lawyers—and the elected officials—the USA slips further away from democracy.

By the 2050s—this volume—the Judges are entrenched. Most of the citizens, especially the juveniles, don't remember what it was like to *not* have Judges. They've grown up knowing that at any moment they could be arrested, convicted and sentenced for even a minor crime, perhaps one they didn't realise they were committing.

In *Necessary Evil*, the Justice Department in Philadelphia is stretched to the limit when a riot breaks out at the country's first city-block on the same day that Chief Judge Fargo is killed.

C. E. Murphy's *What Measure Ye Mete* is the tale of NYPD officer Cera Cortez who now finds herself playing second fiddle to the Judges. When a seemingly random murder hints at a far-reaching conspiracy, Cortez comes to realise that the Judges' image of strength and solidarity might be nothing more than a paper-thin veneer.

Amara, the youthful protagonist of *(In)Famous* by Zina Hutton, believes she has found her own way out of the rat-race, a chance to rise above the mundane and forge her own path through a rotten, unfair system—but it's a path that will pass through some very dangerous territory, and a journey from which she might never return.

My hearty, voluminous thanks to the magnificent C. E. Murphy and Zina Hutton for their massively entertaining and insightful volumes: I strongly urge you to check out their other books! Thanks also to the series' senior editor David Thomas Moore (our Glorious Benevolent Leader!) and his awesome crew at Rebellion, and of course to Judge Dredd's beloved creators John Wagner and Carlos Ezquerra.

Now read on, folks! Here, in these three adventures, we see the Department of Justice from the point of view of the citizens... and as some of them learn—the hard way—that there's a very important question that those in power really don't want the ordinary people to be asking:

"Who will save us from our saviours?"

Michael Carroll
Dublin
October 2021

NECESSARY EVIL

MICHAEL CARROLL

To James Bacon,
First High King of Earth (pending)

PROLOGUE

North Lincoln, Chicago
Monday, December 22, 2025
12:02

FRANCESCO DEACON WATCHED silently as Marisa Pellegrino glided around the busy diner's patrons so smoothly that few of them even noticed she was there. As she approached the corner booth, she shrugged off her jacket, folded it in half and dropped it onto the seat next to Deacon, then sat down opposite him.

She unleashed her full, broad smile at him as she placed her cell phone, keys and wallet on the table. "I'll save time by doing both sides of the conversation. 'You're late, Marisa.' 'Only a couple minutes, Deac.' 'Late is *late*.' 'You said noon, so *I* got here *before* noon. You've kept me waiting.' And so on."

He returned her smile with a scowl. "Marisa, I don't—"

"You don't like it when people put words in your mouth. I *know* that, Deac. It's not my job to make you feel comfortable."

"And what *is* your job, exactly?" He pulled a napkin from the dispenser and wiped the table before resting his arms on it, a habit he'd picked up from his earliest days as a recruit in busy Army mess halls.

Without looking up from the diner's plastic-coated menu, Pellegrino said, "You know him as well as I do. Eustace is single-minded, and that's going to drive him to the top. But that same single-mindedness means that he often can't see outside his narrow path. That's why he needs me: to steer him in the right direction."

Deacon grinned at that. "You're Jiminy Cricket."

She looked up, and nodded. "If that's what it takes. Eustace Fargo is going to change the world, and he'll need people like you and me to protect, guide and occasionally advise him."

"I don't see how I can help. If he wants security, he should look to the FBI or the Marshals. A military police officer is not what he needs. I don't have the background."

She paused for a moment, her lips pursed. "The plans have changed, Deac. We've been talking about it for the past few weeks, come to some conclusions. And decisions... You heard about Glenn Tade Cogan?"

"No. *I've* spent the past few weeks sequestered."

"Right. On a case you're never going to tell me about... okay. Last month, about eighteen blocks west of here, Cogan attempted to rob a liquor store. The owner—Cotton Sutherland—shot him in the head. The locals are hailing Sutherland as a hero."

Deacon nodded. "Go on..."

"Cogan needed cash to pay his rent. Now he's dead. Four police units and a team of paramedics were dispatched. The officers were on site for almost two hours. No charges have been brought against Sutherland. Estimated cost of the investigation so far is one hundred eighty-seven thousand dollars, not counting the twelve-thousand-dollar call-out fee for the paramedics, which the local precinct is disputing because *they* didn't call them."

Deacon began, "Well, if the owner felt that his life was in danger, then—"

"No. Wrong line of thought."

"Hundred and eighty-seven grand would cover Cogan's rent

for a *long* time. Is that where we're going with this?"

"In a way, yeah," Pellegrino said, nodding. She picked up the menu again and gave it a brisk wave to attract the attention of a passing hostess. "Two decafs, no sweetener."

Around her mouthful of gum, the diner's hostess asked, "You want a little somethin' in that to keep out the cold, hun?"

"No, we do *not*," Deacon said. "And if you're attempting to sell alcohol on an unlicensed premises, you've just lost your job."

The hostess sagged, "Aw hell. Cops. That ain't fair—you're s'posta *say* if you're cops!"

"Just get the coffee, please. And tell the rest of your staff to expect an inspection in the next couple of days."

"Thanks," Pellegrino called to the hostess's retreating back. "*That's* what I'm talking about, Deac. She *knows* it's illegal to serve alcohol without a licence. People don't care about breaking the law because everyone else is doing it. Glenn Cogan is dead because he couldn't pay his rent. He couldn't pay his rent because he couldn't get a job. He couldn't get a job because he lived in a slum, and no one wants to employ someone who lives in the sort of place where even the roaches file grievances against the landlord."

"So you and Eustace Fargo are going to fix all that..." Deacon shrugged. "I applaud the sentiment, Marisa, but it's going to cost billions to successfully run for office, and it'll take years. And then what? Eustace finally gets the big chair and has to spend the next four years struggling to keep it, with his enemies fighting every single decision, analysts second-guessing every word, every gesture... And even with all that... Jesus, do I have to spell it out?"

"You do. Say it."

"Eustace Fargo is *cold.*"

Pellegrino sighed. "Cold."

"Don't deny it. Ephram? Sure, he's approachable. Empathic, almost. But his brother keeps his emotions so tightly under control that people don't see him as one of them. Analytically, he's a genius. But can you see him in charge? God knows he'd do a damn better job than anyone else I can think of, but he'll never *get* there if the people can't relate to him."

"Cotton Sutherland had his gun behind the counter, and as soon as he saw what Glenn Cogan was doing, he opened fire. A thirty-eight, at a little under four metres." She put her closed fist next to her temple and abruptly flared her fingers. "Boom!"

Deacon nodded slowly. Another apparent shift in the conversation's topic, but he'd known Marisa Pellegrino for several years—ever since that course they took in Applied Ethics where everyone had clustered around the star pupil Eustace Fargo—and he was used to her way of approaching a point from more than one angle at a time. He could see that she was upset, a little defensive, but also excited and anxious to sort out the problem and then go beyond it. He'd seen this on the battlefield, with soldiers under fire. And with perps, too, when they sensed a gap in the net closing around them.

Marisa accepted her cup of coffee from the hostess, and waited silently until the woman was gone. "Sutherland's being hailed a hero for shooting a man in the head. But one of the local cops knew Cogan. Said he wasn't the sort of guy to rob a liquor store. He was desperate, that was all."

Deacon's heart raced. He knew exactly where this was going now. "Damn. He wasn't robbing the store. He was robbing *from* the store."

With her elbows on the table and her cup close to her lips, Pellegrino gently nodded. "Shoplifting, not a hold-up. Tried to snatch a crate of vodka. Sixteen bottles, would have sold them for maybe twenty bucks each on the street."

"He was unarmed," Deacon said. It wasn't a question.

"Crime of opportunity. The liquor store's door was open, Sutherland was distracted. No one's life was in any danger, but now Sutherland's being praised as a hero, and most of the community are backing him up because there's not one of them who hasn't been mugged or burgled or worse. You know what *that* is, right?"

"Retribution by proxy. They couldn't punish the person who hurt them, so they take comfort that *someone* has been punished."

"There's been a few people calling for Sutherland to stand for mayor. And if he were to do that, there's a chance he could win. A small one, but it's there. Politics is the game of popularity."

And then Deacon caught her glancing at her cell phone. It was face down on the table. *She's recording this. No, it's on a call. To Fargo.*

He reached out, picked up the phone and flipped it over. Pellegrino watched him do it without reacting.

Deacon said, "You're not going to make a run at the presidency, are you, Eustace?"

Fargo's voice said, "No, Francesco. I'm not going to devote my life to becoming yet another figurehead. This country's problems can't be fixed by photo opportunities and pithy slogans. This is going to be something different. Something *new*. I'm not talking about politics. I'm talking about *power*. I intend to create an elite police force. Hand-picked. Highly trained, highly educated. And *very* carefully vetted. They will be the best of the best. They'll know the law inside-out and have the abilities, the power and the backup to dispense instant justice. They will be absolutely unassailable and unimpeachable."

Deacon stared down at the cell phone long enough for Pellegrino to say, "Well?"

He hesitated. "Eustace, that's... that's potentially the most dangerous thing I can think of. The odds of success are tiny, but the potential for corruption is *immense*." He looked up at Marisa. "This won't work. You know that."

"We'll *make* it work," Fargo said. "This country is dying, but for decades we've been going to the store for candy so we can feel better. We should have been going to the pharmacy for medicine."

"Riiiight," Deacon said. "Eustace, from now on, you're

not allowed to do metaphors. Leave the speech-writing to Marisa."

"The point stands. I'm due back in court... Marisa, give him the details. Explain to him how it'll work. And Francesco... You think I'm *cold?*"

Deacon knew better than to try to gloss over the comment. "Yep."

"I guess that's fair."

The call ended, and Deacon said, "I *do* get what you're both proposing. But I'm not sure I agree. How would you even begin to choose these new super-cops?"

"We're not going to choose them. We're going to *make* them." Pellegrino reached out and placed her hand on his wrist. "You're the model, Francesco. The paradigm. When was the last time you broke the law?"

Deacon's gut tensed at that. "I've never broken the law."

"Exactly. I've been looking at your records from elementary school right up to your CO's most recent evaluations. You've rarely been top of your class in *anything*, so a casual observer might conclude that you've got average skills... but the truth is that as an all-rounder you're unsurpassed. You're good at *everything*."

He shrugged. "I put the work in."

"And now you're halfway to a doctorate in criminal psychology. You've put any potential personal life on hold in the pursuit of justice. That's what it's going to take to put this country back on course. People like you, and Eustace Fargo. You're very different, but one thing you do have in common is that you both understand that law and justice are not the same thing. There's a chasm between them, and you both want that chasm narrowed, if not entirely closed. When I told you about Glenn Tade Cogan's death, your instinct was to judge the store owner."

"Death should never be a penalty for a non-violent crime. Especially not when that penalty is dispensed by untrained hands."

"Which is why *you're* going to help train them."

"You and Fargo want *me* to train your super-cops?"

She smiled. "We do. But don't think of them as police officers with the power to pass judgement. Think of them as judges with body armour and guns."

CHAPTER ONE

Hall of Justice, Boston
Sunday, March 26, 2051
11:02

EIGHT DAYS AGO Judge Francesco Deacon had proposed the idea that every Judge—even the most senior—should ride a patrol in the slums at least once every six months.

Deacon was by far the most experienced Judge on the street. Of the first group hand-picked by Eustace Fargo to become Judges, he was the sole survivor. He *knew* the job, he'd trained the rest of that first group and many others since, and everyone understood that. His word carried weight.

If we lose touch with the people we're assigned to protect, it becomes that much harder for us to be objective, he wrote, *and much easier to forget that they are* people. *Our first duty is to them. The Law should serve the citizens, not the other way around. Yes, we need administrators and tutors: they're a vital part of the Department and no one is denying that, but first and foremost we are* Judges, *and Justice begins out there on the* streets, *not at the keyboards of those of us who are so far removed from the job that they haven't made an actual arrest in years.*

Now, as Deacon sat in his windowless office and paged

through the excuses filling his e-mail inbox, he suppressed a sigh. "All right. You *told* me so."

Standing with her back to the door, arms folded, head tilted to the side at a slight angle, Marisa Pellegrino gave him her customary sly smile. "We asked four hundred and eighteen senior Judges whether they believed they were too important to work directly with the lowly citizens... for ten points, how many said yes?"

Deacon cleared the laptop screen with a flick of his wrist, then stood up and reached for his gloves. "One of the marks of a decent human being is the ability to resist being a bad winner. Gloating doesn't suit you, Marisa."

She smiled again. "Please. *Everything* suits me. I'm drokkin' *adorable.*" She nodded towards the laptop. "How many are on board with the idea?"

Deacon clenched his fists a couple of times. The gloves were new, and he was still breaking them in. "A lot fewer than I'd like."

"Tell me. No, wait, I'll tell *you.*" Pellegrino focussed on the wall for a moment, eyes half-closed. "Six. Everyone else thinks it's a great idea for *other* Judges, but they're too busy themselves." She stepped aside as Deacon slid open the door.

He didn't look back as he said, "Almost correct. Eight. Roberts, Shannon, Santana, Lloyd, Desjardins, Kurzweil, Smith and Morrone."

"*Which* Smith? Can't be the one from Acquisitions because *he* hasn't seen daylight in a decade."

A line of thirty cadets walked past as Deacon and Pellegrino stepped out into the corridor, and Deacon caught himself automatically judging their posture and attitude. To Pellegrino, he said, "Brent Smith from the South Atlanta office. I don't know him personally."

"I've met him. He's a good Judge, but he should never have been promoted." She gave Deacon a sidelong smile. "*Some* Judges would be much better off riding a Lawranger than an office chair."

"I know."

"That was a subtle dig at *you*, Deac."

"I know that, too."

They watched the cadets until they turned a corner, then Pellegrino gestured back the way the cadets had come. "We shall walk in silence towards the canteen, each wrapped in our own thoughts."

Deacon responded with a smile of his own. She'd been right, of course. She almost always was. He'd hoped that more than just a handful of senior Judges would agree. Most had just ignored his emails, but some had gone out of their way to shoot down the idea. Joint Deputy Chief Judge Hollins Solomon had told him, "You don't get the farmer to pull the milk cart when the horses are idle."

Not for the first time, he considered going directly to the Chief Judge, but that was a privilege that he didn't want to abuse, or squander. Reminding the Judges that they exist to serve the people was important, but there could come a time when he'd need Fargo for something crucial.

As they waited in line in the canteen, Marisa Pellegrino asked, "How old are you now, Francesco?"

"You're the one who's memorised everyone's files. You *know* how old I am."

"I know you're starting to think that it's time to hang up the badge." She grabbed a pair of trays and handed one back to Deacon.

"Marisa, it's bad enough that you keep guessing my passwords so you can sneak a look at my personal journal, but I wish you'd stop rubbing salt into the wounds by correcting my spelling."

"*And* your grammar."

"That too. You're too smart for your own good. And for everyone *else's*. How come Judge Stone's department has never had you checked out?"

"Who says they haven't? Maybe they—" She flinched.

The Judge standing behind Deacon said, "That was a *gunshot!* Anyone else hear that?"

Marisa Pellegrino was already moving, pushing past Deacon before her tray even hit the floor.

Deacon raced after her, out into the corridor, where a dozen more Judges were emerging from the side rooms, shock and confusion on their faces.

CHAPTER TWO

Broadway East, Baltimore
11:28

ON A QUIET, tree-lined street—ancient patchwork road surface, weeds flourishing in the gutter, houses with more boards than glass in the windows—Judge Errol Quon slowed her Lawranger to a stop. The rookie pulled up alongside her, and they both watched the uniformed police officer cheerfully stride towards them.

"Everything's good here, Judge. All under control."

Officer Fischel looked to be a good ten years older than Quon. Male, white, in good shape, very tall. He had a broad smile that would probably have fooled most people and might even have fooled Quon had he not deliberately positioned himself to block her line of sight.

She climbed off the motorbike and peered past him. On the far side of the street, two other officers held a woman on the ground, face down, one with his knee on her back, the other currently patting her down.

"Seriously, there's nothing for you to do here. Perp was resisting, we're taking her in. Could be she's not our suspect, but we've gotta follow *procedure*, right? The innocent don't resist."

Quon glared at Fischel for a moment. "Where the hell did *you* grow up?" She began to move towards the other officers, but Fischel stepped into her path.

"This is not your concern, Judge."

Quon said, "Judge Kimber, care to weigh in?"

Judge Adam Kimber, twenty years old and two days out of the Academy, calmly said, "Officer Fischel, you're interfering with a Judge's investigation. Step aside. There will be no further warnings."

"*What* investigation? You were riding along and you saw us! That's not an investigation, that's just luck!"

Quon started to move to Fischel's left, and he put out his arm to stop her.

She immediately grabbed his arm and took a step backwards, twisting away from him and pulling him off-balance. As he shifted his weight to compensate, Quon slammed at his left knee with a side kick.

Fischel shrieked as he dropped, an odd sound coming from a man so big, and Quon pushed him aside as she continued towards his colleagues.

From behind her, Kimber called, "Uh, Judge Quon, should I...?"

Still with her eyes on Fischel's nervous-looking colleagues, Quon said, "Just hold him for now." She paused for a second. "But not in the middle of the street, obviously."

One of the other officers—a woman with a stocky build who looked to be in her early thirties—got to her feet as Quon approached. "There was no need to do that, Judge."

Quon looked down at the suspect on the ground. Female, African American, slender build, dreadlocks, wire-framed glasses; wearing faded red jeans and a colourful, loose-fitting, hooded sweatshirt.

"Judge, this is an ordinary arrest. We're just doing our jobs. We've been on the lookout for a suspect matching this woman's description."

The other officer—male, forty, average build—said, "And

now she's refusin' to talk until she gets her lawyer. That's all there is to it. We're takin' her in."

Quon went down on one knee close beside the woman, who was glaring up at her. "You guilty?"

The woman didn't respond, just continued to stare.

In a calm voice, as she reached out and carefully straightened the laces on the woman's sweatshirt, Quon asked, "Got a *name* at least?"

Still nothing.

Behind Quon, the female officer said, "Judge, I, uh, hate to recite you the regs, but procedure is you are *not* supposed to get in the way of the local law-enforcement officers without reasonable grounds."

"I know." She leant closer, peering at the woman's eyes. "This woman's not a user. She's healthy, well-groomed. Skin's just about perfect, I'd say, and her eyes are clear. There's *anger* there, though. That's a look we only see on someone who *really* doesn't like cops. What's the charge?"

The female officer said, "ARV, habitual. Over in Westmall. She jumps people as they're approaching an ATM, forces them at gunpoint to take the max out of their account. Leaves them bleeding on the ground, usually from a head wound. Stabbed one guy, though. At least eight attacks, always the same MO. Perp here matches the description, and we spotted her running."

Quon was still looking down at the woman on the ground, and hesitated for a moment. "Officer...?"

"Vick. Belinda Vick. And this is Forrester."

"Officer Vick, if the description of the perp was 'black woman, colourful clothes,' then you and your colleagues here will have some explaining to do."

The male officer, Forrester, said, "We approached her *calmly*, Judge. She ran. If she was innocent, then she—"

"You and Officer Vick have different stories. She just told me that she spotted this woman running. If I examine your bodycam footage, what am I going to see?"

Vick said, "What I meant was she ran when *she* spotted *us*."

"Is that so?" Quon pulled a handcuff key from her belt-pouch and unlocked the woman's cuffs. "Judge Kimber, call for a wagon. Code nine-zero-four."

As Quon was helping the woman to her feet, Officer Fischel—now standing at the side of the street and nursing his wounded leg—called out, "You can't just release her! This is a legitimate arrest!"

"Judge, Fischel's right," Vick said. "We have to follow procedure, same as you do. She is a suspect, and we have to take her in. Anything else would be dereliction of duty."

Still holding onto the suspect's arm, Quon asked her, "Are you a forty-seven-year-old named Elandra Theodora Barros who's already spent a total of eighteen years in prison?"

For the first time, the suspect spoke. "*What?* Hell no! My name's Salmon Davidtz, and I'm only twenty-five!"

Quon smiled. "Salmon? Nice name. You're free to go, Ms. Davidtz, and of course it's your right to file a complaint against these officers. Judge Kimber, what would she accuse them of?"

"Abuse of power, racial profiling and excessive force."

"Correct."

"There's no point!" Davidtz pulled her arm free of Quon's grip. "I make an official accusation, I'll either end up on a slab, or have my life torn apart by the IRS or the DEA. That's how power *stays* in power. You got each other's backs. Always put yourselves *above* the people you're supposed to be protecting!" She stepped back, still glaring at Quon. "You Dreadnoughts always talk about justice as though it actually *exists*." She turned and briskly walked away.

As they watched her go, Quon said, "Elandra Theodora Barros was arrested late last night, caught in the act of committing another ATM robbery."

Vick looked away, swearing under her breath, and Fischel said, "Well, no one told *us!* That shoulda been on the morning briefing!"

"It *was*," Judge Kimber said. "Item eight. Westmall ATM

robberies. Suspect was apprehended in the act, full confession, case closed."

Vick said, "Oh, come on! You know how long those briefings are. Sometimes we have to pull double shifts, and it can be hard to focus."

"That's no excuse for negligence and incompetence," Quon said. "You attacked a civilian without cause. That's unprovoked assault."

The other male officer, Forrester, started backing away. "No. No *way.* This is bullshit. We were just doing our jobs!"

Kimber said, "It's *not* your job to run down an innocent woman, throw her to the ground and put her in cuffs."

"We didn't *know* she was innocent! She fitted the description! You ask *anyone* in the precinct, they'd have done the same!"

"Forrester, last I heard, 'fitting the description' isn't a crime." Quon looked at each of the officers in turn. "You all have a choice. The Department of Justice runs an intensive retraining course for police officers—or Judges—deemed to be operating below acceptable standards. The course runs for eleven weeks, and the next one starts tomorrow morning. So, I advise you to leave *now* because it's in Jacksonville, Florida. Or you can choose to hand in your badges."

A large, black Department of Justice truck pulled to a stop behind the Judges' Lawrangers, and two more Judges climbed out.

Officer Fischel said, "You can't force us to go to *Florida!* You throw your weight around all you want, Judge, but I'm not doing that."

"I'm *not* forcing you to go. It has to be your choice."

"Then I refuse."

Quon nodded. "Understood. I accept your resignation."

Fischel looked from Quon to the approaching Judges and back. "All right. I'll do the retraining course."

"Too late, you've quit. All three of you will be taken back to your precinct. Vick and Forrester, inform your families that you'll be away for the next eleven weeks. Fischel, you'll turn in your badge, sidearm and uniform. You're a civilian now. I advise you to stay out of trouble."

Fischel—pale-faced and slightly trembling—said, "You can't *do* this!"

"It's already done," Quon said. She walked towards her Lawranger, and Kimber fell into step beside her.

As she climbed onto the bike, she thumbed the switch to activate her helmet's radio. "Central Control, this is Quon. What have you got for us?"

"Standby, Quon."

As Kimber climbed onto his own bike next to her, Quon glanced towards him. "Your first encounter with local law-enforcement?"

He nodded. "Yeah. First on the streets, anyway. They don't much like us, do they?"

"That's a sign that we're doing our job. Most cops aren't corrupt, but a lot of them have become *comfortable*. That can make them lazy, inclined to protect their own interests."

"What that cit said about justice not existing... People don't *really* think like that, do they?"

"The lower someone is down the social ladder, the less likely they are to believe in justice. And the higher up they are, the less likely they'll *care* about justice." Quon glanced down at her Lawranger's control screen. "This is taking too long..." She thumbed the switch again. "Central Control, this is Quon."

A pause, then a new voice, a man. Voice trembling slightly, as if in shock. "All units... This is Joint Deputy Chief Judge Solomon. It is with great sadness that I must inform you of the death, earlier this morning, of Chief Judge Eustace Fargo."

CHAPTER THREE

Hunting Park, Philadelphia
12:13

"So, CAN I get onto the roof?"

Sitting in the doorway of their compact—and thankfully temporary—prefabricated home, Beatriz Graziano looked up from her book and brushed her hair from her eyes to scowl at her thirteen-year-old brother Hardy. "No."

"Shaze said we should take a snap every day from the same spot, looking in the same direction, right? And when it's done, we run them all together to make a *movie* of the block going up! So, can I get up onto the roof and see how it looks from there?"

Beatriz pulled the elastic band from her wrist and used it to tie back her hair. "Hardy, what did I *just* tell you?"

"*Mom* said I could."

Hardy was a good kid, but he'd always been a terrible liar. Not just in his delivery, but the actual lies themselves.

"Did she really?"

He nodded vigorously. "Yes. She absolutely really did. She said, 'You *can* get up onto the roof, Hardy, but'—um—'you have to wait until me and your father are at the church on Sunday.'"

"Oh, right, I remember now," Beatriz said. "She told *me*, 'If Hardy wants to get up onto the roof, he's allowed, but he has to eat a handful of gravel first.'"

Hardy looked down at the compacted gravel on which the hut was resting. "No, she didn't!"

"I'm pretty sure she *did*... but you might be right." Beatriz pulled her cell phone out of her pocket. "Hold on, I'll call her."

"No, don't. It's all right. I don't need to go up there now anyway. But... *You* could climb up and see if it's safe." He pointed off to the side. "Some of those people are lying out on *their* roofs!"

"They're adults, Hardy. Now get lost. I'm trying to read."

Beatriz was well aware that her brother was just bored, but he had friends here—why couldn't he go and annoy them instead?

Right now, this was *her* time, what she thought of as her Golden Hour. Mom and Dad were at the church, her chores had been done—not that there was much to do now that they didn't have an apartment any more—and everyone else in the community was wrapped up in their own business. Beatriz's only responsibility was to make sure that Hardy was still alive and intact by the time their parents got back.

Around her, the park's other inhabitants were tidying the plots around their own huts, or wheeling five-gallon bottles of water in from the truck, or just lying out enjoying the sun, their music thumping away in the background. The picnic atmosphere was still there, most of the time; that permeating sense that everyone was sharing in an adventure. The feeling wasn't as strong now as it had been back in October, when this all started, but winter had been pretty mild, and now summer was around the corner, this wasn't really a hardship. Well, except for the cramped living conditions. Most of their stuff was in storage, even their clothing. This morning the only clean clothes Beatriz had been able to find were her faded-peach *uperstar* T-shirt—the first S had peeled off—and her old jeans with the patches on the knees.

Hardy was still talking, telling her something dumb about something even dumber, and then he abruptly stopped, and slowly turned to face her, his cheeks darkening.

She grinned. "Sorry, *what* was that?"

"Umm..."

"Was that the first time your voice has cracked?"

Speaking softly, and carefully, Hardy said, "No. Happened last week too. But no one noticed. Bea, please, don't make a big deal about it!"

She closed her book on the subway ticket she'd been using to mark her place, set it on the wooden step beside her, and stood up. Arms folded and head slightly tilted to the side—in a manner she knew made her look like her aunt Georgia—she peered at her brother and noticed for the first time that he was almost as tall as her. "Do you remember six years ago when you realised I was getting zits and you laughed and laughed and laughed for a whole *week* and you pointed them out to everyone you met? And you only stopped when Mom gave you hell for it?"

Hardy began, "That's not true! I would never—" but cut himself off because his voice shrieked on the first syllable of "never."

"You *did*, squeaky. You made my life a misery. Now I get to do the same to you."

"Well... I was just a kid. You're seventeen. I didn't know any better then, and if—"

"*Relax*, will you? God, you're so gullible you haven't even noticed the *I'm Gullible* sticker on the back of your shirt."

As Hardy tried to pull his T-shirt around without taking it off, Beatriz looked out along the row of evenly spaced huts and realised that she hadn't *really* looked around for the past month—maybe a little longer.

At first, it had been exciting to see the new block going up where their old neighbourhood used to be—especially when the workers brought in the huge machines to dig the foundations. One of the construction supervisors had told her dad that they need to go down at least half as deep as the building's final height. The dirt and rocks extracted were hauled away in a never-ending line of trucks while the foundation machines constructed huge pillars from bundles of carbon nanotubes. "Each one's stronger than a diamond, thinner than a human hair," the supervisors had told Dad. "You build a building out of this stuff, it *stays* built."

It had been all anyone could talk about for months. Luxury accommodation in a giant state-of-the-art block. Free Wi-Fi, no utility bills, greater security. All they had to do was sign the right forms and move out so that the neighbourhood could be demolished. The homeowners and landlords would make a fortune, sure, but the tenants would benefit too: part of the agreement with the SkyBlock Corporation was that their rent would be frozen for the first ten years and would not increase more than two per cent per year thereafter. All they had to do was sign.

The first few weeks had been traumatic, fraught with problems as over three thousand families learnt how to cope with camping in the neighbourhood's small parks and vacant lots. The Judges had to step up their patrols, and the SkyBlock Corporation employed a whole cadre of former cops as private security guards.

"We'll get along," Father Howland had told everyone at one of the many community meetings in the soon-to-be-demolished local movie theatre, "because the sacrifices we make today are really investments in the future. Just like the adversities we endure in this life are rewarded in the next."

Sitting beside Beatriz in the second row, her mother had whispered, "No playin' video games 'til after you do your homework. Amen." Beatriz had snorted a laugh and quickly turned it into a cough that didn't fool anyone.

Dad hadn't heard, or if he had, he'd chosen to ignore it. He was staunchly religious, Catholic to the extent that the holy pictures in their apartment had outnumbered the family photos, but Mom was, in her own definition, "agnostic, but only because being an atheist is too much trouble. It's not my job to deny someone else the comfort of an imaginary friend."

When she'd declared that at the dinner table, Dad had said, "Go on, then. Make your jokes. We'll see who has the last laugh when you're stuck outside the pearly gates looking in."

She still helped out at the church, though, and even Father Howland introduced her to others as, "God's favourite non-believer."

They'd be back soon, their weekly obligations completed, then the family would all get started on the Sunday meal, which was considerably more basic now that most of their utensils were in storage and they had to cook everything on a hotplate. They sure were having sandwiches for a lot more meals these days.

The guy from the SkyBlock Corporation had offered everyone in the neighbourhood temporary accommodation in other buildings they owned, but most of them were thirty miles away on the far side of Trenton, so very few people took them up on it. A lot of the time living in the prefab huts was a pain, but there was always something going on with the block to keep everyone focussed. The thing was going up *fast*.

Hardy said, "I wonder where *we'll* be? Which floor, I mean?" He was shielding his eyes against the sun as he stared up at the block.

"Mom said it'll be a lottery. Except for the really old and sick people, who'll get the lower floors."

"Yeah, but there's already lots of *offices* in the lower floors. With people in them, I mean. The builders and the SkyBlock people."

"That's just temporary. This is their first one, so the SkyBlock people have to be here to supervise the build. They'll move out when most of the work is done."

Hardy nodded, still looking at the many-wheeled and clawed machines constantly crawling up and down the block, hauling up arm-thick cables and huge metal brackets and four-metre-square panels. As he'd declared to the family many times, he liked the hovering machines the most, but Beatriz was always a little unnerved by the way they drifted about, as easily as balloons, even though they weighed several tonnes.

Hardy said, "Suppose it makes sense if the oldies are on the lower floors. If the elevators are out, you don't want to have to climb a million stairs if you're in a wheelchair."

"The elevators *won't* break down, though," Beatriz said. "The guy from the place said that they're guaranteed to keep going for a hundred years."

The new building would be a cube three hundred and fifty metres to each side, with up to seven hundred apartments on each of the most densely populated floors. In total, the block would contain almost sixty thousand apartments, housing about two hundred thousand people. There'd be four movie theatres, two shopping malls, plenty of parking, and seven schools.

The country's first mega-block—but it certainly wouldn't be the last.

The expensive-looking brochures showed the gleaming, spotless cube standing proud over the old neighbourhood, its name elegantly painted across the side. *Indira Knight Block*, chosen by the local community in honour of the first interstellar astronaut, even though—as her father Dio had pointed out—she wouldn't even reach her destination for nearly seventy years. "For all we know, we could be naming it after someone who's already dead," he'd told the family. "And she knew that when she left. *That's* what makes her a hero."

The block's name was one of the areas in which the SkyBlock Corporation had significantly misjudged the mood of the city. The project to send Major Knight to another solar system had cost hundreds of billions of dollars. The authorities never revealed *exactly* how much, but just about everyone agreed that it was money that could have been invested in healthcare or education. The conspiracy theorists were more excited about the mission than anyone else: they knew that the authorities were hiding the evidence of intelligent extraterrestrial life and concluded that Major Knight's mission proved them right: 'You wouldn't go visit a friend in another city if you didn't know they'd be home, would you?'

After several half-hearted attempts to have the block renamed—mostly in honour of local sports teams—SkyBlock's spokespeople announced that the original name would be kept, telling the world, "A lot of the technology we use was developed from the tech created for the interstellar program. The gravity insulators that lifted Major Knight's craft into orbit with minimal fuel expenditure were the basis for the engines that drive our lifters and seam-welders. This block is a testament to the space programme's engineers as much as it is to the major herself."

The more cynical pundits suggested that the SkyBlock Corporation didn't want to change the block's name because they'd already printed all the brochures and posters.

At the last cookout before the removal trucks showed up, one of their neighbours had said, "Everyone's makin' out like bandits here! I don't get it!" He'd turned to Beatriz's father and asked, "Dio, you *ever* heard of a scheme invented by rich white guys that was to the benefit of people like us? Ever? Even *once?*"

Dio Graziano had replied, "The tide can't be against us *all* the time, Tommy. Sometimes, things will go our way."

Tommy had shrugged at that and backed away, never willing to be drawn into a conversation with someone who didn't already agree with him. "I'm just sayin' that this puppy is cute and friendly right now, but one day it's gonna sink its teeth in. Hope I'm wrong; don't believe I am."

But Tommy had already signed the agreements, of course. They all had. And so far the SkyBlock Corporation was keeping to its promises. They'd been pretty honest and open from the start, telling the locals, "Look, this is going to be an inconvenience for you, we won't deny that. But it'll be worth it in the long term. You'll get a brand-new apartment for next to nothing, and the company will make a *lot* of money out of the project—the apartments in the top ten floors will be initially priced at a million dollars *minimum*. Everyone wins."

Hardy asked, "How much longer, do you think?"

Beatriz watched one of the mechanical builders—it was shaped like a squashed car crossed with an octopus—halfway up the structure shooting a perfectly horizontal line of plastic rivets into the wall. "Five months, maybe. They said we'd be in long before Christmas."

Again, she looked around at the rows of huts, which had been supplied by the SkyBlock Corporation free of charge. Over on the left, a trio of their security guards were leaning back against a wire mesh fence, watching the kids playing basketball. In her experience, the guards were mostly friendly, really only there to be sure that none of the neighbourhood's old gangs started making trouble. Officially, the gangs had been driven out, but there were always rogue elements, mainly teenagers, whose experience told them that the only way out of the poverty trap was to ignore society's rules. Beatriz knew who they were, too, because her father always had a stack of pamphlets in his pocket and wasn't shy about handing them out on the street, accompanied by a friendly lecture about the afterlife that he persisted with against the tide of jeers, profanities and mild threats.

Almost always, Dio Graziano would return to the same spot a half-hour later and pick the crumpled pamphlets out of the gutter. If they weren't in too bad condition he'd smooth them out and use them again next time. He'd once told Beatriz, when she was very young, "If I can only save *one* of those kids, it'll be worth it." She hadn't really understood what he meant, and asked, "Which one?"

From somewhere on the right a half-muffled voice shouted, "Oh my god!" and moments later the door to the Bridwells' hut was pulled open. Mr. Bridwell was wild-eyed, looking around in shock. He spotted Beatriz and Hardy looking back at him. "You heard the *news?* Just now! It was on the radio—he's dead. Fargo, the Chief Judge!"

Hardy said, "No way!"

"It's all over the news!" Bridwell said. "It was a drive-by. In Boston, I think they said. He was arresting someone, car speeds past, they're firing. Fargo pushes this woman and her kid out of the way, blam, he takes one in the chest."

Hardy pushed past Beatriz into the hut, and switched on the TV. Already, Mr. Bridwell had moved on to another neighbour, his shock at the news matched only by his eagerness to be the one to break it to everyone else.

Beatriz stood in the doorway, watching the small screen over Hardy's shoulder.

Every schoolkid knew who the Chief Judge was. He was the man who made the rules they all lived by. Even President Pierce didn't have as much power as Eustace Fargo.

And he was a good man, everyone said. Firm but fair, that's what they said about him on TV, just about every time he was mentioned. Firm but fair.

On screen, the image cut to shaky, hand-held footage from a cell phone. Downtown Boston, a pedestrian saw a Judge in the process of arresting a perp, so she filmed it, because the *PerpCatching* show paid two hundred dollars for a good clip of the Judges in action. She didn't know it was the Chief Judge himself until he was on the ground, bleeding from a hole in his chest the size of an orange.

"What does this mean?" Hardy asked, still glued to the screen. "Bea?"

"I don't know." She knew from history class that Fargo had been head of the Department of Justice for twenty years. He'd founded the department, pulled America back from the edge of self-destruction, saved it from the corrupt and incompetent politicians who'd clawed their way into power on platforms of hate and greed.

And now he was gone.

Hardy said, "There's two *Deputy* Chief Judges, right?" He turned around to look at her. "One of them will take over, won't they?"

Beatriz shrugged. "Probably."

"Because if there's no Judges... I mean, I hate them like everyone else does, but you know those movies about the *old* days, before the Judges? If the Judges are gone, will everything go like that again? Dad said that when he was a kid, they had to move out of the city because of the riots, and that's why Gramma never comes back here to visit."

She gave him her best reassuring smile. "It won't ever get that bad again. I hate the Judges too, but I think we'd hate *not* having them more."

Hardy said, "Yeah, maybe," and turned back to the TV set. His voice had squeaked again on the first syllable of *maybe,* but Beatriz chose not to comment on it. He had enough on his mind right now.

CHAPTER FOUR

Southwest Center City, Philadelphia
12:59

DALLAS HAWKER RAN an address over and over in his head, hoping that he wouldn't forget it. He was tempted to write it down, but that would be against the rules. Nothing written, nothing digital, nothing that can be traced, hacked or copied. You keep your notes only in your head. That way, if the Judges are getting too close, you can *erase* all those notes with a single round from a forty-five.

"You don't get caught by chance," Romley was fond of saying. "You get caught through *carelessness*."

A half hour ago Dallas had been sitting in his own apartment watching the news. Everyone was talking about the Chief Judge, how he died, how he'd lived. And speculating on what was coming next. A former Judge who claimed to have been a very close friend of Eustace Fargo told the news anchor, "Fargo's one of the architects of the Autonomy Act. I'm not saying he was assassinated *because* of that, but it's no secret that many people think grouping the country's major coastal cities into three self-governing 'mega-cities' is yet another nail in the coffin of the United States of America."

As the news anchor paused to consider his reply, Dallas's cell phone buzzed and displayed Romley's number.

"Dallas, I need you to talk to one of my other people. *Today.*" Romley was in his usual hotel room, fixing his tie as he addressed the camera. "You don't know him, and he doesn't know you, so you'll need to play this with caution. He can be paranoid—maybe *flaky* is a better word."

Dallas was already pulling on his sneakers. "Understood."

"The news media is going to be swamped with stories about Fargo for the next few days, and that's triggered something in one of my other ventures." Romley glanced at the camera again. "I'm putting a *lot* of trust in you, Dallas. You'll be my voice, my deputy. He'll resist that, but stand firm. I know you won't disappoint me."

Now, as he made his way on foot across the city—something he hadn't done in a long time—Dallas could feel every one of his fifty years weighing him down. Especially the past decade.

Back when he and Gwen had been dating, they'd loved coming to Philly, even talked of moving here. But that was a lifetime ago, and now, sometimes, it felt like it was all he could do to walk upright.

He'd dressed casually for the occasion. T-shirt, sneakers, sweatpants. Muted colours, no logos, nothing to make him stand out among the crowd. Just another unremarkable middle-aged man on some trivial errand. Another rule: you don't do anything that might help casual witnesses remember you.

Someone pushed open the door to a bar as Dallas was passing and the words "...Chief Judge Eustace Fargo is dead..." drifted out from a TV set. Dallas automatically glanced in and saw Fargo's customary scowl on the screen.

The newsreader was saying, "...while intervening in a vicious drive-by shooting."

Dallas wanted to go into the bar, to hear more, but he was on a schedule. He kept moving.

Fargo's dead. It was an awkward, cumbersome concept.

The man had been around for so long... A drive-by shooting seemed like such an ordinary way for a man like Fargo to die. You'd think that someone who'd managed to reshape an entire country would meet his end on the rim of a volcano, or battling aliens, or something like that. You don't acquire power without also acquiring enemies; that was one of the fundamental laws of the universe, and someone as powerful as Fargo would surely have *thousands* of people wishing him dead.

In some ways, it felt wrong that Fargo had lived this long without succumbing to an assassin's bullet.

But then, Dallas could say the same about Irvine Romley.

EIGHT YEARS AGO, after Romley had somehow tracked him down and confronted him, Dallas had seriously contemplated a strong vodka-and-barbiturates cocktail, but he couldn't do it. Even when Romley forced him to go against his strongest beliefs, Dallas hadn't been able to terminate his own existence. A long time ago, Gwen had put it very succinctly: "If your life's on the wrong track, you don't fix it by blowing up the train."

That was what broke him, in the end: not Romley's threats, not Gwen's arrest and incarceration, not the knowledge that he would never see his children again, but the realisation that his attempts to make things better for everyone else had resulted in the absolute devastation of his own life.

In his days as a vigilante he had personally executed fourteen perps who'd evaded the law. He'd recovered millions of dollars from criminals and donated it to charitable causes. He'd anonymously tipped off the Judges and cops to maybe forty major crimes... but somehow *he* was the bad guy.

I am *the bad guy*, he told himself.

Romley's first task, the night he confronted Dallas in that hotel in Indiana, had been to completely and bluntly outline his operation. "I arrange for the manufacture and distribution of the narcotic known on the streets as T.T., or Trance-Trance, or sometimes just Trance, or Dust. Probably a lot of other names too. You know how the junkies love to concoct and apply nicknames. I am the *only* person who knows exactly how it's made, Mr. Hawker. The only one in possession of the list of eleven secret herbs and spices and the formula used to combine them. A lot of people have attempted to duplicate my process—or take it in a new direction, which has not always gone well—but mine is the original and best."

Standing by the window in Romley's modest hotel room, while the man himself constantly clicked the remote control at the muted TV set, Dallas still didn't know whether this was real. Since he'd fled Golgotha in the August of 2041, he'd been waiting for the thick-gloved hand on his shoulder—or more likely the bullet in his back—that meant the Judges had found him. He'd not figured on another wanted perp getting to him first.

"I lost some of my best go-to guys around the same time the Judges descended on your little group of would-be do-gooders," Romley told him, still rapidly flicking through the TV's channels. "We had a very cosy and profitable set-up that was destroyed when your friend Mealing stole a marked fifty-dollar bill from one of my people."

Dallas said, "No, the Judges were on to your people anyway. If anything, we *distracted* them. If they hadn't been closing in on us, more of them would have been available to take down your people in the bar."

Romley turned to him and stared, half of his face in shadow, the other half blue with light from the TV. "So I should *thank* you for stealing from me?"

"I just meant..."

"Dallas, you know more about avoiding the Judges than most, and you're good at it. You're going to help me shore up my empire. What happened in Alabama was a major setback, but I'm rebuilding already, and you'll be a large part of that. If you refuse, you'll live only long enough to see the proof that your wife and children have been—for want of a better phrase—viciously butchered." Still staring at Dallas, Romley pointed to the TV screen. "Take a look."

His heart pounding in a dry throat, Dallas slowly turned to look at the television set mounted on the wall. It showed a still photo, a high-angled shot looking down on a blank-walled room where an old woman with straggly grey hair sat on a harsh metal bunk.

It took him far too long to recognise the woman.

Romley said, "The Judges call their prisons 'Isolation Blocks,' not because the prisoners are kept in solitary confinement—although that does happen—but because for most people the concept of isolation is quite terrifying. Gwen will almost certainly never see you or your children again, Dallas, and that knowledge has shattered her. I've seen photos from before you deserted her. She was an attractive woman. Not *my* type, personally, but undeniably good-looking. Healthy, strong, confident. And now look. It's only been two years, and she looks like she's aged at least *ten*."

The worst part—the real butt-kicker, as Gwen herself might have put it—came next.

Romley nodded towards a full-length mirror close to the hotel room's door. "Take a look at yourself."

He didn't want to do it, but Dallas didn't have anything left in him to refuse. He walked to the mirror and looked. Sharp suit, pressed shirt, neat tie. Hands manicured, hair expertly styled to hide the thinning spots.

"You've been taking good care of yourself," Romley said. "I expect you've used the excuse that you *need* to do so in order to fit in, but the truth is you took your running-away money and cried your little eyes out at abandoning your family even as you were doing it."

Romley moved closer to Dallas, stood behind him, looking over his shoulder and peering at their reflections in the mirror. "Brendan Dallas Hawker. Is he a noble vigilante who took down the scum that evaded the system, now in hiding because the Judges just won't understand that sometimes a good man has to stand up for the little guys? Or..." Another step closer, and now Romley was standing side by side with Dallas, one hand on his shoulder. "Or is he a coward who had a plan to get himself out of trouble, but not one for his wife and kids? A self-deluding narcissist who saved only himself and spent the next two years wallowing in self-pity in one fancy hotel after another? Always absconding before the bill was due, leaving even more people to deal with the mess he's left behind?"

Romley's hand squeezed tighter, and he leant a little closer to Dallas, almost whispering in his ear. "You think you're better than me. I make and sell addictive narcotics, and yes, that's bad. But you're a *murderer*, Dallas. A stone-cold killer. You can tell yourself—and everyone else—that those people deserved to die, but the truth is you killed them because you *wanted* to kill them. They're dead because killing them gave you a thrill."

"It's... it wasn't murder. It was *justice*. They—"

"Shut up." Romley stepped back. "You work for *me*, now. You betray me, and your family will die. It's that simple. And every time a part of you starts thinking that this is unfair, that you don't deserve this..."—another click of the remote control—"I want you to remember April Susan Dunstall."

Dallas turned to the TV set again. It was now showing a high school yearbook photo of a smiling young woman.

"The Judges unearthed her body last year. Scratches on her skull matched the blade of a screwdriver found in your garage. You remember April, don't you? Sure you do. It was a high-profile case. Out of her mind on Trance-Trance, she'd left her three young children home alone for almost a week. The ravenous gutter-media eagerly lapped up the story, especially when her oldest boy went to live with his father but April managed to retain custody of his siblings. Oh, what a miscarriage of justice *that* was. You decided to take the law into your own hands. You abducted her, murdered her, buried her body in the woods."

"That..." Dallas dry-swallowed. "She was a junkie. She abandoned her *kids*."

"Be careful you don't slip on the irony, Dallas." Romley pointed to the screen again. "April Dunstall was not a junkie. Grud knows she wasn't the best mother in the world, but she did love her children. And she didn't abandon them by choice. Her former boyfriend—a man with serious impulse-control issues and a large collection of knives—abducted her and dosed her with Trance-Trance. And one of that drug's frequent side effects is an overwhelming desire to please the people you're with. April had no *choice* but to stay with him and his friends... until his supply of the product ran out, and she sobered up."

Romley tossed the remote control onto the bed. "You *murdered* an innocent woman. Remember her, and her children, next time that little whiny voice inside your head starts telling you that you don't deserve this."

DALLAS HAD DONE this sort of thing many times before, but he was still impressed with Romley's paranoia. The man had dozens of people working for him, maybe hundreds—maybe thousands—but almost none of them knew that. Most had never heard of him.

Romley had once told Dallas, "Crime does pay, but *bragging* about it is a lot more expensive than people realise."

Each person in the organisation was a link in the chain, but most of those links could only see as far as the next link. If the average dealer on the street only knew the name of their supplier, but not their *supplier's* supplier, then it was a lot harder for the Law to follow the chain to its anchor. Romley called it 'insulation through ignorance.'

Dallas's destination was all the way over on Cherry Street, where a large U-Haul truck pulled up outside an apartment building just as Dallas arrived. The truck disgorged five burly men who immediately started to carry bulky sofas and armchairs into the building. A sixth man emerged from the cab and approached Dallas. "You the guy?"

"I'm *a* guy."

"*Better* be the guy," the driver said. Charlie Kibbs was a skinny, full-bearded man wearing a high-visibility jacket, with bare arms covered in thick black hair. "So the man says he can't come and see me in person, so he's sending you. Helluva a day, huh? You hear that sumbitch Fargo finally got what's been coming to him? Helluva day."

"We're not here to talk about the news," Dallas said.

"I know that." Charlie nodded towards two of the workers who were hefting a sofa out of the truck. "It's all there. Now why'd he send you to talk to me? I got this in hand. I always do."

Romley hadn't given Dallas a description, but this was definitely Charlie Kibbs. "You've been coming up light."

"Hell I have." Kibbs glanced at Dallas. "I do it by the book. The product goes out, and when the money comes in, it all goes to the pickup guy. All of it. Every single cent."

"That's all I was told. It's not my job to find out who or how or why it's light, it's *yours*."

"Not a chance." He shook his head. "No way." He tapped his forefinger against his temple. "I got it all in here. I know the figures. And I vet all my people. I'd *know* if something was wrong."

"Then you're going to have to dig a little deeper and find out who it is. Start applying pressure."

Charlie Kibbs shook his head. "No. This isn't right. He's never sent someone else before. You go back and tell him that I run a tight ship, and I make damn sure *everyone* knows that."

"Yeah, that's part of the *problem*, Charlie."

The man almost wilted. "Aw, man. No names. There's never supposed to be *names*."

"*No one* should know that you run a tight ship. He says you're getting a reputation, and that's not good. That's what's made him take a closer look at your numbers."

One of the builders—almost two metres tall and built like someone had mashed two wrestlers together—approached them with a scowl creasing his forehead. "Everythin' okay here, boss?"

"We're cool," Charlie said. "Old friend with a bit of bad news, that's all." He nodded towards the back of the truck. "Almost done?"

"Gettin' there." The big man backed away, still looking at Dallas.

"Charlie, he told me to say that you have two days to make amends. And then you're off the books. Four months at least. No contact of any kind. When he wants you, when he feels it's safe, *he'll* make contact."

Charlie leant back against the door of the truck. "Jesus. Look, tell him that I'll find whoever's skimming and deal with it. And I'll keep my mouth shut. But he can't cut me off!"

"Not our problem. You know the rules, just like the rest of us." To himself, Dallas said, *And now he's going to threaten me.*

"You're making things *difficult* for me," Charlie said. "I don't like that, and I'm feeling kinda moved to *do* something about it."

It was how people in this game operated. When you feel threatened, you threaten someone else, just to feel like you have some kind of control over your life. Early on, Romley had told him to expect that, and to use it. "In any conflict where you know you have the upper hand, you leave a little gap through which the enemy can retreat... but only if they back down. And you allow them to take that path with *dignity*. The dead don't respond well to pressure, Dallas. You want your people to keep paying, then they have to be alive. If they come out of the conflict feeling relieved and grateful to you, then they owe you, and they know that."

He told Charlie, "Look, I was just told to meet you here and warn you that the numbers aren't adding up, and that you've maybe been talking too much. That's all I got."

Charlie ran his hands over his face and said, "There's no one skimming. I swear. I don't know *why* he thinks we're coming up light. My people understand the consequences—I make sure of that. And they're not using the product themselves. I'd *know* if they were."

"What would *he* say to you?" Dallas asked. "Right now, what would he say?"

"He'd... remind me of the consequences." Charlie nervously ran his tongue over his lips. "Look... what's your name?"

"I don't have a name."

"Okay, right. Look, the thing is, it's all checks and balances. The guy tells me where to pick up the product, I pass it on, make a little profit. Steady income. You know how it is. And that all works, no problems there. But..." He waved his right arm as though he was presenting the truck. "I have other businesses. *Legit* businesses. Well, mostly. I'm in hock for damn near a *million*. I don't keep up the payments, certain other people are going to come *looking* for me."

Dallas felt his heart start to race. *How the hell could someone working for Romley be so* stupid? "You owe money to a loan shark?"

"Yeah. If you cut me off, I'm gonna default on the payments. And they know about my sideline with our mutual friend. They know about the Trance. They might decide to take a shipment or two in lieu of what I owe them."

Charlie was still talking, and Dallas wanted to grab his shoulders and tell him to shut the hell up, but then he reminded himself that the man was a key part of the distribution network process of a drug that had already killed millions. *Let him keep digging his own grave here.*

But he knew he couldn't do that. *Shut him up. Someone could overhear.* As firmly as he could, using the same voice he used back in the old days when he wanted Jason to focus on his homework, Dallas said, "Charlie, stop talking. Right now."

The skinny man abruptly pulled away from Dallas. "Aw,

no." The look in his eyes told Dallas he finally understood what was going on.

"Charlie, just *relax*, will you? I'll talk to him, and we'll clear this up. I don't know where you sit in all this but, c'mon, he wouldn't send me to talk to you if he didn't think it *could* be straightened out, right?"

Charlie nodded for a moment, then his expression went slack, and he slowly turned back to face Dallas. "You *have* to say that. You have to say it because you're not his trigger-man. That'll be someone else, and he's not here, and until he *does* get to me, I'm still a liability."

His right hand darted around to the back of his jeans, and a moment later Dallas was looking down the barrel of a gun.

"I'm a *dead man*! He's got the idea that I'm skimming—and I'm *not*—and that's all he needs. You ever try to convince him he's wrong about something? He never changes his mind. *Always* has to be right... How much time do I have? Minutes? Hours? If I'm already marked then what's to stop me from blowing your goddamn head off right now, huh?"

A powerful voice from behind Charlie called out, "Boss?"

Dallas risked a brief glance over to the right towards the building's entrance. All five of the burly men were approaching.

With his wide eyes still on Dallas, and the gun still in his face, Charlie called out, "Sumbitch here is trying to get me *killed!*"

"Charlie... I swear you've got me wrong. But this can all still be fixed, okay? You put down that gun and let's just talk. Seriously, man, put the gun away. Someone will see, they'll call the Judges, then we're *screwed*. We don't want that. Do you understand me? The way out of this is right in front of you. A simple step, Charlie. You just put the gun away."

The removals men were spreading out around them now, keeping their distance, calmly pleading with him to put down the gun. "Don't do anythin' stupid, Charlie," the largest one called. "We got your back, all right? Whatever *this* asshole's problem is, you don't wanna go killin' him. You know that."

Charlie's gun arm wavered a little for a moment. "He always made it clear that if I betray him or let him down, then he'll send someone after my family. He'll *do* it, too. I saw him do it to someone else. One time he made me *watch* when..." Charlie sagged again. "You don't get past seeing something like that."

Dallas said, "Charlie, believe me, I *know* what he's like. He's not accusing *you* of anything. He—"

"Why didn't he come himself? He's *never* sent someone else before. Never. And now you know I owe money, so *he's* gonna know..."

A voice from behind Dallas yelled, "Drop the gun!"

Charlie Kibbs's face drained of any remaining colour. Softly, he said, "Judges." He looked back at Dallas. "Working for him... It's a *death sentence*. You know that." He smiled. "Now he's *your* problem, asshole. I get to be a hero. Gonna save my kids' lives." Charlie placed the muzzle of his gun under his chin and pulled the trigger.

CHAPTER FIVE

HARDY SAID, "SOMETHING'S happening out there, Bea. A whole bunch of the SkyBlock guards just got outta a truck, and now there're two Judges. They're just sitting there, though."

Beatriz moved closer to the doorway and looked out in the direction her brother was facing, towards the east. Six SkyBlock guards at the park's gate were greeting another two coming from the south, and four more from the north. "Hardy, gimme a boost up."

"What?"

"I want to look from the roof."

"But you won't let *me* go up on the roof?"

"Just do it. This is important."

Hardy interlaced his fingers, and Beatriz first used his hands and then his shoulder as steps while she scrambled up onto the flat roof.

Below, Hardy backed away a little to look up at her. "What can you see?"

She turned in a slow circle and counted. Fifteen more SkyBlock guards, at least seven cops, most of them doing their best to look casual. On the average day she might see one or two. And four Judges now, too, rounding the corner on their Lawrangers.

She jumped when her cell phone in her pocket buzzed, and pulled it out to see her father's name.

"Honey, is Hardy with you?"

Beatriz glanced down at her brother. "He's right here, Dad. What's—"

"I want you to grab the bag with the wallets and your mom's purse, okay? Take your brother. Come here to the church. Just walk casually, don't run. Don't tell *anyone* what you're doing, got that? And if someone tries to stop you... anyone at all, even a Judge... *then* you run. Whatever it takes, you get yourself and your brother away from the park right *now*. Tell me you understand, Bea."

"Yeah, but..."

"Just *do* it. If you can't make it here, go to your grandpa's, okay? *Now*, Beatriz! Get moving!"

Beatriz had been five years old when her parents told her what it had been like growing up in the city before the Judges came, and they'd covered a lot of it in school. She knew what to do. The old skipping song went, 'Rich and white, you'll be all right. Poor or brown, keep your head down.'

She sat down on the edge of the roof and squirmed around until she was resting on the edge on her belly, then allowed herself to slide down. She dropped the last metre, landing lightly on her toes.

"So what's happening?" Hardy asked.

"We have to go." She grabbed his arm, kept hold of it as she reached back into the hut, into the alcove above the door.

"Get off me!" Hardy said, struggling to pull his arm away.

"That was Dad. Something's happening. I don't know what, but we have to leave." She pulled him closer. "Hardy, all those cops and Judges aren't here to have a picnic." Her fingers touched the straps of the small backpack and she hauled it out.

"We're not supposed to leave the hut with no one to guard it!"

Still holding onto Hardy's wrist, Beatriz looked to the left and right again.

More guards, more Judges, more cops, all casually clustered around the park's entrances. "We are not gonna get out..."

Not both of us. She looked down at her little brother. He was still trying to pull away from her, but now his expression leant more towards fear than annoyance. Beatriz handed him the backpack. "Put this on. We're going to walk calmly to the gate. If it looks like they're going to stop people leaving, I'll distract them and you slip away, all right? But don't run if there's any cops or Judges or guards around. Just be as casual as you can. If you run, they'll call it aggression—even if you're running *away* from them—and then shoot you in the back."

Hardy paled. "Oh God. Really?"

"Really. I want you to walk behind me, okay? About five metres. We don't want to look like we're together. If they stop me, you don't even look up. You keep going as though you didn't even notice."

"What if they let *you* through but stop *me?*"

"Then I'll distract them from the other side." She crouched a little and looked into her brother's deep brown eyes, wondering if that would be the last time she saw him. "Are you ready?"

He nodded a little too vigorously, then said, "You're supposed to tell me that everything is going to be fine."

"I know. But that's not a promise I can make."

DALLAS WAS A dead man. He was certain of that. As certain as he had ever been of anything else.

Running would not have been an option. The Judges immediately locked down the scene, scanned and printed everyone. Standard operating procedure: assume everyone is guilty until the evidence proves otherwise.

His fate was sealed as soon as they scanned his DNA.

He was wanted for fourteen murders, as well as countless acts of vigilantism and evading the law. The Judges wouldn't just put him away for life; this was a death-squad situation.

Romley had said to him once, "If it ever looks like capture

is unavoidable, then you fight back. The Judges will respond to that with deadly force, and that's what you *want* them to do. Better to die quickly on the streets than to suffer their interrogation methods."

Now, in the empty, windowless three-metre-cubed concrete holding cell in the Philadelphia Central Precinct, Dallas knew that even if by some miracle the Judges didn't execute him, then Romley would find a way to silence him. He had people *everywhere*. It could happen at any time, even here and now. *Especially* here and now. There were Judges on his payroll.

Dallas looked up at approaching footsteps. The door's lock clunked, and it was pulled open.

A tall, broad-shouldered, Caucasian female Judge filled the doorway. "Brendan Hawker. Also known as Dallas, after the city of your birth. Formerly of Golgotha, Alabama. Disappeared ten years ago. Captured today in Philadelphia at the scene of another killing. That's *fifteen* that we know of."

"I didn't... that guy did that to himself!"

"When I saw your name on the manifest I nearly *wept*, Hawker." She smiled. "You're the biggest fish I've ever caught. You know you're on the top forty most-wanted list?" She stepped into the cell and stood directly in front of him, and he saw the name *Gaines* on her badge, next to the two pips that indicated she was a senior Judge. "So citizen Charles James Kibbs has a gun on you, and when confronted by the arresting Judges he takes his own life. Why?"

"I don't know. I never met the guy before today."

"Not according to his employees. They said you and Kibbs were involved in a brief but intense conversation. Kibbs told them that you were endangering his life."

"I've no idea who he was. I saw the removal truck and he was clearly supervising, so that meant he was the boss, right? So I asked him if there was any work, and then he just went crazy."

Judge Gaines sighed. "You're already under a death sentence for your past crimes. But... congratulations. You've actually extended your life a little, at least until I solve this."

With more courage than he felt, Dallas said, "Then I have no incentive to tell you anything."

"Oh, you *will* talk. We'll be bringing in our best interrogators to extract it from you. You *are* going to die, Hawker. It's up to you whether you'll be unconscious or screaming when it happens."

"I... want to make a deal." Dallas felt his throat constrict even as he said the words. This was a step that couldn't be reversed. Even if the Judge turned down the idea, the damage was done. He knew that. He'd always known it.

Romley had spies everywhere, and there was no reason to assume that this precinct was exempt. The second Romley found out that Dallas had been arrested, long-standing plans would have been triggered. Someone would get to Gwen, wherever they were holding her. Someone would get to Evie and Jason.

They might be dead already. They probably *were*—people like Irvine Romley don't take chances.

So, if they were already dead, and the Judges were going to execute him anyway... then he had nothing to lose and maybe he could help take down Romley. End all this as it began: getting a scumbag drug dealer off the streets.

Judge Gaines said, "No deals."

"Then... I just need time because I can give you someone you've been after for a very long time. Someone far worse than me."

"Give me a name."

"Irvine Desmond Romley."

"I've no idea who that is."

"Look him up. And then get back to me."

The Judge looked at him steadily for a few seconds, then straightened up. Without a word, she moved to the door and closed it behind her.

For the first time since Charlie Kibbs had put a bullet through his skull, Dallas felt a glimmer of hope.

* * *

Errol Quon felt more eyes than usual on herself and Judge Kimber as they rode back to the precinct, the citizens understandably curious as to what was going to happen next.

For years the left-wing TV and web pundits had been speculating on the fate of the Department of Justice if Eustace Fargo left the office, by whatever means. Would everything just collapse back into the old ways? Would someone else take over and maintain the status quo? If so, how do we know that the next Chief Judge won't want to make even more radical changes? Would Fargo's successor increase the pressure on President Pierce to sign the Autonomy Act into law?

And now Chief Judge Fargo's face was on every news display, every billboard, and it seemed to Quon that the whole city—hell, the country, the entire world—was holding its breath.

She'd never met Fargo, but she had once walked past his office in the Boston East Academy, and she was pretty sure he'd been inside because there had been guards outside the door.

The closest she'd come to meeting him was her instructor at the Academy, Judge Deacon: everyone knew that Fargo and Deacon had been friends since before the new Department of Justice was even founded.

Some people even said that Fargo had been so impressed with the way Deacon handled himself—and other people—that he'd used Deacon as the model for the first Judges. The story goes that Fargo told his advisors, "You find me a thousand men and women just like Francesco Deacon, and I'll save this country from its own toxicity."

They scoured the police ranks, the military, and the judiciary, but they couldn't find nearly enough people like Deacon, so they had to make their own.

Once, she came close to actually asking Judge Deacon about it, but chickened out at the last second. He wasn't the sort of tutor you felt was open to casual conversation.

But in one of the course's lessons, Deacon brought up the subject himself. "The story goes that during the space-race in the middle of the last century, the US and the Soviets both needed astronauts. The US Air Force took their best pilots and made them into scientists. The Soviets took their scientists and trained them to be pilots. That's not *strictly* accurate, but it's a fair analogy. Judges must know and understand every aspect of the law. They must be able to make instant and accurate judgements. They must be in peak physical, emotional and mental condition. You will be tested... and you will *fail.* And every time you fail, you will get back up and you will try again. There is no room in the Department of Justice for the weak."

Unlike most of her fellow cadets, Errol Quon had never wanted to be a Judge. She didn't believe that an all-powerful Department of Justice was the way to go, and she'd said so at her entrance interview, which was conducted by a Judge named Hearn—a middle-aged man missing his right arm and with severe facial scarring—and a woman whose name was never given.

Hearn had told her, "You have an exceptional record, Quon, and in all respects you have the makings of a good Judge, but if you don't want to be here... why *are* you here?"

"Because the Judges are the best chance this country has of avoiding self-destruction. But once that's been accomplished, someone will need to save it from the Judges."

The unnamed woman had smiled at that. "The old, 'You're all a bunch of fascists' argument? We've heard that before. But fascists seize power for their own gratification. We are going to save this nation, and for that we will receive no reward and very little recognition. That's not fascism, Quon. That's *altruism.*"

Quon had understood her words, and her meaning, and she was sure that the woman believed what she was saying. But she was still wrong. On the wall behind Hearn's desk, an impressively large painting of Chief Judge Fargo loomed over the room, his expression grim and stern, his eyes invisible behind his helmet's visor. He didn't look like a saviour. More like a dictator.

And now he was dead. Gunned down in the streets, according to the radio chatter. She knew that the conspiracy theorists would be already wetting themselves with excitement. In their world view, famous people can't possibly just die by accident or coincidence, only as the result of a complex, nebulous plot.

Senior Judge Trimble was waiting on his Lawranger outside the entrance to the precinct's underground parking lot. Trimble was forty-six, a former lawyer, and there was a strong rumour that he was one of the very few Judges who had a family, although no one had ever seen them. According to the stories, when Trimble was approached to join the department, Fargo had strongly urged him to divorce his wife and cut all ties with the children. "The country needs you more than they do," he was alleged to have said.

Quon doubted that was true but wouldn't have been completely surprised if it was. As Quon slowed down, Trimble told Kimber to go inside and see the duty sergeant. "Quon, got something else for you."

She pulled to a stop alongside his bike. "Sir, what's the situation—?"

"How's the kid working out?" Trimble asked, gesturing towards Kimber's retreating Lawranger.

"He's a little impatient, but I think he'll make a good Judge. He's ambitious, though. Has a lot of his own ideas on how things should be done."

"Why do you think I assigned him to you? You'll straighten him out." Trimble removed his helmet. "You've heard, obviously. About the old man."

"Chief Judge Fargo was hardly *old*, sir."

"He was older than me. Certainly *looked* it." Trimble shrugged. "All leave is cancelled, and everyone is pulling a double shift. The analysts are predicting trouble in the usual hotspots. Could be bad. The Deputy Chiefs are trying to keep things running smoothly, but..." Another shrug. "You've always wanted the Judges gone, maybe this is how it happens."

"It's not that I want them gone, sir. I want them to be *unnecessary*."

Trimble leant over and peered down at her Lawranger's engine. "Huh. How'd you do that? *Mine* doesn't have a back-pedal function."

"Very funny, sir."

Trimble grinned. "Humour keeps us human, Quon. I had you and Kimber down to do another twelve on the waterfront, but there's been a request from on high, so I'm putting him with Hills and Cignoni instead. You're being reassigned to Philly Central for the foreseeable."

"Philadelphia? May I ask *why*?"

Trimble shrugged. "Fire away, but it'll be a waste of ammo because *I* didn't ask." He nodded towards the precinct. "They're sending a copter. You've got twelve minutes to pack up, so get moving. And when it's over, make sure you come back to us."

BEATRIZ COULD SEE what was happening, but didn't know how to stop it, or even how to get away.

Hardy had managed to get out before everything went to hell, at least that was something. When she'd been within ten metres of the park's side gate, two of the SkyBlock guards—adults who looked like they could be sister and brother—had stepped out to block her path, their faces friendly but their body language resolute.

"Better stay put, little lady," the man said. "The Judges are saying everyone has to wait here a little while."

She'd stopped and looked up at them. "Why? Because of what happened to the Chief Judge?"

"They didn't say. Probably just a false alarm, but it's best to be safe, right?"

On her left, a boy of about her own age was also being stopped, and beyond him several more people were being calmly but firmly herded back into the park. But on her right, Hardy was staring up at the still-growing Indira Knight Block as he very casually sidled towards the gates.

"My mom and dad are at the church," Beatriz said. "They just told me to meet them there."

The female guard said, "Sure, and you will, just as soon as we get the all-clear."

Hardy had drifted to within two metres of the gate, still looking like he was focussed solely on the new block and the giant machines that were steadily building it, and no one was paying him any attention. Beatriz pointed off in the opposite direction and, far-too-loudly, said, "Oh, that's them over there!"

She'd caught a last glimpse of her brother darting out behind a police officer who was directing people into the park, and then he was gone.

Safe, she hoped. He'd certainly have reached the church by now, she was sure of that. It was only a few blocks, and this was Sunday afternoon, probably the safest time in the whole week.

Over the next half hour, more and more people filed into the park, herded by the cops, security guards and Judges, and Beatriz half expected to see her parents and Hardy among them, but as yet there was no sign.

And no call, either. All around her, people were repeatedly pulling out their cell phones and looking at them, hoping that this time there'd be a signal.

Beatriz was back at her own place now, standing in the doorway and constantly looking around. Their neighbours on the left, the Ramiz family, weren't home, but Mr. and Mrs. Bridwell on the right were there, looking as concerned as Beatriz felt.

Now, Mrs. Bridwell called out to her, "Dio back yet? Or your mom?"

Beatriz shook her head.

"Whatever's happening, it'll be okay, I bet. There's *Judges* here."

Beatriz wanted to say, "Yeah, that's not a guarantee of safety," but the Bridwells believed wholeheartedly in the Judges—kept talking about how everyone 'owed' them after the 2047 lockdown—and she didn't want to get drawn into *that* conversation.

She turned at the screech of bicycle brakes to see her friend Nina's older brother Pip slowing to a stop in front of her.

"You heard anything, Bea?"

"No. You?"

"Nothing definite. Someone said that it was someone *here* who killed Fargo, and the Dreads are going to tear the place *apart* until they find them." Pip made an expression of disgust. "Someone *else* said that this has nothing to do with the Judges and the SkyBlock people are gonna make some announcement." Pip sat up straight on the bike and gave a deep shrug that Beatriz knew was so that he could show off his chest muscles. "Could be nothin', could be something."

"That narrows it down, all right. Is Nina home?"

"I don't know, she—" Pip flinched slightly, then pulled his phone out of his back pocket. "Signal's back."

Her own cell phone was also buzzing, and from the activity of the other neighbours, so was everyone else's.

As he swiped at the cell phone's screen, Pip said, "I was beginning to think that... that... What the hell is *this?*"

Someone in the distance started swearing, and at that moment Beatriz's phone buzzed to signal an incoming e-mail. It was from the SkyBlock Corporation. She'd never received a message from the company before and was sure she hadn't signed up to any of their mailing lists.

To all potential residents of Indira Knight Block.

It is with great regret that we must inform you that due to financial difficulties beyond our control, and despite our best efforts, the SkyBlock Corporation is to be dissolved immediately. Our assets—including but not limited to the Indira Knight Block currently under construction—have been acquired by Melchior Kenway, a conglomerate of other companies who have pledged that the construction work will continue without pause, and will likely be completed in advance of the original estimated date.

Unfortunately, and to our considerable regret, the Melchior Kenway Conglomeration is under no obligation to honour any previous agreements into which the SkyBlock Corporation may have entered with former residents of the area upon which Indira Knight Block is being constructed.

However, as a gesture of good faith, all such residents will be offered the opportunity to purchase apartments in the block on a first-come, first-served basis.

Apartments are expected to be available for purchase within the next two months, with prices starting at US$690,000 (excl. all relevant and applicable state, city and local taxes) for a two-roomed apartment with a footprint of approximately thirty square metres.

The shouts of anger began long before Beatriz had finished reading, and the first shots were fired approximately seven minutes later.

CHAPTER SIX

Beatriz watched from the roof of her family's hut, looking south towards the new block, its building machines still working on automatic, the block's height increasing at the same speed it had for months, over a metre per day. The robots didn't care that the people on the street below were rioting.

There was another burst of gunfire from the south side, and Beatriz once again dropped down flat on the roof.

She'd never seen a dead body before today. Certainly never seen someone die.

It had started with the e-mail. No, it had started with the increased security. The SkyBlock people had clearly called in reinforcements before they released the e-mail because they knew it was *not* going to be well received.

We gave up our homes on the promise of a better life, and they've just taken it away from us. Just like that. No brand-new apartment, no future.

When the news broke, Mr. Bridwell from next door had told Beatriz that they shouldn't be surprised. "This is always the way. The poor get screwed over because money makes money."

"But they can't just *do* that!"

"They *have* done it, Beatriz. And we were fools not to see

it coming. Fools." He'd looked at her then with tears in his eyes, and stepped back into his prefabricated hut, and quietly closed the door.

Beatriz had followed Pip towards the south gates, joining dozens of people with the same idea: confront the SkyBlock representatives in their offices and demand to know what was happening.

The guards and cops at the gate had closed ranks. They were now three deep, all facing into the field, all with their hands resting on their batons. Beyond them, a line of seven Judges.

It might have been resolved peacefully, maybe, if one of the guards hadn't been stupid. As the people screamed and swore at them, the guard—an overweight, red-bearded man Beatriz had never seen before—said, "I want you to all go back to your homes and cool off. It's probably just some dumb mistake. Things like that happen all the time. Probably just some schlub in their office hit the wrong button or something. I guarantee you that everything will be straightened out soon enough and your original agreements will be honoured."

A woman in the crowd yelled, "*You're* not a resident here... Did *you* get that e-mail?"

"No. But that's—"

"If you didn't get one, how'd you know what it says?"

He didn't have an answer to that.

Standing next to Beatriz, Pip said, "They knew in advance—that's why extra security was brought in! And if they knew in advance, then it couldn't have been a mistake!"

That had triggered more yelling, and in response the guards had drawn their batons.

A man had pushed his way through the crowds, a baseball bat in his hand. Beatriz recognised him immediately as Stafford Holzer, one of her father's friends. Bat held down by his side, Holzer had said, "You let us through, or this ends badly."

The red-bearded man had replied, "Dude, they're not even *in* there."

"Their cars went in this morning, same as every morning.

Saw them myself. And they haven't come out yet. What were they doing? Wrapping everything up before they threw our agreements in the garbage and sold the company to themselves for a huge profit?"

"Don't know, don't care. That's not the *SkyBlock* people in there, just the builders. You take one step closer with that bat, and it'll be an act of aggression. We will respond in kind."

"You got a big mouth when your friends are backin' you up."

"Just stand down. This doesn't have to get fatal."

Holzer had tightened his grip on the bat. "Are you *threatening* us?"

Beatriz hadn't seen it happen: she'd grabbed Pip's arm and was dragging him back through the crowds when they heard the shot.

Now, crouched on the roof, she could see Stafford Holzer's body on the ground, not far from that of the red-bearded guard, and at least thirty other people and guards.

She still wasn't sure who'd opened fire first, her side or the guards', but she didn't suppose it mattered. With the gunshot acting like a starting pistol, half of the crowd had surged forward—but the rest had scattered, sweeping up Beatriz with them.

She'd let go of Pip somewhere along the way but was too scared to look for him.

Some of the people had rushed back to their homes, others had run for the other gates, but there were guards and cops and Judges waiting there too.

Someone kept shouting, "Non-lethal! Non-lethal!" and she wasn't sure whether that was a Judge giving an order, or a civilian begging for clemency.

The phone signals had gone down again, of course. Mr. Bridwell had told her that it was part of the Judges' strategy: the people can't call their friends for help if they can't get a signal out.

As they'd rushed towards the east gate, a tear-gas canister sailed over the guards' heads and towards the crowd: a freckled teenage boy she didn't know darted out and hit it with his cricket-bat, sending it back out into the street. The boy's gleeful cheer of victory was cut short by a bullet to the throat, and four more to his chest.

Lying on the roof, Beatriz repeated something she'd done a while ago. How long, she couldn't tell; it felt like hours, but it was probably only minutes. She rolled onto her back, and stared up at the sky. Last time, she'd been able to pretend for a few minutes that despite the noise—the gunfire, the screams, the screech of metal as a stolen truck was rammed into the park's heavy railings—everything was peaceful. Looking straight up, all she could see were a few white clouds against the blue sky and a small flock of pigeons.

Now, though, there was also smoke. Thick, black smoke roiling up from the south side.

And the noise was a lot harder to ignore now. Judges bellowing orders through their loudhailers, people on the ground fighting back, sporadic bursts of gunfire, screams, crying, Lawranger sirens approaching from the distance, and helicopters, too, getting louder and closer.

This has to end soon! It can't... it can't go on forever!

There was another crash from the south, much louder and harder than before, and Beatriz rolled onto her side again to look. A truck from the Department of Justice, so large it took up both sides of the road at once.

It slammed into the stolen truck, crushing it like a paper cup, and kept going. Over the downed railing, across the open area—its massive tyres churning up the dirt and bodies indiscriminately—the black truck didn't slow when it hit the first hut, or the next, or the after that.

And Beatriz knew from the screams that those huts had not been empty.

CHAPTER SEVEN

The Department of Justice owned a fleet of seventy-one heavily customised Chinook CH-47F copters, and right now five of them were racing from Boston towards Philadelphia. The first four carried ten Judges each, headed for Hunting Park to help quell the riot.

Alone in the back of the fifth copter, inside a double-insulated bubble that cut out almost all of the noise from the copter's twin rotors, Francesco Deacon looked at the cell phone in his hands and again cursed the timing of all this. "It's the first strong lead we've had on Romley since Golgotha," he told Marisa Pellegrino. "If this is real... The last person we apprehended who had direct contact with him was Niño Aukins—and that was eighteen years ago. I *have* to go."

Marisa nodded. "I understand. And Eustace would too. If we can take down Romley, it would cut Trance production by eighty per cent. Maybe more. You take him down *hard*. And alive, if you can. What's the situation with Hawker? How can we be sure that Romley doesn't have someone inside the precinct?"

"He possibly does—but I had the precinct locked down as soon as Romley's name surfaced."

"There's a covert holding facility in Philadelphia. It's vacant right now. We could have Hawker transferred there."

Deacon rolled his eyes. "Another one of your pet projects?"

"I *saw* that, Deac. Do you want the place or not?

"Send me the details."

"You'll need someone solid to handle the relocation. Senior Judge Gaines has an immaculate record. She's... spirited, and takes a bit of getting used to, but she's a good Judge."

"All right. I've already assigned the lead on Hawker's case to someone I know I can trust."

"After what happened with Crow, I'm surprised you can trust *anyone*. But you're talking about Errol Quon, aren't you? The cop from Golgotha? Yeah, she's the right choice—Unity Kurzweil's still singing her praises. I've actually been looking at Quon for something else, but that'll probably be a few years away." Pellegrino paused, and looked into the camera. "Or maybe not that long. Everything's changed now."

"Marisa, I wish I didn't have to leave you there alone to deal with the fallout."

"I know. But I've talked to Goodman and Solomon, *and* the President. They're thinking that Solomon will take over as Chief Judge. Clarence Goodman is content with remaining Deputy."

"That's *not* what Eustace would have wanted. Goodman's the better option."

"I agree. But both President Pierce and Mayor Rivera get on better with Solomon, and in general the public sees him as more human than Goodman, who they think is just one of Fargo's lackeys. When the Autonomy Act kicks in—and with Eustace out of the picture, that's probably going to happen a lot sooner than we'd like—Pierce wants Solomon on his side to help negotiate with the Texans and Californians." Marisa smiled. "You know, a few years back, Eustace told me that if anything happened, he wanted *you* to take over."

"He once told *me* that his biggest regret was that he'd never been able to persuade you to put on the uniform. You could have been a great Judge, Marisa. You could still be."

"You're deflecting, but I'll let that slide given the circumstances." She looked away from the screen for a second.

"I never wanted to be a leader, Deac. Nudge people in the right direction, sure, but not take charge. Besides, I'm too old now to get through the training." He and Marisa and Fargo had known each other for three decades, and worked closely together for most of that time, but they didn't often speak of their personal lives. Not that any of them had a lot of free time anyway. They hadn't even discussed the recent discovery about Fargo's 'external interests'—as Marisa had put it—other than to fight fires.

Deacon had made a mental note to bring it up at the next appropriate opportunity: there hadn't been many people in the world who could sit down with the Chief Judge and tell him to his face that he'd been a fool. There were even fewer who could say that and have Fargo actually listen to them. But now the chance was gone. "I keep thinking that if I'd *talked* to him..."

"I know. Clarence said that he and Solomon did what they could. Deac... I asked you earlier whether you were thinking it was time to hang up the badge. You *have* been thinking that. Don't deny it. And so have I. When this period of... *transition* is over, I'm stepping back. There's a whole new generation of Judges who don't even know who I am."

"You can't quit if you don't officially have a job, Marisa."

"Eustace needed people like us to get this whole thing started. But now..."

Deacon said, "We'll talk when the dust has settled. Properly, I mean. There's... a lot of things we've left *unsaid*, things we've pushed aside because the job always came first. But the job doesn't last forever."

"I disagree," Marisa said. "The *job* lasts forever. But *we* don't."

On the roof of Philadelphia's central Department of Justice building, Judge Quon had to shout her name to be heard over the roar of the copter's rotors.

The Judge guarding the precinct's roof entrance looked her up and down for a moment, then unclipped a small scanner from his belt. "Helmet off," he yelled, though the noise from the departing copter was already subsiding. "Submit to a retinal scan."

As the device's low-powered lasers flickered over Quon's eyes, a Judge pushed open the door behind the guard and stepped out. "Olivia Gaines, Senior Judge. I prefer to be addressed as 'Sir,' not 'Ma'am,' in deference to my rank rather than my gender. So what the hell's all this about? No one but *you* in or out, every phone and comm line for three blocks is down. We've had to divert all cases to the outlying precincts."

Quon asked, "Judge Gaines, my orders were to report here and speak to you. Privately."

The Judge guarding the door stepped aside. "Identity confirmed, sir."

Judge Gaines pulled the door open further. She was a head taller than Quon with a very broad build, a crew-cut hairstyle that was now growing out, and a face that could clearly switch from scowl to smile in microseconds. "Good to have you here, Quon. We'll talk in my office. And we're still on lockdown?"

"That's my understanding."

"Wish it was mine. Clearly you have friends in Olympus. That's Boston, the seat of power, before you ask."

Quon replaced her helmet and followed the woman down through the building. The place reminded her of her high school back in Merrion: roughly finished walls made smooth by decades of thick off-white paint, tiled floor with peeling duct tape over the cracks, rails in the stairwell polished by countless hands. A strong odour of antiseptic cleaning agent lingered in the air: someone had recently mopped the floors.

"I've been here since the beginning, just about," Gaines said. "We had to do some pretty heavy structural work when we converted this building, but it holds up. And it makes more sense than a new building because of the *atmosphere*. You ever read Eloise Thallheimer's study on the psychological impact a precinct can have on the citizens, Quon? She said if you have a new building, that makes them unsettled because everything about it is alien. But you *convert* a building, that gives them the impression that the Department of Justice is adapting itself to fit in with what's already there. Makes them feel safer. Is this your first time in Philly?"

"Yes, sir." She had to pick up speed to keep up with Gaines.

"You'll like it. Best city in the world, and that's *official*." Gaines looked down at Quon. "The birthplace of America. The cradle of modern civilisation, if some of the local historians are to be believed. On the other end of things, there's even a bunch of survivalists out in the hills who've overanalysed the Bible and come to the conclusion that the End of Days begins right here in Philly. The Lord himself will come down from the sky in a golden chariot and save them. Are you a believer, Quon?" Without waiting for an answer, Gaines said, "Not that it matters. We are Judges, our individuality is inconsequential. We're here to serve the people, and that's all. The big problem is that the average Jane on the street doesn't seem to be able to grasp the simple truth, which is that 'serving the people' means giving them what we know they *need*, not what they've convinced themselves they *want*. Wouldn't you agree?"

I might if I could get a word in, Quon thought, as Gaines continued. It was nerves, and that was understandable. When they arrested Brendan Hawker, they'd stumbled into something bigger than they'd been expecting.

She glanced up at Judge Gaines, who was still talking. *She's taking me the long way through the building so that as many people as possible see her with me. Showing them she's on board with whatever's going on and her authority hasn't been undermined.*

The unofficial tour ended in an office that looked like it had been converted from an old bathroom: the wall behind Gaines's desk even showed regularly spaced holes where the stall walls would once have been bolted to it.

Gaines dropped into her chair with a grunt. "All right. Speak."

"I've been sent to interrogate a prisoner, Brendan Hawker."

"Of course you have. That SOB says a name and everyone up on Mount Olympus wets themselves in panic." She nodded towards the computer on her desk. "Tried to look him up, but everything's locked out. That name Hawker mentioned... You going to tell me who he is?"

"No, sir."

"Good." Gaines again glanced at her computer. "Worth remembering, Quon: even the tightest ship can have leaks." She ran her hands over her face. "God, I miss *coffee*... Look, it's obvious that the top brass are in a bad way right now. Fargo wasn't a legend for no reason. The man was a gruddamn hero no matter which way you look at it. I met him back in thirty-nine. Huh, that was *twelve years ago* now... Replacing him is gonna be a tough task."

"Sir, the prisoner?"

"Right, yeah." Gaines pushed herself out of her chair. "I've moved him to a secondary holding site that even *I* didn't know about until an hour ago. Makes sense. Hawker's on the most-wanted list, so you snag someone like that, you don't advertise their whereabouts. We'll keep this place locked down so if anyone *does* come a-knockin' for him, they'll be a-knockin' on the wrong door."

Gaines led Quon back out into the corridor, and they walked side by side out to the street, where two Judges at the main door had to unlock it to let them out.

An unmarked car stood waiting for them. "Get in. It's not far, but best to drive."

Quon settled into the passenger seat and clipped her seat belt into place, which drew a slight smirk from Gaines. "Safety first, right? But take off your helmet—don't want anyone seeing me driving a Judge around and wondering where we're going. So you came in from Baltimore?"

Quon removed her helmet. "That's right."

Gaines nodded, and pulled out into the street without checking for oncoming traffic. "Never been there. But we kicked your butts more times than you kicked ours, and you *hate* us for that."

"I don't..."

"The Ravens and the Steelers, Quon. *Football.* Guess no one follows it much any more, but my old man was a die-hard supporter." She turned left, then right, heading into the Bella Vista district. "Steelers all the way, that was Pop. Got the logo tattooed all across his back after the play-offs in 2010, but it was kinda crappily done so he never showed anyone."

Six minutes later, on a quiet street in a mostly abandoned industrial area, Gaines turned a sharp left into the partly demolished shell of old red-brick building, slowing the car down just enough to avoid scraping the passenger side along a metre-thick pillar.

Deep inside the building, in a stained-concrete clearing surrounded by discarded girders, rusting construction equipment and giant lumps of masonry, Gaines hit the brakes with the same abruptness as every other part of the journey. The car screeched, and Quon was glad she'd put on the seat belt.

"This is our stop. Let's go."

Quon climbed out. "Judge Gaines, I could fine you for reckless driving."

The older woman laughed. "That's true, I guess." She gestured towards a wide concrete stairwell sealed off with recently installed bars. "This way. So, the department took over the building a long time ago with the idea of building an Isolation Block here, but everything is behind schedule." She shrugged. "That's the *official* line, anyway, which I totally absolutely believe one hundred per cent. Quon, you should know that comms are out here too. Cell phones, radios, whatever. But you won't be on your own: I've got my best Judge down there."

At the stairwell, Gaines touched a keycard against a reader, and a section of the bars swung open. "This is the only way in or out, and I've got the only key with the right codes, apparently." She thumped one of the bars as she passed through. "Seriously, you'd need a *tank* to get through this."

The holding area was two floors below ground level, past two more sets of bars. "*Told* you it was secure," Gaines said.

The final door opened on a converted underground parking garage, with walls erected between the pillars to form cells. There were still bay numbers and direction arrows painted on the sloping concrete floor, and in an alcove to the left, a large collection of rusting scaffolding poles, ancient planks, and a dozen large, ancient metal signs bearing the messages *Pay Fee Before Returning to Vehicle*, *Exact Change Only* and *Management Is Not Responsible for Damage, Loss or Theft* were stacked up against the wall.

The cells were windowless; the only light came in through the barred doors.

A slender male Judge stood outside the only cell with a closed door, one hand resting on the 'Lawkeeper' gun at his hip, a closed cardboard box by his feet. Past him, through the bars, Quon could see the prisoner sitting on the floor in the middle of the room, peering back at her.

"Sitrep?" Judge Gaines asked.

"We're flying true, sir."

"Good to hear it. Prisoner's all yours, Quon. I need to check in, but Judge Cusack will stay here on guard duty. He was supposed to be off today, so even his own colleagues don't know he's here. Right, Cusack?"

"Hundred per cent, sir."

As Judge Gaines left, Cusack used his foot to slide the cardboard box towards Quon. "The prisoner's effects." He nodded towards the closed door. "You sure you don't want me in there with you, Judge?"

Quon scooped up the box. "No need. Just lock the door behind us. And step back out of earshot."

As the cell door closed behind her, the prisoner began, "So who are—?"

"Quiet." She waited until Judge Cusack had locked the door and stepped back, then looked down at the prisoner.

He'd been stripped down to his underwear and was sitting on the floor with his wrists and ankles cuffed and connected by a fifty-centimetre-long chain—too short for him to even stand upright. The only defence he had from someone outside the cell was the barred door. Sure, the bars—like those on the gates between floors—were almost as thick as his wrists and would probably take someone a long time to cut through, but they weren't going to be much use if the would-be assassin had a gun.

Quon pinned a tiny microphone to her collar and tapped it. "This will record everything you say and transmit it back to the Department of Justice." There was no need for him to know that right now they were in a comms blackout zone, so the microphone was recording instead of transmitting. "I'm Judge Errol Quon, formerly of Golgotha PD."

Dallas's shoulders dropped. "Ah." After a moment, he asked, "Were you on *my* case?"

"No. I was co-opted by the Department of Justice to help arrest Sullivan Reidt." She dropped the box in the corner, crouched down next to it, and began to remove its contents.

"I remember that name. One of my targets—" He hesitated, biting his lip. "I guess you'd prefer 'victims.' Anyway, one of them mentioned Reidt, said he was her boss's supplier, but I checked him out. He was a useless drunk. Could barely stand up most of the time. So, I figured my target or her boss had been lying. The boss was Deborah Rozek—you got to *her* around the same time it all went bad for me, didn't you?" A shrug. "My memory of those last few days is a little hazy. There was a *lot* going on."

Quon looked down at the line of Hawker's personal items. Pair of sneakers, heavily used, two or three years old. Plain light-grey cotton T-shirt, old but clean. Black sweatpants, also cotton. Wallet containing nothing but one hundred and twelve dollars in bills: no driver's licence, credit cards, store receipts or anything else that could be used to incriminate him. His cell phone was a Pleiades Vosburgh WD750Ti, fifteen years old at least. Perps loved them because they could download a software patch—now banned by the Department of Justice—that completely disabled all tracking features and could even fake the caller's location. The only other item in the box was a manifest list produced by the precinct when Hawker was arrested: it specified that the cell phone's memory had been cloned and uploaded to the department's servers.

She placed everything back in the box. "You're facing a death sentence, Hawker. The only reason it hasn't yet been carried out is that you mentioned Irvine Desmond Romley. There's no way you could know the name if you don't know the man, and we know you weren't working for him back in Golgotha."

"Of course not." Dallas looked down at his cuffed hands. "I was one of the good guys. Or *trying* to be. If you *were* there, Judge, then you know what it was like. So much corruption, so much poison. My group did a lot of your work for you. If not for us, crime in Golgotha would have been much worse. We saved hundreds of lives. Maybe *thousands*."

"You can paint the past any colour you like, Hawker, but that doesn't change its *shape*. You killed at least fourteen people. Regardless of what they were guilty of, that was still premeditated murder. But... I've been authorised to inform you that you can avoid the death penalty if you supply us with sufficient information that leads to the apprehension of Irvine Romley."

"I don't believe you, Judge Quon. I think you'll just execute me anyway. But that doesn't matter. I worked for Romley because he was blackmailing me. It was clear from the way he found me that he was powerful enough to get to my wife and children. And the second *I* was arrested..." Dallas looked away, shaking his head. "They're dead now. He'll have given the word. Probably has a dozen assassins trying to get in *here* right now, to shut me up."

"Because he knows you *can* lead us to him."

He shuffled about a little. "Romley's very intelligent, but he sometimes forgets that other people can be smart too."

"What name is he using these days? Or *names*, if there's more than one?"

"None. I mean, he made it clear a few years ago that I wasn't to address him by *any* name. He phones, and I don't say, 'Hi, Mr. Romley.' I just say, 'Hi.' Same with the other people who work for him, I think. That guy who killed himself today, Charlie Kibbs, he only referred to Romley as 'the guy.'"

"Where is Romley right now?"

"I don't know *exactly* where. But I know he's here in Philly because that's why I'm here. I go where he tells me, and a few weeks back, he told me to come here. I met up with him in Washington Square four days ago. He didn't say *why* he was here, and I know better than to ask, but it was some important business. I mean, more important than Trance stuff. I know because he had his best suit on. He normally dresses well, but this was, y'know, *tailored*. I've only seen him wear it a couple of times."

Quon looked around the bare cell, then crouched down about two metres from the prisoner. "What reason do you have to think that he's *still* here?"

"When he called this morning, he was in his hotel room—I could tell from a painting on the wall behind him. I don't know *which* hotel he stays in, but it's always the same room. He doesn't have many habits, but that's one of them."

From the outside of the cell, Judge Gaines's voice called out, "Cusack, I'm back. Everything all right down there?"

"Yes, sir," he yelled back. "Everything is both hunky *and* dory."

"Good to hear. I'm going to get the prisoner's lunch. Ask Quon if she's okay with that."

Cusack moved closer to the door and looked in through the bars.

"Sure," Quon told him. "But we want pre-packaged food *only*, and I want to see it first."

"That's SOP," Cusack asked, "but I'll tell her."

When Cusack stepped away from the door again, Quon

turned back to Dallas. "So, he's in Philadelphia. Maybe it's *not* a hotel room. Maybe he has an apartment here?"

"No, I'm sure it's a hotel. The room is always spotless. No socks left out, the little desk is always tidy. No piles of books by the bed. I don't get the impression that he lives there."

"Some people are just neat-freaks," Quon suggested.

"I know, but..." Dallas frowned. "It *feels* like a hotel room."

"You ever get a glimpse through the window?"

"Couple of times, but I didn't recognise anything. Just a building across the street. I suppose that tells us it's not a very high floor."

"Day or night?"

"Day."

"What time of day? Which way were the shadows falling?"

"So you can work out which way the window faces. Makes sense..." He closed his eyes. "The building across the street. Tan-coloured blocks, square windows, no fire escape... the sunlight was coming from the right, around midday."

"So the room faces east," Quon said.

"Yeah, I guess so." He suddenly sat back, staring at Quon. "Hold on... The *wall sockets* in his room. You know how they are in a lot of hotels: you get your desk and a mirror on the wall above it, but below that you have the power points and charging ports. Someone could have that same set-up in their home, too, but in hotels, the ports have labels on them. You wouldn't do that in your own home. So, yeah, definitely a hotel. And if he's always in a hotel when he comes to Philly, then that means he doesn't live here. That doesn't narrow things down very much, though. That part of his life is sewn up pretty tight."

"Describe him."

"He's... ordinary. Male, white guy, mid-sixties at most. Keeps himself fit. A little above average height. Grey hair, clean shaven." Dallas pointed to the microphone pinned to Quon's collar. "I suppose you're building an identikit picture, right?"

"Close your eyes, Hawker. Try to picture the last time you saw him." Then she turned on the pressure with a series of rapid-fire questions, forcing him to answer without thinking too much about it. "Does he resemble anyone famous? Any identifying marks? What colour are his eyes? Does he have any moles, old acne scars, freckles, tattoos? What about chin- or cheek-dimples? Eyebrows—thick or thin? What colour? Is his nose straight? Bumped? Crooked? Nostrils both the same size? Are his teeth white? Any discolouration? Are they all straight and even? Does he have a lot of beard-shadow? Any marks on his hands? Scars? Age-spots? Fingernails—neat or ragged? Manicured or just clipped? What about body hair? Does he have excessive hair on his fingers, or on his arms poking out of his cuffs? Is he left-handed or right-handed? When he's standing, does he tend to put his weight on his left foot or his right?"

Quon had done this before, many times, and although Dallas was clearly rattled by the barrage of questions, he did better than most. Every solid answer would help to whittle down the list of suspects. "All right. If you think of anything else that might be relevant, just say it. You'll only get your sentence commuted if we're able to apprehend Romley. Do you have any access to his personal files that might—?"

From far above there came a series of loud metallic clunks as the barred doors were opened and closed one by one, then Cusack called out, "Food's here, Judge Quon."

She stood up and stretched. "Go ahead."

Cusack unlocked the door, then stepped aside. Judge Gaines entered carrying a cardboard tray containing four candy bars, three small bags of chips, and two cans of soda. "Hope you like diet root beer, Hawker, because that's all the store had that doesn't contain sugar or caffeine."

"Not a fan, but... thanks. And I need to use the john."

"Not yet," Quon said. "You can last a couple more hours. If your bladder was full, you'd be squirming more."

Gaines placed the tray on the floor, and straightened up.

"Judge Quon, you've got a visitor up top. Judge Deacon."

Quon glanced at her watch. "Has he been waiting long?"

"Few minutes. Asked me to check whether it was okay to bring him down."

Quon reached for her Lawkeeper, but for someone who grunted when she leant over or got into or out of a chair, Judge Gaines's reactions were surprisingly swift and fluid. She had her own Lawkeeper out and firing before Quon could take aim. The shot struck Quon's gun-arm, knocking her gun clear across the room.

Gaines wheeled back and fired at Cusack—who was already in the process of drawing his own weapon—hitting him in the chest, then, still moving, swung her arm to aim directly at the prisoner's head.

CHAPTER EIGHT

THE JUDGES CAME swarming in after the truck, most on foot, some riding their powerful motorbikes over the wreckage of the fence.

Beatriz immediately swung herself back down from the roof, but there was still nowhere to go so she did the only thing she *could* do, something her parents and teachers had taught her from an early age: find a spot that's out of the way, but where people can see you, and lie face down with your hands visible so they won't have any reason to assume you have a weapon.

As she lay on the floor of her family's temporary home, she hoped that the Judges understood what she was doing. Not resisting. When the cops come, you *never* resist. Resisting is the same as attacking, and that's justification for a couple of shots in the back of your head.

Once, when she was about eight, Grampa—her mother's dad—had told her that it used to be different. "We had drills in school for when a shooter came. Hide, keep still, make no noise. You could pretend to be dead already, but they might just put a couple of rounds in you anyway, just to be sure. It's different with the *cops*, though. For them, it's all about us making sure we know our place. The school shooter wants to be famous, so's he can get whatever dumb-ass message he has out there, but the cops want us to call them 'Master.' Can't do that if we're all dead." Bea's parents had admonished the old man, but he'd refused to apologise or tell Beatriz he'd been exaggerating.

And now she could hear them approaching, heavy footsteps, doors being kicked open, stern voices calling out, "Clear!" or "Live one! You—hands where we can see them!"

There were gunshots, too. Not many, but they came one at a time, the sharp bark of a Judge's Lawkeeper. That was worse than when there was an exchange of shots, which indicated people were fighting back. One shot at a time meant the Dreadnoughts were carrying out executions. Beatriz couldn't help counting the shots. Each one was another funeral for the community to attend.

The footsteps were getting closer now. Loud voices from Mr. Bridwell's place next door: she could hear him desperately trying to explain that he had nothing to do with the riot. Then a sharp crack followed by a heavy thump: she pictured that as a rifle-butt striking Mr. Bridwell across the head, and him hitting the floor.

Immediately outside Beatriz's door a man's voice said, "Live one... You, citizen! Do *not* move. Understood?"

She nodded her head very slightly, and said, "Understood."

"Is there anyone else in there? Anyone armed? Bear in mind that at this time I've got my sidearm aimed at your head. Any sudden movement and I *will* open fire."

"I'm alone, I promise!"

"Better be."

Something light and plastic bumped into her arm.

"Zip-tie. Don't move until I give the word. Then, keeping your hands where they are, you will roll onto your side so that you're facing away from me, with your arms behind your back, wrists together. Do you understand? Yes or no."

"Yes."

"Do it—slowly!"

Her arms trembling, Beatriz rolled onto her side, but not

before she looked up at the Judge who was pointing his Lawkeeper in her face.

He couldn't have been more than two years older than her.

DALLAS KNEW IT was more luck than skill that saved his life. He'd flinched as Judge Gaines shot at Quon, then as she spun to shoot at the Judge outside the cell, he'd tried to roll away—but his hands and ankles were still chained to the floor. Just as she fired at his head, he reached the extent of the chain and jerked forward.

Half a second later and the bullet would have struck him square in the forehead, but instead it buried itself in the concrete wall behind him, and then Judge Quon body-slammed Gaines, knocking her off balance.

Unable to get away, ears ringing from the gunshots, all Dallas could do was watch.

Before they hit the ground, Quon had grabbed Gaines's gun-arm, forcing it up and away from Dallas as Gaines fired again. This shot struck the ceiling, quickly joined by two more.

Quon had the much larger Judge on the ground, face down, her left arm around her throat, her right—the wrist already drenched in blood—balled into a tight fist that she jabbed into Gaines's side directly beneath her armpit, four powerful punches in rapid succession, while at the same time Quon repeatedly and forcefully slammed her helmeted forehead into the back of Gaines's head, bouncing Gaines's own forehead against the floor.

He looked over towards the other Judge, Cusack. The man was lying on his back, unmoving, a growing crimson pool around him.

He knew that the Judges' uniforms had built-in body armour, but at that range it wouldn't have helped much more than a thick sweater.

Gaines heaved herself up off the floor, Quon still on her back trying to strangle her, and turned to face Dallas again. Blood sprayed from her shattered nose and torn lips. The Judge still had her Lawkeeper in her hand, though her aim was unsteady. She looked like she was on the verge of blacking out, her muscles straining against Quon's grip.

Another shot: he flinched to the side as the bullet grazed his temple and tore a chunk out of his left ear, but even before the pain registered, Gaines had fired again. The shot passed through his right shoulder just above the collarbone.

He must have passed out because suddenly he was on the ground, on his side, looking to Judge Quon as she climbed to her feet. Gaines lay between them, her eyes closed, blood and drool spilling from her mouth.

From far above came indistinct shouts, then a high-pitched electronic whine that he felt was familiar but couldn't place.

He looked down at himself. Blood still oozed from the hole in his shoulder and was now making its way down through his chest hair, soaking into the waistband of his underpants.

Quon had her right arm clutching the collar of her uniform as she limped over to Cusack, and then towards Dallas, and he could see why: Gaines's shot had passed clean through her forearm, leaving a hole you could almost poke a finger through.

"You're hit," Quon said. "How bad?"

"There's not as much pain as I thought there'd be."

"Not yet. You're in shock. Raise up your hands." She pulled a handcuff key from a pouch on her belt and unlocked the cuffs. "Same key will unlock your ankles."

As he fumbled to insert the key into the lock around his ankles, Quon used her own cuffs on Gaines.

"What about Judge Cusack?"

"He's dead," Quon said. "So Romley had something on Gaines... Did *you* know that, Hawker?"

"If I did, I'd have mentioned it, wouldn't I?" As he was getting to his feet, he put his right hand down—and a wave of agony rushed over him from his shoulder.

"Did I say you could get up?" Quon asked. "Just stay put, let me take a look at your wounds."

"Judge Quon, we're sitting ducks in a barrel here... If Romley had Gaines in his pocket and she was the senior Judge, then there'll be others. He never has only *one* plan—there's always a backup. And a backup for *that* backup. That's why you've never caught him." He flinched as the Judge placed a steri-patch on his chest, and again when she did the same with the exit wound.

"Your ear will have to be stitched, but right now that's not a priority—the bleeding's mostly stopped. Whoever's up top will get through the doors soon—that's a laser-cutter from the sound of it. We have to not be here when they get through."

"What about the other one, your friend? Gaines said *he* was waiting for you upstairs."

"She was lying, trying to get me out of here so she could deal with you. That's what tipped me off—Judge Deacon's not due to reach the city for another"—she looked at her watch again—"twenty-four minutes."

"So if we can hold them off until then, we're safe?" Dallas said.

She took hold of Dallas's left arm and helped him to stand. "I'm not letting him walk unprepared into a potentially lethal situation. He's worth more than both our lives."

"Not to me."

Then Quon was shoving Dallas towards the wall with such force that he'd have tripped over his bare feet had she not been holding his arm. He hit the wall hard, on his bad shoulder, and a fresh blast of pain radiated through him.

Quon leant close, her teeth gritted. "One more crack like that and I'll remember that you've already got a death sentence, Hawker. We don't need you nearly as much as you need *us*. Do you understand? Yes or no."

"Yes."

She shoved him towards the box containing his clothes, then went to retrieve her Lawkeeper. "Get dressed. We've got to find a way out of here."

CHAPTER NINE

WITH HER HANDS tied behind her back, and a thick cloth bag over her head, Beatriz Graziano had to rely on the Judge tightly gripping her upper arm to steer her through the wreckage of the park. From all around came the voices of the other residents—some crying, some pleading, most angry—and the barked orders of the Judges.

This wasn't going to end well, she was certain of that much. When the Dreadnoughts came for you, that was pretty much game over. Everyone knew that.

The Judge jerked her to the left. "Step up. *Up!*"

Beatriz raised her right foot and gingerly set it down on what felt like a wooden platform. It gave a little under her weight, sagged a lot more when the Judge stepped on it too.

He steered her around the uneven platform and along the way her foot collided with something small and metal that rotated out of the way. *A door handle... we're walking across the remains of someone's home!*

"Step down. One metre ahead. *Watch* it, citizen!"

She blurted out, "You try watching where you're going with a bag on your head!"

The Judge shifted his grip a little, then the back of his hand smacked into the side of her head hard enough to almost knock her off her feet. As she staggered, a woman's voice from a few metres away shouted, "You *bastard!* Hitting a girl when she's blindfolded!"

A different Judge, gruffer, almost breathless, snarled, "Shut it!"

"Drokk you," the woman said, her voice steady, but hard. "Drokk *all* of you. We didn't do anything wrong, but you're treating us like—"

A sharp crack cut her off, then Beatriz heard the gruff Judge mutter, "Goddamn it." Louder, he said, "Winters, Kinsella... bag this one and get her to the med-truck. Tell them to check for concussion and a possible fractured skull. And *watch* her. She's a troublemaker. She's already down for two years for resisting."

The Judge steered her further away. The steady murmur of voices was increasing, the smell of sweat growing stronger. She brushed against someone else, who yelped and flinched away.

They reached a grassy area, and the Judge let go of her arm. "Stay put. Say nothing. You get the order to march forward, you march until you're told otherwise. Understood?"

Beatriz nodded.

"I said, is that *understood*, citizen? Answer me."

"Yes, sir."

She heard the Judge move away, then more and more people were deposited around her. On her left, a woman smelling strongly of lavender and urine was rapidly but quietly muttering a prayer.

On her right, a man's hairy arm brushed against hers, and he softly said, "Susannah... Susannah... is that you?" He swayed a little into her. "Susannah? It's me, Daddy."

She wanted to tell him that she wasn't his daughter, but the Judge had ordered her not to talk. This could be a trap. The Judges did that sort of thing. They didn't *need* an excuse to hurt a citizen, but it made things easier if they had one.

Louder, the man said, "Susannah, it's Daddy. Are you *there*, honey?" Louder still, his voice cracking, "If you can hear me, *say* something!"

Someone else whispered, "Jesus, shut *up*, will ya? They'll take it out on alla us!"

The man yelled, "Susannah! Are you all right? Did they *hurt* you? Just tell me you're all ri—"

A scuffle, and the man was silent, then there came a grunt and two heavy thumps, and the scrape of something heavy being dragged away.

For several minutes, the only sound came from Beatriz's own breathing, and the woman on her left who was repeating the same short prayer over and over: "In Jesus's name, protect us from all harm and guide us into your arms in the Kingdom of Heaven forever and ever. Amen."

A young man on the far side of the woman said, "Give us a break, huh? Jesus ain't real, and if he *was*, then he lets stuff like this happen to us, so what's *that* make him? Evil, that's what. You got the power to help people and you don't? Then you're an asshole."

Don't, please, Beatriz said to herself. *Stop talking—or they'll take it out on all of us!*

A strong female voice from somewhere on her right called out, "Listen up! My name is Judge Guzowski, and you citizens are now in my care. You'll be taken to a safe place for processing. If you're innocent, you've got nothing to worry about. You give us any trouble, well, then you *won't* be innocent. You got any questions, I don't wanna hear them. In one minute, we're gonna start walking forward. Slow and steady. Bear in mind that someone ahead of you might be old, or slow, or they might trip, so you don't want to rush."

There was a pause, then Judge Guzowski's voice came again, a lot closer to Beatriz this time. "Any of you thinking about making a run for it, you reconsider that. You can't see where you're going, and every Judge here is an excellent shot. Is that understood? I want to hear a *Yes, Judge* from all of you. Right now."

Beatriz said, "Yes, Judge," but she couldn't hear her own voice over all the others.

"Good enough. Judge Schonning, that citizen on your left is angled a good fifteen degrees off course. Correct her. All right. Counting down. On my word."

From somewhere ahead, an old man with a strong Jamaican accent called out, "Someone just tell me what laws we broke!"

Guzowski, now standing so close to Beatriz that she could smell the Judge's deodorant, yelled, "No talking!"

"You'll pay for this in the next life, woman! The Almighty is the only one who can sit in judgement. You people are an affront to him!"

"Judge Schonning, if that citizen speaks again, you'll take him out of the line and make an example of him."

"Sir!"

The man with the Jamaican accent said, "On Sunday. On *God's* day. Shameful!"

"Always one," Guzowski muttered, then louder, "Schonning?"

There was a scuffle ahead, and Beatriz mentally pictured a strong, scowling Judge pushing through the crowd and dragging the old man out.

"They're gonna kill me!" The old man yelled. "This is *murder!* They took our homes and now they're takin' our *lives!* My name is—"

A gunshot triggered a wave of screams and crying. Someone crashed into Beatriz from behind and she would have been knocked to the ground if Judge Guzowski hadn't grabbed her arm and held her steady.

After a few seconds, Guzowski yelled, "Enough! Judges, get them back in line! He's not dead—that was a *warning* shot!" Softer, she said, "For cryin' out loud, Schonning, what'd you do that for?"

"Sorry, sir."

Beatriz softly said, "Judge, I don't want to *die*."

There was a tiny pause, then Guzowski said, "Shut up."

"Just tell me what we did *wrong*."

"I said, shut *up*. Won't tell you again." The Judge moved away, and yelled, "Get ready to move. On my word... March."

* * *

QUON HAD ALREADY stripped both Gaines and Cusack of their weapons, ammunition and supplies, and as she was double-cuffing Gaines's wrists and ankles, a shock wave of pain rippled through her wounded right arm. She tentatively peeled back her right sleeve and bit down on her lip to stifle a gasp.

The good news was that Gaines's shot hadn't shattered either the radius or the ulna. Instead, the bullet had passed between the bones, scraping them both as it made its way through her arm. She'd never be this lucky again. If the shot had hit her wrist or her elbow, she'd be out of commission for a long time.

From behind her, Gaines—her voice weak and cracked—said, "That's gonna take *years* to heal. Sorry."

Quon turned to face her. "Romley got to you."

"*Someone* did..." Gaines shrugged as well as she could against her cuffs, then looked towards the stairwell. "I guess he has fingers in *every* pie, huh? They followed me back here. Said they just want Dallas Hawker dead. They *know* stuff about me... things I thought I'd buried a long time ago. I was told to blame you, say you'd gone off the rails." Gaines sniffed, then raised her hands to brush her nose with the back of her wrist. "And... I have a sister in Tampa. She and her partner have a little girl." Again, she looked towards the stairwell. "Those men upstairs... they showed me live camera feed from a cell phone. If Hawker doesn't die, my niece does."

Standing next to Quon, with his blood-drenched T-shirt in his hands, Dallas said, "Do it." He turned to Quon. "My life is over anyway—they'll find a way to get to me—so *do* it, Quon. Put your gun against my head and pull the trigger because I'm not going to live with a little girl's death on my conscience."

The tutors in the Academy of Law had spent a lot of time discussing morally ambiguous situations, and the official line was that Judges would never bow to threats or blackmail. *Cornered perp, threatens to kill his hostage if you don't let him go. What do you* do? *Cadet Quon?* She had answered that the correct action was to shoot the perp. *Just like that? And what about the* hostage? *You'd risk an innocent person's life? Why not let him go and take the chance that you can catch up with him later?* Quon had replied, *Because we might* not *catch up with him, and a lot more people could die.*

Now, Quon looked down at Judge Gaines—*former* Judge Gaines, she reminded herself—and her stomach churned, but she knew the right thing to do. "I'm not going to kill you, Dallas. You're our best shot at getting to Romley."

Gaines said, "Please. My niece! She—"

"Enough." Quon pulled the knife out of the back of her boot, then crouched down next to Cusack's body, and cut a long, wide strip from the sleeve of his uniform.

"You do this and you're *killing* her!" Gaines yelled.

"Then I'll regret my choice. But if we don't stop Romley I'll regret it even more. It's simple math. Better one than many."

"Jesus, Quon! You are one cold-hearted, class-A *bitch!*"

"I've been told. But *you're* the one who's just murdered her friend, and tried to kill me and Hawker." She stepped behind Gaines, and tied the strip over her mouth, gagging her, tying it as tight as her wounded arm allowed.

"You need help over there, Hawker?"

"Can't get my shirt on."

"Hold on." She placed steri-patches over the entry and exit wounds on her wrist, and hoped they'd hold long enough to get out. If there *was* a way out.

This place had once been a parking garage, but that was before the Department of Justice took over the building. It was a certainty that they'd filled in the entrance and exit ramps. She closed her eyes, and tried to picture what it would have looked like originally.

Parking garage under a disused building, two floors down. Steps up to the ground floor, doors locked at each floor. Gaines said she had the only keycard... which is why whoever's up there is cutting their way in now.

Dallas yelped again, and Quon walked over to him. With

one good arm each, they managed to pull his T-shirt on.

"So, what do we do now?" Dallas asked, as he picked up one of the cans of root beer and awkwardly cracked it open.

"We need a way out." Quon unclipped her holster from her belt and attached it to the left side instead.

"You're ambidextrous?"

"No. But I can manage."

Dallas nodded towards Judge Gaines. "Have to hand it to her... I've never seen anyone shoot like that before. She was *fast*. She—"

The whine of the laser-cutter abruptly stopped.

"That's not good," Dallas said.

"They still have another two doors to get through. We have time."

"To do *what*? There's no other way out!"

"Sure there is."

CHAPTER TEN

Someone behind Beatriz grabbed her arm again and roughly steered her across a flat, echoing floor and into a specific spot.

"Sit. And stay put."

She did as she was told, and all around her she could hear more footsteps, more voices giving the same orders.

They were inside, she knew that for certain—the air-conditioning was a giveaway. The echoes and the slight spring in the floor made her think of a school gymnasium. A newly built one too: the air was laced with the scents of freshly sawn wood and drying paint.

A woman's voice came from somewhere behind Beatriz: "Please... my children are terrified! Why are you *doing* this to us?"

From in front of Beatriz, Judge Guzowski said, "No talking."

When the footsteps and scuffling settled down, Guzowski said, "This is the situation. Some among you chose to attack police officers, Judges and private guards employed by the owners of this building."

We're inside the new block, Beatriz realised.

"We know you're not *all* guilty, but what kind of Judges would we be if we allowed the perpetrators to go free because we didn't want to inconvenience you?"

From the left, a man's voice said, "You pigs rammed your truck through the crowds and into our *homes!*"

"That wasn't us," Guzowski said. "Rogue elements took control of that vehicle."

Beatriz called out, "That's a lie! I watched it happen! I *saw* the Judges getting out of the truck!"

"*Enough!*" Guzowski yelled, her voice closer than Beatriz was expecting. A thump of footsteps coming even closer as the Judge barked, "There will be no more talking!"

Then Beatriz felt a strong hand grab her left arm, haul her to her feet. "Got your first interviewee here, Ryburn! Take her up."

She felt another hand grab her right shoulder, and this time she tried to pull away. "Struggling is resisting, citizen!" a male voice said, almost in her ear. "You're just adding to your sentence. Shut up and do as you're told."

Judge Ryburn started pushing her ahead of him across the floor, his grip on her shoulder shifting until he had his hand on her neck, holding on firmly enough to make it clear what would happen if she tried to run.

A door was pulled open in front of her, then there was thick carpet underfoot, and the sound changed. They were in a corridor, and they weren't alone: they passed a man who smelled of engine grease, and he muttered, "Ryburn." Then two women, talking softly to each other and apparently unperturbed to see a Judge driving a teenage girl ahead of him.

After eighty or ninety steps, another door, another corridor, quieter this time.

Then tiled floor again, and a wide, echoing stairway, leading up. The steps were hard, definitely tiles or concrete. Beatriz counted fifty-four steps, not that that helped her; she couldn't tell how many steps there were between floors.

Judge Ryburn said, "Last step," and Beatriz was surprised to hear that he was slightly out of breath—until now, she'd only been focussed on her own breathing.

"On your left."

He steered her into another room, and again this one felt quite large. There was a smell of scorched plastic, and beneath that a hint of cinnamon, which—despite her fear—triggered a pang of hunger.

Ryburn stopped walking, then, from a few metres ahead of her, a man's voice asked, "Who's this?"

There was nothing for a few seconds, then the Judge roared into her ear. "Answer him!"

Beatriz took after her mother when it came to her temper. She could put up with a lot, almost anything, but if she was pushed too hard, she would suddenly snap. "How stupid *are* you? I didn't know he was talking to me because you drokkers put a *bag* over my head!"

Ryburn tightened his grip on her neck, his fingertips pressing deep into her flesh like steel pokers, and she tried to flinch away from him.

The man calmly said, "Scan her prints and DNA."

She felt something cold on her hands, then a few seconds later there was a soft beep from behind her, and Ryburn said, "Beatriz Maria Graziano, born January eighth, twenty-thirty-four. Student at Jermaine Andoh High. No previous. No warnings. No citations... Analysis of the securicam footage shows her at the scene of the first attack."

"Hmm. Clean record until today. What *triggered* you, Graziano? What makes a seventeen-year-old girl suddenly decide to take up arms against the Department of Justice?"

"I didn't! We weren't there to cause trouble—we were just looking for answers!"

"I'll remind you that lying to a Judge is a serious offence."

Doing her best to remain calm, Beatriz said, "I know that. I'm *not* lying. I'm not here because I did something wrong. I'm here because other people did something wrong and we complained about it. A Judge came into my home, pointed a gun at my face and put a bag over my head. Since then I've been pushed, pulled, beaten and screamed at. You're treating us like criminals, but we're *victims*. The SkyBlock people—"

"Enough. We've got over twelve hundred cases to get through today. Rioting, five years. Resisting arrest, one year."

Again, Beatriz tried to pull free of Ryburn's grip. "No! I didn't *do* anything!"

"Take her for processing. And tell Guzowski to pick up the pace. We don't want to be here all day."

The Judge started to steer Beatriz away, back the way they'd come, but as they turned she ducked and stepped backwards at the same time, then managed to twist around, breaking Ryburn's grip on her neck.

She knew it was futile, but she darted forward anyway.

Everyone had always told her that when it came to the Dreads she should offer no resistance, ever. Always do what a Judge tells you. Never give them even the slightest reason to think that you're more trouble alive than dead, because they're just waiting for an excuse to take you down.

But today she was learning that if someone has the power and the will to convict you without cause and to sentence you without evidence, then you've been fighting a losing battle from the beginning. The system is corrupt; it's not just your right to disrupt it any way you can, it's your duty.

As she blindly surged forward she felt Ryburn's grasping fingertips brush against her arm, then slip away, and for a second she thought she might just make it, somehow. If she could get out of this room—

Her left shin hit something hard—she later realised that it was Ryburn's boot tripping her up—and she pitched forward, cracked her head on the cold floor.

In more shock than pain, she lay still, on her side, as the man said, "For Christ's sake... Get her *up*, Ryburn. Make sure she hasn't fractured her skull."

She was again hauled to her feet, then the bag was pulled from her head. The sudden burst of light hurt more than the bump on her forehead, and she forced her eyes shut for a moment. As she carefully and slowly opened them again, the first thing she saw was her own distorted reflection in the Judge's visor.

"She'll be fine," Ryburn said as he stepped back. "Minor bruise, that's all."

Beatriz looked around the room. It was a large windowless office, still unfinished—bare walls, loose power cables, no furniture or decorations—and sitting on a crate in the centre of the room, using another pair of crates as a makeshift desk, was a middle-aged Judge. Male, Caucasian, ordinary-looking. He had tidy grey hair and glasses. She stared at him for a moment.

He stared back. "What?"

"You... you don't *look* like the kind of man who'd send an innocent person to prison for six years just because he's too drokkin' lazy and corrupt and incompetent to do the only job he's *supposed* to do. Which—because you've clearly forgotten—is to protect the innocent."

"Get this punk out of here, Ryburn. Before I add another couple of years for sedition."

EIGHTEEN MINUTES OUT from Philadelphia, Francesco Deacon contacted the Department of Justice's Central Control. "Give me a sitrep on the riot in Hunting Park."

"Stand by."

While he waited, Deacon scrolled through the notes on his datapad. There was always a riot *somewhere*. Or if not an actual riot, then a demonstration of some kind, and every demonstration had the potential to turn violent.

But you can't satisfy everyone. It pretty much came down to something Pellegrino had said, way back even before Fargo came up with the idea of Judges: "Some people won't be happy as long as they believe that there are others who refuse to regard them as superior."

So much hate *in the world...* That was what had bothered Eustace Fargo the most.

One of the first cases Fargo had prosecuted was that of a middle-aged Caucasian man who had beaten a young Haitian man to death with a golf club because he was offended that the Haitian man was playing on the same course. At his hearing, the defence claimed that the accused was a victim of 'involuntary exposure to a lifetime of systemic and sustained racially-biased imagery in the media' that had brainwashed him into believing that his life was in danger from people with brown skin. Therefore, his attack was motivated only by self-defence and the real perpetrators were the TV and web news channels who had deliberately and wilfully selected content designed to garner viewers and hits rather than present a fair, balanced and accurate portrayal of the real world.

As part of his closing arguments, Fargo said, "I agree with the defence that the media is biased and unbalanced. That's inevitable when the media is run by corporations who are more concerned with the bottom line than with truth. But hundreds of thousands—perhaps *millions*—of other people have been exposed to the same news stories, and the vast majority of them are *not* triggered to savagely murder innocent people. If the members of the jury have even an *ounce* of common sense, they will convict. The evidence is overwhelming and indisputable."

After almost four days of deliberation, during which the jury were unable to reach the unanimous verdict required to convict, an independent investigation revealed that close relatives of three of the jury members had received very credible death threats. A mistrial was declared, and the whole process had to start again.

Deacon's radio buzzed. "Deacon here."

"Judge Deacon, this is Judge Phoebe Guzowski, overseeing the clean-up in Hunting Park."

"How are we doing today, Guzowski?"

"It's a mess, sir, but we're getting through it. The backup Judges you dispatched are hitting the streets now, so we can concentrate on the aftermath of the riot. Civilian figures so far... twenty-eight fatalities, about the same number of serious injuries, dozens of minors. Also five members of the SkyBlock's private security forces. No fatalities on our side. A lot of injuries, though."

Deacon hesitated. "On *our* side?"

"Sorry, sir, just a turn of phrase. We didn't lose any Judges in the conflict. Right now, we're processing the civilians. A lot of their homes sustained damage in the conflict so I've ordered the conversion of unused apartments and other rooms here in the block itself. I don't suppose these people will appreciate the irony."

"I suppose not," Deacon said. He tapped at his computer pad. "You've still got all civilian comms blocked in the region."

"Yes, sir. Planning to lift them once we're done processing."

"Give me an ETA on that?"

"Three hours. Four at the most."

"Not good enough, Guzowski. Today of all days we need Judges on the *streets*, not shepherding civilians."

"Yes, sir. We'll do what we can to speed it up. We've been analysing all the street-cam, body-cam and cell phone footage from the riot, running facial recognition to find the instigators."

"What about the *trigger*? I'm reading here that the SkyBlock Corporation filed for bankruptcy. Their last act was to inform the citizens via a mass e-mail."

"That's how I understand it," Guzowski said. "I've passed that on to Financial Forensics to investigate. They're not done yet, but their initial report suggests that it's all pretty clean. There's some suspicion that the SkyBlock Corporation's directors are guilty of masking the company's true financial state from shareholders, but as yet no evidence to confirm that. If it *is* true, they'll be looking at substantial personal fines."

"All right. I can see you have your hands full—keep Central posted of any major updates."

"Will do... Sir, about the Chief Judge? I know you were friends. I just want to pass on our condolences."

"Appreciate that, Guzowski. We'll talk again. Deacon out." He disconnected the call, and stared down at the datapad for a few more seconds. *Eustace would know what to do now. He'd tell everyone to focus on the job. Roll up your sleeves and get the work done—wallowing in pity is the sort of thing you do in your spare time.*

"THEY'LL HEAR IT moving," Dallas said to the Judge. "And then we really *are* trapped."

Between the two of them, they'd managed to lift the scaffolding poles, planks and parking lot signs out of the alcove next to the door.

Now, they were facing a set of closed elevator doors. The panel that once would have housed the call button had been removed, and a blank plate crudely welded over the hole.

"The elevator will be a lot less noisy than that laser-cutter," Judge Quon said, jamming the point of her knife into the wafer-thin gap between the doors. "Assuming that it still has power."

The doors hissed open a few centimetres, and Quon shoved the left door the rest of the way, then the right, revealing a dark, empty elevator shaft. She leant in and shone her flashlight around. "Elevator's about six metres up... That's the ground floor."

When the Judge stepped back, Dallas leant in and looked up. "There's no way either of us can climb that far, and even if we could, how would we get past it?"

She pulled him aside. "We *don't* get past it." Quon groped around the wall inside the shaft, at the back of the now-missing call button panel. "Got it. They removed the button, but not the wiring." She pulled a bundle of wires free, then handed him the flashlight "Hold this steady so I can see."

"They really teach you to hot-wire elevators in Judge school?"

"Yes." Quon peered at the bundle of multicoloured wires, separating them one at a time. "How come *you* never signed up, Hawker, if you were so concerned about justice?"

"Call me Dallas." As he watched her work, the thought occurred to him that he'd never spent this much time with a

Judge before. She seemed more *real* than he'd expected. With their visors and detached manner, it was easy to forget that they were people. Maybe that was what they were going for. "I didn't sign up because I had a wife and two young kids. I know some Judges did have families back in the early days, but I wasn't willing to put mine at risk."

Quon looked up at him. "Good job there."

"I did what I felt I *had* to do."

"Really." Quon used her knife to slice open two of the cables, revealing their copper cores.

Dallas had to admit to himself that he was impressed. Wearing gloves, with her dominant hand severely wounded, and the threat of death pressing down on her, she still had more focus and fine control than he'd have on his best day. "Judge, my only regret about that time is being caught. But before your people came for us, we did a lot of good. Got a *lot* of criminals off the streets."

"And *after* we came for you? When you fled and went into hiding and ended up in Romley's employ? Did you do a lot of good then? Or did you aid and protect a huge criminal organisation that fed on the pain of millions?"

Dallas felt his anger rise, but he forced himself to keep calm. She was right. He knew it, and she knew it. There was no need for her to *say* it. "I had no choice."

"There's *always* a choice," Quon said. "What you mean is that you didn't like the alternative. Same as with Judge Gaines."

"He would have killed my family!"

"So instead you helped him kill *other* people's families." Quon twisted two wires together. "I think we've got it." She stepped back, and pulled her Lawkeeper from its holster as the elevator above hummed into life and started to descend. "Back against the wall, Hawker, just in case they're already in there."

"*I* should have a gun."

"You really shouldn't."

The elevator car's own doors opened, and the Judge lowered

her gun, but didn't put it away. "Cutter's still going—I don't think they heard anything."

As he looked into the elevator, Dallas realised he was drenched with sweat, that his hands were trembling. He turned around to face her. "Judge... we don't stand a chance! This is *suicide!*"

"It's only suicide if we die."

JUDGE RYBURN BROUGHT Beatriz up two more flights, to a part of the block that looked to be almost finished. The walls had been painted with an immaculate ombre effect—a deep blue colour at the floor fading quickly into white, then a rich bronze closer to the ceiling— that was so perfect it could only have been done by a machine. Everywhere was carpeted, all the doors had been hung, many already bore small plaques ready to be inscribed with company names.

Beatriz was glad the Judge hadn't replaced the bag on her head, but her arms were still tied behind her back, and Ryburn still had his hand on her neck as he steered her through the wide corridors.

He stopped at a cross-junction, and softly swore under his breath before unclipping his radio. "Judge Guzowski, this is Ryburn. Half of these corridors don't have signs up yet. What room am I looking for?"

A sigh. "Hold on."

Beatriz took the opportunity to turn around and look at the Judge. She'd only barely seen his face before, and still couldn't see much because of the helmet, but now it was clear that beneath the uniform he was just an ordinary man. She didn't like that. It was easier to hate them if they were monsters.

Or maybe it *wasn't*. Ryburn wasn't a monster, he was just a thug. And that meant that somewhere along the way he'd *chosen* to be like this, to hurt innocent people under the banner of protecting them. It made him feel safer to keep other people down.

"Room eighteen twenty-two. And pick up the *speed*, Ryburn."

"Yes, sir." Ryburn started pushing her forward again.

More than once, Beatriz had thought about joining the Academy of Law. It was a solid job, and you got to make things better for people. Sure, there was no money—the Judges didn't get *paid*, as such—but the Department of Justice took care of their housing needs and every other expense.

But even though she still didn't know what she wanted to do with her life, she was very sure about the things she wasn't willing to give up. A career, a family, friends, relationships... All the things that made life worth living.

Ryburn had made that choice—and every other Judge had, too—and she found herself wondering how hard it had been for all of them... and how they justified their initial idealism against what they had become.

"Judge Ryburn, I'm being punished for something I didn't *do*. I'm going to end up in an Isolation Block, and by the time I get out, I'll be a hardened criminal. That's how it works. You're not upholding the law, you're just setting up future crimes."

He didn't respond, and she wasn't even sure that he was paying attention. A glance back over her shoulder confirmed he was facing straight ahead; it was hard to be entirely sure which way a Judge was looking, under the visor.

Justice was supposed to be blind, and impartial, but the Dreadnoughts' justice was hidden and inscrutable.

In a wide, unfinished corridor—bare walls, uncovered pipes and conduits, plasticrete floor, flickering lights—they found the open double-doors to room 1822. Compared with the corridor, it was immaculate, a perfect replica of an old dance-hall, with an expensive wood-effect flooring, seating around the sides and even a stage for the band.

A few metres inside the door, a Judge was arguing with a tired-looking middle-aged man and a prim, much younger woman, both wearing business suits.

"This is *not* acceptable," the woman said. "The terms state that portions of the block that have not yet been assigned to specific purposes will be made available to the Department of Justice. This room *has* been assigned!"

Calmly, the man said, "It's fine, Isobel. No one's going to be using this room until the residents move in. Judge Peyer, my team will ensure that any structural changes required by the Department of Justice can be reversed without lasting impact, and that your use of these facilities doesn't impact on our ability to deliver on spec and on time to the client."

She snorted. "Huh. *Which* client? The SkyBlock Corporation or Melchior Kenway?" She turned to the Judge again. "Out of the blue, the SkyBlock board tell us they're dissolving the company and now these Melchior Kenway people are the new owners. Just like that. Is that even *legal*?"

The Judge said, "Corporate law is not my speciality, Citizen Bowers, but..." He shrugged. "Probably, yes."

"So the SkyBlock executives trigger a riot outside, *we're* stuck in here until you Judges tell us it's safe to leave, and now you want to turn our ballroom into a prison? Do you have *any* idea how much it cost to furnish this room? The parquet *alone* costs nineteen hundred dollars per square metre! And you're okay with a bunch of prisoners locked up in here for weeks on end? Why can't they be housed in one of the gymnasiums?"

"It's a matter of *security*," Judge Peyer said, turning in a slow circle. "There are no windows, we can barricade all the entrances but one, the bathrooms are just across the corridor and we can convert that back room into a kitchen. And..." He stopped, looking towards Ryburn and Beatriz, still standing in the corridor, then threw a glance at the woman as he started to stride towards them. "Now we *are* behind schedule."

As Peyer stepped out into the corridor, Ryburn said, "Got your first prisoner here for processing," and handed him a small datapad.

Peyer briefly looked at the datapad, then at Beatriz, then back to the Judge. "She's a *minor*. No one said anything about facilities for juveniles. Hold her here. I've got to straighten some stuff out with Guzowski." He stalked away, back along the corridor, talking into his radio.

Ryburn called after him, "Judge Peyer, wait!" but the other Judge was still talking.

He dragged Beatriz over to the corridor's wall, then unclipped a set of handcuffs from his belt, hooked one cuff around Beatriz's right wrist and the other onto a metal pipe running along the wall at waist-height. "I'll be back. Do *not* move from this spot, inmate."

As she watched him trot after Judge Peyer, that last word hit her like a knife in the heart. "Please... no..." With her arms still tied behind her back, she couldn't even brush away the tears.

A minute later, the businessman and woman exited the ballroom, passing Beatriz without apparently noticing her.

"There'll be *hell* to pay, George," the woman said, her teeth clenched in anger. "Whoever released the news is to blame. And they *knew*, too. In advance, I mean. They *knew*."

"I don't follow you."

"Those documents they sent through about the SkyBlock Corporation's assets being bought up by Melchior Kenway? One of them still listed Xou Brant Caragay as a subsidiary of SkyBlock. Xou Brant Caragay ceased trading seven *weeks* ago, which means SkyBlock prepared those documents before that. And you know, of course, that at least half of the SkyBlock directors also sit on the Melchior Kenway board."

Beatriz stared after them. *They planned this! They were waiting until a big news story came along so that they could bury it!*

They screwed us all over just so they could make a profit!

CHAPTER ELEVEN

THE SHOOTING STARTED even before the elevator doors opened on the ground floor.

The noise of the gunfire was almost deafening, and as she crouched next to Dallas Hawker at the back of the elevator Quon had never been more glad of her Department-issued earplugs.

She'd had doubts that this would work, but had tried to keep them from Dallas. The perp was shaken enough as it was, and exhausted from the effort of carrying the parking garage's discarded metal signs and the thick scaffolding planks into the elevator.

Now, a volley of a hundred or more rounds of high-velocity ammunition slammed into their makeshift shield, and it held.

The final element in Quon's plan had been the most risky: they'd waited until the others—whoever they were—had cut through the last door before riding the elevator up.

Dallas had argued that they should ascend while the others were busy cutting through the doors—that way, there was a chance that they could sneak away. She'd told him, "They'd follow us. We're both injured. Do the math. This way is better, trust me."

As the elevator doors closed, they'd heard a male voice

shout, "Elevator! Get back up there!"

That had been less than sixty seconds ago. Now, the elevator doors—riddled with holes—slid open and the same man's voice shouted, "Drokk! Hit 'em *again!*"

Quon was sure now that these people were not Judges. A Judge would have remembered their lessons from the Academy: you don't fully unload your sidearm unless you have no choice or you're absolutely certain that the threat has been eliminated. An empty gun is useless in a firefight.

Quon's Lawkeeper was *not* empty: she pushed her left arm out from behind the barrier and squeezed the trigger. Rapid-fire, emptying the whole clip in less than two seconds. She immediately tossed the gun to Dallas and picked up Judge Cusack's, emptied that too, then Judge Gaines's.

As Dallas passed her gun back to her—now with a fresh magazine—Quon listened. Nothing from beyond the barricade.

"You think we got all of them?" Dallas whispered.

"Quiet."

Still nothing from outside.

"Just load the other guns." She'd already recoded Gaines's and Cusack's Lawkeepers to match the Justice Department ID code embedded in her gloves.

With her left hand holding the Lawkeeper ahead of her, and ignoring the stabbing pains in her right wrist, Quon squirmed out past the bullet-riddled barricade.

On the cracked and stained concrete floor outside, three people were dead, and a fourth was slowly crawling away, leaving a wide trail of blood and gore.

"All clear, Hawker. Get out here."

She walked past the survivor and stopped in his path, crouched down so that she could look him in the eye. He was a middle-aged man, about the same age and build as her father. He'd taken shots to both knees, his stomach, at least two to his chest, and one to his left eye.

"Name of the person who sent you."

"Go... go to Hell..."

"You're dying. Give me a name and I'll debate whether you're worth saving."

He reached up a trembling, blood-drenched arm. "Hel... help *first*... then names."

"Debate's over. Your side lost." Quon pulled out her boot-knife. "Attempted murder of a prisoner. Attempted murder of a Judge. The sentence is death."

The knife went in easily, through the hole where his left eye had been.

Standing at the elevator doors, Dallas Hawker was staring at her in disgust.

Quon wiped the knife on the back of the man's jacket, then put it away. "They'll have a transport. Check the bodies for keys, cell phones, wallets."

Hawker still hadn't moved. "God... Judge, you have a *gun*. Hell, *he* has a gun. Using a knife to execute him is just... just..."

"It's *quieter*. We'd be fools to risk drawing any more attention. Get moving."

DEACON WATCHED THE copter lift off, then turned towards the building's roof-entrance.

"Sorry, sir," the Judge at the roof door shouted. "No one in or out, 'less they're on the list. We're on lockdown."

"I know," Deacon said. "I'm the one who *ordered* the lockdown. Tell Judge Gaines I'm here."

"I believe the Judge is off the premises right now."

"You know this but you're on lockdown? There should be no comms in or out of the building."

The young Judge nodded. "Yes, sir. That's right. But I heard her leave."

"We're six floors up, Judge. Your hearing is so acute that you can tell who's leaving the building just from the *sound?*"

"Only Judge Gaines, sir. She drives like a lunatic."

"Then where is she?"

"I expect she's with the Judge who came in earlier, sir. Judge Quon."

Deacon nodded and turned away as he pulled out his radio. "Central Control. Deacon."

"Go ahead, Judge Deacon."

"Amend the lockdown instructions at Philadelphia Central to give me full access to the building."

"Wilco."

"And give me the location of Senior Judge Olivia Gaines."

"Stand by."

Deacon walked to the edge of the roof. It had been a long time since his last visit to Philadelphia, and it hadn't left him with good memories. The gangs here were mostly under control now—or at the least, they were corralled, to a degree—but thirteen years ago things had been different. Unemployment was the catalyst, as always, the first link in the chain. Unemployment leads to poverty and despair, both hi-octane fuels for the fires of revolt.

It was here in Philly that Deacon had killed his first Judge. He'd trained former cop Earl Hockin himself. Knew him well—or so he thought. Deacon and Hockin had been stationed here for five months when Deacon noticed discrepancies in Hockin's reports. From a distance, everything looked fine: Hockin was diligent and balanced, just about a model Judge. But close analysis of his sentencing showed otherwise. He was much more lenient on the members of Jerboah Flax's gang than any others.

A deep investigation into his past showed that Earl Hockin's family records had been doctored to hide that he was a first cousin of Jerboah Flax himself. The gang had placed him in the police academy first, and then the Department of Justice, and from there he'd buried evidence, tipped off the gang whenever possible, steered investigations in the wrong direction.

Deacon had wanted to confront him on his own, somewhere out of the way, but Hockin had discovered that they were on to him. In the middle of one of the city's busiest streets, Hockin had pulled his gun on him and Deacon instantly went for the kill-shot. And in response, the Flax gang—now the strongest in the state—ran riot. It took two weeks to calm the city down.

Deacon's phone beeped. "Go ahead, Control."

"Judge, you now have full access to the Philadelphia Central Precinct, and we've located Judge Gaines' vehicle: it's at South Eleventh and Christian, Bella Vista district. Currently stationary."

"Appreciate it, Control."

Deacon returned to the roof door, where the young Judge was already stepping aside.

"It's open, sir. Sorry about that."

Deacon pulled open the door. "A Judge shouldn't apologise for doing their job."

"No, sir. Sorry, sir."

UNDER THE FLICKERING lights of the unfinished corridor, Beatriz Graziano prayed that this was all a nightmare and soon she'd wake up.

She hadn't seen or heard anyone since Judge Ryburn left her here, handcuffed to this pipe. That had been five minutes ago, maybe ten. Maybe longer.

She'd heard stories about the treatment of prisoners in Isolation Blocks. Horrible stories. And some of them were true. A friend of Nina's mother had told them, "A lot of the inmates use the term 'time-stretcher' because in the cells there's no natural light, and the overhead lights are on all the time. Every day, the same routine. You get the same thing for every meal, so you can't even use that to mark the days. You can't sleep. Might not sleep for two or three days. And then you can't wake up. Your body-clock goes haywire, like, the worst jet lag you can imagine. Except worse even than *that* because you'll be thinking, 'It's morning, I *know* it's morning' but everyone's acting like it's early evening. It's called temporal deprivation, or something. So the guy who told me about it says, anyway. And it doesn't take long to kick in. A couple of months and you'll be going back and forth between thinking that you've been there for *years*, and that you only got there a week ago. And there's no one you can ask, because the other inmates are in the same boat, and the guards don't care. They *want* you to suffer."

Beatriz looked both ways along the corridor. Still nothing. All she could do was wait there in the sporadic darkness. Or pace a little, though cuffed to the pipe and with her arms still zip-tied behind her back, she couldn't go far.

The pipe—bare metal, about as thick as her wrist—seemed to run the length of the corridor, fixed to the wall at waist-height, with brackets about every three metres: the limit of her freedom.

It was only when Beatriz actually tried to walk from one bracket to the next that she realised this wasn't a continuous length of pipe: halfway between the two nearest brackets there was a gap about the thickness of her finger. The threaded ends of the two pipes suggested that there was a connecting piece that hadn't yet been fitted.

The gap between the two sections was too narrow for the cuffs to slip through, but only just, only by a few millimetres.

If the brackets are just holding the pipe up, but not actually attached *to it...* She grabbed the pipe with both hands, tried to slide it back. Nothing. Whoever had attached this to the wall had made sure it wasn't going anywhere.

But the other section of the pipe was looser. It didn't slide left or right, but she could twist it a little. Only a few degrees, back and forth.

She kept twisting. Something would give. You put enough pressure on *anything* for long enough, and you can break it.

Back and forth, back and forth, until her wrists and arms ached, the sharp edge of the zip-tie scratching into the flesh of her wrists.

She paused to flex her hands a little, then started again. Back and forth. *Don't stop.* She conjured up a mental image of herself as a worn-down middle-aged woman. Lank grey hair, mottled dry skin, wearing an orange prison jumpsuit. That woman was telling her, "If you don't want to become *me*, do not stop."

Nina's mother's friend had been full of stories about the Dreads, and all of them negative, but Beatriz had always thought they were like ghost stories. It's fun and thrilling to frighten each other with them, but you're not supposed to *believe* them. They're not supposed to be *true*.

But Beatriz had watched that huge truck being driven through half a dozen of the park's prefabricated huts.

She understood now that it had been a lesson from the Department of Justice. A lesson that firmly stated, *We are in power here, not you. You live or die at our whims. We control every aspect of your lives, and if it suits us, we can and we* will *snuff out those lives. There is nothing you can do. We will punish those who resist, or speak out, or even ask uncomfortable questions. If you stand against us, we will take you down and destroy all that you love.*

You are our *subjects, and without us you are* nothing.

We are Judges.

We are the Law.

There was a sharp *snap*, and the pipe was now loose.

CHAPTER TWELVE

"THERE'S *NOWHERE* SAFE," Dallas said to Judge Quon as she calmly drove the killers' car—an ordinary rented Ford saloon—westwards along Philadelphia's Tasker Street.

He didn't like this much. Quon seemed like a good person, but Romley had already sent four professionals and a Judge to kill him. *He can get to anyone.*

"I know a few places..." Quon said, and glanced at the fuel gauge. "But not in this part of the country. We could go *south.*"

Dallas snorted at that. "Right. Take us back to good ol' Alabammy... and back in *time* ten years too. Wouldn't *that* be something? Judge, we're going to have to ditch this car. Public transport is best. Philly's not big enough to lose ourselves. We should go to Manhattan. You'd have to switch to civilian clothes, though. You must know people there who can hide us. After that... Are there any Judges other than you who you're sure aren't corrupt?"

She began, "*Most* Judges are—"

"No. No, you don't get to do that after what happened with Gaines! She's the senior Judge in the whole of Philadelphia and she tried to kill us! She *did* kill that other Judge, and he was her friend!" Dallas glared out the window. "We left her alive. That was a mistake."

"You don't get to decide who lives or dies, Hawker."

"And you do because you're a Judge. Fantastic. You're a stormtrooper for a fascist organisation set up two decades ago to solve problems that are still with us. Actually, no, they're worse than *ever.* This country is... dangling over the edge of a cliff, and the Department of Justice is trying to solve the problem by hammering nails into its hands. You Judges carry out executions on a whim. In Indiana, I saw a Judge shoot a fleeing perp in the *back*. The perp was a vagrant. Absolutely harmless. The worst thing he ever did was panhandling. Shot in the back for asking for spare change. What kind of justice is *that?*"

"You work for the largest manufacturer of deadly narcotics in the country."

Dallas was silent for a while. She was right, sure. Of *course* she was, he knew that. But she was forgetting that he didn't work for Romley by choice. "Great. So we both kill people. But at least when *I* do it, they die happy."

Something beeped, and he fished his cell phone out of his pocket. "We're clear of the blackout zone."

"You could phone him," Judge Quon said, her attention on the road ahead.

"Him who? *Romley?*"

"Phone him. Tell him that his people got you out, but they didn't make it."

"You want me to phone the guy who's trying to *kill* me?"

"We'll pull over. You get in the back, lie down, and call him. Tell him that you're hiding out and you want him to send someone to pick you up."

He could tell from her expression that she was serious. "Judge, he's not an idiot. And he knows that *I'm* not an idiot. That wouldn't fool him."

"Maybe not, but it'd definitely rattle him."

"What good will *that* do?"

Quon shrugged. "People like Irvine Romley get their kicks from being in control. We show him he's *not* in control. It's a little victory, but it might be the only one we get." She glanced in the rear-view mirror. "Hold that thought. I think we're being followed."

Dallas resisted the urge to look around. "How certain are you?" He didn't know this part of the city. Narrow streets, residential, not much cover.

"Forty per cent," Quon said. "White Toyota. It's been on us for the last three turns... and it's gone."

Dallas asked, "You feel up to running? Because there's a trick I know—"

"I'm sure anyone tailing us knows it too. I need you to make a call." She recited a fifteen-digit number.

Dallas keyed it into his phone, and was instantly looking at the logo for the Department of Justice.

"Hold it up to me."

When he did so, Quon said, "Code eight. Authorisation one-six-bravo-bravo-three. Judge Errol Quon."

A voice said, "Acknowledged," and the call ended.

"What was *that* about?"

Before Quon could reply, the phone rang.

"Answer it."

Dallas thumbed the answer button and saw the face of a middle-aged African American Judge staring back at him. "Hawker. So clearly everything has gone south."

"I, uh... Hold on." He aimed the phone at Quon.

"Quon, we just got a data-burst from your recorder. We're analysing it now."

"Sir, Judge Gaines has been turned. She's still breathing, but I can't say the same for her colleague Judge Cusack—Gaines's work, not mine—or the four unknowns backing her up. Ex-military is my guess. Sir, right now I'm at a loss. Don't know where to turn."

"Or who to trust. Understood. I'm in the precinct, Philadelphia Central. Pick somewhere and I'll meet you."

"Yes, sir. I'll keep—*Damn it!*"

Quon slammed on the brakes and jerked the wheel to the

left, causing Dallas to crack his head against the window as the car went into a stomach-lurching skid.

He hadn't even recovered when she floored the accelerator again, sending the car screeching along another narrow residential one-way street, not caring as she clipped the wing mirrors of almost every parked car they passed.

"It's them," Quon said. "White Toyota."

They shot through a cross-junction at three times the speed limit, with Quon's knuckles white on the steering wheel, narrowly missing a city bus.

Dallas squirmed around in the seat in time to see the white car swerve around the bus and pick up speed. "They can outrun us!"

"I know."

Dallas heard another voice and realised that the call to the other Judge was still connected: "Where are you?"

"Don't know this city," Quon said. "Bit busy to read out street-names." She briefly swerved into oncoming traffic to overtake a slow-moving pickup truck.

Dallas said, "Sunday market on the left... That's Bucknell, I think. Means we're headed towards the expressway."

"No good," the other Judge said. "You need to lose them before that."

"Agreed," Quon said, her face expressionless, eyes darting back and forth as she checked the mirrors over and over. "Dallas, reach past me. Take the Lawkeeper from my holster."

"I don't... I'm not *that* kind of criminal."

"What kind of *corpse* do you want to be?"

The Judge on the phone asked, "You *have* fired a gun before, Hawker?"

"No!"

"Do as Judge Quon says. Take the gun." A tiny pause. "She said reach *past* her. So she switched her holster to her left. She's been wounded."

"Actually, we *both* have. I was shot in the—"

"Just get the damn gun."

Dallas placed the cell phone on the dashboard, then he had to unbuckle his seat belt and duck down under Quon's right arm. As he groped for the gun, the car served again and he had to grab onto Quon's seat belt to avoid rolling off her lap and into the foot-well. "I can feel it, but it's—"

"Release catch on the near side," Quon said, "where my thumb would grab it."

"I got it." With the gun in his right hand—and both his shoulder and ear aching from the exertion—Dallas managed to pull himself back upright. "But it's coded to—"

The other Judge said, "Eject the magazine part of the way, about the thickness of two fingers."

Dallas's hands were already shaking. "Okay..."

"Now *push* the trigger forward, towards the muzzle. It'll resist at first."

"Got it. It just buzzed like a cell phone."

"You've disabled the gun's ID-check. It'll now work for you. Hawker, if you even *consider* using it against Judge Quon, I will hunt you down and kill you very, *very* slowly. Understand?"

Dallas was still staring at the gun. "Yeah. Yeah. I understand."

"He's trembling," Quon said, "Deacon, I don't know if this is a good idea!"

"They still there?"

"Yeah, but they've not fired on *us* yet."

"Romley will want Hawker *alive*—he has to be sure he hasn't talked. Hawker, you're gonna need to roll down your window. And watch the sides—more vehicles will come. They're going to box you in, try to herd you where they want to go."

Still looking at the heavy gun in his hands, Dallas said, "Then... then let me go to them! That'll buy us time. Romley's going to kill me anyway, but if you let them take me, maybe you can follow them back to him."

"Lower the window, Hawker!" Judge Deacon yelled. "Right now!"

They were speeding along a much wider road now, heading south-west, judging by the position of the sun, and as Dallas fumbled for the switch to control the windows, Deacon said, "You give yourself up to them, they wouldn't let Quon live. Besides, Romley wouldn't tell his goons to take you to him. Just somewhere that they could torture you in peace."

"On the right," Quon said. "Dallas—on the *right!*"

Dallas looked around in time to see a heavy old panel van—brown, with blacked-out windows—come racing out of a narrow side street, swerving to make the turn, its rear end almost fishtailing into the side of the Toyota before the unseen driver corrected its path. Its engine screaming, the van accelerated towards them and in seconds was parallel to their Ford—then started drifting closer. Five metres away, now four, now three.

"Trying to force us to turn left... Dallas, *shoot* the damn thing!"

Holding the Lawkeeper with both hands, Dallas aimed and fired. The recoil jerked his hands up, and the noise was like a punch to the ears, but he saw a nickel-sized mark appear on the van's window.

It wavered a little, then resumed coming closer.

"Bullet-proof glass..." Quon said. "But not at *point-blank*. When it gets close enough to touch, press the muzzle right against the glass and keep shooting until the clip is empty!"

He tried to keep the gun steady as the van drifted closer. He was almost able to reach out and touch it now. He found himself wondering who was in there. Was there a passenger? Just the driver, maybe? Could be—if there was a passenger, surely they'd shoot back.

There was shouting from far away, over and over, and it took him a few seconds to realise that it was two voices, Quon and Deacon, screaming at him to keep shooting.

"Do it!" Quon yelled. "The other drokker's right behind us!"

Judge Deacon said, "Hawker, they're trying to force you into a side-road that they'll have blocked off. If they manage that, they will *kill* Judge Quon. Right now, she's the only one who can protect you from whatever Romley has planned. So you've got to protect her first. Do you understand?"

"I don't know if I can—"

Something hard cracked into Dallas's jaw, knocking his head back: Quon's elbow. "Give me the damn gun."

He passed it to her—placing it into a hand that was still coated with dried blood from her wounded wrist—and Quon, still steering with one hand, leant past him, jammed the muzzle of the Lawkeeper against the van's window and emptied the magazine.

It slowed, swerved, then mounted the sidewalk and slammed into the wall of a fast-food outlet; Dallas had just enough time to see the tight cluster of holes in the van's driver's side window.

The Judge dropped the gun into his lap and snapped, "Reload!"

"Sure, yeah." He glanced at Quon, then at the phone with Judge Deacon's face still glaring out at him. "What... what about other Judges? They'll come, won't they? Someone shoots up a van and it crashes, the Judges come."

Deacon said, "There's a shortage of Judges on the streets right now."

"And we don't know who we can *trust*," Quon said.

"Agreed. I've put a few calls in, but to be frank it's unlikely you'll get backup for the foreseeable. And... Quon, I know you understand how important it is that we get to Romley."

"I do, sir."

"But if it comes down to it... you put your *own* life ahead of the prisoner's. I won't have you dying just to save *this* drokker."

Dallas almost protested at that, but then he remembered April Susan Dunstall. She had a tendency to crop up whenever he started to feel sorry for himself.

He held the Lawkeeper up. "Loaded." He squirmed around, looking out the back window. "It's still there. Should I...?"

"At this distance you'd need armour-piercing rounds to get through that glass."

Judge Deacon said, "Quon, you need to shake that tail before more show up."

"Very much aware of that, sir."

"Remember your training. What was the very first thing I told your class at the academy?"

"You said, 'Nobody wants to die.'"

"Bear that in mind. Keep this number free—I'll be in touch." The call ended.

After a second, Dallas said, "He's right. I don't want to die."

"He wasn't talking about you, Hawker." Quon again glanced in the rear-view mirror. "He means the perps. People like Romley use other people—like you—as though they're disposable. They often forget that even the most psychotically loyal henchman is a person underneath all the muscle and body armour. Road's clear ahead... Hold on, because this is going to hurt."

"What?"

She pressed down hard on the accelerator. "Put your belt back on. Now!"

Dallas made a grab for the seat belt, wincing at the fresh wave of pain from his shoulder. "Damn it! Okay, I've got—"

"Too slow—brace yourself!"

Quon slammed on the brakes and the last thing Dallas felt was his body being whipped forward, then back, as the car behind ploughed into them.

CHAPTER THIRTEEN

BEATRIZ DIDN'T KNOW where she was going, but she didn't care as long as it was away from the Judges.

And if Judge Ryburn got into trouble for losing her, that was a bonus. Maybe they'd even fire him.

But even as that thought crossed her mind, it was followed by another: that wouldn't happen. The Dreads took care of each other. Ryburn wouldn't be punished, but they'd take out their frustrations on the other prisoners.

She hadn't seen anyone since she'd worked the handcuffs free of the pipe. She'd immediately run into the ballroom and across to one of the doors on the opposite side, shouldered it open, and peeked out into a wide, brightly lit empty hallway.

In a narrower side-corridor she'd found an incomplete section of aluminium wall-plating with a sharp edge. It had taken several terrifying minutes to use the edge to cut through the cable-tie, then for the first time in what felt like hours she was able to properly move her arms.

Now, having climbed four sets of stairs throughout the block, Beatriz was carefully making her way through a maintenance corridor that ran along the back of what would eventually be a row of small apartments. It was barely a metre wide, criss-crossed with dozens of struts and cables and air ducts and conduits. Unfinished edges snagged at her clothing and scratched her arms, and at one point the dust was so thick she'd had to pull her T-shirt up over her mouth and nose. Tiny orange and white LEDs overhead showed the way, but only just: she'd already hit her head three times.

There's no going back now, she thought. *No matter what happens, I'm a criminal in their eyes. Escaping from custody is a crime, just like resisting arrest is a crime. It won't be long before* scowling *at a Judge is punishable by death.*

There were stories about *that* too. Rumours that the Justice Department had special covert divisions that used psychics or magic or voodoo to find their perps. Nina's mother's friend had known all about that: "Soon, if you even *think* about committing a crime, that'll be a crime."

They want to control every aspect of our lives. They won't be happy until we're slaves.

The maintenance corridor reached a T-junction, and for a moment Beatriz was frozen with indecision. She figured that the left path would take her deeper into the building, but the right would be safer, closer to the outside wall. *Or* is *that safer? The Judges will come looking for me, and they'll be able to detect my body-heat. That'll be easier to do if there's less stuff around me.*

She turned left, and fifty metres along saw that one of the apartments' back walls was missing several panels.

She stepped through, and the apartment's overhead lights blinked on.

Though empty, the apartment didn't seem that much bigger than the prefabricated huts out in the field. *For one person, maybe*, she thought. *Two at a push*. It was really only one room, maybe four metres by five, and windowless—she remembered from the SkyBlock brochures that the apartments with windows would be a lot more expensive. To her left was an alcove for a tiny kitchen at one end and a bathroom next to it.

She turned on the faucet at the kitchen sink and almost cried with relief when water trickled out. She drank from her hands, getting water everywhere, but didn't care.

If there was food, I could live here for a while.

In the tiny bathroom was a shower/body-drier combination. The temptation to use it was almost overwhelming, but she couldn't take the chance that it would be heard. She moved on, back out into the maintenance corridor.

Maybe there'll be food in another one. Maybe one of the builders left their lunch behind.

Ahead, the corridor widened a little to make room for a very narrow set of metal stairs, rising to an identical corridor. Another set of stairs took her further up into the block, but this floor was empty except for support pillars every thirty metres and several high stacks of the pre-formed plastic panels that would eventually become the walls of new apartments.

Beatriz slowly turned around. There were wide, rectangular windows on every side, but she was almost in the middle of the floor, so from this distance they resembled a row of lights.

How long can someone hide out inside a place like this? She wondered as she walked towards what she figured was the south-facing wall. *If I'm careful, and keep clear of any workers, maybe I could stay hidden long enough that they'll give up looking for me.*

And then when Mom and Dad get their apartment, I could sneak down through the maintenance areas and visit them at night. We'd have to tell Hardy, but he could probably keep his mouth shut. He...

No. That won't happen, because they won't be getting *an apartment here because the SkyBlock scum went back on their promises!* She reached the windows to see that she was facing not south but west, looking out over the park.

This morning it had been filled with neat, tightly packed rows of prefabricated huts. Now, it looked like a landfill site. Several of the huts were charred and smouldering, dozens had been collapsed, and people were swarming all over everything—she couldn't tell whether they were residents trying to reassemble the shattered pieces of their lives, or scavengers looting the wreckage.

It took her almost a minute to find her own hut. It seemed to be intact, and for a second she thought she saw someone inside, passing the doorway, but this high up it was hard to be sure.

Her family would be down there somewhere, though, she was sure of that. And when they found out what had happened to her... Beatriz smiled. She wouldn't want to be the Judge who got caught on the receiving end of her mother's wrath. Her family used to joke that Maria Beatriz's righteous fury could blister the paint on a wooden door.

That's not going to happen either, she told herself. If her mother did complain to the Department of Justice, they'd do as they always did: pretend to investigate and then return a report absolving the Judges of any wrongdoing.

Her father's friend Tommy once said, "Life is simpler nowadays. When we were kids, things were complicated. Now, *so* much simpler. We're playing a *game* with the Jays, and we can't win because they keep changin' the rules. We'll never break even—'cause that's, like, *next door* to winning—and they won't let us quit. All we can do is *lose*. It's like... It's like we're parked at the side of the street and there's a traffic cop coming along, and we're feeding quarters into the meter—remember that?—but we're only gettin', like, ten seconds for each quarter, so we have to keep feeding it over and over, because if we walk away, then sure as Christmas we're gettin' a ticket. And eventually, we're gonna run out of quarters, so we're gettin' that ticket anyway. Bingo-bango-bongo, QED, ipso-facto, the system is totally loaded against us and we are *never* gonna win."

"We are never going to win," Beatriz said aloud, then darted back from the window as one of the hovering construction machines drifted down in front of her. Hardy would have loved to get this close to one, but they left her feeling cold. It was the *silence* that creeped her out. A metal-and-plastic machine the size of a family car should not be able to silently float around like a helium balloon on a calm day.

Hardy would have particularly liked this one, though. It was one of the block's three seam-welders, and he'd spent hours watching them in action. They drifted over the surface seemingly of their own free will, checking and rechecking the joins between girders and panels, reinforcing them when necessary, automatically avoiding the crawling riveters and lifters.

The seam-welder moved on, and Beatriz looked around the almost-empty space again. This was how it was going to be from now on, she was sure. A bunch of people who'll never come here designing buildings that will be mostly constructed by machines. *They'll give us movie theatres and shopping malls and schools and a ballroom and* everything *we need to stay here so we don't have to bother the* better *people.*

She looked down at her arms. Red marks and deep scratches from the zip-tie, handcuffs still attached to her right wrist. *Even if this hadn't happened today, even if we did get our new apartments in this block... we'd still be prisoners.*

After the Judge had cuffed her to the pipe, that man and woman from the ballroom had walked out past her without even noticing. *What kind of person* does *that? How self-involved do you have to be to not even notice someone handcuffed to a pipe with her arms tied behind her back?*

They're still here too, she realised. From the conversation they'd been having with the older Judge, it sounded like they were from the construction company. *They have offices here. That means they might have food.*

IN THE PUBLIC lobby of the Philadelphia Central Precinct, Francesco Deacon lowered his cell phone long enough to order the Judges to unlock the doors, then raised the phone to his ear again. "She talking?"

"Not yet. But she *will* be, soon. The team I sent to interrogate Hawker has her now."

Deacon began to pace back and forth across the lobby. "The others?"

"No IDs, nothing on any database. If *my* contacts can't find someone, then they were buried *deep*. Someone paid a lot of money to shut Hawker up. What about Quon?"

"Unknown, at present. She's resourceful, though. I have faith in her."

"Agreed," Marisa Pellegrino said. "For someone who despises the Department, she makes a damn good Judge. What's the situation there in Philly Central?"

"With Gaines out of the picture, Phoebe Guzowski is in charge, but right now she's stuck out at the mega-block. From what I've heard, it's been a total dumpster fire. Guzowski tried to handle everything herself and when it started to fall apart, she doubled down rather than stepped back. They even managed to lose a prisoner. I'm heading out there now."

"You're lifting the lockdown?"

"Already lifted here, but I'm leaving it in place in the block until I assess the situation for myself."

One of the Judges at the door signalled to Deacon. He nodded towards him, then strode outside where a small Department of Justice truck was waiting, passenger-side door open. "What's happening back there, Marisa?" To the driver, he said, "Hit it."

"This one's also a dumpster fire, except *this* dumpster's full of toxic waste, body-parts and used diapers. We've got the media hounding us, demonstrations breaking out all over the country, politicians from both sides trying to get the president to put pressure on Solomon in the hope that he'll be easier to push around than Eustace was, and at least thirty senior Judges vying to fill Solomon's role as Deputy Chief. On that score, I've talked with both Solomon and Goodman, and they have *you* on their short-list for the job."

"Not interested. I'm too old to play politics."

"If you *don't* play politics, Deac, then politics plays *you*."

He smiled. "You do love your little sound-bites, don't you?"

"They help to paper over the bottomless void in my soul. Maybe I should get a cat." Marisa sighed. "We have to talk about the *arrangements*. The funeral. And... other things. Fargo's legacy."

"I know. But that's for tomorrow. We tackle today's problems first."

After ascertaining that Dallas Hawker wasn't actually dead, Judge Errol Quon sliced through the car's airbags with her boot-knife, grabbed the Lawkeeper out of Dallas's limp hands—ignoring the fact that it was now splattered with his blood—and pushed open her door.

She'd jarred her right arm in the crash, and right now it felt like someone had pierced it with a red-hot iron bar and was trying to twist it enough to snap her bones.

She wasn't naturally ambidextrous but had practised a lot with her left hand until she was almost as good as with her right. At the Academy, the tutors had put that down to what they referred to as her "condition." It wasn't that she *had* to have everything neat and symmetrical, but it made things easier.

Across the street, a pair of civilian women had been staring at the Toyota almost embedded in the back of the Ford, and now that they saw the driver of the Ford was a Judge, they took out their cell phones.

"Don't," Quon barked, holding her gun steadily at the Toyota's windscreen. If the driver wasn't dead or unconscious, they'd know she meant business. "You upload any photos or video, you're interfering with an ongoing Justice Department investigation. That's a three-month sentence minimum."

On the edge of her vision Quon saw the women lower their phones, then begin to back away.

There had been no sign of life from the Toyota since the crash, just a slow, steady metallic ticking from its engine.

For a moment, she considered just opening fire. These people had clearly been sent by Romley, and he would have his tracks as well-covered as he always did. Interrogating whoever was in the car might yield a name, but the person attached to that name would be long gone.

But people like Romley didn't only get perps to do his work. Sometimes they used victims. "Open the door. Count of three. One. Two. Th—"

The door opened a crack.

"*All* the way."

A weak voice. "Can't."

Trying not to wince at the pain, Quon used her bad arm to jerk open the door the rest of the way.

A woman—Caucasian, maybe fifty years old—was slumped back in the driver's seat, her face covered in blood, hands limply by her side. No seat belt, no airbag.

"Name!" Quon barked.

The woman opened one blood-drenched eye. "Tabitha Stermer... Told to watch the place. Follow the *men*. Same car... sure of it."

"*Who* told you?"

"The *guy*... I've never learnt his name. He called me... said do this, he'll clean the slate." She gave a short laugh that turned into a cough. "I used to be a *cop*, a long time ago. Went up against one of his people... he didn't *like* that. Made it clear that I owed him."

"Have you got the phone he called you on?"

"Jacket, in the back..." The woman slowly rested her head back again, and as Quon opened the back door and pulled out an old denim jacket, she said, "I didn't know there was a *Judge* in the car, I swear. The four men... Saw them meet up with another Judge, a white woman, my age. She led them to the old building. There was a lot of noise, like construction work? Then gunfire... I thought I was following *them* back out."

Quon found the woman's cell phone. "What's the PIN?"

"Four-one-three-zero. But I *need* it..."

"Tough. You carrying?"

"No. No guns, nothing illegal."

Quon took hold of the woman's left arm and cuffed it to the steering wheel. "Paramedics will cut you free. If Judges or police officers get here first, tell them Judge Errol Quon has sentenced you to five years for abetting a known criminal and a further three for reckless driving." She stepped away, then looked back. "I find out you *failed* to tell them, I'll double that sentence."

Back in the Ford, Dallas was regaining consciousness. Quon put away her Lawkeeper then pulled open the passenger-side door and caught him before he hit the ground.

"Goddamn it, you nearly killed me..."

"Come on, we need to get out of here."

He slumped back into the seat. "Can't... Go without me."

"I need you *alive*, Dallas. You have to help us get to Romley, remember?"

He nodded, then inhaled and exhaled deeply a couple of times. "All right... But where can we go? Where's safe?"

Quon straightened up, turned left and right. "Ah no... Sirens, getting closer. *Police* sirens."

"Yeah?" Dallas asked. "What *model* sirens?"

"Sounds like Ryettotechs. Model 400-B, I think. Sixty watts, one hundred twenty-two decibels. And they're definitely heading this way." She grabbed Dallas's arm. "Out. Come on. Right now."

He had to hold onto the top of the door to steady himself. "I'm not going to be able to run... My shoulder was bad before, but now it feels like it's on *fire*."

Quon took a moment to check the soaked-through steri-patches on Dallas's shoulder. "Yeah. I'm seeing a lot of inflammation."

"I'm *feeling* it."

She looked at him for a second. "We can't run and we don't know who's coming. We might not get another chance to talk about Romley before his people get to you. Is there anything else that might help us to find him?"

Dallas leant back against the car, slowly shaking his head. "I don't... I can't *think*." He looked back at the Judge. "He has people everywhere, that's the thing. *Everywhere*. Even inside the Department of Justice. Remember the riots in Dayton a few years ago? We were caught in the middle of that, Judges coming in from all angles. All roads blocked, the cell phone networks completely dead. And he was *still* able to make a call and arrange for his car to get through a roadblock unchecked." He shrugged, then winced as he straightened up. "Quon, Romley always wins because he's smarter than everyone else."

Ahead, a police car screeched around the corner, then skidded to a stop. It was immediately followed by a second.

Dallas said, "If he was here with us right now, he'd have a way out of this. Half of these cops could be working for him and not even know. *Most* of his people don't know."

A third car appeared behind them, then a fourth. Boxed in.

Quon said, "You're one of the few. You've met him, and all you can really tell us is that he's Caucasian, about sixty, short grey hair, blue eyes, always very neat. That could be one of ten million people in this country."

"I know. You could pass him in the street and you'd never guess he was a criminal mastermind." Dallas tried on a smile. "He could even be a *Judge*."

"We *have* thought of that."

An amplified voice from the left roared, "Judge... do you require assistance?"

A fifth police car arrived, screeching to a stop behind the first two.

"This is a sensitive situation," she called back. "I want the senior officer present to make themselves known to me."

The passenger-side door of the fifth car opened, and an older man—Latino, strong build, shaved head but with a tight grey beard—stepped out. "Sergeant Caparros, Philly Central." He put on his cap as he started to walk towards Quon, his hands casually by his side. "I got word a Judge was involved in an RTI."

Quon said, "That's close enough. Who sent you?"

Caparros glanced around. Then he looked back and raised one hand to his ear and stepped closer. "Forgive me, Judge. Little deaf in this ear. I need to be closer. You'll notice that I'm not reaching. Don't mind if *you* are, as long as you're not feeling too jumpy right now."

He looked Dallas up and down. "This one all right? He seems—"

Quon placed her hand on her gun. "You will stop walking right now, or I will consider that an act of aggression and respond accordingly."

Sergeant Caparros stopped, hands empty and arms spread a little as he faced her. "I think we're all fine here. Don't need so many officers, right? I'm reaching for my radio, and we're all *casual*, no stress. No muss, no fuss, not need for a truss." He unclipped his radio from his belt. "All's good here. You can all clear out, resume patrol." He turned to face the way he had come. "Not you, McKeever, you're my ride back."

The cars began to back away, and Caparros returned his attention to Quon. "You know, *I* applied for the Academy, soon after it all started. They turned me down. Not immediately, though. I got through the training—this was back when it took only *two* years—and then after my final assessment they brought me into a side-room, sat me down. Told me I wasn't suited to the uniform."

Quon began, "Don't care. We need medical assistance and transport—"

The Sergeant talked over her, his voice raised. "Two *years* in training, and they spat me out." He snapped his fingers. "Just like that. Two years of my life wasted. For what? For nothing. And you know who was behind the desk at that final meeting? A civilian woman who didn't say anything—Grud knows why *she* was there—and the same Judge I saw marching through the precinct less than an hour ago. Francesco Deacon. You don't forget someone like *him*. Here..." Caparros reached into his pocket and pulled out a quarter, held it up for Quon to see. "Ordinary quarter. Catch this."

He flipped the coin at her, and she snatched it out of the air—

—then saw that he had his gun aimed at her face. "And now the other officers are gone, and the only witness is Officer McKeever, and *he's* not going to say anything, so..."

He fired six times in rapid succession.

CHAPTER FOURTEEN

BEATRIZ HELD HER breath and tried not to move. On the other side of the wall, a woman's voice said, "We've already *been* down here. Twenty minutes ago."

"Are you sure? All these corridors look the same to me." A man asked. "I'm getting a heat signature right there. Very strong, too."

"Correct. That's the same water-heater that you were surprised to find was there last time."

"Right, yeah... But shouldn't it be insulated, though? I mean, if they're trying to conserve energy. A properly insulated water-heater shouldn't show up at all on a thermal scanner."

"The block is not even halfway finished yet. They probably don't put the insulation on until they're sure everything is working. Besides, I figure she got out."

"How? There's forty of us searching the block for her and the exits are sealed." The man's voice began to fade. "There's no way for her *to* get out. You know what I think? I think Guzowski just made her up. Pretend there's a lost kid in the block and that way we have an excuse to snoop around. Or she's doing it just to keep us occupied."

Beatriz remained where she was—sweltering, with her back

to the water-heater—until she was certain that they'd moved on.

She'd found a flashlight in one of the upper levels, and that had made things a little easier down here on the fourth floor, where almost everything had been finished and decorated. About a quarter of the floor was occupied by small companies, most of them connected to the construction of the block in some way, but only one had people who were working right now, on a Sunday—Beatriz guessed they were the builders.

Sure that the Judges had moved on, Beatriz continued on her way towards the offices. If she'd been out in the corridors, she could reach them in a matter of minutes, but inside the walls and under the floors the going was a lot slower, especially as she had to do it without making any noise.

She was on her side now, pulling herself along the wall through a gap not more than forty centimetres wide, by now almost oblivious to the fixings and fastenings that seemed to draw fresh scratches on her arms, back and legs with every movement.

I can do this, she told herself for the hundredth time. *They're going to give up looking, because what's it worth to them? They'll spend* days *searching for me, and they'll look like idiots in the process.*

She conjured a mental image of the ordinary people—the other prisoners, the people from the neighbourhood—learning that she'd escaped from the Dreadnoughts. Her victory would be theirs. The people would always know that a seventeen-year-old girl with no training had managed to escape from the most efficient, most ruthless law-enforcement agency on the planet. Whenever the Dreads rode through the neighbourhood, the people would jeer and laugh and call out, "Hey, you ever catch that chica? The one who got away? Maybe you put *another* hundred Jays on the case, then you have a chance!"

But that wouldn't happen. There was no neighbourhood any more.

And the Dreads would never admit that someone had

escaped. They'd just claim that Beatriz had been moved to some Isolation Block, or maybe that she'd died in custody. Then they'd go to her family and tell them, "You hear anything from your daughter, you tell us immediately or you'll disappear too."

She stopped crawling. The thought hadn't occurred to her until now that maybe her family *weren't* worried about her. Maybe they didn't know she was missing yet, because the Judges had come for them and they were too concerned about their own safety.

For all she knew, they were dead. Maybe they'd even been caught up in the riot.

She shook herself. *No. Can't think like that. That's not going to help.*

A man's voice echoed through the underfloor area from somewhere far ahead. It was indistinct, but steady.

He didn't sound strident and bullish, like a Judge throwing his weight around. And he wasn't scared, either, like one of the civilians they were interrogating.

She crawled a little closer, and after about fifteen metres the passageway opened up, and she was able to stand again.

As she moved closer to the sound, a woman's voice interrupted the man's, and Beatriz froze again. She'd heard the woman's voice before.

"We have been under *immense* pressure here! Do you know how many suspects I've had to process today?"

"Yes," Deacon said. "You already told me. Over twelve hundred. And you *lost* one."

Judge Guzowski shook her head dismissively. "Not lost. Misplaced. We will find her. I've already reassigned Judge Ryburn and circulated the perp's description to every Judge in the block. We *will* find her. And in the meantime I've got to organise holding for almost three hundred inmates, and negotiate with the builders, the SkyBlock Corporation and

Melchior Kenway to get the space and resources that we need for those inmates. *And* Judge Gaines has gone dark. Deacon, one missing girl who won't be able to escape the building is *not* top priority."

"It's *her* top priority," Deacon said. He looked around the office. Thick carpet, painted walls, pictures, ornaments, expensive furniture. A private bathroom, and next to that a smaller room equipped as a gymnasium. It was nicer than the Chief Judge's office back in Boston. Several of the desks were currently home to the remains of lunch: trays of tiny sandwiches, plates of even tinier cookies, pots of expensive coffee.

Judge Guzowski was sitting on the edge of another desk—one that looked like it had cost more than a standard-issue Lawranger—and Deacon thought she looked tired. That wasn't a surprise. The day had started badly and rapidly plunged down-hill. And she didn't even know the worst of it.

"What do you *need*, Guzowski?"

"A week's vacation. But aside from that, I need a bit of *cooperation*. Nothing against you personally, Deacon, but out in Olympus you don't have to deal with the same day-to-day crap that *we* do. Gaines is great at keeping on top of things, but like I said, she's gone dark."

He ignored the *Olympus* dig—that one had been around for a few years. "That's twice you've mentioned Judge Gaines going dark. What have you heard?"

Guzowski paused, and tried to mask it by turning a little and picking up a half-stale bite-sized sandwich from the tray on the desk. "Nothing, but I tried to contact her several times. She normally responds within a few minutes at most."

"What have you heard? Don't make me ask a third time."

Guzowski swallowed the sandwich. "That prisoner we took in this morning... Hawker, the fugitive. That triggered a lockdown. Then Judge Gaines took him off-site. Came back when the other Judge came in from Boston. The one with the Asian name?"

"Quon."

"Right. Gaines took her out, too, and that's it. No official word from or about Gaines or Quon since then." Another sandwich followed the first.

"And *un*officially?"

Guzowski shrugged. "Just that some Judges from Boston are right now tearing through her office and her apartment, and not in a way that suggests she's missing. They're looking for dirt."

"Will they find any?"

"Sir, I've worked with her for years. She's a good Judge."

Deacon nodded. "Glad to hear that. And... from you, that's the last I want to hear about Judge Gaines for now. Do you understand? No speculating with your fellow Judges. We already lost the Chief Judge today; we need to appear united. If the media or the public think we have a weakness, they'll exploit that."

"Understood, sir."

Deacon turned at a knock on the door behind him. A Judge opened the door and leant in to address Judge Guzowski. "Sir, Mr. Hauser insists on seeing you."

Guzowski glanced at Deacon, who nodded. Then she said, "Send him in."

The Judge stepped aside to allow a middle-aged man and a younger woman to enter.

"Well," the younger woman said. "Thank you for permission to enter our own offices!" She looked at Deacon. "And *you* are?"

"More respectful than you, apparently," Deacon said.

"Do you think that's *funny?* Our entire operation here has been *destroyed* by you people! It's bad enough that SkyBlock has already thrown the cat among the pigeons by going into liquidation and forcing us to renegotiate with those charlatans at Melchior Kenway, but now you want to turn half of this block into a prison!"

"Only temporarily."

The man said, "That's enough, Isobel. The Judges are under a lot of pressure too. Snapping at them won't help us get out of here any sooner." He extended his hand to Deacon. "George Hauser, senior architect, Davy-Artak-Moxon Fabrications."

"Senior Judge Francesco Deacon."

"What can we do to grease the wheels, Judge? We've had a day from Hell—"

Standing at the coffee machine, the younger woman, Isobel, said, "*That's* an understatement."

"—*but* we're always happy to cooperate with the Department of Justice. If you're looking into the suggestions of impropriety by the SkyBlock Corporation, we'll give you what we can, but pressing charges won't be easy. You'd have to prove *intent* to defraud."

"I do know the law, Mr. Hauser," Deacon said. "It's interesting that you do, too."

Hauser smiled. "*I* was a lawyer, back in the old days. Harvard. You're not the only one who had to find a new calling. This is a strange new world we've built." He walked up to the window, and stared out. "I was *tempted*, you know, to join the Department of Justice. But I like my comforts too much." He shrugged, then looked back. "You want to make the world a safer place, and I want to make it *nicer*. So I like to think that I'm still contributing. I understand you've misplaced someone?"

Deacon didn't need to give Guzowski a withering glance: it was clear from her deflating body-language that she understood this was another strike against her. To Hauser, he said, "Correct. Female, seventeen years old. Cuffed to a pipe outside the ballroom. She managed—"

Isobel said, "We saw her. You remember, George? We passed her. The other Judge had left her to chase after Judge Peyer."

"I think there *was* someone there, yes, but..." Hauser shrugged. "I was a bit preoccupied."

"Jeans, orange T-shirt, shoulder-length black hair, pretty but tired-looking. Like she was having a really hard day. Which

I suppose she was." She turned to Deacon. "What was she arrested for?"

"Not your concern. But any assistance helping us find her would be appreciated."

Hauser returned his attention to the world outside the window, and said, "If she didn't get out, she's still here. If it were *me*... I'd be inside the walls, or under the floor. Somewhere within the superstructure. There's a million places she could be hiding. You could run a sweep starting with the lowest level, floor-by-floor, sealing off each possible exit as you pass. But that's going to take a lot of time and effort, and we'd have to completely shut down construction while that was happening. That will cost upwards of nine million dollars per day."

Isobel said, "I could reconfigure the seam-welders to look for anomalous heat-signatures? That might help. And I know this building better than just about *anyone*. You said so yourself, George."

Hauser nodded. "That's true."

"But I'm actually supposed to be off-duty right now," the young woman said. "I'd be giving up my free time."

"And the Department of Justice appreciates that," Deacon said.

"Does the Department appreciate it enough to cancel outstanding traffic fines?"

Guzowski snapped, "Not as much as the Department frowns upon *shake-downs*."

Deacon said, "Fines cannot and *will* not be commuted, citizen. But we'll pay you for your time, and you can use *that* money to help pay what you owe. Agreed?" When Isobel nodded—looking a little subdued—Deacon added, "Good, thank you. Judge Guzowski will tell you what she needs."

When Guzowski and Isobel had left, Hauser gave Deacon a smile. "Young people, eh? Always wanting more. But I suppose we were just the same at that age. You ever regret putting on the badge, Judge?"

"At times, yes."

"It's a thankless calling, I know... But I believe that even when the people are cursing you Judges in the street, deep down they know that you're better than the alternative."

Deacon didn't respond to that.

CHAPTER FIFTEEN

IN THE CRAWLSPACE under the office's floor, Beatriz moved as slowly as she could. It was like the businessman, Hauser, had known she was there, and was teasing the Judges: "I'd be inside the walls, or under the floor."

There has to be a way out of this.

She toyed with the idea of going back to the ballroom and figuring out a way to rejoin the other prisoners without the Dreads seeing her. They'd discover her at the next count and maybe think that they'd been wrong, and she'd been there all along.

Even if they hadn't been looking for her, she couldn't stay here forever.

She reached the edge of the office's interior wall, squirmed through a narrow opening, and was then able to stand up.

She switched on the flashlight again and saw that she was in a wider clearing than most, ten metres long, with a good three metres between the office wall and the next. There was even an old plastic crate left here that she could use as a seat.

Another possibility occurred to her as she sat down. The woman, Isobel, had mentioned the seam-welding machines. They were as big as a car, roughly the same shape, but without obvious windows or doors. *Maybe there's space inside them, and a way to get in. They'd never find me then, and the next time the machine has to land so that it can recharge, I could just get out and run away.*

The men's voices came again, and she thumbed off the flashlight.

"I was sorry to hear about Chief Judge Fargo," Hauser said. "I never met him, but I've only heard good things. That's why this happened, you know."

The Judge asked, "Meaning?"

"It's Isobel's theory. She thinks that the board of the SkyBlock Corporation had *always* planned to dissolve the company before we could finish building the block. It's an old trick, but if you're careful it can be done without breaking the local laws. Basically, you spend every cent you can on slow-burn investments, so you run a big loss; then you file for bankruptcy and sell the assets cheap to your own new company."

"So those hundreds of families who gave their land to SkyBlock in exchange for a new apartment...?"

"They can take it up with SkyBlock, except the company no longer exists. Melchior Kenway is a completely separate organisation."

"Owned by the same people."

"There's no law against that," Hauser said. "Not yet, anyway. You're a Judge—you could *rewrite* the laws, but you're not allowed to apply your change retroactively. Unless you rewrite *that* law, too."

Judge Deacon asked, "What do you mean when you said this was because of Fargo? Are you saying they had this takeover planned and just sat on it until the time was right?"

"Yes. Bury bad news under worse news."

Beatriz stood up. *They really did it. SkyBlock completely sold us out, and there's nothing we can do about it. Nothing even the Judges can do. But even if they* could, *they wouldn't. The Dreads don't want the ordinary people to stand up and make their voices heard. They want us to sit down, shut up and be grateful for their table-scraps.*

She switched the flashlight on again, preparing to move away, and a glint of metal high on the office wall caught her attention. Most of the interior walls were centimetre-thick plastic with plastic fittings, but this one seemed different.

She moved closer. The wall by the discarded crate had a lock on this side, and hinges.

A secret door. Hauser said he was the senior architect for the company... Who wouldn't *include a secret door?*

She grinned in the darkness. *That's my way out.*

DALLAS KNEW HE wasn't dead because his shoulder and ear and face still hurt, but there was something holding him tightly and rocking him from side to side, and for a moment he thought of his mother.

Then Judge Quon said, "He's still with us."

Dallas tentatively opened his eyes. Quon was looking down at him, her face as expressionless as ever. He wondered if he'd ever see her smile. Or if *anyone* would.

He began, "What—?"

"Sergeant Caparros is an undercover Judge," Quon said. "The other officer who stayed behind, McKeever, is suspected to have criminal connections. So, for his sake, Caparros had to make it look like he was executing us—his gun was loaded with blanks."

Dallas realised now that he was rocking because he was in an ambulance. He tried to sit up, but he'd been strapped down.

"You've been hooked up to a glucose pack, and the paramedics have patched your wounds," Quon said.

"Great. Wouldn't want to die before my execution. How do we know we can trust the paramedics?"

An angry voice from the front of the ambulance asked, "Because if you *couldn't* trust us, you'd be dead already."

Quon said, "They're also Judges."

"Well, so was Gaines."

"And *this* is Judge Richter."

A stern-looking woman with a shaved head silently drifted into Dallas's view. In a voice much softer than her appearance might suggest, she said, "Hello, Dallas. I want you to close your eyes. Can you do that for me? Just relax and let them close by themselves. They *want* to close: they're heavy with exhaustion. Not just from today. From eight years of being forced to work for a man you despise, eight years of looking over your shoulder, eight years of being scared. But that's all over. Mr. Romley can't get to you now. So relax and let me in, won't you? Everything is going to be all right. You're safe. You're comfortable. There's no pain. You can't feel any pain, can you?"

"No," Dallas said. *This is hypnosis*, he told himself. *No way I'm falling for that. Can't believe that the Dreads have their own hypnotists. Next it'll be like, 'Dallas, I want you to meet Judge Fraud, he's a homeopath, and this is Judge Charlatan who's going to read your horoscope.'* He smiled at that.

In the warm darkness, Judge Richter's voice asked, "Did you just think of something amusing? Can you tell us, Dallas?"

"You're... trying to hypnotise me, aren't you?"

"Does that bother you?"

"It's a waste of time."

"You could be right about that. It does work on *some* people, though. It really does. Do you think it would work on Irvine Romley?"

"No chance. He's too cynical. Same as me, really."

"Are you alike in other ways?"

He shook his head. It was a little uncomfortable talking into the darkness like this, so he imagined that Judge Richter was standing beside him. "No, we've very different. He's always in control, and sometimes I feel like I'm *never* in control. But I *used* to be."

"Back when you lived in Golgotha."

"That's right. I had my job and my friends and... and..."

Judge Richter gently placed one hand on his shoulder. "Go on. It's safe to say it."

"I had Gwen, and Evie, and Jason. But they're dead now."

"Why do you believe that?"

"Because Romley said if I ever betrayed him, he'd kill them."

"They're *not* dead, Dallas. Gwen and Jason are living in Oakland now, and Evie has just finished college in San Francisco. They had to move after your activities in Golgotha were discovered."

"Romley said Gwen had been arrested."

"Why would we arrest her? She didn't know about your vigilante hobby. She wasn't involved. No, she's safe, Dallas. And missing you. They all are. But we can arrange a visit. Wouldn't you like that? All you have to do is give us enough information to find Romley."

"I've already told you everything..."

"What does he look like?" Richter asked. "Picture him for me now, as he was the last time you met him. That was in Washington Square, four days ago. Take me there, Dallas."

Dallas imagined himself and Judge Richter walking side by side through the small park, where another version of himself sat on a bench waiting for Romley to show up. Not that Romley would be late. He was never late. Always punctual, always perfect. *Unflappable*, that was the word. The man had unrufflable feathers. Even when he was absolutely furious, you couldn't really tell.

The version of Dallas on the bench glanced at Judge Richter and said, "Here he is now."

They turned to see Romley casually striding through the park, wearing his fancy suit, the usual calm, subdued expression on his face.

Judge Richter stepped directly in front of Romley, then walked backwards, keeping pace with him so that their faces were only a few centimetres apart. Romley didn't even notice her, but he slowed way down, almost to a stop.

And after a few seconds of peering at his face, Judge Richter smiled. "*Got* you, you son of a bitch."

She was gone. Romley was gone. The park was gone. Dallas opened his eyes and saw Quon and Richter staring down at him. Richter was still smiling, and at the same time she was sketching with a stylus on a tablet.

Then she flipped the tablet around, and showed it to him. A very good likeness of Irvine Romley. "Do I get a gold star, Judge Quon?"

"At the very *least*, Judge Richter."

CHAPTER SIXTEEN

Standing in the doorway of the ballroom at the heart of Indira Knight Block, Deacon watched as the Judges attempted to herd the prisoners into some sort of order. Many of them had already been shipped out to Isolation Blocks, but there just weren't enough free cells for everyone. Mattresses had been ordered for the rest, but the latest word was that they'd be delayed until Monday evening. Maybe Tuesday.

For the past hour, Deacon had been regularly checking his cell phone for word from Marisa Pellegrino's people. Based on the data that they'd already accumulated and the input from Dallas Hawker, they were narrowing down the list of suspects. But still: white male in his mid-sixties was far too wide a field. The facial descriptions reduced the list a little, not enough.

As he watched, Judge Guzowski barked orders at the Judges, who in turn barked at the inmates. Guzowski's latest idea was to get sheets of pliable insulating foam from elsewhere in the block and use them as makeshift beds. The young woman, Isobel, was insisting that was a bad idea: the insulation foam was hugely expensive, and it would be easier to send Judges out to the park below and take mattresses from the damaged huts: "Oh, and some of the inmates might even get their own mattresses back! I wonder what the odds of that happening are?"

This is wrong, Deacon said to himself. The inmates—mostly adults, but a few juves too—had been ordered into one corner and were now sitting on the floor, all facing the same direction, under strict orders not to move or talk. And the people who'd put them in this situation were going to get away with it.

His datapad beeped again. He pulled it out of his pocket, looked at it, and swore under his breath as he grabbed his radio. The likeness was close. Not *exact*, but more than close enough to warrant suspicion.

"Central Control, this is Deacon."

"Go ahead, Deacon."

"I want a complete comms lockdown on Indira Knight Block!"

"What, *again?* I mean, acknowledged, Deacon. That's in place now."

He put away the radio. "Guzowski!"

She looked up from the plans of the building she was pouring over with Isobel. "Sir?"

"Seal the building's exits. Freeze the elevators. *No one* gets in or out until I give the all-clear."

"You *found* her?"

"Just do it—now!"

He was already running, and grateful that his target wasn't far, especially given the size of the block.

Up one flight of stairs, left along the corridor.

Ahead, George Hauser was emerging from his office. "Judge Deacon—I was just coming to see you. The phones and web are down again."

"I know," Deacon said, slowing down. He stopped ten metres from Hauser. *Damn, it's close. But not close enough.*

"Something wrong?"

He's the right age. And his job takes him all over the world dealing with imports and exports. That's a perfect cover.

"Judge?"

"I don't know. Hauser... You bear a strong resemblance to someone I've been trying to find for a very long time."

"*How* strong a resemblance? Scale of one to ten?"

"I'd say... seven. Maybe eight." He held out his datapad, in his left hand, allowing his right to drift down close to his Lawkeeper. "You tell me."

Hauser took a step back, frowning at the datapad. "That's my *brother*. That's Robert. Why are you looking for him?"

"You're positive this is your brother?"

"Yes, but I haven't seen him in years. Not since our father's funeral, and that was back in thirty-eight. We were never close, Robert and I. Never really had time for each other." He took another step back towards the door of his office. "I have a photo of us together. We were a lot younger, but you can clearly see that it's him."

Deacon followed him into the office. *This feels wrong... He's stalling.*

Hauser pulled open a drawer in the nearest desk and poked through it. "Just between us, Robert was always a bit jealous. I got into Harvard Law, he ended up in M.I.T. Not that there's anything wrong with that. It's a *fine* school." He moved on to the next drawer. "But he decided he wanted to be a biochemist, specialising in toxicology, of all things. Here it is." He withdrew a small photo framed photograph and smiled at it. "This is the one." He held it out to Deacon. "I'll get that back, right?"

"Of course," Deacon said, watching Hauser's hands as he reached for the photo. "We'll just need to scan the photos and—"

Hauser leapt back as the photo flared in Deacon's hand, a glare so hot that it instantly seared his skin through his glove, so bright that it would have blinded him if not for the visor on his helmet.

Deacon automatically dodged to the side as he shook off the scorched, flaming glove—an instinct he'd later realise saved his life: in the second of distraction triggered by the thermite-laced photo-frame, Hauser had snatched a gun out of the drawer and fired four times.

The first shot missed entirely. The second shot clipped the right side of Deacon's neck. The third pierced his right arm at the bicep. The fourth hit him in the side—he felt his ribs shatter.

As he dropped, he opened fire at Hauser, but the man was already moving, heading towards the back of the office.

One of Deacon's shots struck Hauser's left arm, jerking his body enough that his next shot at Deacon ricocheted off the Judge's helmet.

Deacon hit the ground on his back, shooting again. Three shots, close-grouping, hitting Hauser in his left side and passing through to strike the door to his small gymnasium.

Hauser crashed against the door, half falling through it.

Deacon saw the man scrabbling away across the carpet, his hands slick with blood as he pushed the gymnasium door closed.

Deacon rolled onto his side, his left arm screaming with the pain—the skin was scorched raw, with blisters the size of golf balls already appearing. His neck, right arm and right side felt almost calm in comparison. He fumbled his radio out of his belt. "Guzowski... Hauser's office. Now."

He felt himself growing heavy, slipping away.

"GET UP! IT won't be long before they come!"

The man—Hauser—was heavy, but Beatriz was sure she could get him through the small gymnasium's secret door and into the space beyond.

She had been standing on the other side of the door when it opened and Hauser collapsed backwards into the room, crashing against a sit-up bench, smearing blood over everything.

"Can't... can't make it."

"You have to!" She hooked his arm over her shoulder, tried to stand up.

He slipped again, and looked up at her with a smile. "The girl in the crawlspace. I was right... They're looking for you."

"This is *your* secret door, isn't it? I'll help you!"

"Too late... Deacon's a good shot. Hit me three times and each one... is a fatal wound. What... what's your name?"

"Beatriz."

His voice was weakening. "Good name. I'm Irvine... well, that's *one* of my names... heh..."

She stared down at him. *The Judge shot him in the* back. *They don't care what they do, who they hurt!*

The man's breathing was erratic now, wheezing. "You... you do yourself a *favour*, Beatriz... Go back to the crawlspace. Close the door. Then you... you go down to the lowest level, north-east corner... Arrow on the ceiling. Small, but you'll see it if you look for it."

"Come with me!"

"I'm already dead, Beatriz..." He grabbed her hand. "The arrow points to a box. Fake power-junction. Open it. There's money. A passkey for every lock in this building. And..." Another smile. "You want to get the Judges back for what they did to you today? Info's on datachips in the box. *Hundreds* of files on the Judges. Every single one of their atrocities... Enough to bring them *all* down."

His hand slipped from hers. "Go, Beatriz... Use those files... Set fire to the Department of Justice... and burn it all to Hell."

CHAPTER SEVENTEEN

Indira Knight Block, Philadelphia
18:40

ERROL QUON STEPPED back from the doorway as the paramedics wheeled Judge Deacon's stretcher out of the offices of Davy-Artak-Moxon Fabrications. The stench of blood and scorched flesh was almost gone now, whipped away by the new block's efficient air filters.

Judge Guzowski said, "Don't worry, I'm sure he'll make it. He's strong, takes care of himself. He—"

"I don't need reassurance." Quon re-entered the office and looked towards the door to the small gymnasium where Judges specialising in forensic detection were running their scanners over the body of George Hauser.

"So it's confirmed?" Guzowski asked. "That's your guy?"

Quon nodded. Photos of Hauser had been sent to the only two people the Judges were certain could identify Irvine Romley. "Both Dallas Hawker and Niño Aukins confirmed it. Aukins became... very emotional. He's due for release in a couple of years and every day since his arrest back in thirty-three he's been expecting a shiv in the kidneys. Romley had a *lot* of people in his pocket."

Guzowski sat down on the desk and stared at her hands. "Including Judge Gaines. I've worked with her for years. I didn't think she could crack like that. And I can't get past that she killed *Cusack*—she trained him pretty much single-handedly." Guzowski looked up at Quon. "You're sure it was deliberate? She wasn't just trying to wound him?"

Quon held out her wounded arm. "Gaines is an *excellent* shot. She knew exactly where to hit him to do the most damage. She disarmed me, killed Cusack, turned on the prisoner. It was only luck that she missed him—and that gave me time to recover and stop her. Once Hawker was dead, she'd have finished me." Quon hesitated for a moment. She knew what she had to do next, but given the events of the day this wasn't going to be easy. "Judge Guzowski... Securicam footage of the riot and its aftermath is being analysed. The evidence is pointing to heavy-handedness on behalf of the Judges, and questionable decisions on your part."

Guzowski slid off the desk, stood with her feet solidly planted, arms folded. "Is that so?"

"It is. The missing citizen?" Quon asked.

Judge Guzowski scowled. "Inmate. She's a *prisoner*, not a citizen."

"You think that makes it better or worse that she vanished under your watch?"

"Who the hell are *you* to question me? I've been a Judge for sixteen years. Five of them as second-in-command to Judge Gaines."

"Are you proud of what happened here today?"

"I stand by my decisions."

"The evidence is suggesting that you were informed in advance that the executives of SkyBlock Corporation were preparing to release news that would trigger a violent reaction from the citizens of this neighbourhood. You chose to prepare to meet that violence rather than act to prevent it. One of your orders involved Judges driving a Department of Justice vehicle into several places of residence without first checking whether they were occupied. Three citizens died as a result."

"Bullshit—they had guns. They were taking cover in those huts." Guzowski pointed to the window. "The people out there *rioted.* It was *their* choice to behave like that. You've seen the footage—*they* fired the first shot!"

"*All* of them?"

Guzowski froze. "What?"

"They *all* fired the first shot?"

"No, that's *not* what I—"

"Did Beatriz Maria Graziano fire the first shot? Or any shot? Did that seventeen-year-old girl take up arms? Did she raise her fists? Did she raise *anything* other than her *voice*?"

"Drokk you, Quon! You weren't there!"

"Neither were you, Guzowski. You showed up after the riot had been quelled. *Why* did your Judges arrest Beatriz Graziano? You must remember. She was the first one you sent to be interrogated and sentenced."

"She's a *perp.*"

"Seems to me that she made you uncomfortable by speaking out. Effectively she was sentenced on the charge of resisting arrest." Quon stepped closer. "That is *not* how this is supposed to work."

"It's the *law.*"

"No, it was a bruised ego. I'm sure you've heard that the Department runs an intensive retraining course for Judges deemed to be operating below acceptable standards. Eleven weeks, starting tomorrow morning, in Jacksonville, Florida. The last flight from Philadelphia to Jacksonville leaves at twenty-two-hundred. If you returned to your quarters now, you'll have time to pack."

"I outrank you, Quon! You don't have the authority—"

Guzowski's radio beeped.

"I'd answer that if I were you," Quon said. She left the office then, without looking back. Later, she'd get her arm properly examined, but right now she had work to do. Someone had to break the news to Dallas Hawker that Judge Richter had lied about his family in order to gain his cooperation. And someone was going to have to oversee the mess here in Philadelphia, go over all of Guzowski's work. Re-interview and reassess the almost three hundred prisoners arrested today.

The route back through the block was longer than she'd remembered, and by the time she reached the ballroom her wounded arm was screaming for a painkiller, but you got the painkiller at the *end*, that was how things were done. You did the work first and *then* you got the reward. Anything else was wrong.

So no reward yet, because this still wasn't over. Beatriz Graziano was still missing. Somehow, she had managed to get out of the block. Her family were still holed up in the local church—apparently one of the private guards employed by SkyBlock had grown up in the area and warned Beatriz's father that something bad was about to happen—and they had no idea that she was missing. Someone would have to tell them.

You're being a fool, Quon told herself. *Just get the damn pain-killer now and it'll be easier to focus on work!*

On the heels of that thought came an old favourite, always in the voice of her younger self: *You could just* quit, *Errol. You know that you* can't *make everything perfect. There are just too many factors, too many variables.*

And you never wanted *to be a Judge.*

So why are you still here?

She smiled to herself, because she knew the answer even though her younger self would never have believed it.

Because I like it. And I'm good at it. And I can make a difference.

EPILOGUE

Hall of Justice, Boston
Wednesday, September 6, 2051
09:43

"Francesco. Come in. How's the hand?" Deputy Chief Judge Goodman asked.

"A lot better, thanks," Deacon said. "Still feels like a rubber glove filled with chicken bones and sand, though." He passed Goodman and looked around the Chief Judge's office. Last time he'd been in this room, Fargo had been behind the desk.

Now Hollins Solomon sat in the big chair as he paged through a document on his monitor. "With you in a second, Deacon..."

Goodman brought over a chair and Deacon tried not to let out a grunt as he sat down. *I am* so *out of shape.*

"Are you ready to come back to duty?" Goodman asked.

"That's what I'm here to talk about. A lot has happened since then."

"True. Indira Knight Block has been officially opened."

Deacon nodded. "And the citizens who'd been screwed over by SkyBlock are still in temporary accommodation that looks like it's well on the way to becoming a permanent shantytown. Meanwhile, the SkyBlock executives who defrauded them have made *millions* and have yet to be prosecuted. We're sheltering the guilty and punishing the innocent."

"That's *enough*, Deacon."

"Don't give me the intimidating voice and glowering eyes. I *invented* that damn trick."

"Justice *will* be done," Goodman said. "But sometimes the wheels turn slowly. You know that. In the meantime, take comfort in the successes. Since Irvine Romley's death, Trance distribution has almost completely dried up. No one else knows how to make it." Then, slightly softer, he added, "Grud knows they're *trying*, though. We're taking another Berserk off the streets every few months." He shook his head. "And there'll be two more mega-blocks within the year. Atlanta and The Bronx. Before the split happens we're going to be looking at marking the city into sectors to make it easier to manage. You've heard that, right? Each sector will get its own Sector Chief. Deacon, we want you to run Atlanta."

Deacon sat back, smiling. "I don't want the job."

"You *do* want the job."

"No. This is not the way things were meant to be." He looked at the portrait of Eustace Fargo on the wall. "*He* didn't want this."

On the other side of the desk, Hollins Solomon pushed the monitor aside. "This again."

"Yes. This again. Fargo always said that we're a means, not a solution. We've taken apart the old way, now we need to learn how to *build*."

"We *are* building, Francesco," Solomon said. "We're building a *mega-city*."

"You know that's not what I mean." He reached up to his tunic, and pulled his badge away, placed it on the Chief Judge's desk. "I will no longer be a part of a government that feeds on the citizens' fear."

Goodman said, "We're stopping the people from *killing* each other!"

"If you believe that, then someone's feeding you doctored crime stats." Deacon pushed himself to his feet. "We're not protecting the people. We're just teaching them to hate us more. This will all come crashing down one day. We're building on unstable ground and expecting the structure to last forever. That's not just foolish. That's pushing the problems down the line for someone else to tackle. That's negligence."

"Deacon, the people need us," Solomon said. "You can't deny that."

"I'm not denying that they need something, but *us?*" He glanced up again at the portrait of Eustace Fargo. "I'm to blame just as much as he is. How *arrogant* we were, to assume that we knew what was best for everyone else."

Solomon sighed. "Deacon, you are sailing dangerously close to sedition."

"*That* is the battle-cry of the cowardly, Solomon." He took a deep breath and exhaled slowly. "Look... I'm just saying that we can't lose sight of the original goal, which was to save the nation from itself. We were supposed to be the *path* to salvation, not the destination." He stepped back. "If you want to talk, I'll be available. But I won't be putting on that badge again."

He was halfway to the door when it opened and Marisa Pellegrino strode in.

Chief Judge Solomon said, "For crying out loud, don't you *ever* knock?"

"No." She looked at Deacon as she pushed the door closed. "So you're ignoring my advice?"

"Your orders, you mean? Yeah. I am."

"Good for you. But wait for a few minutes, will you? You can walk me out as your last official act as a Judge, or some crap like that."

She reached into her jacket pocket and withdrew a datachip, tossed it to Goodman. "There's a solution to *one* of your problems." When Goodman didn't reply, she added, "Go on, don't be shy, gentlemen."

Solomon said, "I don't know why Fargo ever let you talk to him like that. But it doesn't work on *me*, Pellegrino."

"Just look at the damn datachip, Chief."

Goodman passed the chip to Solomon, who dropped it into the slot on his desk. A fresh document opened on the monitor.

Pellegrino said, "That's my plan—which you *will* adopt, because it makes sense—for a new internal division. We've been growing too fast. I understand that it's necessary, because there are a lot of external factors, not least of which is the impending dissolution of the United States, but nevertheless, we *are* growing too fast. We need internal checks and balances. Irvine Romley was able to blackmail Judge Olivia Gaines because no one looked closely enough at her personal life to spot the potential weaknesses. At least seven Judges under her command in Philadelphia proved to be at the very least incompetent, if not downright corrupt. And that's just *one* precinct." She pointed at the window. "We've got some unknown faction out there regularly supplying the media with proof of corruption within our ranks and absolutely *shredding* our reputations in the process. Well, the honeymoon's over; faith in the Judges is at an all-time low. Whoever it is out there who's been hanging us out to dry... well, *we* should be doing that! *We* should be cutting out the poison that's killing us."

Solomon said, "You're talking about an Internal Affairs division."

"Correct." Marisa glanced at Deacon. "The Judges who judge the Judges."

The Chief Judge shook his head. "I don't know if that's even *feasible*. We've always managed to self-police without—"

"It *is* feasible," Marisa said, pointing to the monitor in his desk. "And if you read the research and the conclusions, you'll see that our track record for self-policing is atrocious." She stepped closer to the desk. "Hollins... we *have* to do this. There has to be someone to whom we are accountable."

Goodman said, "You *do* know you're not actually a Judge, don't you?"

"*Not* helping, Clarence." She pointed at the monitor again. "I trust you. Both of you. You're good Judges, and I believe you genuinely have the best of intentions for the citizens and the city. But it is *far* too easy to start believing that a position of power implies a higher moral standard. That 'might makes right.' Some of the Judges on the streets refer to this place as Olympus, but we are *not* gods. We are *servants*, and we need a system that will ensure that every Judge understands that we work for the people, not the other way around. My new squad will fill that role."

"And you want Deacon to run this division?"

"*Him?* God, no. He's too old. Besides, rumour has it he's retired."

"I've heard that too," Deacon said.

"Yourself, then?" Solomon asked. "It *could* work. We'd need to deputise you first. But that's just a formality."

Marisa shook her head. "Of course not. It should be a Judge who's been out there on the streets. Someone who will make damn sure you're all doing your jobs properly." She stepped back and pulled open the door. "Come in, please."

The young Judge walked into the Chief Judge's office, and nodded a greeting to Deacon.

Marisa Pellegrino said, "Gentlemen, meet the head of the new Special Judicial Squad... Judge Errol Quon."

ABOUT THE AUTHOR

Michael Carroll is the author of over forty books, including the award-winning *New Heroes* series of Young Adult superhero novels and the #1 Amazon best-selling cult graphic novel *Judge Dredd: Every Empire Falls*. He currently writes *Proteus Vex* and *Judge Dredd* for *2000 AD* and *Judge Dredd Megazine*.

Other works include *Jennifer Blood* for Dynamite Entertainment, *Razorjack* for Titan Books (co-written with artist John Higgins), and the *Rico Dredd* trilogy for Abaddon Books, for whom he has also created the acclaimed *JUDGES* series which explores the genesis of the world of Judge Dredd.

www.michaelowencarroll.com

WHAT MEASURE YE METE

C. E. MURPHY

For Michael Carroll,
thrill-powered inspiration.

CHAPTER ONE

Boston-New York-Philadelphia Autonomous District
Monday, March 17, 2053
04:47

A SPIDER CRAWLED across Cera's face, chanting, "Murder, murder, murder."

She sat up shrieking out of a dead sleep and smashed the bug—it didn't matter that it wasn't technically a bug because *it was a goddamn bug*—smashed it against the concrete wall beside her bed. Only when it hissed and sizzled and sparked instead of just dying did she realise it wasn't even alive.

Didn't matter that it wasn't alive, any more than it mattered it wasn't a bug. It was definitely dead now, either way. Heart beating puke-fast in her chest, Cera picked the thing up by one tiny metallic leg. It dangled in the darkness, glowing faintly with residual heat and a gleam of stuttering neon light from somewhere outside her bedroom's small, high window. She rotated it cautiously, squinting at fine wires, and the thing's gleaming, multifaceted eye gave her an accusing look as it croaked "Murder" one more time before its heat died.

Cera, shuddering, threw it across the room to smash against another wall, and got up, put a boot on, and stomped on it for good measure.

Because that was what a steady-minded, calm, cool, and collected police detective should do when a bug whispered *murder* in their ear.

Not that Cera could remember the last time she'd solved a case, or done anything but mop up after Judges, but that wasn't the fucking point, was it.

One boot on, ragged pyjama cuff hanging over it, Cera Cortez sat on her bed, rubbed her face with her hands, then dropped them to dangle over her knees as she stared at the spiderbot body across the room.

Murder. Murder. Murder.

When she'd started on the force, more than two decades ago, if somebody had sent a message containing only the word *murder* to any cop, it would have been taken as a threat. Now... Well, now nobody gave a shit about actual cops. Half of New-DCadelphia, or whatever they were calling the new self-governing region this week, didn't even know actual cops still existed. Some days Cera counted *herself* among that oblivious half, even though she technically still collected a pay cheque from the NYPD and would until what passed for retirement arrived, or—more likely—she got her ass killed because she was following Judges around as a 'softening presence.'

That's what cops had come to: cooling people down for the Judges. Cera lowered her head, fingertips pressed against her eyes until red sparks danced behind her lids. She had gone into the academy still holding on to the idea of a better style of policing, despite the uninhibited police-based murders, despite the demands to defund the police, despite the daily protests that had begun when she was a teen and hadn't fully ended until the Judges finally suppressed them. She'd swallowed the copaganda line and had honestly believed she could be one of the good ones. Good enough to make a difference: to a precinct, a whole department, maybe even a whole country.

No one was that good. All the cops Cera looked up to in her rookie years died, retired or retrained as Judges, but she never pulled on the jackboots herself. Probably mostly because she wasn't cut out for it—*spiders* scared her, for Christ's sake—but maybe she still believed, somewhere down deep, that she could make a difference as a cop, with investigations and due process instead of a helmet and a gun.

Maybe somebody else believed that too.

She lifted her gaze again, scowling at the spiderbot body. If it hadn't been a threat, then it might have been delivering information.

And hardly anybody let a cop know they were going to murder somebody *ahead* of time.

Cera got up. Her right foot was sweating inside the boot and her bare left foot felt frozen through. She told herself that was why she was shivering as she went to pick up the spiderbot again, but honestly, the little thing just creeped her the hell out. Its spark had faded entirely, whatever powered it thoroughly crushed by her booted enthusiasm. Even a scan with her phone didn't find its network. Cera said, "Fuck," to the world at large, and went to try harder.

Two hours with a soldering iron, the smallest eyebrow tweezers she could find, and a dozen video tutorials on repairing delicate electronics later, Cera had accomplished squat-all beyond a raging headache and a still-frozen-ass left foot. Spiderbot wasn't coming back from the dead without somebody a lot more skilled than she was at resurrection.

Which meant it wasn't coming back at all, because as best Cera could figure, the only kind of person who would come tell a cop about a murder these days was somebody who didn't want Judges to know about it. It wasn't like the Judges meant crimes went unsolved; it just meant if somebody got caught red-handed, they didn't get to walk on a technicality. So, all she had to do was a little detecting. Figure out where the body was, who the body was, and why somebody didn't want the Judges involved.

Either that or the Judges were already involved, and somebody knew that they weren't going to detect a damn thing. Either way, Cortez had a case on her hands for the first time in more years than she cared to think about. And like it or lump it, the best place to pick up any useful dirt on the topic was at the precinct, so somewhere around seven, irritable with lack of sleep and her left foot barely warmed up from a quick shower, Detective Cera Cortez stomped into work trying to pretend she wasn't walking on eggshells. The Judges had frowned on cops doing anything even resembling police work for most of a decade now. She knew a dozen cops who—once upon a time—would have had her back in a covert investigation. Now, she ran through the list of names who hadn't gone on to become Judges themselves, and realised she thought most, maybe all, of them would rat her out, in the world as it was. She hated that the idea of even trying to ask—or investigate on her own—sent her heart into another rabbit-fast arrhythmia.

She remembered when the precinct had been, if not exactly friendly, at least more... *human.* Back when some of the lighting was still incandescent, adding a warmth that LED couldn't. Back when the institutional walls at least had a layer of coloured paint slapped over them, instead of alternating between concrete grey and glaring white.

Back when you could see all of your co-workers' goddamn *faces*.

Some of them, she still could. Cops like her, who were assigned as a Friendly Community Face backing up the Judges, or who were the Judges' clean-up crew—often literally. Cops *less* like her, who followed the Judges around like bloodthirsty puppies hoping to get a chance to shoot somebody without consequence. Most of those wanted to be Judges; none of them could cut it. They were thugs wearing a badge to validate their murderous tendencies, insufficiently dedicated to the Law—Judges always managed to say it with a capital L—to pass the rigorous training. And then there were a few who were just afraid, and inclined to suck up to anybody with power. Whole regimes had been built on that in the past; whole countries had fallen to it.

Every single day of her life for the past fifteen years, Cera Cortez had wondered if she was one of the latter, and if it mattered that she thought she wasn't. She tried to do what job she had left well, but you didn't—*couldn't*—argue with someone whose word was literal law. It didn't matter how true and noble and righteous you were, how pure your ideals, how honest your heart. If you crossed a Judge, your life was over, and any good you might do was lost forever.

There was a word, after the fact, for people who supported the Nazi regime, not out of ideology, but out of ease or convenience or fear: they'd been called Nazis, because history didn't care *why* they didn't fight the rise of fascism, only that they hadn't.

Cera honestly didn't know if she was a Nazi.

She *absolutely* knew that a bunch of her co-workers were, though, and she still nodded, waved, said hello, and bantered with them on her way through to the office she shared with the Judges she supported.

Just like a Nazi would.

Her shared office was nicer than the open-plan desks or even the individual offices of the higher-ranked cops in the department. The Judges' chairs were high-quality, their desks ergonomic, their computers the latest, fastest tech available. Cera's stuff was almost as good, which made her office more comfortable than her actual apartment. She pushed the door open, threw her coat over the back of her chair, and fell into it with a grunted greeting that got an actual cackle out of her favourite of the two Judges she worked with.

"Cortez. You look like shit."

"Thank you, Whitlock, you look like a knob." Truth be told, Cera had no idea what Whitlock actually looked like. She'd known him eight years and only seen him from the upper lip down, although she'd seen a *lot* of him from the upper lip down. A *lot*. Not on purpose. It was just the changing rooms were unisex, and Whitlock's sense of personal modesty only applied from the lips up.

It was faintly possible that was why she liked him better, of her Judges. The other one, Webb, took her helmet off sometimes, but it didn't help. Webb had cool eyes that reminded Cortez of a shark, and short-cropped pale hair that didn't seem to have any particular colour to it. She generally remained more buttoned-up with her helmet off than Whitlock did with his on. She barely lifted her chin in acknowledgement as Whitlock, still chuckling, said, "Where's our coffee, Cortez?"

"What, is there a law about me getting you coffee now?"

"Could be."

Webb turned her head, staring at Whitlock, who laughed again. "Could be one of Solomon's new laws."

"For Grud's sake." Webb turned her attention back to her paperwork. "I don't have time for another Solomon spiel today."

"Why?" Cera tried to ask it casually, but her voice cracked. Both the Judges lifted their gazes to stare at her, Webb with her shark's eyes and Whitlock's visor reflecting Cortez's own face back at her.

She wasn't *sure* if the Judge helmets could read vital signs. Maybe she just wore every emotion she had on the surface, as a cold sweat, or a visible pulse, or a grimace, like she had a bad case of gas. Her distorted expression in Whitlock's helmet looked like all of those things, plus guilt, were broadcast across her features. "I'm just saying, what, you got an interesting case or something this morning, or are you just trying to avoid another two-hour lecture on why Chief Judge Fargo was best and Hollins Solomon is worst?"

Whitlock's jaw tightened, a flush of anger creeping up to stain his dark golden skin to a fiery warmth as he spat, "Solomon's a *politician.* Fargo was a—"

"*Visionary*," Cortez chimed in. "A man with a *plan*, cut down in his prime by the kind of *common criminal* he hoped to *eradicate*—"

Cera would have paid real cash money to see if Whitlock's ears were as red as his jaw had become. He never would have let his opinions slide into the open around other cops, but they'd worked together a long time, and she guessed he trusted her enough to let politics slip out. "Hollins Solomon should never have become Chief Judge," she prompted. "We needed someone with the *foresight* to develop *new divisions*—"

"Not a *politician* willing to let *Internal Affairs* start interfering with Judge discretion!" Whitlock roared over Cortez.

"SJS," Webb said, "not Internal Affairs. Special Judicial Squad. And there are Judges out there who need that oversight, whether we like it or not. Not everybody is as dedicated to Fargo's vision as you are."

"Or to the law as you are." Cera nodded at Webb, who shrugged one shoulder in mildly pleased acceptance.

"It's crap," Whitlock said. "The new divisions, the increasing hierarchy, the political strategy, it's all crap. We don't need new badges issued. When it started out, we were *all* street Judges. Why muck it up—?"

"We were not," Webb said patiently. "Technical and medical Judges always existed, Whit, even back in the early days. You know that."

"What do you mean, new badges, when are you getting new badges?" Cortez leaned around her computer interface to look at Whitlock's chest, where *STR9928* now gleamed on his ID. "Oh, look, you already did. S-T-R for street? M-E-D for medical, obviously, and, what, T-E-C for—?"

"T-E-K," Webb said, and rolled her eyes as Cera arched an eyebrow at her. "Don't ask me, I didn't decide on it. Talk to marketing."

"Talk to Chief Judge *Solomon*," Whitlock growled.

"Sure, I'll just get on the line to him now. I'll bitch about the SJS while I'm at it, okay? Just for you, Whit." Cortez mimicked picking up her phone, and the helmeted Judge managed to give her a filthy look even with half his face covered.

See, they were *human*. That was the problem with fascists. They were terrible people as a class, but individually, they got their panties in a twist over the new boss or somebody's fashion sense, just like anybody else, and while you couldn't quite *forget* they were the boot on everybody's neck, it wasn't so hard to cut this or that *particular* Judge some slack. Grading them on a sliding scale, in exactly the way they'd never do for you. Cortez's humour faltered, although she still 'hung up' her pretend phone, as if the game hadn't caught up to her emotional state. Whitlock smirked at her, and she sighed. "So anything good today?"

"What are you, a dog with a bone? No, there's nothing interesting. Go get coffee like Whit wants, if you wanna get out of the office."

"Not gonna arrest me for unauthorised use of work hours?"

Webb smirked too. She had a good laugh, when she used it, but her smile had bite. "Not if it's what a Judge is telling you to do. Besides"—she eyed a clock—"you don't *have* to be here for another seventeen minutes. Why so early?"

"Freaked out when a spider crawled across my face and couldn't get back to sleep."

Whitlock cackled. "No wonder you're not a Judge. Can't believe you've even got the stones to be a rent-a-cop."

"You know what, when you two are off on assignment somewhere and I'm not wiping your leather-clad asses, I'm *still* a pretty good cop. I don't know how to break it to you, but I've never had to arrest a spider." Although if she was ever going to, the one that morning had been a contender. Its tinny, tiny *murder* chant crept through her mind, and she fought off a shiver.

"It's not *leather*," Whitlock complained.

At the same time, Webb lifted her gaze, cool again, to give Cera a warning look and said, "Watch your mouth, Cortez. You know what kind of penalty slandering a Judge carries."

Cortez lifted her hands, palm out, in an apology she didn't want to voice. Webb looked mollified, and Cera let herself hang on the edges of wishes for a few seconds. Her best days at work really were when the Ws were on other assignments, but it had been three or four months since Whitlock had been out of office, and longer for Webb. The last time they'd *both* been, a couple years ago, had been a breath of fresh air, like the whole wretched Judge organisation had temporarily disappeared and left a functioning democracy in its place.

They'd come back, though, of course, and every day since then, there was something that reminded Cortez that it would be fine if Judges were maybe a little less dedicated to upholding the law. Especially when it came to sensitivity about personal insult.

That would undermine the whole point of Judges, of course, but that was kind of Cortez's favourite scenario. At least the SJS existed now; at least there was *somebody* out there to deal with Judges who crossed the line.

Cera grabbed her coat, a bad taste in her mouth. "Gonna get coffee."

A chorus of "Decaf" followed her to the door, as if she hadn't been getting coffee for these two buffoons for four years, and other Judges before that.

The door swung open, and a broad-chested, ill-tempered Judge snarled Cortez back into place. Cera's heart contracted, and she backed up, returned to her chair, and kept her head down as the Judge stepped in and closed the door behind her.

"What're you two nimrods still doing here? Didn't you get the call?" Judge Moore had a high-pitched, squeaky voice that, by its nature, undermined any authority she could possibly command. She made up for it by being a stone-cold bitch. Cera would cross Whitlock and Webb a thousand times before she risked getting on Moore's bad side.

Whitlock and Webb seemed to feel the same way. They both scrambled for a response as Moore flicked data to their screens, Webb going red as the file came up. Normally so pale she would sunburn on a rainy day, Webb could flush a shade of red that looked like a mistake in the Day-Glo factory. Cortez watched the colour spread across her whole scalp, between the strands of her pale hair.

Moore saw it too, a nasty smile forming under the helmet. "Looks like you're wasted as a Judge, Webb. There's a lighthouse out there somewhere waiting for a beacon like you."

"Why was this information held back this morning?" Webb sounded like she'd gargled a garbage disposal, but she didn't otherwise rise to Moore's mockery. "We've lost precious time towards apprehending the criminal."

"Don't ask me. I don't make the rules. I just follow them." Derision filled Moore's tone. "Isn't that what we're supposed to do? Now get your asses out on the street."

"You're a street Judge too," Whitlock said, though he was collecting his gear as he said so. "Why us?"

"I've got better things to do with my time." Moore turned and left, ignoring the loathing glares that followed her out.

"One of these days..." Whitlock said.

"Shut up before I have to arrest you for threatening a Judge." Webb pulled her helmet on and threw a bag full of recording equipment at Cortez. "Guess you got your case."

Cera grunted, catching it. "Yeah, just what I wanted. What's the deal?"

Webb looked over her shoulder on the way out the door. "A Judge has been murdered."

CHAPTER TWO

Cera had a decent motorcycle, paid for by the department, but using it to follow a couple of Judges on their massive Lawrangers always made her feel like someone's little sister desperately trying to keep up with the cool kids' bikes. The streets tended to clear for the Lawrangers, though, and she stuck close enough to them that the crowds didn't swirl back into place until she'd cleared them. She felt the weight of angry, fearful stares following them all, and sympathised with those who were afraid of the Judges and their badges and their implacable adherence to the law.

The housing business was booming, in the newly self-governing super-city. Blocks were going up faster and faster now, since the first couple lawsuits had died. Between them, older high-rise buildings still reached for the sky, reflecting just enough light to remind citizens that somewhere up there in the world, the sun continued to rise and shine on the lucky. Everything below about forty storeys was dank, dark, dim and grim.

Cortez lived on an eighth floor.

The Ws pulled up to a glimmering, glass-sided building with a goddamn door attendant. They read as female to Cortez, and wore a Kevlar suit that didn't try to hide what it was. Her jaunty top hat had a face guard, but she still was a goddamn door attendant, a throwback to a lifestyle that Cortez barely even realised still existed.

She pulled the door open gracefully, murmuring, "Judges," in a politely respectful tone that disappeared into a withering look as Cortez quickstepped to catch up. "Officer."

Cortez said, "Thank you," with a polite nod, and a trickle of appreciation wiped away some of the guard's disdain. Once she was through the door, Cortez hissed, "This place is fucking *decent*," at the Judges. "I thought you all lived in monastery cells."

Whitlock's lip curled, and Cortez regretted saying anything even before he said, "Solomon thinks *some* Judges are worth the higher upkeep."

"According to her file, Dr. Carla Rigney has lived here since long before she joined the Technology Division," Webb said coolly as they strode through a marble-floored lobby. "No one actually tells us to move out of the digs we've got when we become Judges."

"Nobody tells us *not* to either." Whitlock punched an elevator button so hard Cortez was surprised it didn't crack. A bellboy with a security tag under his name plate winced at the Judge's unnecessary rigor, but obviously didn't say anything. "Under Chief Judge Fargo—"

"Dr. Rigney *was* a Judge under Fargo, Whit. Give it a rest."

"I'm just saying we're all supposed to be equal under the Law."

"Maybe you should ask Chief Judge Solomon for a fifty-fifth-floor apartment then." Webb stepped into the lift, which had brass rails worth more than everything in Cortez's apartment, and waited stoically for her companions, Whitlock spluttering with outrage, to join her.

"What do we know about the victim?" Cortez asked over Whit's fuming. She rarely got answers to that kind of question, but the spider's *murder, murder, murder* chant kept crawling up and down her spine, bothering her, and she had to say something to push it away.

Webb turned her head towards Cortez, her expression unreadable within the helmet. Cortez looked at her reflection in the visor and was relieved to note she looked reasonably calm and professional, and not like her molars were rattling from the speed of her heartbeat.

Apparently the Judge thought answering her was better than listening to Whitlock grouse, because finally, around the twenty-third floor, she said, "Mid-fifties. Lived alone. Joined the Department way back in the early days, after completing both medical and computer science degrees. Never worked the streets, though, always Technology Division." Webb paused and Cortez could all but hear her rolling her eyes. "Sorry, 'Tek-Div.'"

"Any known enemies?"

"Jeezus, Cortez, whaddaya think you are, a cop?" Whitlock interrupted his own diatribe to curl his lip at her.

"Don't like enclosed spaces. Just trying to pass the time." Elevators weren't really a problem for her, but it was a sure way to distract Whitlock from thinking she was trying to do actual police work.

And it succeeded. Whitlock sneered. "How'd we get stuck with the most everything-phobic cop left in the Mega-City?"

Webb shrugged and answered Cortez instead of her partner. "No known enemies, beyond everybody hating all of us."

"Yeah," Cortez said under her breath, "doesn't that bother you?"

"Not really. Rigney was well-liked at Technology. She was a junior tech on the program that gave us our DNA-locked Lawkeepers. That was her kind of gig."

The elevator *dinged* with a deferential, old-world bell, as if afraid to offend, and the doors opened on the plushest hallway Cortez had seen in thirty years. A whistle escaped her, and although Webb's glance was sour, Cera figured she agreed with the sentiment.

"Look at this *drokking* place," Whitlock growled. "Nobody needs this kind of luxury." He stalked down the hall, heavy-duty boots muffled on the thick carpet, and let himself into the apartment guarded by pale-faced cops. Cortez recognised one of them and jerked her chin in greeting. He gave her a sick smile as she brushed by, following Whitlock into the apartment.

"Do we know what she died of—oh." She all but swallowed the last word, staring at the scene in front of her.

Even lusher carpets covered the floor, the legs of real leather chairs and tables sinking into them. Huge windows lined with heavy, sound-muffling curtains opened onto a large, deep balcony that overlooked a growing mega-block and the city streets beyond. There were other doors leading into different rooms—*entire* rooms, not just a kitchen offset into one corner in a shared living/sleeping area, with only the toilet and shower being really private. Everything visible was decorated in tasteful, expensive shades of white and highlights of gold.

Carla Rigney's body was stretched in bloody ribbons across the whole place.

CERA MANAGED—BARELY—to keep her breakfast behind her teeth, mostly because she hadn't eaten any. She heaved, though, and through a rush of blood in her ears heard Whitlock say, "Swear to God, you puke in here and your guts will join hers on the floor."

After a couple of bleary-eyed moments, the worst of the nausea passed, and Cera dragged a hand across her face. The Judges had spread out around the room, using tech Cera didn't get to even touch to investigate. "No sign of forced entry," she said, trying to clear her mind. "Any defensive wounds?"

"Why don't you take a look?" Webb's cool voice somehow also sounded condescending, as if she didn't expect a mere detective to notice anything her scans couldn't.

Which was pretty likely, but Cortez steeled herself and went to look, asking, "Who found the body?"

"Maid service. They called the apartment management,

apartment management realised the vic was a Judge and called us."

As if they would have called anybody else anyway. The cops outside were for decoration, although Cortez said, "Anybody send those guys out there to talk to the neighbours?"

"She really does think she's a cop," Whit said to Webb. "Hey, cop! Go door-to-door and talk to the neighbours!"

"Yeah, okay, in a minute." Cortez waved her hand in acknowledgement as she studied the body.

Someone had drawn and quartered Carla Rigney with great care, either before or after flaying her. Her fingernails were technically still in place, just... not very close to one another, or to her knuckles. Cortez hadn't known tendons and ligaments could stretch that far.

She wished she still didn't.

Neither her own ordinary scanning equipment, nor a tweezers or a swab, were able to come up with anything under the woman's nails. Her skin was too, uh, disembodied, to tell if there was any real bruising around her wrists, ankles, or even her mouth, to indicate she'd been tied up and gagged for the duration of her dismemberment. Cortez, breathing through her teeth, stood back from Rigney's head and stared down the length of the apartment at the spread of her body. "It's almost fucking artistic. Somebody was *freakishly* careful."

"Room's clean," Whitlock growled. "Nothing in here that isn't Rigley."

"*Rigney*, Whit, *Jesus*," Webb said. "You're right. There's *nothing* here that says she ever had friends over, noth—"

Cera blurted, "Do *you?*" and both the Judges turned glassy helmeted gazes on her. "Well, *do* you?" she asked again, despite herself. "Do you *ever* have friends over?"

Webb snapped, "Do you?" but gave it some thought, finally shrugging the question off. "Not often, and mostly Judges. I don't sterilise the place after, though."

"Maybe Tek-Div was all she had." Cortez found the nickname easier than Webb did, maybe because it obviously annoyed Webb so much. "I'll sweep the other rooms, if you want."

"With your crappy tech? I told you to go talk to the neighbours." Whitlock shouldered by Cortez, saying, "Flip you for the bedroom," to Webb.

"Ugh. Gross." Webb went into the bathroom while Whit took the bedroom, leaving Cortez alone in the living room with the body. She liked the phrase 'strung-out' better as a fun way of saying 'hopped-up junkie' than as an accurate description of someone's remains. The blood was slowly browning on the carpets, but the smell wasn't as bad as the visuals. Not yet, anyway. She stepped over a meat-covered femur and prowled cautiously across the apartment. The whole exterior wall of the apartment was windows, but only the balcony doors had handles, one of which had a key in it. Blood splatter suggested the entire wall had been closed off to outside view when the murder took place, but somebody had opened the curtains in front of the balcony before Cortez and the Judges arrived.

Stomach clenched, Cortez edged towards the balcony doors. Intellectually, she knew she wasn't going to spontaneously crash through them and fall fifty storeys to her death. She still hated even *knowing* she was that high up, never mind voluntarily approaching the balcony, even if the doors were closed. She tried one from as far away as she could: locked.

Locking a balcony door hundreds of feet in the air seemed ridiculous, except Cortez knew she'd absolutely do it herself. It was just that extra level of protection between herself and five seconds of terror ending in a giant *splat*. She shuffled a little closer, trying to keep her breathing steady as she looked through the doors, as if something in the ever-expanding city outside would give her a hint as to what had happened to Dr. Carla Rigney.

Ants plodded along the balcony, stymied by the door seals but still apparently finding something worth crawling up fifty-five storeys to collect. There was no blood visible through the glass, or on it, and if there had been, presumably the Judges would have found it anyway. Butt clenched and movements stiff, Cortez unlocked the door and pushed it open, scattering ants and waking a primal part of her brain that gibbered in unintelligible panic. She shuffled one step forward, pushing her toes onto the balcony without lifting her weight at all. Another shuffle, and her heels were on the outside edge of the door frame.

The view of the city from there wasn't significantly different from the view one step *inside* the doors. If she looked up, out, straight across, it would be slightly less bad than if she looked down. But she had to look down to see anything potentially useful. She edged another half step forward, hands clenched in sweaty fists and uninvited cursing sliding between her clenched teeth.

"What the *drokk*, Cortez—?"

Cera shrieked at Whitlock's voice and threw herself back into the room, landing on her hip and palm hard enough to jar her elbow.

Whitlock fucking smirked as she awkwardly climbed up off the floor, stopping at her hands and knees. He sighed. "I can't believe you even made it as a *cop*, Cortez."

Cortez didn't answer. A spider, right at eye level on the curtain, stared at her as, still on her hands and knees, she pulled the doors closed and locked them again, then leaned against them, eyes shut, as she tried to calm her heartbeat. The heights were bad enough. The creepy little bug had the same glittering faceted eyes and finely jointed legs as the spiderbot she'd smashed that morning.

Obviously, she should mention it to the Judges. She didn't know why their scans hadn't found it, but she should still mention it.

Except the first spider had come to her, not the Judges. She could imagine this second one had too. It made her feel like *she* was supposed to solve the case, not the Judges.

Besides, it would be nice to do something that proved to them that she wasn't useless.

Cera peeled her eyes open to glare at Whitlock, and decided if she was going to solve a case under his nose, him continuing to think she was inept wouldn't hurt her chances. "Guess I'm a real ground-pounder. All my old cases were street level." She turned her gaze away, working at not focusing on Webb as the other Judge came out of the bathroom. The spider moved up a couple inches, drawing her attention, and whatever Webb had to share was lost in a rush of blood in Cera's ears.

The spiderbot had gathered itself and leapt easily from the curtain to her shoulder. It ran down her arm and inside her sleeve as she repressed a shudder.

"Come on." Webb wove her way through Rigney's remains and offered Cortez a hand up. "I don't much like these high-rises either. Guess the air's better up here, though. You okay?"

Cera, her hands tense with the sensation of the spider skittering up her arm, croaked, "Yeah. I'm gonna go talk to the neighbours," and hurried out of the apartment.

All she wanted to do was take the spider out and interrogate it, but there were cops—actual cops like her, not Judges—in the hall, standing around in the same kind of performance role she had. Friendly neighbourhood cop faces, and all that crap. Cortez, her heart beating too fast, croaked, "Hey, Kelly, you wanna come help me talk to the neighbours?" to the cop she'd recognised earlier.

Relief swept his expression, and he stepped away from door duty, voice lowered to say, "Anything to get away from that apartment. Did you see what they did to her?"

"Yeah. Nasty." Cortez shivered. "How're you? I haven't seen you since, I don't know, it seems like not since the fucking academy."

"There was that retirement party for Detective Elliott a while back, but yeah. I'm okay." Kelly slid a glance over his shoulder, voice dropping even farther. "As okay as you can be as a lapdog for the Judges."

"Yeah, I feel that. You take this side of the hall, I'll take that side?" They moved to opposite doors, knocking on them and identifying themselves. Nobody had heard anything. Nobody had seen anything. Nobody wanted to look past their own door frames, afraid the Judges would notice them.

Judge Rigney kept to herself, according to everybody who would say anything at all. Some of them hadn't even known she was a Judge. The woman directly next door had talked to her in the elevator a few times, but she'd never seen Rigney with anybody, or heard any sounds from her apartment that suggested she had visitors. Cortez sighed. "Was anyone in the building friends with her?"

"Friends?" the neighbour asked disbelievingly. "With a Judge?"

Cera breathed, "Yeah. Okay. Thanks for your time," and went back, with Kelly, to report a total investigative bust to the Ws.

CHAPTER THREE

Whitlock gave her a ration of shit about her fear of heights, her failure to get anything useful out of the neighbours, her imaginary dislike of elevators, and everything else he could think of on the way back down to the thirteenth floor, where building security was located. Cortez took it all with about as much grace as she felt, which was none at all, until Webb said, "Shut up, Whit," as the doors dinged open. Cortez thought maybe she liked Webb better after all.

The building's security team waited for them, all shoved into a computer lab made up mostly of screens. It felt cramped, and Cortez wondered why they used one single boxy room when they had an entire floor available to them. The team was made up of about two dozen people built like slabs and a scrawny guy in a wheeled office chair who ran the computer system. One of the slabs was the doorkeeper, whose Kevlar suit turned out to be standard wear for the security crew. The top hat, however, was apparently just for the door job, because nobody else was wearing one. Together, they looked like a well-dressed football team.

They tried to come across as intimidating, but it didn't stick. They were obviously nervous. Judges had that effect on people, even when they hadn't done anything wrong, and somebody had drokked up colossally last night, or Dr. Carla Rigney wouldn't be dead.

"The security footage is *clean*," the scrawny guy squeaked before either of the Ws had anything to say. "I swear to God, I've looked through every minute of it, every backup we've got, I can't find any sign of anybody being here who isn't *supposed* to be here. I got it all ready for you to send over to Technology Division, maybe they can find some way it's been tampered, but I swear to God I haven't touched it, and none of these nitwits know how to do anything that sophist—"

"So you're saying you *do* know how," Webb said in a deadly tone. "Do you know what the penalty for tampering with security footage is?"

Sweat poured down the guy's face in rivulets. Cortez, her own spine icy with the slick streak of fear she'd earned on the balcony, sympathised, but she kept her mouth shut. The spider had crawled up to inside her collar, under a wrinkle of shirt. She couldn't even really feel it, but she knew it was there and knowing made it itch like a bastard.

The security guy squeaked, "I dunno, I don't know, but I swear, Judge, I didn't tamper with it, I wouldn't do that, I like my job, I'm no Judge, but I just wanna help keep people safe, I—"

"How many entrances does this building have?" Whitlock would already have the specs available, but Cortez didn't know, and if the security guy's answer differed from the Judges' knowledge, it wouldn't go well for him.

The guy—his name tag read Alfie Q in poor handwriting—said, "Six," without missing a beat. "Two elevators and two staircases from the underground parking garage, the main front entrance and a goods entrance at the back. There are another six emergency exits onto the alleys, but they don't open from the outside and make an unholy noise if they're opened at all."

"Can that be turned off?"

Alfie looked nonplussed. "I mean, I guess, maybe, but I've never tried. There's security cameras on all of them, though, and I swear to God the cameras all work and nobody's messed with the feeds. See, look." He wheeled across the floor, punching buttons to show everyone the feeds. Maybe that was why they were cramped into such a tiny space: so a single person could oversee the whole multitude of screens at once.

At a glance, none of the alleyway emergency exits had been used in years: the grime built up on the ground outside the doors looked inches thick, an impression enhanced by sticky footprints near one of the doors. Pointy-toed, flat-heeled prints that read as expensive men's shoes to Cortez walked down the alley, with equally pointy-toed high heels next to them with greater frequency and less stability. Right next to the door, the men's shoes turned to face the wall and the women's disappeared. Cortez bet if the camera angle was a little different, she could see the print of a woman's back against the mucky wall.

"Who'd you let into the building?" Whitlock growled.

Alfie Q paled. "Nobody. I swear it, nobody. I'd never let anybody in. Neither would the crew."

Webb turned her visored face towards the top-hat-wearing door attendant. "Were you on duty last night?"

"Yes, ma'am." Top Hat's voice was almost as cool as Webb's. The spider in Cera's shirt shifted, like it was trying to get comfortable against her collarbone. She nearly smacked it.

"And?"

"And what, ma'am?"

Webb took a dangerous step towards Top Hat, who failed, spectacularly, to look endangered. Cortez wished *she* could do that. "Are you hampering my investigation, Miss— Zel?" The momentary hesitation suggested she'd read the woman's name tag.

"No, ma'am," Zel replied calmly. "'And' is a leading, but non-specific question. I want to answer your questions accurately but can't without more direction."

Cortez imagined steam rising from Webb's helmet. "Did anyone unfamiliar to you enter the building last night?"

"No, ma'am."

Whitlock took over, turning the interrogation back to Alfie. "How'd you wipe it?"

"What?" Alfie's voice cracked. "I didn't. I didn't! I wouldn't!"

"Felony tampering with evidence carries a sentence of one to twenty years," Whitlock said flatly. "I sentence you to fif—"

"*No!* I didn't, I swear I didn't, I wouldn't, I *promise* I've got everything here for Technology Division to look at, I *hope* they can find something that explains it, but it wasn't me, it *wasn't* me, I *swear* it—"

"He'll still be here tomorrow," Webb said to Whitlock. "And if he's caught lying, you can add another five years on to his sentence."

Whitlock's lip curled, but he didn't carry out the sentencing. Alfie sagged in his chair, so visibly relieved Cortez expected to smell fresh urine off him. Webb jerked her chin at Cortez, who stepped forward, palm open for Alfie's data drive. "You'd better be telling the truth," she warned him.

He whispered, "I'm not brave enough to lie to Judges," hoarsely, and Cortez, feeling that strongly, left him alone with his computer screens.

A TECHNOLOGY DIVISION facility lay only a couple of blocks away, although the 'blocks' were bigger than ever before, with the new mega-block-city thing going up. The Ws took the long way around for intimidation's sake, their helmets' communications set to the police band to make sure Cortez could hear every smart-ass comment Whitlock made about her panic attack up in the apartment. "That Zool woman back there would make a good Judge," he yelled at Webb. "Cool, calm, collected. Not like Cortez here."

"*Zel!*" Webb yelled back. "Why don't you go recruit her while I do our damn job?"

Whitlock revved his Lawranger's engine, the sound thundering across the street and making the bones in Cera's ears hurt. It was hard to remember she'd been a decent cop fifteen years ago. Heights hadn't bothered her as much then. Neither, maybe, had spiders. Above the ragged edges of the growing block city, the sky shone a brighter blue than Cera could remember seeing in ages. She couldn't remember if it had always been brighter back then, before Judges were everywhere, or if that was rewriting an ugly past into something more palatable. And if she could do that, it didn't bode well for how she'd remember today, a couple of decades down the road. Maybe she'd made all the good choices she could, and still ended up licking fascist boots and accepting being the brunt of their jokes. Maybe twenty years from now, this would seem like a happier time, too.

The Technology Division building had that particular grim stamp of Judginess to it, the corners seeming more brutally shorn, the windows more bunker-like, and the employees more shut off from the world than the rest of the new super-city. Which took some doing: most of the people of the ever-growing mega-city seemed to have hunched their shoulders and turned their backs on the changes settling in around them. Most days, Cortez couldn't even blame them. You could fight corrupt police, you could vote out bad governments, you could stand against the institutionalised *isms* that haunted them all. People hadn't, generally, which was how they ended up here, but they *could*.

You couldn't really fight some asshole in a helmet whose word was the actual law. There'd been some quote, century before last, about power corrupting, and absolute power corrupting absolutely. Cortez figured they didn't know the half of it.

Her stomach clenched at that idea, like her whole body was trying to hold back a thought she couldn't afford to have right then. She put it aside, because it wasn't going to leave her, and swung off her motorcycle to follow the Ws into the building. A blank-faced employee wearing a badge walked by, and Cortez bit back a smile. *TEK1333*. She would enjoy the name *Tek-Div* all the way up until the day Webb stopped saying it with a cringe. After that she wouldn't care any more. It would just be one more way the Judges had shaped the world, something else they'd all got used to.

Tek-Div didn't wear helmets the way street Judges did—less to hide and fewer people to intimidate—although Cera wouldn't be surprised if it got to where they were expected to wear them, too, if they weren't in their offices. Faceless justice, and all that, although she was old enough to remember when Justice was only blind, not anonymous.

A few confused glances, and more disdainful or scathing ones, were thrown her way as she trailed in after the Ws. She was still technically a detective, which allowed her to wear civilian clothes, but experience had taught her that wearing a uniform both separated her from, and united her with, the Judges. Sometimes being almost-but-not-quite on the inside proved helpful.

Now, for example, they just let her through without asking for identification or explanation. She swept by on the power of Judges, and for once, she appreciated it. There were elevators in the ten-storey building, but the Ws took the stairs up two flights, which meant Cortez had to too. There were worse fates—like climbing the eight flights to her own apartment—so she didn't complain, even when Whitlock glanced over his shoulder like he was checking she could do it. Cera tried again to remember why she liked him better, but it basically came down to preferring an angry pit bull to a shark. The shark would eventually eat her, while the pit bull probably wouldn't do more than bite her a bunch of times.

Second floor Tek-Div looked like a nightmare's idea of a mad scientist's lab. The walls and lighting were hard white, except where intense sprays of colour rained down, presumably to help scientists see something they couldn't under the normal spectrum. Glass walls half the height of the tall ceiling separated everything and noise bounced off them, creating a loud, distracting environment Cera absolutely could not imagine working in.

On the other hand, saying no to anything Judges wanted you to do was a good way to get dead, so maybe she'd make do, like everybody else. Webb stopped a small brown woman with tightly contained curls and said, "Judge Rigney?"

"Genetic imprinting," the woman said without emotion. "Other end of the room." She went back to her job, and Cera followed the Ws through a maze of glass-lined walls and occasional explosions.

A tall black man in a lab coat looked up as they approached, then straightened away from his work, saying, "I knew something was wrong," to the group at large. Half a dozen other geeks poked their heads around data displays and scientific instruments, looking like a herd of meerkats. Or maybe a pack. Cortez didn't know what the group names for meerkats was, because who the hell knew that kind of shit in a world where the only surviving meerkats were the ones in those stupid insurance commercials?

The Tek-Div guy—*TEK2887*, according to his badge—stepped forward. "Rigney's dead, isn't she?"

"Why would you say that?" Webb asked, frost in her voice.

"She'd literally have to be, to not come to work. She's usually here early, stays late, forgets to take lunch. The kind of dedicated developer they hold up as a shining example. What happened to her?"

"That's what we want to find out. What was she working on?"

The man shrugged. Cortez didn't want to think of him as 2887, but didn't think the Ws would look kindly on her if she interrupted their questions to ask his name.

He didn't care, either way. He had answers to offer the street Judges, and nothing else mattered. "We work with genetic imprinting down here. She did half the development on the code for your guns, and I know she was looking for ways to improve that, but it's not our current assignment. We're working on—" He shut up suddenly, and all his co-workers slid back into their places with affected artlessness, abruptly much more interested in their jobs than the Ws' conversation. After a few seconds, the tall Tek-Div man spoke again. "I'd need clearance to tell you, and don't give me that street Judge *I make the law* thing."

A little to Cortez's surprise, the Ws exchanged glances and let it go. The tech guy sighed in quiet relief, then said, "I can tell you it's a similar application to the genetic coding for your new guns"—he indicated Whitlock's Lawgiver—"and that Rigney's talents were being wasted on a project of this calibre. She was *good*," he said with a note of urgency. Behind him, chairs rolled again as several of the other techs reappeared to nod agreement. "Do you know what *good* means, when you're talking about people like us?"

"Nah," Whitlock said, "we're meatheads. Explain it to us."

"It means we'd been working on the genetic imprint for *years* before she came along. It's not like fingerprints, it's checking your DNA. It sends a signal, and if it doesn't get the right answer, kaboom." He 'exploded' with his fingers, splaying them out.

"No, that's not right," Cera protested. "It reads palm prints. Everybody knows that."

The tech guy gave her a look somewhere between sympathetic and exasperated. "How many Judges you see running around bare-handed, Officer?"

Cortez, under her breath, said, "It's 'Detective,'" and aloud, said, "None, really," as she shook her head.

"So you wanna tell me how the Lawgivers read palm prints through a quarter inch of leather?"

Cortez opened her mouth and shut it again. The tech guy's eyebrows shot up and back down. "You tell somebody it's a palm print, they think maybe they'll luck out, maybe their print matches a Judge's, maybe they can shoot the gun. Then: boom." His fingers 'exploded' again. "Drives home the point, doesn't it? Tell everybody it's a genetic match, and you don't get so many demonstrative examples as to why it's a bad idea to try."

Nausea boiled in Cera's belly. "You mean they're *letting* people blow their hands up as an object lesson?"

The Judge's look this time suggested she'd gone soft in the head. "The whole point of Judges is that they make every infraction an object lesson, Detective."

Cera's nausea burned away into the cold panic Judges tended to engender in everyone. This one hadn't been meant to hear the comment about her rank. He hadn't, up until that moment, seemed *scary*, but now, all at once, he was One Of Them. Somebody on the other side of fascism from where Cera hoped she still stood. The goddamn spider shifted on her collarbone, tickling.

The Technical Judge turned his attention back to the street Judges. "Anyway, we were stuck on the code. We had all the pieces, but we couldn't get them talking to each other. Rigney walked in, and four weeks later, the first Lawgivers hit the streets. She was a genius, and I kept expecting her to move upstairs. But she liked the genetic work. Excelled at it. So here she stayed. Did you check her home computer?"

"Hard drive was missing," Whitlock said. Cera hadn't known that.

"What was she working on?" Webb clearly didn't care about Rigney's ambitions, or lack of them. Cera did, but not enough to interrupt them.

"Same thing we all are, which I still can't tell you. Get clearance from the Chief Judge's office—"

Whitlock actually *spat,* shocking everybody into just staring at him for a few seconds. Then the most enraged robovac Cortez had ever seen buzzed down the hall at a genuinely dangerous pace, rolled over the spit, and smashed into Whitlock's ankle with obvious intent to injure. He lifted a foot to step on it and an entire phalanx of razors popped up from its top.

Cortez, Whitlock and Webb all stared at the furious little vacuum in faintly horrified astonishment. Whitlock, cautiously, put his foot down well away from the angry robovac, then took his Lawgiver out.

"I wouldn't," the Tek Judge said mildly.

Whitlock looked at him.

"Tek-Div is very fond of Stabby."

Helmet or not, Cera could see Whitlock weighing his odds: take vengeance on an infuriating suck robot and risk having the entire technical division of the Judges turn against him, or back down and live with the humiliation of having been defeated by a six-pound automatic vacuum cleaner.

Whitlock forced a chuckle. "'Stabby', huh? Ain't that a thing?" Casually, as if it was meaningless, he holstered the Lawgiver and turned his attention fully back to the Technical Judge.

Stabby slammed into his ankle two more times for good measure, then zipped off with an audible and undeniably mocking cackle. Whitlock's jaw clenched, cords standing out in his throat, and Cera bit the inside of her cheek to keep from grinning. She felt Webb slide a sideways glance at her, but Cera couldn't tell whether the Judge shared her amusement or condemned it.

Which was why she was a Judge, and Cera was the Friendly Neighbourhood Police Face.

"I'll be happy to tell you what I can, if you get clearance," the Tek Judge said to Whitlock. "Until then, I just want to know if you think the rest of us are in danger."

"I hope so, 'cause if you get killed, I'm coming back for Mr. Stabby there."

"Not as far as we believe," Webb said more diplomatically. "We'll let you know if that changes. In the meantime, this is below your pay grade, but we've got security footage that needs to be examined for tampering."

"In Rigney's building? We'll take it." The Tek Judge put his hand out. "We can run specs as well as anybody, and she was one of ours." He curled his hand over the data drive when Webb handed it to him, hesitating. "How did she die?"

"Slowly," Whitlock said, which Cera thought was unnecessary.

The Tek Judge recoiled, then recovered with a brief nod. "We'll get this checked for you and be in touch."

"You know where to find us." Webb turned on her heel and Whit fell into step with her, leaving Cera to trail behind, as always.

For once, she really didn't mind. Out of their sight, out of their minds, she could afford to let herself follow up on the question of absolute power that had been bothering her. The Ws hadn't asked a single question about Rigney's enemies, or about who could have tampered with the security footage successfully, or potentially threatened Alfie Q into lying to Judges about doing it himself. They hadn't asked who could possibly have got into a well-secured, high-rise building without being detected.

And the only reason Cera could think of for not asking those questions was that the answer was *Judges*.

CHAPTER FOUR

Opening a murder investigation about, and under the noses of, Judges, probably wasn't the *worst* idea Cera had ever had, but she was hard pressed to think of many that topped it. Maybe the teenage thing with the train track bridge, but at the very worst that could have ended up a good, quick death, whereas if this went sideways—and it was *going* to go sideways—it would be a slow, horrible death, probably in a jail cell. Because Judges *were* the law, and if she got caught investigating them by the *wrong* one… well, it wasn't like Judges were notoriously comfortable with people treading on their territory.

Just a couple years ago, Chief Judge Solomon had started the Special Judicial Squad that Whitlock hated so much. Not, Cortez thought, because Whit was corrupt, but because he loathed the idea that *any* Judges could be. It was like a personal affront to him. Cera thought he genuinely loved the idea of Judges. Not the jackbooted thuggery actuality of them, but the *idea*, that individuals could carry the breadth and width and depth of the law within them and make correct, unbiased judgements based on that law and the evidence at hand. Impulses to shoot robovacs and general dickheadedness aside, Whitlock and Webb both embodied the concept of Judges as well as anybody could, and for Whit, it was like a religion. It made sense of the world for him, and nobody liked it when you questioned their religion, so he hated the SJS.

Unless, of course, Cera was wrong and he hated it because he *was* corrupted, or corruptible, too. In which case, cold fish Webb might well be, too, and squeaky, violent Judge Moore seemed almost textbook-primed for corruption, and...

...and that was why Cera wished she could somehow just magically transport herself into the SJS offices. Somebody with the power of the Law behind them should be investigating the possible murder of a Judge *by* a Judge. It was out of Cera's league. It was whole *orbits* beyond her league.

But there wasn't anybody else to do the job, because she couldn't ask one single Judge, whose duty it might be, just in case it turned out they were the bad one.

At least if she barfed from nerves while investigating, it would fit right into the Ws' image of her. She went out to get their lunches like a good little lap dog and as soon as she was no longer under their noses, found herself a shadow to hide in so she could scrape the spiderbot out of her pocket.

It glittered faintly in the curve of her palm, small and creepy, but silent, when she hissed, "Where the hell did you come from? Who sent you? Why? Why to me?" at it. She scanned it, trying to find a signal, but like the one she'd crushed, it didn't seem to have one.

If it couldn't answer, at least it could go somewhere other than her hair. She kept it in her hand until she got to the food cart, where she took a condiment tub from the stack of them and slid the bot inside before putting it in her pocket.

She interrupted an argument about whether Whitlock not arresting Alfie Q on the spot for obstruction made Judges look weak, when she got back. Cera figured that had more to do with Stabby the Robovac routing Whit in front of a bunch of Tek-Div geeks than Alfie himself. She handed out food and kept her mouth shut as she sat down at her desk.

She could do exactly no research on anything about Dr. Carla Rigney from her desk, because anything she did would be logged. She couldn't afford to leave a flaming trail suggesting she didn't trust Judges. The day crawled by: a few perps being dragged into the precinct by other Judges; a few lunatics coming in to lodge complaints, as if they *wanted* to draw the attention of the Judges; Webb taking Whit out for a few random traffic violation arrests to make him feel better about losing a standoff with a vacuum; Moore sticking her head in and demanding to know why Cortez wasn't with them; Cortez scrambling for an answer that wouldn't get her convicted of rudeness to a Judge. She crawled home later than the clock said she had to, afraid if she bolted out of there at the appointed time, somebody would suspect her of not trusting the Judges around her.

She emerged from her apartment a lot later than she usually did, wearing the least cop-clothes she owned, which inevitably made her feel like she was instead advertising that she was Definitely Not A Cop, Don't Look Here, I'm Not A Cop, Why Are You Looking At Me, Cera Cortez, Who Is Not A Cop. The goddamn spiderbot broke out of its condiment tub and crawled in her hair when she was changing clothes. She pulled it out again and put it back in the tub, then shoved it back in her pocket. She thought she could feel it tapping at the seal, trying to push the tub open again, although that was probably her imagination. Probably.

Surveillance cameras were everywhere, but one of the few good things about hanging out with Judges all day long was Cera had long since learned the tricks to avoiding them. Some of it was easy enough, changing her physical profile by layering shirts, putting her hair up, grabbing a wig off a street vendor's stand and tossing five bucks on the table in exchange. Other things were harder, like changing her gait or making sure not to leave any trace DNA behind, but she did what she could, until she was deep enough in the city that even surveillance became unreliable.

The cost of an anonymous internet connection could only be paid in untraceable cash. Cera parted with a fair chunk of her hard-won stash and sat at a glassy terminal in a dark room that smelled like decades' worth of unwashed teenage boys, then activated a privacy mode for her terminal cell that she had, of course, had to pay extra for. It didn't matter: she couldn't afford to have anybody reading over her shoulder. Not this time.

Once upon a time, somebody had developed the tech to scatter a web search so that it only collated at the querying terminal. Cera thought of it as every single key stroke going somewhere different and pulling back together when it hit her screen. She had no idea if that was how it really worked, but the concept satisfied her modest need to know.

The Judges, obviously, really *hated* that tech, and had gone to great lengths to stamp it out, but even after seventy years of existence, one thing was still true about the internet: once something was on it, you couldn't take it out again, just like pee in a pool. Anonymity could still be bought, at the right price.

Searching for a specific Judge still seemed risky. Or maybe that was the spider crawling through her clothes again and giving her the creeps. Cera checked her pocket; the tub was open again, and the spider missing. "Dammit." She pawed through her clothes, but the horrible little thing was good at hiding, and she didn't want to draw too much attention to herself by looking too hard.

With a sigh, Cera pulled up what she could about Tek-Div, landing on both official sites and various opinion pages. Officially, what was now Tek-Div had originally been the Technological Research and Development Judges' Program, formed when the Justice Department had nationalised Thurgood Industries. The R&D Program had picked up the obvious acronym of TRAD, and the whole program had been rebranded immediately because the last thing the Judges wanted was to be mistaken for their traditional counterparts. Anyway, whether TRAD or Technology Division or Tek-Div, its job was, in essence, to make cool shit for the Judges, which had been well-received by those who saw any technological developments as positive, and poorly received by those who saw anything to do with Judges as negative.

There were descriptors in the articles, though, that made Cera look harder at how Tek-Div had developed. Nobody, not even the authors who disliked the program, actually *said* the scientists, engineers, and medical personnel were conscripted. They used phrases like 'answered the call of duty' and 'selected' and 'recruited', and Cera, following those deeper into the web, became increasingly certain that while *some* Technical Judges were definitely hired, an awful lot more of them had been 'volunteered.' Tech Judges weren't like the street Judges. They didn't need to have a certain personality, or respect for the law, or ability to keep going against overwhelming odds. They just needed to be really freaking smart.

They also apparently had to not care who got credit, because while in the first several years after the Judges were formed, Cortez found announcement after announcement about new developments from Tek-Div, there were very few details about who was responsible for those developments. After the first decade or so, even those disappeared, as Judges closed their collective fist on America and information started to flow through them. Better to surprise the enemy—i.e. the people—with tech they didn't even imagine existed, rather than give them data to fight back with.

The fucking spider crawled across Cera's nape. She slapped at it without thinking, and a hand caught her wrist before she made contact.

Cera spun out of her seat, sliding her hand around her assailant's wrist and slapping her free hand on top of theirs. A quick twist locked their wrist and she drove them to the floor, pushing their hand up between their shoulder blades and dropping her knee onto their spine.

The guy howled and slapped the sticky floor, not even pretending to be macho or fight back. Cera tugged his arm a little farther up, and he screeched again. "What the hell, what the hell, you crazy bit—aaargh!"

Cera got down close, hissing in his ear. "You picked the wrong vic, asshole. You think just because there's no Judges around—"

"Jesus Christ, I'm *here* because there aren't any Judges, who the actual hell do you think made that *spider*—"

Cera let the guy go, jumping back into a defensive stance as he got to his feet, an expression of disgusted dismay etched on his features as he stared at the gummy, street-trodden grime now coating his front. He was tallish, oval-faced, and white, with pale eyes and light hair; the specific colours were distorted by the various screens and privacy shields in the internet cafe. Cera let herself take one hasty glance around the room, pleased to see that every other person in it was taking a studious disinterest in the sudden commotion.

Her assailant raised his unhappy, slightly betrayed look on Cera, who barked disbelief. "Shouldna fucking grabbed me, asshat. Who the hell are you?"

He mumbled, "M'name's Durrell," and rubbed his shoulder. "What the hell was that?"

"Aikido. What do you want, Durrell?"

His eyes shifted nervously. "Can we talk somewhere else?"

The surge of panic that had thrown him on the floor was fading, things he'd said finally clicking. He'd implied he'd made the spiderbot, and the fact he even *knew* about it supported the statement. It crept from Cera's hair down her spine, bringing a chill with it. She said, "Yeah," reluctantly, all too aware she'd paid for a lot more anonymous internet time than she was gonna end up using, and that she'd never get the cash back. She jerked her chin towards a back door, not caring that it said *fire exit*. Odds of it being alarmed were about the same as the odds of her getting her cash back. "That way."

Durrell lifted his hands a little, like he was mildly protesting an arrest, and went the way she told him to. A minute later they were in a skanky back alley, dark as pitch except for a few squares of light well above them, from ragged apartment windows. Durrell's skin was pale enough to be a faint white shadow in the darkness. She could see him straining to see her browner skin and darker hair. "You killed my bot." He sounded petulant.

"Why'd you set it on me?"

"Nothing personal." The petulance faded into a very faint superiority. "I've got 'em on all the cops assigned to a Judges unit."

An illusion Cera didn't even know she was maintaining melted, at that. So much for being the lone hero sought out by a… well, she didn't know what Durrell was. Not a damsel in distress, anyway. She hardened her voice, not difficult, as anger surged through her. "Why are you spying on cops?"

"Because it's less dangerous than spying on Judges, *obviously*." Durrell shuffled away in the darkness until he was barely a blur against the alley wall. He was in his fifties, Cera reckoned, a decade or so older than she was, and had a hunch to his shoulders that suggested either too much time keyboarding or too much time trying not to draw notice. She suspected both.

"Do you do that too? Spy on Judges?"

His gaze flickered towards her and away again, ghost glances in the murk. "Only the smart ones."

A cackle escaped Cera before she could stop it. "So, not my unit." A penny dropped at the back of her mind—or maybe it was the fucking *spider* crawling down her *spine* again—and she said, "But Technical Judge Carla Rigney, maybe, huh? You know who murdered her."

"No!" Genuine distress sliced through the word. "No, my bots only crawl her place every few days. They're on an untraceable network, but I still wouldn't risk one for long around somebody of her capabilities. I found her like that. Or the bot did. And then I contacted you, and you *squished* George."

"Why me?" That question came out hard, professional, the way it should, but then she totally wrecked the vibe of *cool badass cop* by asking, "Why *George*? Do you only have a few of those things and they all have names?"

"Of course not," Durrell said, audibly offended. "It's just

yours hung out there so long I had to call him something other than 'Cortez's spider', so I started calling him George."

"You know my name." Of course he did, but the words came out with a dead weight that made Durrell back up another couple of steps.

"I told you, I have spiderbots on all the Judge unit cops. Most of 'em want to be Judges. You don't. I don't know if you actually give a crap about justice, but you don't want to be what they are. So you're Rigney's best chance *for* justice."

"Who *are* you?"

When Durrell didn't answer, Cera sighed and jerked her head towards the alley's mouth.

"Come on. Let's find something to eat and you can tell me the edited version of your story."

THEY ENDED UP at Durrell's apartment, which, given he'd been spying on her for some indeterminate amount of time, was outright creepy. On the other hand, Cera didn't quite dare trust the Judges she worked with, and trusting the guy who'd tried to notify her about a murder seemed like her best option for the moment.

Besides, he clearly knew a lot about staying off the Judges' radar, and his apartment was almost certainly safer than some random diner where she couldn't verify the functionality and placement of every single security camera.

Apartment turned out to be an overwhelmingly grandiose term for the space Durrell occupied, though. The building was condemned. Most of the *block* was condemned. People still lived in it, because where else were they going to go, but Cera had no doubt the whole place would be levelled, sooner rather than later, for a new block. In the meantime, the entry to Durrell's home was through literal heaps of trash and debris from where half an old brownstone had collapsed, and some enterprising souls had jury-rigged a number of increasingly unstable apartments above it.

Something similar had happened on the other side of the street, too, buildings tilting towards each other until the sky was a narrow slit between them. The people in the top apartments could probably reach out and shake hands with one another, if they felt like it.

Durrell lived in the basements below them, in a warren of forgotten technology and heaped, rotting clothes. He pointed out more than one place where she couldn't step on the floor, or where putting her hand on the wall would bring it all down. "Keeps other people from moving down here," he said, as she squeezed by a weak spot in the concrete floor.

"You mean you've booby-trapped it."

"Yeah." The living space he brought her to looked like Hell on the surface, but within a few minutes, Cera realised the shambles disguised fully functioning, even high-quality, kitchen equipment, seating, and bedding. She still wasn't sure she wanted to sit in a couch that looked mouse-ridden, but Durrell sank into it and exhaled. "I'm brighter than most."

A lot of people Cera knew would have said that in an almost aggrieved tone, challenging her to disagree. Durrell obviously didn't give a shit, which made it a much more effective statement. She sat in a kitchen style chair and opened her hands, inviting him to continue.

"You're what, forty-seven? Forty-eight?" he asked her. "Old enough to remember when Fargo started this whole mess. I'm old enough to have written think pieces on how the technology the Judges were gonna use would change the world for the better. I was well-meaning and really naive, back then." He paused a moment, not looking at her. His eyes were blue, it turned out, and his short-cropped hair, white. It looked like he cut it himself. "A lot of very smart people are weirdly naive. It's so *obvious* to us how things could be better, the fact that other people don't see it is dumbfounding. So when someone comes along who seems to see it... Anyway, when I realised how dangerous they were, how it was a straight smooth road to fascism... You're the first person I've told my name in fifteen years."

"Jeezus." After a moment of uncertainty, Cera said, "Well, I'm Cera. Cera Cortez. I guess you know that, but if we're doing the polite thing and exchanging names and all..."

Durrell smiled, a brief, thin thing that disappeared as quickly as it had come. "Nice to meet you, Detective Cortez. Sorry about the spiders. They're how I watch the world. Mostly they're the only way I see or communicate with anybody."

"Why? How? I didn't get a signal off, uh, George, or this one." She started looking for it again, and it ran down her sleeve to cling to her wrist. It took everything she had not to screech, shake it off, and stomp on it.

"Yes, for spiders they're remarkably not web-savvy." Durrell smiled again, and it lingered a moment this time. "I developed a tech cloak a long time ago, a signal array that bounces data in a way that makes them look... not invisible, because that would be obvious, but like they're just carrier networks."

"That sounds like the tech I was paying through the nose for at the internet cafe."

Durrell's glance skittered away, and Cera's eyebrows rose.

"Right. *Right*, uh, okay, so look, why me? And why Rigney? And... why me? Or did you send like fifty spiders going *murder murder murder* to every cop in Newbaltington or whatever we're calling this, this—"

"'Autonomous District,' according to the Autonomy Act. People are calling it the *Mega-City*," Durrell said, sounding tired. "Pretty soon it won't have any other name. Or I guess they'll need to distinguish it from California and Texas; maybe the 'Eastern Seaboard Mega City.' No, it was just you. I had to place my bets because I couldn't nudge an investigation to more than one Judge unit, and I thought you might... care."

"You mean you spied on me and I seemed nice, so you thought I might like a murder investigation that could get me thrown in jail forever dropped in my lap?"

"It sounds like a bad thing when you put it that way," Durrell admitted.

Cera pinched the bridge of her nose, then leaned forward,

elbows on her knees, and sighed. "But you're not wrong. I used to be good at this. I used to like it, even. So what was Rigney working on?"

Durrell's lip curled, and he shook his head. "I don't know. My spiders have really limited capabilities and copying data drives isn't among them. I know she protected what she was doing, though. Her bedroom had a negative pressure seal on it."

"A what?"

"A negative pressure seal. It's where you're spitting out a lot more air than you're letting in to a room. I got spiders into her bedroom a couple times, but they got blown out when she sealed it. Any other kind of bug that wasn't fixed to something would get blown out, too, so whatever she was working on, she wanted it kept private."

"Why would she have it at home at all?"

"Now that's a very good question. You hungry?" Durrell rose and got cheese from the fridge, slicing chunks off and plating them with some crackers. "Cold food only, no coffee, sorry. I can't have anything that smells good in here."

"Hell of a way to live." Cera took the plate and had some cheese, which was surprisingly good. Real milk had gone into it. "You must have a weird network."

"Weird but diverse." Durrell got his own food and a couple water bottles, one of which he gave to Cera before sitting back down. "My guess is she was working on something the Justice Department hadn't sanctioned."

Cera stopped chewing a mouthful of cheese and crackers, staring at Durrell dumbly for several seconds while the food dried out in her mouth. After a swig of water, she asked, "How much trouble could she get in for that?"

Durrell spread one hand, as if indicating murderous amounts of trouble, but shook his head. "I wouldn't normally think they'd kill her for it, but if it was dangerous or important enough, and she wouldn't share... but they could just requisition it, so I think whatever it was, Technology Division didn't know about it."

"We're calling it Tek-Div these days—T-E-K, so it fits on the badges," Cera informed him with a certain glee.

His mouth twitched. "Not bad. Anyway, you figure out what she was working on, you'll figure out why she's dead. But that's your job, not mine."

"Her hard drive was missing."

"Well, then, your job is gonna be hard."

CHAPTER FIVE

Your job is gonna be hard. The helpful comment rode Cera like a black dog all the way back to her apartment at four in the morning. If investigating Judges were easy, the whole world would be different. It seemed wildly unreasonable of Durrell and his fancy spiderbots to expect her, a boots-on-the-ground grunt cop, to be able to do what he couldn't.

On the other hand, she had direct access to a couple of reasonably decent Judges, if she could just figure out how to leverage that.

Somebody pounded on her door way too early, and she answered it in her underwear, gun in hand.

Whitlock leaned on the door frame, a disposable cup of coffee on display. Cera stared at him for a second, then took the coffee and stumped back into her apartment. Whitlock took it as invitation and followed her, his immaculate Judge uniform making him seem larger than life in her dingy grey space. And in her dingy grey underwear, for that matter: the fitted sleeping shorts and tank top were passable for company clothes, if the company wasn't too picky, but they looked like the low budget, department-mandated underthings that they were. "Whaddaya want, Whit?"

"Consider it an apology for being a dick yesterday."

"You're a dick lots of days, Whit. You don't usually apologise." The coffee was pretty good.

"Yeah, but sometimes I do."

"Yeah. I guess sometimes you do." Just like a pit bull feeling bad after biting the hand that fed it. Cera rubbed her face, trying to wake up. "Thanks."

"No problem." He hesitated. "You all right?"

"Oh, sure. Great. There's a uniformed man in my apartment and I'm mostly naked, but I'm great."

"I've seen you a lot more naked than this, Cortez."

"The exposure is mutual. You gonna give me a lift to work, or what?" Cera gestured at the couch, but Whitlock didn't sit. She hadn't expected him to. She dropped into a scratchy armchair anyway, determined to try enjoying the coffee.

"On the Ranger?" Whitlock actually smirked, close to a laugh. "That'd go over great, wouldn't it?"

"It would start rumours, Whit. It would start such rumours. Webb would look so disapproving. Moore's head would explode." Cera grinned into her coffee. "Might be worth it for that."

"Moore's not so bad."

Moore was a heinous bitch, but saying that to another Judge wouldn't earn Cera any friends, so she only shrugged. "Ever investigated a Judge's death before?"

"No, and I hate it." Vehemence leaked into Whitlock's voice, and Cera figured she'd landed on the real reason she'd got an apology. He started pacing, which meant about four strides across Cera's tiny apartment before he had to turn again. "Judges don't get murdered. We get *killed*, but not murdered, not like this. Usually one of us is right there, or there's surveillance to tell us who did it, and it's all—"

"Over and done with," Cera supplied around a sip of coffee. "There's none of this investigation crap. Not that Judges don't investigate, but... well, you said it. Not usually murders of other Judges. You got... anything?"

"Not until the security tapes come back. Webb believed that

twit yesterday."

"Webb didn't think he was innocent. She thought there would be proof to condemn him with, when the security footage came back. And you knew she was right, or you would have just sentenced him right there." Cera shrugged one shoulder as Whit glanced her way, light bouncing off his visor. "Am I wrong?"

"Nah." Whitlock sighed and threw himself into Cera's couch after all. It scooted back four inches, feet screeching on the barely carpeted concrete. "I'm not thought police. Can you imagine how drokked up that would be? Arresting people for what they were thinking about doing?"

"I dunno, it'd cut the snake's head off, wouldn't it?" Cera didn't believe that, but she kind of wanted to see what Whitlock would say. He sat up so straight, staring at her so hard, that for a second she actually thought he was going to take his helmet off so she could make eye contact.

"You can't mean that. Where's your due process and evidential arrests, with that? That's the whole reason you hate Judges."

Cera finished her coffee and stood up with a sigh. "I hate the *idea* of Judges, Whit. Individually, I guess some of you aren't so bad. I'm hitting the shower before we head out. There's some bread if you want toast."

"What, you're not inviting me to join you?"

"*Ew.*" Cera looked over her shoulder with a laugh as she stripped off her tank top on the way into the bathroom. "Seriously, would you even take your helmet off? I don't think so. Ew."

"You'll never know what you're missing, Cortez!"

"This is workplace harassment, Whitlock!"

"We're not in the workplace!"

Cera said, "Well, shit," philosophically to that, and took her shower.

* * *

WHITLOCK WAS GONE by the time she got out, which was fine, because somebody would certainly make a noise about her showing up to work *with* him, and that would only lead to tears. As far as she knew or cared, all the Judges she worked with stuck to the celibacy rules, and she did *not* want to be caught in the middle of an accusation that one of them wasn't. Bad enough that when she left her apartment, the nosy old lady next door poked her head out and said, "New boyfriend, Cera?"

"Yeah," Cera said. "I'm definitely banging a Judge."

The old lady sniffed. "He's got a nice jawline."

"All Judges have good jawlines, Mrs. Garcia. It's a requirement, or something."

"You should come by for tamales and tell me all about him, later."

Cera put a hand over her face. "I'm glad to come by for tamales, but he's not my boyfriend, Mrs. Garcia. I don't have a boyfriend and if I did, it wouldn't be a Judge."

Mrs. Garcia sniffed again. "Well, you should have somebody. These walls are thin, and you haven't got laid in way too long."

Cera, mortified, said, "Oh my God," and slunk off to work.

Boyfriend or no, the coffee Webb had brought helped her get through a morning of snooping around on the computer, trying to find out more about Technical Judge Rigney. Friends, family, acquaintances: anything useful to the case. She'd been given a higher-than-usual security clearance for it, which made it a hell of a lot easier than trying back channels in stanky internet cafes, but even the official files were pretty scant. It was like somebody didn't want people knowing much about Judges, or something. Even with the coffee, Cortez's eyes crossed a couple of times, so she was grateful for Whitlock's early morning apology.

She was *also* glad to know she wasn't the only one uncomfortable investigating the murder of a Judge. On the other hand, Whitlock hadn't touched on the possibility that a Judge had done the deed, either. She didn't know if it hadn't occurred to him, or if it was such a crappy thought he couldn't voice it. Either way, if there were Judges who hated Rigney, Cera couldn't find it without something closer to Judge-level security access of the files. As it was, there was only one lead that looked like it might go anywhere.

Webb came in after lunch and slammed her helmet on her desk, jaw set with anger. Whitlock looked up from where he was working at his desk, coat loosened, gloves set aside, but helmet, as always, on. Cortez felt vaguely undressed compared to them, without her coat and with her shirtsleeves rolled up.

"Headquarters won't give us clearance to find out what Rigney was working on. How the he—" Webb inhaled sharply, censoring herself, and started again without a curse on her lips. "How are we supposed to know *why* she was killed if nobody will tell us what she was working on? They say it's not relevant. So somebody's just flaying Technical Judges for fun, then? That's supposed to make us feel better? Knowing what she's working on gives us a potential list of people who don't like it, people who might see killing her as a way to stop it. Otherwise it's just personal enemies, and—" She swung around to Cera, who had to stop herself from jumping to parade attention.

"Rigney went to CalTech when that still meant something, then followed it up with Stanford medical school. Scholarships on both; her family didn't have money. She had a few social media accounts back in the day, but she almost never posted on them, and hasn't at all in over a decade now. Between them she had maybe fifty exclusive contacts, none of whom, with one exception, has she had contact with in the past five years. None of them have tried reaching out to her, either; she seems to be a part of their life they've readily left behind."

"Who's the exception?"

"A college girlfriend she kept in touch with for a while."

"Girlfriend or *girlfriend?*" Whit asked.

"The latter, I think. The girlfriend has a greater social media presence, although it's pretty outdated now. Still, it suggested an intimate relationship. They travelled together a little and exchanged emails occasionally up until about three years ago, when Rigney stopped answering them entirely." Cera flicked images up onto a shared screen on the wall, showing Carla Rigney and a strong-jawed blonde woman at the edge of the Grand Canyon. "That's Kaz Mahoney. She's currently in her fourth year of Judge training."

Dropping that little bomb got the attention it deserved: the Ws both sharpened, looking from the images to Cera, who shrugged. "I can't get past security clearance beyond that. If you can give me dispensation, I'll spend the rest of the afternoon on it, but it's the only thing like a lead I've got. I want to know how it went down with them, anyway, and where Mahoney is undergoing training."

Webb exchanged a glance with Whitlock. "I'll see if Moore will give you access. That's good work, Cortez. Thanks."

Cera was a full grown-ass adult, and a word of praise from the institution that had rendered her job obsolete shouldn't have made her want to wiggle like a happy puppy, but it did. She managed to keep it to a nod, and Webb left to talk to Moore about her access.

Less than two minutes later—not long enough to have argued with Moore over it—she came back in, her expression bleak. "Technology Division says the security tapes are clean. They haven't been tampered with."

"No *way.*" Whitlock rose, colour crawling along his chin. "No freaking way. We should've given it to their security people, not those genetic egg-heads—"

"Rigney was one of their colleagues, Whit. They had every reason to get to the truth about the footage."

"Unless one of them killed her! You heard that Tek Judge. She came waltzing in and finished their projects without breaking a sweat. That's gotta cause some kind of tension, don't it?"

"You want me to track everybody on her team for the past forty-eight hours?" Webb demanded. "They're Judges, Whit. We know where they've been."

"You think Tek-Div can't wipe its footprints?" Whitlock demanded incredulously. "You think under *Hollins Solomon*, they *wouldn't?* You think they couldn't get away with it? Not on Fargo's watch, they wouldn't have, but—"

"This is not *about* Chief Judges Solomon *or* Fargo, Whit, this is about a bunch of Technical Judges who—"

"Everything is about the Chief Judges!" Whitlock roared.

"Almost nothing is about the Chief Judges! You have *got* to get over this, Whit, people *die*, even *Fargo* dies, it's not some massive conspiracy to drag the Judges in a different direction, it's just what *happens*. It's what happens to *Judges*, man, it's our *job*. Fargo *died protecting civilians*. What else do you want from him? Immortality? Wouldn't that be a perversion too?" Webb stepped around Whitlock's desk as she shouted, getting right in his face, a move Cera wouldn't have dared even if she *had* been a Judge. Right then, all she wanted was to be anywhere else; having front row seats to this was not a picnic.

"I'm not looking for gods, Webb! I'm looking for consistency in our mission, and Solomon's gonna bring the whole system down! What's going to happen to the civilians then? They're gonna depend on people like *her?*" Whitlock jabbed a finger in Cortez's direction. "That's how we ended up here in the first place!"

Cortez, despite knowing better, said, "Hey," weakly, and Whit turned on her, his fury flushing his skin from collarbone to cheekbone.

"Like I'm wrong? You can't even go up a high-rise without pissing yourself, Cortez! Your heart's in the right place, I gotta give you that, but you're one in a hundred who tried to do the right thing, and even if every single cop in America was decent, the rest of the system was broken, *and you know it.*"

Cera, softly, said, "Yeah," and fell silent again as Webb lifted her voice.

"Yeah, but that's not about Solomon or Fargo or whoever comes after Solomon, Whit! *Our* system's adapting, it's got to, that's why we've got the SJS coming in—"

"*Because Judges like we saw in Tek-Div can't be trusted,*" Whitlock bellowed. "Because they've never *been* street Judges, they don't know what it's like, they don't care if the system breaks down, we've got to hold the line, Webb—"

"What if it's Mahoney?" Webb snapped. "What if the ex-girlfriend joined the Judges *just* to find a way to get back at a broken heart? What if the *street* Judges are corrupt, Whit?"

"If that's the only reason she joined, she'll wash out!" Whitlock slammed his fist into his desk, then went shockingly pale and lifted his hand, cradling it against his chest. He snarled when Webb made as if to look at it, turned his back on her to get his uniform jacket, and stalked out of the office in a white-faced fury.

A long silence followed him slamming the door, broken, eventually, by Webb saying, "Well. That went well," and Cera choking on a laugh. "Moore won't give you access," Webb went on evenly. "I might go argue with her about it, but I figured the security footage was more important... Jesus, he dented the drokking desk."

Cera got up to look at where Webb's gaze was trained: three knuckle-shaped grooves in the metal desktop. Her own knuckles ached sympathetically. "I broke all the blood vessels in my palm flat-handing a wall a while back," she said. "Wonder if Whit broke any knuckles."

"I wouldn't give him much grief, if he has," Webb warned.

"No shit." Cera backed up, leaning against the edge of her own desk. "Is Solomon really that bad?"

Webb sighed explosively and went to her own desk. "Not that I know the man, but he's more of a politician than Fargo. He's committed to Fargo's vision, but Fargo didn't have a compromising bone in his body. Solomon reckons there's more ways to skin a cat, and as long as he thinks the overall goals of the Judges are being achieved, he'll make changes to support those goals. Whit..." She shook her head. "He doesn't like it when the rules change. He'd have been a good soldier, back in the day. And I think he truly believes Judges can't be corrupted.

The idea that this might have been a Technical Judge, or even that kid—Mahoney. I think it's really hard for him."

"What do you think?"

"I think Judges are only human."

Cera made a show of surprise. "My illusions are shattered."

"Hah! No, they're not. But Whit's might be, so tread lightly around him, all right?"

"Oh, yeah. Because I usually make like a bull in a china shop around Judges. Look, Moore's not gonna let me at the files, so how about I go put on the Friendly Neighbourhood Cop face at the security guy and see if he lets anything slip when he's not terrified for his life and/or future?"

Webb's expression cooled. "You'll let us know if he confesses to anything?"

"I know the penalty for obstruction of justice, too, Webb." Cera picked up her uniform jacket and left the office in Whitlock's wake, grateful she wasn't actually following him.

CHAPTER SIX

THE DOOR ATTENDANT at Rigney's building was the top-hatted Zel again. She obviously recognised Cera, and looked past her for the Judges unit before her gaze returned to Cera, questioning.

"Just me today. Nobody's getting arrested or sentenced. Not right now, anyway. Is Alfie at work?"

Zel frowned and shrugged. "As if he'd be anywhere else. We live here. Where else are we gonna get digs this nice?"

Cera guessed that explained why the security rooms were crammed into a couple hundred square feet on a floor that spanned acres. "I thought the floor was unfinished. Unlucky thirteen and all that."

Zel's gaze went shifty, and Cera put her hand up. "Must be super uncomfortable living with all those bare pipes and open wires."

The woman's eyes came back to Cera's, and she smiled faintly. "Yeah. Yeah, it totally is. Look, if you go up and head to your left, through the fire door on that floor, you'll find, uh..."

"The best a squatter can do?" Cera suggested, and Zel's smile grew.

"Yeah. Third door on the right. That's where Alfie squats."

And that, Cera thought, entering the thirteenth floor a minute later, was why cops could do what Judges couldn't.

Of course, it was also a textbook example of why Fargo had concluded Judges were necessary in the first place, but that wasn't a useful thought right then. Cera took the left and the right as she'd been instructed and walked into a nicely appointed apartment eight times the size of her own. Alfie, lounging in his underwear on a couch that cost more than Cera's monthly salary, leapt up with a shriek. If he'd had a blanket, he'd have cowered behind it like a cartoon housewife afraid of a mouse.

Cera patted the air, trying to calm him. "Just me today," she repeated. "This is your chance to come clean about any infractions you don't want a Judge to hear about."

"I swear to God I didn't do anything." Alfie collapsed in the couch, tears streaking his face without warning. "Once, when I was new here, I let somebody's boyfriend in 'cause he asked so nicely, this was a guy I knew, he'd been in and out of the building with his bae a million times, but it turned out they'd broken up and he beat the crap out of them, and I didn't sleep until they got out of the hospital. I've never screwed around with the rules since, I swear I haven't. I honestly don't know how somebody got into Dr. Rigney's apartment. I don't know how to convince you."

Cera sank into the far end of Alfie's expensive couch and rubbed her face. "How long ago was that assault?"

"I dunno, twelve years? Fifteen?"

Way, way beyond the statute of limitations, then, especially for someone who was only an accessory. Not even deliberately, in this case, which would carry an even lighter sentence, if any at all, in a fair and reasonable justice system. Not that Judges gave one good goddamn about things like that. "What happened to the perp?"

"Their partner's family threw him off a roof." Alfie paled, as if he realised too late he was talking to a cop, but Cera couldn't help laughing.

"Well, it's hard to argue that wasn't justice, even if vigilantism is frowned on. Look, Alfie, I can probably keep my Judges off your back. You screwed up, but not seriously, and it was a long time ago. Justice, like it or lump it, has been served, assuming the victim was satisfied?"

Alfie looked at the ceiling. "They might not have, uh, known."

"Good enough for me. I just need to know the absolute truth. Have you seen *anything* that explains how somebody got in and killed"—he'd called her *Doctor* Rigney; he might not know she was a Judge—"Dr. Rigney?"

"I swear I haven't," Alfie whispered. "Zel was on door duty and says nobody unknown to us came in, the security tapes show she's telling the truth, I didn't see anybody, nobody saw anybody! I *swear*, officer."

"I believe you." Cortez stood up with a sigh. "But if I *ever* find out you're lying to me, Alfie..."

"You won't. I'm not. I'll be good. Just don't tell the Judges on me."

Cera nodded and left him, not feeling good about herself at all. Intimidation tactics were par for the course, maybe, but using Judges as her stick seemed about half a step from being one herself. Whitlock would probably be proud of her.

She reached the elevators and went up, on an impulse. All the way to the fifty-fifth floor. She tried the door of Judge Rigney's apartment, just in case. Just in case of *what*, she didn't know, but the locked door stuck.

Cera looked up and down the hallway, checking the security cameras, then took tools she wasn't supposed to have out of a deep pocket and picked the lock. A moment later, the door opened, and she stepped through the police tape to stand just inside the apartment, examining the room.

Rigney's body had, thank God, been removed, but the stains hadn't been. Cera walked to the Judge's bedroom, careful to avoid the brown marks, and closed the door behind her. A light flashed beside the door, and she covered her fingers with her sleeve, then pressed it.

The air pressure changed immediately, causing her ears to pop. She stood there a minute, feeling air rushing in and out until it equalised at a distinctly different level than it had been before.

Nothing else exciting happened. She realised she'd half expected a secret door or compartment to slide open when the negative pressure seal had finished isolating the room. With that thought in mind, she circled the room, looking for any seams that didn't match up, or extra drawers in the dressers, or anything untoward that a...

...that a Judge, equipped with the highest-end technological sensors, might have somehow missed. She said, "What the hell, Cortez?" aloud to herself, and left the room again with a sigh. It had been a nice idea, just not grounded in reality.

The problem was, though, the Judges with all their cool tech *had* missed something. Somehow. They'd missed Durrell's spider, for example. She'd given up trying to keep it in its condiment box and accepted that it lived in her cuff now. As long as it stayed still, she didn't care that much.

And aside from the spider, they'd missed... *something* else. The killer had got in somehow, without leaving a digital trail.

Hardly anything in the modern world didn't leave at least a ghost of a trail. Even her own careful descent into the inner city last night could be traced, if somebody wanted to badly enough. There had to be *something* that would point to Rigney's killer.

Either that, or something that could wipe it completely.

Cera left Rigney's apartment as quietly as she'd come, stopped at home to change out of uniform, and went into the depths of the growing mega-city again, taking a different route and ending at a different internet cafe. This time she couldn't shake the feeling she'd been followed, although God knew Judges didn't follow people subtly, and she moved on before she'd found out anything useful.

The trouble was, she needed Justice Department files. If she'd been granted clearance earlier in the day by Moore...

But she hadn't been, so there was no point in agonising about it. Regardless, anything useful about what the Technological Division had developed was unlikely to be public record, and she needed dirt. Details. Unfettered data. Durrell could probably get it for her, but he was deep in hiding, and had already risked himself once by meeting with her. She doubted he'd do it again.

He'd talked like he'd belonged to Tek-Div back when it started, though. Like he'd got out, as if anybody *got* out of the system. They *washed* out, yeah, but nobody walked away, and Cera couldn't imagine they had twenty years ago either.

If they had, though, she could believe they'd have to live in a garbage heap underneath a collapsing building. Maybe he *had* got out.

Cera let it go; she'd find him again later, if she couldn't get what she needed without him. In the meantime, she didn't have contacts in this part of the city, but she did still have some cash.

A few dollars convinced a street corner junkie to sell out his buddy 'who knows people.' The buddy was so afraid of being busted he gave up the name and location of a 'guy who knows everything about the old city' without Cera even paying him off. Before midnight, she slipped into an internet cafe so buried in back alleys and byways that she never would have found it on her own, and approached the proprietor, a skinny black man with glasses that reflected the screens around him.

His face went wary as soon as she walked in. Cortez guessed that even in a world with Judges, something about her still said 'cop.' Voice low, she said, "I don't give a shit what you're up to here, pal. I'm here for information and word on the street is that you can provide it."

The guy's gaze flickered over her shoulder, looking for Judges, and came back to her, still cautious. His voice was a light tenor that probably sounded great in song. "What are you looking for?"

"Paper archives. Old ones. Shit that hasn't been digitised, or is digitally buried."

Sly interest flickered over the cafe owner's face. "Who you digging up dirt on?"

"None of your fucking business."

"I don't trade information for free, bitch."

Cera palmed a substantial chunk of cash where he could see it, and a slow, thin smile spread over his face. "You must want it real bad."

"Can you give me what I'm looking for?"

He leaned in, uncomfortably close, and took the cash. To her surprise, he smelled fantastic. "I got a key. A key to an archive that nobody knows about any more. You want old data, it's there. More information than you'll ever find online. You bring the key back, though. This is a, ah, this is a rental fee, you get me?" He fanned the money, then pocketed it, and, from the other pocket, withdrew a key that he dangled between them. "Sixty steps back up the alley. Turn left. Go right. Just a crack in the wall. It goes deep and tight. Hard to fit through. Even kids don't bother. But it'll have what you want."

Cera took the key. "If this doesn't pay off, I'm coming back for my money."

The guy smiled and turned away. Cera bared her teeth at him, but left, following his directions through a rubble-wrecked building and through spaces she wasn't surprised kids didn't bother with. She wasn't big, and there was still hardly enough room to breathe. But eventually the crush opened into narrow, chimney-like chute, just about big enough to stretch her arms out in. It rose upwards five or six storeys before a chunk of concrete lay across its top, blocking access from above. Its only exits were the path she'd squeezed through, and a door that had turned as green as ivy with disuse. The key fit its lock, and it creaked open like she was the first person in eternity to use it.

There was a fucking *library* on the other side of the door.

Cera breathed an astonished curse and shoved the door shut behind her, making her way through the building with a flashlight and a gun, not sure which was more useful. The whole place was unbelievably well sealed: she didn't even see evidence of rats, much less squatters. A calendar at the front desk suggested it had been locked up for fifteen years, which meant any information it held was incredibly dated.

But it might also be completely untouched.

There were machines in the basement like she'd never seen, with *microfiche* and *microfilm* stencilled on the sides, and stacks of actual physical newspapers that had apparently been recorded on the film right up until the day the library closed. Cera had to look up how to use the damn things on her phone, which referred to them as antiquated, old-fashioned, embarrassing, and—critically—borderline indestructible. Things on the web disappeared all the time, but her phone said micro-stuff would last centuries.

Old newspapers, it turned out, had a lot more to say about the creation of the Justice Department and the Judges than the internet let on. Cera hunched over the readers, spinning through spools and zipping past sheets until her vision blurred, but the little indexes gave her enough to go on, with more and more information about the nascent Technology Division revealed with each page. Things Cera couldn't even imagine being public record *were*. It highlighted how much things had changed in the past twenty years, and she knew, vaguely, that they'd been much more restricted in the years of her childhood than in the decades before it.

She'd ended up deep in the weeds of a cross-section of Technology Division and digital surveillance, reading until her eyes crossed, but one of the blurring words caught her attention and she stopped abruptly, backing up to read the article with her full, focused attention.

The article's author clearly despised the Judges and what they could do, and had done a deep dive into what Tek-Div was up to. Among their sins was what the author called an 'all-access pass,' one that not only unlocked any door, but rewrote digital footprints on the fly, so original files were never tampered with: they just collected the wrong information from the outset.

Apparently in the early 30s, that was still too much for the populace to bear. The 'AAP' got shouted down without ever being implemented. Even now, Cera wasn't familiar with Judges having such a thing, and after eight years as the police ride-along for a Judges unit, she thought she'd probably know if they had.

But unlike any modern articles about tech advancements out of Tek-Div, this one gave credit to the individual network engineer and scientist who had begun work on the all-access pass before it was scuppered. *Engineer Bryant Durrell recognises the potential danger of this development...*

Cera lifted her cuff and shook the spider out, turned its little face towards hers, and hissed, "We need to talk *right now*," at its creator.

CHAPTER SEVEN

BARELY A MINUTE after she demanded to talk to Durrell, a bell rang in short, sharp bursts somewhere in the library around her. Cera, headachy from staring at the microstuff all night, nearly jumped out of her skin, then stomped through the library in search of the noise. It stopped and began again before she found it: an old-fashioned telephone. *Really* old-fashioned. It had a circular dial and vibrated visibly with the clanging of its bell. Cera picked up the heavy receiver and put it to her ear cautiously, honestly not quite sure what would happen.

Durrell's voice came through, sharp and surprisingly clear. "What do you need?"

"What the hell is this 'all-access pass' thing I found, *Bryant?*"

The engineer's gasp could have cut her eardrum. He held it for long seconds, so quiet that if there hadn't been a faint hiss on the line, Cera might have thought he'd hung up. "Where did you find that information?" he finally asked.

"Microfiche."

"Micro—Jesus, I didn't think that stuff existed any more."

Something in his tone suggested arson was on his mind. Cera said, "Don't you dare," and somehow his next breath sounded guilty.

"I won't. But you shouldn't have been able to find that. Any of that. Yeah, I developed the AAP. It's what my bots use, and a variation on it is what does the search scatters. But I dismantled everything I'd ever done for the Justice Department on it before I left. They shouldn't have that tech."

"And yet." Cera sounded portentous to her own ears.

Durrell made a dismissive sound. "Maybe, but it would take a lot of work to redevelop it. They've been working on other stuff. Maybe somebody in Tek-Div used anti-grav to get in the balcony."

"Anti-grav? Like the big block construction sites use?"

"Yeah. If the Justice Department got their hands on it and isn't developing it for individual use—Lawrangers, maybe, or drones—what are they even doing over there?"

"Drones fly already. But maybe they need somebody with your technical genius," Cera said, not sure if she was serious or not.

"Maybe it's what Rigney was working on." Durrell was definitely serious.

Cera's stomach lurched. "If somebody stole something like that from her, it would explain how they got in and out of her apartment unseen. And..." She turned around in the darkness of the library, looking towards the distant door. "And we only looked at ground floor surveillance, Durrell. And indoors."

"Guess you've got your work cut out for you." Durrell hung up without further commentary, leaving Cera with a buzzing phone line in her ear. It brought back a visceral childhood memory of playing with the landline, a thing she'd never seen before or used since, at her grandmother's house. She hung up more gently than she meant to, shaken by the strength of the memory. She hadn't thought of that in decades.

Dawn was going to catch her in the library if she kept standing there being wracked by old memories. She slipped out, debated keeping the library key, and instead stopped to get a copy made with the last of her cash before returning it to the owner. She gave up on discretion and took the subway back to her part of town, shedding layers with each change of train, until she looked—she hoped—like somebody else as she emerged into the early morning light.

At best, she had time to run home, shower, and change before work. No way could she get any sleep. And she needed to be sharp today, because she'd be investigating Judges right under other Judges' noses. After a shower, in uniform, and just about blind with exhaustion, Cera stopped for a large coffee, drank it on the way to work, and got a second smaller one to help her through the morning.

Whitlock threw an information packet at her as she came through the office door. Cera, given a choice between dropping her coffee and catching the packet, ducked to the side, knocking it out of the air with her shoulder. "Dude!"

"List of contacts for Kaz Mahoney. Call 'em up and find out the story behind her break-up with Rigley."

"Rig*ney*, Whit, for Grud's sake, Rig*ney*." Webb sighed. "I don't know if you get names wrong on purpose because you're an asshole, or if you've got the memory span of a goldfish, but it's not a good look. Get it right or I'll put you in for memory evaluation. Can't be a Judge if you can't remember names."

The two Judges glared at each other while Cera set her coffee safely on her desk and picked up the info packet.

"You coulda emailed this."

"I wanted to throw something at you."

"What'd I do?" Cera threatened to throw the packet back, but sat instead, flipping her screens on. "How's your hand?"

"'Sfine." Whit sounded like a sullen ten-year-old, so Cera took him at face value and went to work, interspersing calls to Judge-Candidate Mahoney's friends and family with searching security footage from the highest exterior cameras around Rigney's building that she could find.

Everyone immediately related to Mahoney said variations on, "Oh, Carla? Yeah, I remember her, she and Kaz were friends for years. I wonder whatever happened to her, do you know?" After about the fourth call like that, Cera looked up where

Mahoney was from. Small town Mid-West, where apparently 'queer' hadn't settled in as an identity option yet, but hey, it had only been like forty years since marriage equality passed. No rush.

The college friends were more forthcoming, although most of them had the same *Oh, yeah, whatever happened to Carla?* vibe. "They ended up fighting," one person finally said. "Carla joined the Justice Department's Technology Division pretty much out of college. She was always gonna, but Kaz wanted to do the whole settle-down-and-have-babies thing. They were on and off for *ages*, like she thought she was gonna talk her out of the Judges, but she finally gave up on that dream a few years ago. I think she joined the Judges herself so she could maybe get with Carla again, like, *spiritually*, if not, y'know, boning down."

"Five years of training to be somebody's *spiritual* partner?" Cera asked disbelievingly.

"I dunno, I guess. Kaz has always been really all-or-nothing, you know? I think the last time they talked they broke up for real and good, though. I think Carla was maybe seeing somebody else? But Kaz hasn't dropped out of the Judges program, so I guess she's serious about it. Who'd you say you were again, anyway?"

"Detective Cera Cortez with NYPD Outreach, adjunct to the Judges Unit. Thank you for your time."

"Ooh, are you doing a background check on Kaz? Do you need to know about the time she—?"

"I don't at this time. Thank you again for your ti—"

"Does the NYPD even exist any more? I thought it was just all like mega-city cops kissing Judge ass—"

Cera muttered, "Bye," and hung up, cheeks flushed with anger. Anger because it was true, mostly, and that she was impotent to do anything about it. Her screens finally came back with security footage from around Rigney's building, offering a kind of distraction.

Unsurprisingly, most of the cameras pointed down,

and nothing much over the third storey even existed. Not officially, anyway. Shocking numbers of people just straight-up voyeuristically filmed their neighbourhoods, and almost none of those people had the technical knowledge to make those feeds secure. Or cared: they didn't imagine anybody would be looking, so they didn't firewall or even password-protect their data streams. Cera fast-forwarded through an awful lot of what amounted to home porn, trying to stay alert enough to catch anything more useful. Whitlock, coming back into the office, snickered loudly enough to make Cera blush. "Anything good?"

"Just your grandma making the rent." Cera switched to another feed, trying one from farther down the street, and tossed Whit her notes about Mahoney and Rigney's relationship. "I haven't found anything in Mahoney's finances that suggest she took out a hit, but I can't get into the Judges database to find out if she's gone off campus without permission."

"She wouldn't still be in training if she had." Whitlock flipped through her notes, nodding at bits. "No salacious personal details? No wonder you're watching home porn."

"Shaddup." The feed Cera was watching went staticky, a whole hiss of visual information corrupted in the distance. She checked its location—fifth floor, as high as any official surveillance she'd found, and way the hell down the street from Rigney's high-rise, which gave it a wider angle on the distant image than anything else she'd seen—then watched the footage again. The visual hiss pixelated everything near Rigney's building, all the way up its street-facing side.

A cold fist plummeted through her gut, sending a wave of goosebumps and heat over her simultaneously. Every part of her wanted to call her superiors—well, the Judges—over to have a look at the footage. *Not* doing so could get her thrown in jail for obstruction. But if Durrell was right, if Rigney was working on human-scale anti-grav units, if a Judge had got hold of them and had killed her for it, the *last* people Cortez could alert to the blurred footage was her Judges unit. She requisitioned a copy of the original tapes with a note that she'd collect at the appointed hour—that, at least, she could do without Judge oversight—and cleared her screen after noting the building, and the time of the interference. "Got anything about Mahoney's movements?" She was almost certain her voice didn't shake as she asked.

"Hasn't left the training facility since entering"—Webb checked her screen—"three years, nine months, two weeks, six days, seventeen hours ago. As is expected."

"What, don't you have the minutes and seconds?"

Webb moved just far enough for Cera to see her flat expression. "Twenty-eight minutes, eleven seconds. Nineteen, by the time I'm done saying this."

Cera grinned and held up her hands in apology. "I should never have doubted you, Webb."

"You absolutely should not have." Webb disappeared behind her screens again.

"I gotta walk or I'm gonna fall asleep," Cera announced, still grinning. "I'll pick up lunch. What do you want?"

"I wanna know what you're up to that you're so tired. Didja have a hot date last night?" Whitlock asked.

"So hot," Cera said. "With your grandma."

Whitlock cackled. "Musta been after I saw her, then. Get me a soyburger."

"Webb?"

"I'm good."

"Arright." Cera grabbed her uniform jacket and left the office, figuring she had less than an hour to pick up the clean security footage, get food, and get back again. She needed to run the footage on a machine that wouldn't trace back to her, but getting somewhere truly anonymous would take too long. Besides, she was pretty much out of cash.

The guy at the security camera company let her borrow his media scanner, though—"Just to make sure it's the right footage," Cortez said—and she took a couple of minutes to skim through it.

There was sure as hell something on the tape where the pixelated blur had been before, but the camera was too far away for any clarity. She leaned over the desk, putting on her best smile. "You probably know all the angles around here, don't you?"

"Somebody's gotta."

"There any other clear shots of this high-rise?" Cera threw an image of Rigney's building up on her phone, showing the guy. "Especially of the higher floors?"

"Do you care how official it is?"

Cera's eyebrows rose. "I checked every local feed I could find on my own. As long as I can see it, I don't care where it came from."

"What's in it for me?"

"I don't tell the Judges I work with that you've got a lead on illegal security feeds."

The guy's mouth flattened, but he nodded. "I'll pull the footage for you. It'll be ready around five."

Cera thumped the desk in thanks, got Whit's soyburger and a hot dog of questionable provenance for herself, and spent the afternoon searching serial killer databases, going through the residents of Carla Rigney's building, and trying not to watch the clock too obviously. The Ws went back to Tek-Div and returned fuming; strong-arming fellow Judges hadn't got them any more information on what Rigney'd been working on, or who she hung out with after work.

"I liked the guy who talked to us," Cera said absently, and sighed when Whitlock leered. "I liked him for a possible after-work colleague," Cera clarified. "He seemed impressed with her. You want me to look into his movements?"

"You really think a Judge did this, Cortez?" Whit's mouth twisted beneath his helmet.

"Honestly?" Cera's heart thumped at the word, because she didn't have much intention of being honest. Whit expanded his hands, inviting her commentary, and even Webb rolled away from her desk to see Cera more clearly. Cera kicked a foot up on her own desk and exhaled heavily. "I think a medical doctor or something did it. The way she was... dismembered... I don't know, it's like a modern-day Ripper."

"Ripper just removed his victims' internal organs," Webb protested. "He didn't... strew them."

"Sure, but the point is somebody with medical knowledge had to have done that, right? It was so careful. So I was looking up serial killers, seeing if anybody'd done this kind of killing in the past twenty years, and checking Rigney's building for medics and doctors. I've got nine hits on that besides herself, but nothing on serial killers. You guys got anything better than the NYPD databases to look at?"

Webb and Whitlock exchanged smirks, then Webb said, "Good thinking," as they both turned to their screens and started data-diving on the Justice Department's servers. Cera went back to tracing the movements of the other medical residents of Rigney's building. More than half of them were home the night she'd died, but the footage they'd got from Alfie Q's surveillance said no one had left their apartments or approached hers.

Cera put her head on her desk and groaned. "I dunno. Do we believe in ghosts?"

"Occam's razor says there's a more obvious solution," Webb replied dryly. "Go visit Alfie at the high-rise and run a couple of visualisation tests. See if there are any dead spots in the halls that somebody could have moved through."

"Yeah." Cera stood up with a sigh. "I'll text if I find anything."

"Don't let him know we're coming." Whitlock sounded like he still wanted to arrest Alfie, and right then, Cera didn't care, as long as she got out of the precinct building without any further questions.

Half an hour later, burdened with a handful of data drives and one promise that she owed the security company guy a favour, Cera *did* go into Rigney's building, and ordered Alfie out of the surveillance room so she could go over the files she'd got. He went, with the rest of his security team, to try to sneak around the building without the cameras catching them. A couple minutes later, the whole building looked like a French farce, people popping in and out of sight on the cameras. Cera grinned, watching them.

There clearly weren't many dead spots, if any, because mostly the security team was just going from one camera angle to another, crossing screens like it was a natural progression. Either way, she didn't have to watch too hard: they could run the footage back themselves and see if and where they lost each other. Cera pulled up the data from the security company responsible for keeping an eye on the street from the outside and started speeding through the footage from the night of Rigney's death.

Somebody, it turned out, had a high-quality personal security camera mounted near the top of a building just down the street. The footage from that *was* encoded, unavailable with Cortez's regular police access, although she bet the Judges would have found it, if they'd been looking.

There it was. A *contraption* climbed the side of Rigney's building. Cera zoomed in as closely as she could, and still could barely tell what it was.

Or rather, she could tell *what* it was: it was a kludge of drones lashed together in a rectangle roughly the size and shape of one of the old, dilapidated phone booths that could still occasionally be found on the city streets. It rose, steadily but shakily, from an alley halfway down the block: by the time it got to Rigney's building, it was at least ten storeys up, and had been above streetlight-level since coming out of the alley. Cera watched, fascinated, as it kept far enough away from the building to avoid apartment lights.

Drones usually had lights of their own, of some kind. These ones had been extinguished. It was hard to count them in the dark, but there had to be at least twenty of them, four each at the rectangle's top and bottom, and a host of them along the sides, generating lift. Cera wished the camera had sound, but she doubted they *made* any, from this distance: they were Technical Division-quality drones.

An unidentifiable figure shrouded in shapeless layers stepped out of the frame onto Carla Rigney's balcony. Rigney opened the door from inside, her body language welcoming, as the drones, relieved of their burden, suddenly shot up out of the camera's view. The door and curtains to Rigney's apartment closed behind her and her visitor, and Cera skipped through the next two hours of footage, until the drone booth suddenly dropped into sight again. Carla's visitor, still swathed in layers, stepped into the booth and flew away again.

Hands shaking, Cera put another data drive in, hoping to get a better angle, to make out the killer's height and build, or even a shot of their face. The second drive had a worse angle; the third had a better one and went back weeks. *Months*. At no time did Carla's visitor ever reveal themselves beyond a general bulk that Cera cautiously concluded was probably male. Probably; the only known romantic relationship Dr. Rigney was known to have had been with a woman. Cera checked Kaz Mahoney's stats as she slotted in the next drive, but she was too small to be Carla's visitor, even with footwear mods.

The last piece of footage looked like it was from the apartment next to Rigney's, although it was probably a bit farther away than that. The picture was much clearer, although the assailant remained every bit as disguised as in every other security feed. This one, though, showed the way the drone booth bobbled as their weight transferred into it.

And it showed something small falling out of their pocket, as their hip checked a drone's hard curved edge when the booth wobbled.

The booth fell away, retracing its flight path back home again, but Cera's gaze followed the bit of debris as it bounced in the building's updraft, and landed on a balcony a few floors beneath Carla Rigney's.

CHAPTER EIGHT

CERA LEANED IN until her nose was almost against the screen, counting the floors and tracking the sideways drift of the glittering bit of tech as it fell again and again, and shrieked as her phone rang, taking her completely off guard. Whit's helmeted mug came up on the screen when she answered, his colour bad in the precinct's buzzing lights. "Where you at, Cort?"

"Rigney's building. I've got Alfie and his team trying to sneak past the cameras." That was true, as far as it went. Cera hoped her voice didn't shake. It felt like her heart was trying to rattle it out of her throat. "What's up?"

"Got a delivery for you. Another camera angle, the guy said. Of what?"

Her heartbeat changed, turning into a heavy pounding that was worse than the frantic buzz. She wasn't supposed to be investigating Judges. Not that Whit *knew* she was investigating Judges, but Cera felt like it was blazoned across her face. "The outside of Rigney's building. I'm trying to figure out what I'm missing."

"Any luck?"

"Yeah. So far, I've figured out I'd be a lousy murderer, 'cause I can't figure out how they did it."

Whit chuckled. "All right. We'll drop it by. Talk to Alfie Q again, maybe."

"He'll piss himself," Cera warned, and hung up.

She ducked her head between her knees, trying to steady her breathing. Nobody, not even Judges, could know what she'd found. Assuming she'd found anything. Not until she knew what it was and could figure out how to *use* it.

Because there were two kinds of people who might have access to enough drones to make the jury-rigged flying monstrosity in the videos. One kind was people like Durrell, who were hiding from the Judges but clearly had some inside channels.

The other—much more likely culprits—were actual Judges.

It meant nothing that the Ws were coming over to back her up. Nothing. That was their job.

Unless it meant everything.

"Durrell." Cera's voice cracked on the whispered syllables. She checked her cuff, then rubbed her fingers through her hair, looking for the spider. She'd kind of got used to the horrible little thing. Maybe she'd wear it on her ear, like an accessory. It clung to her fingertip when she found it in her hair, then crawled onto her palm when she turned it upwards. "Durrell, I don't know what to do. No, I *do* know what to do. I've got to go see what Rigney's murderer dropped. My Judge unit is coming here. I don't know if they—" Her voice broke again, and she laughed. "I don't know if they *suspect* me of anything. Of investigating Judges. Whit won't like it, if that's what he thinks is happening, but I don't think he's gonna stop me. Unless he does. I don't know why he would. For the image of the Judges, maybe. I don't know."

Her phone rang again, and she nearly crushed the spiderbot, who crawled out through a gap between her fingers and looked at her with what she was sure was rebuke.

This time Webb's helmeted face came up, her mouth downturned and serious. "I watched that footage. You can't get involved in this any further, Cera. Anything you do is going to put you between Judges and the truth, and I don't want you stuck there. Stay where you are. Wait it out. That's an order. You know the consequences of disobeying a Judge."

"Yeah. I know." Cera nodded, and the phone screen went blank again.

Cera put it down carefully on the security centre's desk, rose, and took the elevator up to the fifty-second floor.

THE FUNNY THING was, even after twenty years of Judges, nice, law-abiding citizens still opened the door to a friendly smile and a police badge. "Sorry to bother you," Cera told the woman in the apartment below and on the diagonal to Rigney's. "I'm Officer Cera Cortez, part of an ongoing investigation—"

"I know," the woman said cautiously. "The whole building's talking about it. What do you want?"

Cera put on her best smile. "If you don't mind, I'd like to have a look at the view from your balcony."

Surprise furrowed the woman's eyebrows. "Sure. What's it going to tell you?"

Cera's smile weakened. "Probably that we're very high up and that even monkeys think they should be closer to the ground than this."

The woman laughed. "I guess, but any closer and I wouldn't be able to see over that horrible block city thing they're building. Come on in."

"Well, there is that. Sure changing the city, aren't they?" Cera made it to the apartment's glass balcony doors before her stomach rebelled and her hands went into a cold sweat. She couldn't fall down gibbering, though. It wouldn't be professional. "Sorry, 'Autonomous District.' I can't even remember the name they gave it."

The woman gave a mournful sigh. "I don't know. I'm a seventh-generation New Yorker, so I hate that it's changing at all, but most people just call it the Mega-Town or something like that. Oh, you really *don't* like heights, do you?" She chuckled sympathetically and offered a hand. "I can stand inside, if you want. So you feel anchored?"

"That's really nice of you," Cera said hoarsely. She took the woman up on the offer, uncomfortably aware that her hands were clammy, but the woman didn't seem to mind. She held on to Cera's hand firmly, a nice solid connection to a world that wasn't made of howling updrafts and long drops. Cera took a couple of shaky steps onto the balcony, then pinched a smile over her shoulder at the woman. "Okay, I'd rather hold on, but I'm gonna need a minute out here alone."

"I'll pour you a shot of whiskey," the woman offered, and stepped away from the door.

It felt like a lifeline disappearing. Cera, taking short, shallow breaths through her teeth, carefully knelt on the balcony floor, searching it. There were a couple of potted plants, a wicker chair, as if somebody actually wanted to *sit* out there, and—

—and beneath the chair, a faint glimmer of something hard.

It balanced on the edge of the balcony, where one shaky-handed mistake could send it bouncing five hundred feet to the ground below. Or even worse, to another damn balcony that she'd have to go out on, if she could even figure out which one it *was*.

She didn't try to pick it up with her fingertips. That way lay disaster, since she couldn't control the trembles jittering through her whole body. She just lay the flat of her hand on it as much as possible and scraped it toward herself, expecting it to somehow independently eject itself in a fifty-storey fall.

It didn't, and in a couple of seconds, she had it folded into her sweaty palm. All too aware how it would look if she just crawled backwards into the apartment, she made herself stand, eyes clenched shut so she couldn't see the world rising around her. Then she backed up into the apartment, heart hammering so hard she swayed with dizziness.

"Oh, hon," the woman said as she came back with the drink. "You're pale as a ghost. Are you gonna puke?"

"Probably not now." Cera gave the woman a puny smile

and accepted the shot of whiskey as the balcony door closed. "Please tell me it's after five."

"You're in luck. It's after six."

"Thank God." Cera threw the shot back in a single, body-shuddering gulp, then gave the woman another wan smile. "Thanks. I appreciate it. And I've seen what I needed to, so I'll get out of your hair."

"Is this about the woman upstairs?" Worry creased the woman's face. "Are we in danger?"

"No one else in this building is in any danger," Cera said with a little more confidence than she felt. "We believe someone targeted Dr. Rigney specifically."

"'We'?"

"The Judges unit that I work with and I."

Most of the woman's friendliness fell away. "Judges?"

"Yeah." Cera glanced towards the door. "They may drop by later. Answer any questions they have honestly, of course. You'll be fine, citizen." She left, took the elevator down several storeys, then, with a sense of deadly premonition, selected the next floor as her destination and exited before sending it on its way.

A few seconds later, it froze, with a pleasant warning chiming up the shaft. "All elevators are temporarily out of service. We apologise for this inconvenience and ask that you wait a little while before trying again."

There was *no good reason* for the Ws to try trapping her in an elevator. *No* good reason, nothing at all, except the obvious, which Cera couldn't even look at head-on. They were both big enough to have been the figure in the security footage, and she was increasingly sure whoever built that flying frame was a Judge.

She didn't know anything about their personal lives. She didn't even know what Whitlock *looked* like, for God's sake. Neither of them seemed more likely than the other to violate the Fargo-directed rule about Judges not having romantic relationships. Whit wouldn't violate it because he was fanatical about Fargo's directives, and Webb—well, Cera guessed sharks probably had sex lives, but they were presumably, she didn't know, cold, slippery, and not deeply personal.

Not that she even knew if it was *romance* driving one Judge to go to great lengths to sneak into another's apartment, but in the one clear surveillance video, Rigney had embraced her guest, which was at least suggestive.

Her feet had taken her down the hall while her thoughts raced. Now she pushed an emergency stairway door open, swaying again at the sight of tightly turning steps angling sharply downwards. The thing she'd rescued clinked against the door handle as she pushed it open, and she actually looked at it for the first time.

A data drive. A surprisingly large one, like an actual hard drive backup, with every element copied.

If it wasn't romance, the answer lay on that drive.

Cera started down the stairs as fast as she could. There were surveillance cameras in every corner. If she was lucky, both the Judges were on the hunt for her, but they weren't stupid, and she'd have been stationed on the thirteenth floor with the security feeds, if she'd been with them. One of the Ws was probably there now, watching her every move, until they could get one of the building's security personnel to do it for them. Cera missed a step, had to jump to land it, hit the metal floor with a bone-jarring *clang* that must have reverberated through the whole building.

When she was a kid, she would run down stairs like these by grabbing the railing, swinging wide around it, jumping the next set entirely if she could, or using the railings to slide-jump down them.

She'd never been forty storeys up when she started, though, and the deep hole in the middle of the tiny twists of unending flights scared the shit out of her in a way it hadn't then.

A door banged above her. Cera decided the height wasn't as scary as Judges, and put on a burst of speed, using the railing to control her swings and jumps. Within a couple of flights, she was moving twice as fast as she had before, the childish glee of reckless abandon fuelling her more than fear.

A gunshot exploded off the railing behind her, and she screamed from the bottom of her diaphragm, the sound blasting through the tight stairway nearly as loudly as the shot had. Webb bellowed something—so it was Webb chasing her, but she didn't know if that meant anything except probably Whitlock would meet her on the thirteenth floor—and fired again, this time hitting the steps above Cera's head. "What are you running from, Cortez? I just want you not to get involved in Judge problems!"

Cera yelled, "Then stop *shooting* at me!" back and willed her feet faster, as if she could somehow make it past the security floor before Whit got to the door. She was already on the seventeenth floor and descending fast. She didn't know where this set of fire stairs was in relation to the security centre, or whether the security team's self-built squatting apartments would slow Whit down between where he was and where he needed to be to catch her. Hope sprang eternal, though. She spun out on the fifteenth floor, losing her footing, and heard Webb catching up, above her. At least she'd stopped shooting, although she shouted, "Evading pursuit carries a fifteen-month sentence, Cortez! Stop now so I don't have to arrest you!"

"Stop chasing me and I won't *be* evading pursuit!"

Something that sounded suspiciously like a laugh bounced off the walls, but Cera didn't take it as meaning it was safe to slow down. She cornered on the thirteenth floor, nearly vomiting with relief as Whitlock didn't burst through the door and tackle her.

She'd made it down another two floors when he *did* burst through, and in a spectacular move that she'd have applauded if he hadn't been chasing *her*, he threw himself over the railings, hit the rails on the next floor hard enough to bounce off, landing only one floor above Cera as she screamed and pushed more desperate speed into already-burning thighs. Whit lost some momentum and scrambled to his feet, giving her almost enough time to gain another floor on him, then came down using the same swing-wide-and-jump technique she'd perfected in the last dozen floors.

He was bigger than her and stronger. He was going to catch her, and she didn't really even know why she was running.

He was half a floor behind her when the landing-level railing he grabbed bent and broke under his grip, and he tumbled down the stairs to hit the wall like a sack of concrete. Cera shrieked again, but couldn't have stopped if she wanted to: momentum and panic had her in their grip, and she made it the last half-dozen flights without immediate pursuit. She burst through the door at the bottom of the stairs, then stopped dead in wheezing, chest-aching dismay.

She'd gone too far. She'd gone *underground*, into the building's bowels. Pipes and storage boxes, radiators and metal blocks that meant nothing to her, sprawled everywhere, offering hiding places that would be temporary, at best.

The spider in her hair tugged on a few strands and said, "Left."

Cera, almost blind with fear and exhaustion, went left because she didn't have any better ideas, and listening to a spiderbot was better than just standing there waiting to die.

It led her into a closet that opened more easily than she expected, and told her to crouch behind a boiler almost too hot to touch. It would help disguise heat sensors, although unless her heaving breath slowed, it wouldn't do enough good. She squished herself into it anyway, then sobbed in absolute horror as spiders started to crawl out of the shadows onto her. Mostly little clicky spiderbots, their metal legs tickling and digging at her, but enough real spiders, too, that she clamped her mouth and eyes shut, trying not to breathe for fear of inhaling one. The real ones started re-spinning the webs she'd disturbed, but the bots vibrated slightly as they crawled. Tears rolled down Cera's face in absolute silence.

More time than she could count passed before the basement door opened. Her breathing had slowed by then, and the terror of being crawled on by spiders had settled into an awful kind of calm. It had got very dark, but she didn't know if that was outside of her or part of the weird calm, and didn't much care. She heard Webb complain about the lights and concluded it wasn't just her, which was good. It would make her harder to find.

"Don't matter," Whit said. "Sensors will pick her up."

Or maybe not.

A long time passed.

"She must have made it out the ground level," Webb finally said, from almost right in front of Cera. "There's nothing here. We must have missed her."

Whitlock growled, "We didn't miss her," but a minute later they left, arguing about which way Cera had gone.

She stayed where she was, trembling, confused, sweating, sick, until a spider said, "Go south."

Cera hissed, "Which fucking way is *south?*" and shuddered her way out of the spider nest, trying not to think as she brushed them off in scads. They tinkled to the ground and scattered, although a handful of them banded together, obviously to lead her south. A minute later they brought her to a door with a massive valve wheel on it. It squealed horribly when she turned it, a sound she'd heard when the Ws were looking around earlier. Once it was open, she saw why they hadn't gone any farther: the floor beyond it was thick with muck, and clearly no one had crossed it in years, probably decades.

Cera stepped across the threshold, sealed the door shut behind her, and crouched in the muck to muffle screams into her arms.

The spiders were bad. Whitlock and Webb coming after her like that was a lot worse. Maybe they just wanted to protect the Judges in general, but the reality was, that kind of enthusiasm meant they had to be her prime suspects. And now they *knew* they were her suspects. That she was investigating Judges. That she *knew* a Judge had gone into Carla Rigney's apartment and hadn't come out again until Rigney was dead.

Honestly, Cera had always figured she'd get killed running around after Judges. She hadn't really ever imagined she'd get killed because Judges were running around after *her*.

Her muffled cries had stopped on their own. Cera took a deep breath, stood up, and whispered, "All right, spiders. Get me out of here."

CHAPTER NINE

THE SPIDERS BROUGHT her out of the underground far enough away that she had to walk several blocks before Cera even knew where she was. Then she turned and went the other way, because the one person she could bring the data drive to safely was Bryant Durrell, who probably didn't want to see her, and who *didn't get a say in the matter*.

She got food on the way to Durrell's hovel, doing her best to disguise her path and her person with an increasingly foggy mind. Forty-eight didn't recover from a sleepless night as fast as twenty-eight did, or from knee-jarring leaps down stairs, or from being shot at and hunted by people she thought were her friends, or... anything. The food helped, though, and if it was rat on a stick, at that point, Cera just didn't care.

It was *late* by the time she got to Durrell's. It was late and her feet hurt, and she'd done something to the small of her back with all the jumping, as evidenced by a low throbbing pain that hadn't been there earlier in the day. She edged her way through the booby traps until she reached one she couldn't remember how to avoid, and just stood there dumbly until Durrell came to get her. From its far side, he said, "Were you followed?" and Cera looked over her shoulder like a Judge might pop out of the shadows.

"I don't think so," she said after a while. Probably too long, but her brain wasn't working very well. "I came out of the sewers way off the beaten path. I don't think they could have found me." She turned her focus back on the tense-looking technician. "Thank you. For the spiders. You saved me. I dunno how, but you did."

"I told you they bounce signal. It makes a kind of empty spot where they are, so Judge tech can't see them. Or you, if you're covered with them. Step on that brick, then that piece of cloth. Yeah. All right." Durrell led her through the rest of the warren, and, once within its confines, handed her a tightly sealed insulated cup.

Cera cracked the seal and the scent of coffee wafted up. Her eyes widened and she sipped quickly before sealing it again, capturing the strong odour inside. "Thanks."

"You were obviously gonna need it. What'd you bring me?"

Cera silently handed him the drive. "You tell me."

Durrell grunted and tugged a precarious-looking stack of rags and paper to the side, revealing fancier-looking computer servers than Cera had ever seen. The whole raggedy pile of junk folded neatly down, a sort of camouflage net. Cera stared at it as she shuffled over to Durrell's side and sat down.

As soon as she did, she was sure she'd made a mistake. Getting up would probably not be *impossible*, but it would be difficult and painful, and she already didn't want to. She groaned, and Durrell gave her a brief, sympathetic grin. "Getting older sucks, doesn't it?"

"Better than the alternative." Cera hunched her shoulders and huddled over the coffee while Durrell plugged the drive in and, from Cera's limited technological background, proceeded to work arcane magic to open it. After a while, data spilled out all over his screens, first a rush of blueprint-style images that flashed up too quickly to get a good look at, then innumerable strings of code—nothing more than esoteric numbers and letters held together by some brackets, from Cera's perspective.

Durrell, though, leaned in, and breathed, "Oh, no... oh,

wow... oh, shit," for a minute or so, then saying nothing else for an aggravatingly long time as he flipped through hundreds of pages of code faster than Cera thought anybody should be able to. Just as she was about to press him on it, Durrell sat back with an expression bordering on envy. "She was a genius. A savant. Transcendental. I could never have done this. Almost no one could. Maybe no one else. What a waste."

"What did she *do?*"

He threw the technical specs and code to the side, revealing the blueprint pages. "What do those look like?"

"Like what's-his-face's anatomical man. Except mechanical."

"Da Vinci's *Vitruvian Man,* yes. Look." Durrell expanded one of the images, showing Cera finer detail in the blueprints.

She shook her head and shrugged.

"It's networking," he said. "It's not just how muscles connect, but how nerves do, mapped to every point in the brain. She's built a chip to make it work."

"So she's building fancy robots?"

"Nah," Durrell said softly. "She was gonna build fancy *people.* Real, honest-to-God cyborgs. And Tek-Div didn't greenlight the project."

"Cyborgs." Cera stared between the blueprint and Durrell, understanding the word but feeling like she was missing the importance. "Don't we have cyborgs already? People with implants? Pacemakers? Fake legs? All that?"

"Crude facsimiles of an idea as old as robotics," Durrell replied dismissively. "The brass ring has always been a computer chip sophisticated enough to mimic and bond with the human nervous system, but"—he judged his audience and concluded with—"brains are complicated."

Cera grinned, accepting that was about the right speed for her understanding. The coffee was starting to help, although she was going to have heartburn for a week, after the influx of caffeine and adrenaline she'd had today. "Why wouldn't Tek-Div want that?"

"It's hard. Everybody who's tried it so far has burned

out the test subjects. Fried their brains," Durrell supplied helpfully. Cera recoiled, and he shrugged. "I told you. Brains are complicated. So to get to where she's going, we're talking decades of research, billions in testing and development. We've been doing it for decades already," he conceded. "But she's leapfrogged the next best chip by orders of magnitude. She wanted to test human subjects. That's what Tek-Div turned down." He pointed to a dark red X in the corner of one of the blueprints. "They didn't think she could do it."

"And you think…?"

"I think I'd let her put that chip in my own brain."

Cera sat back, somewhere between horrified and impressed. "Damn."

"Pretty much, yeah. All right, look, she's got… Here, these are her personal files, they're not code, you look through them, see what they've got while I study the specs. This is fascinating…" Durrell trailed off, engrossed in his screens, then scowled at Cera when she didn't pick up the pages he'd slid her way.

"I left my phone in Rigney's building so they couldn't track me."

"Oh. Smart." He handed her a screen and threw the personal pages onto it. "Looks like a diary. Dunno if it's more insightful to her process than the code is, but you can read it, so we'll cover twice as much territory. You good?"

"As long as the coffee doesn't run out, yeah." The diary files were date stamped. Cera started at the beginning, skimming through entries that went far enough back to talk about Kaz Mahoney with fondness. She did a word search on cyborg and skipped ahead years for the first entry, which talked about pitching her new chip project to Tek-Div. They hadn't bitten, just as Durrell had said, and for a while the diary entries got cagey about working on it, as if Rigney was trying to hide, even from herself.

She'd got new resources about three years ago, though, and started talking about the project more openly in the diary.

The barest snippets of a personal life came through: she was dating a fellow Judge: *not* Kaz Mahoney, whose entrance to Judge training Rigney appeared to regard as a desperate final attempt to salvage a relationship that had run its course long ago. Rigney and her fellow Judge—Carson, apparently; Cera didn't know her—got away on vacations a couple of times, which confused Cera until she'd read between the lines enough. Technical Judges could apparently take time off, and Carson was occasionally sent on assignment out of the growing mega-city; that was their stolen time together. It'd be sort of romantic if it hadn't all ended in murder.

Assuming Carson was the one who'd killed Rigney, anyway, and that she wasn't out there somewhere having to hide the fact that she was in mourning. Cera said, "Ugh," under her breath, and Durrell lifted an eyebrow at her. "I don't think I'd date, if I was a Judge, is all."

"Well, you're not supposed to." Durrell went back to the technical specs, and Cera went back to the diary, flipping through pages and pausing every once in a while to read one of Rigney's impassioned rants about why she was right and Tek-Div was wrong. *Obviously, yes, animal testing is critical*, she wrote once, *but newsflash: animal brains are not the same as human brains! I haven't developed a chip for a chimp, I've developed a heuristic for a human!*

Cera decided she would have rather liked Dr. Carla Rigney.

Eleven months ago, Rigney's diary, obviously trying to be cautious about details, said *Carson's on assignment out of town. I'm taking the week off so we can meet.* Cera wondered if Carson's street unit Judge partner knew about Rigney, or if Rigney and Carson's affair had been kept entirely separate from Carson's street Judge life. Either way, even with the details elided, Rigney's diary sounded content as a cat for the weeks after she came home. She wasn't even in a rush to find human test subjects for those weeks. Carson must be hell on wheels in bed, to distract Rigney that much. Cera was faintly envious. Durrell mumbled something about more locked files, and began the incomprehensible work of unlocking them.

Five months later, just over four months ago now, Carson and Rigney had met out of town again, but something had gone wrong. Carson was ambushed off duty, without a Judge squad around, and skilled as Judges were, sheer numbers can overwhelm anybody. Somebody had shoved Carson's arm through a metal crusher, chewing it—pulverising it—from the fingers to halfway up the humerus. The rest of Carson would have gone into the crusher, too, if Rigney hadn't been on the way to meet her. Reading between the lines, Rigney had... taken care of... the gang problem; the details were sketchy again, as if Rigney didn't want to think about what she'd done. That, Cera guessed, was a big difference between a Technical Judge and a street Judge.

"She had a test subject," Durrell said, as Cera turned her own page, watching the diary go from talking about *Carson* to *the subject*, like Rigney suddenly needed the distance.

"Yeah, Judge Carson? She nearly got killed, this says, and would have been furloughed as a Judge, with the kind of injury she took."

"She?"

"The only relationship I can find anything about for Rigney was with a woman, so, she."

"Okay, but—"

"No, look, Rigney didn't even report Carson's injury to MedDiv. She knew they'd never let her do it, but it looks like Carson was into it. I mean, as into it as you can be when you're high on pain meds and your arm's been chewed off. I don't get it, though. Was Rigney just carrying around a cybernetic arm, just in case?" Cera flipped through more pages, excitement tingling her hands. "Man, this story's got everything. Romance, danger, state secrets..."

"Yeah, but—"

"Hang on, hold on. No, she didn't have prosthetics *waiting*, but she had them specced out. She printed an arm for Carson, implanted the chip... It worked immediately. Growing the—Ew. Growing a skin graft to hide it took longer. Gross."

Durrell sounded amused. "You don't have a very strong stomach, do you? Afraid of heights, scared of spiders, grossed out by medical technology..."

"Shut up. She had to get Carson a bunch of blood transfusions, but... Damn. Carson went back to work four days later without anybody knowing any better. She's out there somewhere. But Rigney saved her life. Why would *she* kill Rigney?"

"If you'd let me talk a minute, you'd know she didn't. I don't know who Judge Carson is, but she wasn't Rigney's cyborg." Durrell still sounded amused, and Cera finally looked up.

The medical files he'd unlocked had the details about Carson that Rigney's diary lacked: height, weight, trauma, recovery plan, images of the injury, of the cybernetic implant, of the 3D printed arm, footage of the surgery, which had, by all appearances, taken place in a veterinary hospital.

Cera didn't know the face. Square-jawed, like all the Judges, of course, with a broad nose and sharp dark eyebrows, short cropped black hair. Startlingly good-looking. Cheekbones to die for, even pale from shock. Carson was all planes and angles, the kind of face Cera could look at all day.

The kind of face she almost *had* looked at all day, every day, for years. Because even if she didn't know the face, she *did* know the damn body. Rigney's lover hadn't been Judge Carson after all.

It was Judge *Whitlock*.

Judge *Carson* Whitlock.

CHAPTER TEN

Cera, stupidly, said, "I didn't know his first name."

"What?" Durrell did a double-take, from the image to her and back again. "What, wait, you know him?"

Cera put the coffee cup and screen reader aside so she could curl in on herself, head in her hands. "I don't even think of Judges as *having* first names. He's just Whit. Whitlock and Webb, the Ws. They're my Judges unit." She didn't know if Durrell could even hear her, and forced herself to lift her head again. "They were both out of the office a few months ago. Webb got sent down south, but Whit had something in—" Her gaze flickered to Rigney's diary pages, finding the one place where she'd mentioned her latest vacation spot: *the Falls*. "Whit was sent north of Buffalo, right on the border. Rigney said she'd gone to Niagara Falls. And Whit looked like hell when he came back. Said he'd picked up a bug. Jesus. Jesus Christ. He dented the desk. He ripped the railing off the stairs. He's a cyborg. *Jesus Christ.* He killed Rigney. Why would he kill Rigney?"

"Cera." Durrell's voice was very soft and quiet as he began unlinking all of Rigney's data from his terminals. "Cera, you need to take this and go to Quon. Have you got that name? Director Errol Quon. I can cover your footprints, keep you off

Judge radar until you're at her front door, but you need to do this, and you need to do it right now, Cera. Do you hear me? Can you hear me?"

"No." The whisper sounded distant, pushed through a ringing in her ears that made the rest of the world seem very far away. She'd *liked* Whit, been ready to lay her money on *Webb* as the corrupt one, if it had to be one of her own Judges. But Webb had stopped shooting at her, and Whitlock had torn the railing off the stairs. He'd punched the desk hard enough to dent it.

He'd left, cradling his hand, after that. Maybe it wasn't pain that had sent him sulking out of the office. Maybe he'd torn the skin graft and exposed metal knuckles beneath it. Cera hadn't seen him without his gloves on since.

Cera, aloud, said, "I need to go," and Durrell, his voice still gentle, seized on that.

"Yeah. Yeah, you do. You need to go to DC, Cera. You need to bring this to Errol Quon. Do you know who Errol Quon is? The head judge of the new internal affairs squad? I can cover your tracks," he repeated. "But I need you to go now. Take this." He handed her the data drive, actually folded her fingers around it, making sure she gripped it. Cera stared at it, then at him.

"I can't go to Quon. I'm a cop. Nobody cares. They won't let me close to her."

"I can get you close to her," Durrell repeated. "Remember? I hid you from the Judges a little while ago. I can do that. You can do this."

"*You* should go!" It was too much responsibility. Cera hadn't been meaningfully responsible for anything in years. Not since the Judges came in. She'd thought she hated it. Now she thought maybe it wasn't so bad, licking boots and cleaning up little fires. This was a bonfire, set to rip through the ranks. She didn't want to set that match.

Durrell coughed a laugh. "I've been hiding from the Justice Department for most of twenty years, Cortez. I'm not going to waltz up to Quon's office now. You're a good cop," he said more quietly. "So was she. She'll listen to you. But you've got to go now, before Whitlock and Webb get a bead on you. If they come here, I'm screwed."

"Yeah. All right. Okay." The fog of denial didn't exactly burn off, but Cera started pushing through it. Marching orders helped. Having a specific task to accomplish, and someone to protect, was meaningful. Not much in the past dozen years of her life had been. Might as well go out in a blaze of glory.

Which suggested she didn't think she was going to survive this, but that was a crisis for later. Cera nodded a couple of times, gathering herself mentally, then nodded again, more firmly. "All right. Okay. You can cover my tracks?"

"As long as you've got a spider on you, you're golden." Durrell turned his palm up, a bot glittering in his hand. Cera picked it up and put it in her hair without even cringing, and Durrell smiled. "See? You're tougher than you think."

"I'm really not." Cera finished the coffee in a few swift gulps, figuring she'd need every boost she could get, to get to DC safely. The data drive went into her pocket as she headed for what passed for the front door of Durrell's hovel, then looked back at him with a tired smile. "Look, I get that we'll probably never see each other again, so, uh, thanks. I wouldn't have made it through the last couple days without your help."

"Think nothing of it. It was nice to hear somebody call me by my name again. Be safe, Cortez."

"You too, Durrell." Cera walked out of the rubble-filled entryway to Durrell's home, and straight into Judge Webb's arms.

"Did you really think you could hide from me?" Webb sounded like a disappointed parent. "Did you really think you could hide from *Judges?*"

"No." The inside of Cera's head turned into an echo chamber, empty of everything but simple, stupid phrases. Phrases like, "How'd you find me?"

"I followed you, you twit. It took a while to find you on surveillance, but once I had you..." Webb shrugged.

"Where's Whitlock?"

"Coming around the back."

The fact that Webb even told her that indicated how little of a threat she regarded Cortez to be. Cera's heart rate surged anyway, and she grabbed Webb's sleeve. "You don't get it, Webb, he's—*ow!*"

Webb seized Cera's wrist and shoved her to the ground with an expression of genuine incredulity. "What are you doing, laying hands on a Judge, Cortez? You're smarter than that. I thought you were smarter than that."

Well, she was smart enough not to get up again, anyway. "Whitlock killed Rigney, Webb."

Webb actually pulled her helmet off in public to stare down at Cera in disbelief and dismay. "Are you drokking *kidding* me, Cortez? You come out here to the badlands night after night, you spend all your cash on private network terminals and start hanging with a high-priority technical asset, you run from Judges, and then you say you think *Judge Whitlock* killed another Judge? I'm more likely to believe *you* did."

"High-priority...?" She'd blown Durrell's cover then. Or he had, by helping her. Cera crushed the thought away, trying to focus on the more important point. "You know it was a Judge, Webb. You saw the security footage. Who's gonna get hold of that many Justice Department drones besides a Judge?"

"Maybe a *high-priority technical asset*," Webb hissed. She still didn't have her helmet on—4 a.m. in the hinterlands was as safe a time and place as any for a Judge to expose her face—but she unholstered her Lawgiver, training it on Cera.

Cera's guts went liquid, and she held coffee-flavoured bile back by the skin of her teeth. "Yeah, all right, maybe you're right, maybe a 'hi-pri' tech asset could round up and recondition a couple dozen drones—although I don't think even you really believe that; the Department is too careful with its resources to lose that many units—but your 'asset' isn't the one who tore a metal railing in half a couple hours ago, or punched a hole in his desk yesterday. Rigney was working on a cyborg chip, Webb. Whitlock's her first test subject. *I saw the operation*. It was Whit."

"You've never even seen his face. How would you know?" Webb sounded less certain than she had, though. "...Cyborgs?"

"Webb, I've seen him in the changing room a thousand times. He has an inch-long scar right over his carotid artery from a piece of shrapnel. His left pec is collapsed from a tear. They did a good job reconstructing it and he works to keep it in shape, but it's smaller than his other one and he can't do anything about it. He's got three scars across the ribs right below it from somebody using clawed brass knuckles in a fight. There are six stud-sized scars on his upper abdomen fr—"

"Arright, okay, you know his body, what the drok, Cortez, what, is the masked man your favourite fantasy or something?"

A flush ran through Cera. "He was Rigney's, anyway. They were an item, and she was there when he got hurt a few months ago. She put him back together with her chip and her tech and has been keeping test case notes on him. He's a cyborg, Webb. His whole arm is metal and skin graft. Can I get up now?"

"He was never off work for sick leave," Webb protested.

"You wouldn't be either if you were hiding an unapproved upgrade while trying to pretend nothing had even happened! You'd fake it! Remember how shaky he was when he came back from Buffalo?"

Webb said, "Oh," in a thoughtful tone. She put her Lawgiver away and offered Cortez a hand up. "Ah, crap. Crap. I'd think if Technology Division had come up with something that could keep us in the field even after a devastating injury, they'd be all over it. Why's he keeping it secret?"

Cera brushed herself off as Webb put her helmet back on. "Rigney didn't have clearance. Tek-Div didn't want to go to human trials. Too risky, too likely to fail. They put five years of training into you guys. Burning you out on a hope is a bad use of resources. So Rigney went off campus, to prove she could do it. Where the hell is Whitlock?"

Then an explosion blew her off her feet.

CERA HIT THE ground far enough away that she thought for a moment she'd learned how to fly. Webb landed near her, but bounced back up faster. Judge uniforms cushioned impacts a lot better than half-improvised civvies did. The air tasted like fire, heat blooming from what had been Bryant Durrell's underground hideaway. Cera sat up in stages, partly to see if she could, partly because every movement put more of the disaster into her line of vision, and she could only take it in small bites.

It had *not* been an accident. The explosion was too controlled, fire roaring up in gusts that barely touched the buildings leaning over Durrell's hovel. Sprinklers that Cera was certain weren't regulation hissed water from the walls, preventing the billowing flames from catching hold. A pit of some sort had opened up only inches from where Cera had been standing a moment ago. Fire raged deep inside it, smoke rising in black stinking waves.

Judge Whitlock pulled himself from the hole, one slow hand over the other.

His helmet had blown off. Most of his uniform too. Rags around his hips and thighs, dangling from the tops of his fire-greasy boots. *Skin* dangled around his left bicep, gleaming metal shining beneath it. Bits of skin stuck at the elbow, covered his forearm, until the double layer of uniform jacket and gloves protected his wrist and hand from the ravages of fire.

Webb yelled, "What the *actual hell,* Whit?" above the roaring flames.

He grimaced at her, a sort of vicious, unrepentant smile. "The asset had the place booby-trapped. Soon as he knew there was nowhere to go... boom. Headquarters isn't gonna like that. He was valuable. Can you imagine, hiding from us for twenty drokking years and going out like that?" He shook his head heavily, then focused on Cera, behind Webb. "Couldn't leave well enough alone, could you, Cortez? Couldn't leave it to the Judges. That's your *job*. You don't get to be *useful* any more. Not that cops ever were. Corrupt losers, all of you."

"Corrupt?" Cera's voice broke as she struggled to her feet. "I'm not the one who flayed another *Judge*, Whit. What happened? Why'd you... Why? She saved your life. She liked you. Loved you."

Whitlock's lip twitched. "Loved experimenting on me, anyway. Worked, though. Aren't I fancy?" He stretched his cybernetic arm out, all three of them briefly mesmerised by the flames dancing in the steel, and the soot that drifted down to mar its shining surface. "Cyborgs, though, Cort, that's drokked up. That's a crime against humanity. Against God. Fargo never would have stood for it. Drokking Solomon, he's gonna destroy the whole program with this kind of garbage. He doesn't understand," Whitlock said earnestly. "The Judges have to be *pure*. We can't have cyborgs running around. Tek-Div can't have that technology. The Justice Department can't. Can you imagine what they'd do with it? They'd make monsters. Thou shalt not suffer a cyborg to live, Cortez. Rigney brought them to the point of birth, but they are not given delivery."

"...Whit, *you're* a cyborg."

He laughed, high and sharp against the sound of fire and, more distantly, cries for help and of alarm. His eyes gleamed like his arm did, even with the light behind him; with a light of madness, Cera thought. He'd lost his mind, somewhere along the way. "You think I'm a good Judge, Cortez?"

Cera, swaying in the firelight, started to nod, then stared past him at the guttering flames. Bryant Durrell had been a good Judge: one who'd *quit*, who'd tried to work against the system. And he'd got killed for it. Whitlock had killed him.

Cera moved her focus back to Whitlock and shook her head. "I'm not sure there's such a thing."

Whitlock snarled, but Webb spoke before he could say anything else. "You're a good Judge, Whit. I've worked with you for years. You're dedicated to Fargo's vision. You're fair within the Law. You became a cyborg so you could keep serving, right?"

"You understand!" Whitlock's voice became a howl as he turned a pleading gaze on Webb. "I'm a good Judge! It's one thing for *me* to be a cyborg, Webb, you get that, right? Because I'm not going to abuse it. I've got to keep serving the Law." His lip curled again. "But not everybody could be trusted with it. That's why Rigney had to die. I had to kill her, Webb. I had to keep her research out of Tek-Div's reach. It's the only way to keep us all human. We're gonna be monsters, otherwise. You don't want to be a monster, do you? It's just me." He dropped his arm.

"I'll have to kill you, too, now," he said then sorrowfully. "I'll have to kill you so you can't tell anybody about me. Frankenstein's monster. But I've got a plan, Webb. When I'm too old to be any use to the law, I'll take a boat out into deep water and shoot myself. Go overboard. All my tech will be gone too. Everybody will be safe. No more monsters. Her research is gone. The womb is shut."

Webb said, "Whit," very softly.

Cera reached into her pocket to pull out the data drive. "You mean *this* research, Whit?"

Whatever shred of sanity had been holding Whitlock together snapped. He screamed, a genuinely horrific sound above the dying flames, and threw himself at Cortez, both his hands clawed in mindless rage.

Gunfire spattered, and for an instant, Cera thought she was dead. She should have been. Would have been, if Whitlock had remembered he *had* a gun.

But Webb had remembered hers, taken a centre shot with her Lawgiver that dropped the screaming, foaming Whitlock to the ground. He still tried to claw his way towards Cera, who backed away, shuddering with tears, as Whitlock slowly died. When he finally went still, Cera whispered, "Why... you... headshot. Why didn't...?"

Webb, her Lawgiver already holstered, shrugged. "Didn't want to damage the tech in his head. It's priceless."

"Jesus, Webb, that's heartless."

The Judge shrugged again. "Too bad about your friend in there. He'd have been worth as much as Rigney's research." She transferred her attention to Cortez, flames reflecting in her visor. "He was your friend, wasn't he?"

Cera's gut tightened, her voice cracking as she tried for a degree of indifference she didn't feel. "No. I barely knew him."

"Good. Because the evidence suggests you were deliberately consorting with a known criminal."

"He was a source, Webb. Sometimes, they're not the greatest people. I didn't look into the details of how he knew what he knew." Her heart beat so fast she thought she would come apart from it. Every word felt like betraying Durrell. But he didn't have to live in a Judge's world any more, and Cera did. "That's one advantage of being a cop, Webb, instead of a Judge. We're allowed to look the other way when we need information."

"And that's why Judges are replacing cops."

Cera looked at Whitlock's body, and back to Webb, whose expression was, as ever, unreadable beneath the helmet.

Webb followed her glance, though, and came back to Cera with another, almost imperceptible, shrug. "And *that's* why Whit was wrong, and we need the SJS. Do you want to know who Durrell really was, Cort? Do you want to know who you were dealing with?"

"No." The word came after a long, tired silence. "No, I don't think I do."

"Yeah. Didn't think so. Ignorance is bliss. Enjoy it. And give me that data drive." Webb put her hand out, and Cera put the drive into it. "A Judge squadron is on its way. You wanna remind me what you were doing here?"

"Reconnaissance," Cera said, very softly. "Friendly neighbourhood police officer, getting close to a suspected anti-justice source to supplement evidence for my Judges unit to move in with. The suspect immolated himself and nearly killed a Judge instead of being taken in." She closed her eyes. "We believe the suspect killed Technical Judge Carla Rigney in an effort to suppress the cybernetic technology research Dr. Rigney was doing? And that Rigney's first test subject, Judge Whitlock, was driven mad by the pain of his cybernetic implant being exposed by the fire which immolated the suspect. Judge Whitlock's injuries caused him to launch an unprovoked attack on Detective Cera Cortez, forcing Judge Webb to terminate him."

"Very good, Detective. Now get out of the way, and keep your mouth shut unless you're directly questioned."

Moments later, the squadron Webb had called in arrived, the chaos of bodies and shouting filling the air. Webb's authoritative, cool tones cut through it all, making sense of the situation, as Cortez moved to the perimeter of the action.

Not far enough to be accused of running away. No, she was there, doing her duty, providing legitimacy to a regime that had already long-since declared itself the winner and couldn't be ousted by anyone with less power than it had. And *everyone* had less power than it had.

A spider crawled out of Cera's hair and nestled in the collar of her shirt.

ACKNOWLEDGEMENTS

Writing a story set in the Dredd universe has been a dream come true, and I'd like to say thanks to Michael Carroll, who believed I could do it, as well as to editor David Moore, who has been a champion to work with. I must also tip my hat to Kaz, Bryant, & Carl, whose names I made free with in this story. And, as always, all my love to Ted, who has been an absolute star during the pandemic, making sure I get time to write.

ABOUT THE AUTHOR

C. E. Murphy was born and raised in Alaska, where she held the usual grab-bag of jobs usually seen in an authorial biography, including public library volunteer, archival assistant, cannery worker, and web designer. She earned a B.A. in English and History, and now lives with her family in her ancestral home of Ireland, a magical place where it rains a lot but nothing one could seriously regard as winter ever actually arrives. Her hobbies include making jam and fudge, and also... writing. She has been told she does not really understand the concept of 'hobby,' and accepts that as very likely.

(IN)FAMOUS

ZINA HUTTON

To my niecelings, who inspire me every day.
Thank you for letting me run ideas
by you as I worked on this story.

The Mega-City Post
January 12, 2057

In recent news, residents of the in-construction Timm Block have started to question whether apartment life at this scale is really for them. Following a wave of crimes ranging from minor (graffiti) to major (vandalism and theft) over the past months, hundreds of the apartment's residents have recently signed a petition asking for increased security in the building and for their belongings. Some of the residents have even began asking for the help of an even higher power than the in-house security offered by the developers: Judges.

When interviewed, fifteenth-floor resident James Williams told us that, "Things were fine until the building started getting full. Now we have all of these children running the halls. No one watchin' them. I'm tired of having my things stolen and having to watch my back when I go to the park on the upper levels. Someone has to do something about this."

When asked whether Judges should be responsible for potential fighting between neighbours, Williams scoffed and told our reporter to "...mark my words. Things are only going to get worse around here if no one does anything about it."

Another resident, Grace Lim, says that she hasn't noticed anything out of the norm in the building. As one of Timm Block's assistant managers and a mother with two young children whose twenty-fifth-floor apartment is only a hallway away from Timm Block's in-progress educational annex, she insists that the building is better than the apartment her family lived in before.

"Sure, there are little things that go wrong," Mrs. Lim told our reporter in our video interview. "But with a building of this size and dozens of new people moving in every day, that's to be expected. All the incidents we've had so far have been small. While more security is always welcome, the building already has staff in place monitoring the public areas."

When asked about the other residents asking for Judges to patrol Timm Block, Mrs. Lim replied, "I don't think we need any Judges roaming the halls. That'll just make people think our building is too scary to move into. And we can't have that."

Timm Block, a building by developer group Kin Towers Co, is one of the newest 'city blocks' being built in the Boston-New York-Philadelphia Autonomous Metropolitan District. With forty-five floors opening once it's completed at the end of the year, Timm Block will cater to a wide range of income types. While the building *has* seen an influx of families with children—from school-agers that will be taking advantage of the in-house system once construction has completed to teenagers preparing for the future—neither the building manager nor the developer's spokesperson said that there was a rise of disturbances related to those newer, younger residents. We'll keep readers posted about the situation at Timm Block as it develops.

If you're a resident in this city block or any other and you're concerned about a rise in crime in your new home in one of the BNYPAMD's city blocks, reach out to us to speak with a reporter.

CHAPTER ONE

Timm Block
Monday, January 22, 2057
15:12

My first video gets fifty views on my ViewTube channel, Amaramaramara, in the first week.

I wasn't expecting a million—of course not, nothing that high—but only *fifty*? That's messed up. Counting my extremely extended family, the people I hang out with when I'm forced to drop into meatspace interactions, and the people who I'm friends with thanks to the online school session I (thankfully) finished last year—

That's not a lot.

And it's not *fair*.

If it were just the views, I don't think I'd mind so much. After all, this is my first attempt at being somebody online. Ultimately, I *know* I'm a nobody and it's not as if I expected instafame or fortune. But only fifty views after everything? After all the work I'd put into the video—the editing software I'd splurged on with my allowance, the cool mystery script I'd written, having to bribe all of my annoying little siblings into rehearsing *and* performing—

No one cares, but they should've.

I worked so hard on getting everything together: hours of research on ViewTube, making sure that my video fit the ones trending, and had linked to everyone I could, urging anyone with the slightest amount of clout to share the video. It was the perfect video and yet, no bites. Barely any views.

In fact, the only comment on the video after the first few days is from one of my cousins on the other side of the city where we used to live.

So, pretty much nobody and no one.

I stare down at the comment from my cousin, a simple line of text that says *Yo Amara, you're killing it*, and consider deleting it. It's *obviously* not a bad comment and I guess I like my cousin, but—

This isn't what I want.

Before I can click the little X next to the comment, I hear the sudden sound of chaos from the world outside of my tiny cube of a bedroom. First a loud clatter, and then the sound of shouting. It's a familiar noise in our home once my younger siblings disengage from their school sessions and turn on each other for offline entertainment. I hate that I can figure out what time it is based on how loud the rest of the apartment gets every day.

As much as I love my siblings—most of the time—I also wish I wasn't in charge of them all the time these days. Four children, four energetic personalities too big for a single teenager like me to handle. Before we'd moved into the family suite in the massive in-progress complex that our parents would be responsible for managing, I didn't have to spend all my time with my siblings. We'd lived in a smaller building, one with an in-person school for them. Just a few months ago, my siblings—the twins Ria and Darren, Minnie stuck in the middle, and baby Tracey—had *friends*. They had more than each other. Most importantly? They had other, older people in charge of them.

People that weren't me.

But moving to the new building where our parents have

Responsibilities, as thousands of residents file in to fill the apartments as they're finished and furnished, has changed things. Instead of teachers watching my siblings, I have to spend time with them so they don't short-circuit our section of the apartment or set the building on fire. With thousands of people in the building so far, even the parks on the upper floors are off limits for them. So, I'm stuck in here with them more often than not because our parents have to do things like 'work' and 'manage the move-in for all the residents' and a ton of other boring things that I don't exactly keep track of, but that keeps our parents away for most of the day.

And I *hate* it.

The door to my tiny bedroom slides open with a muted hiss that's quickly overshadowed by the sound of every single one of my siblings rushing in and shouting over one another. It's just *loud* and a *lot* all at once.

I wince, resisting the urge to cover my ears with my hands. I know I should be used to this by now because it's an everyday occurrence, but I feel like my head is about to crack open. All of my siblings that can talk *do*. I catch snatches of the complaints, but none of the word spill makes sense.

Not at first.

I minimise the window on my screen and then turn around so that I can look at my siblings with a stern look straight up stolen from our busy mother.

"One at a time or else I kick you all out and put a lock code on my door."

It's a threat that only works because they're all so desperate to speak to *someone* with some kind of parental power. If our parents weren't out of the suite from dawn until dinner time, this wouldn't work. But I'm the only person that can deliver any judgements about the dozens of petty little problems they have across the day, and so they fall in line.

Silence reigns for a moment before Darren, with Tracey on his hip, pushes forward past his sisters and says, "Can you *please* tell Minnie to leave my game alone?"

That sets off the other two, and their volume ratchets up another nearly deafening level until I wince and reach for the headset dangling over the edge of my monitor. The headset is a pricey VR one someone got me as a gift for graduating. It's the kind that blocks out everything, and the kids clock the threat for what it is. If the headset goes on, I won't surface from the VR communities I have been haunting until it's past all of their bedtimes.

I thrust the headset out at my scowling siblings, brandishing it almost like I would a weapon, and say, "If you're going to be loud like this..."

Silence follows the dangling end of my warning as the sullen quartet in front of me tries to show that they're capable of being quiet.

I sigh loudly and let the headset drop down to my lap. Here's the thing: I *know* that my siblings won't simply go quietly into the rest of the apartment. If I don't go out with them, they'll be back within the hour and louder than before.

"I'm only doing this because I want you all to stop arguing," I say, directing a sharp and scathing look at the kids in front of me. "Give me ten minutes to check my messages and shut down, and I'll be right out," I say.

When Ria opens her mouth wide to complain, I snap my fingers and then point sharply at the door to their bedroom. "Ten minutes of quiet out there or I put the headset on and pretend you goblins don't exist until it's time for us to eat. Choose wisely."

The kids nearly trample each other on the way out, returning me to the dark silence from before. It should feel good to be respected, but it doesn't.

That's the thing, though: I only feel seen and surrounded by my siblings. And even then, they're seeing me as a parent replacement, not as Amara-as-a-person.

At every other point—even more so with this ViewTube thing—it feels as though I'm trying to be seen in a crowd and no one's looking in my direction.

With that on my mind, I'm prepared for more of the same when I glance back at my monitor and then prepare myself to delete my cousin's comment on ViewTube page. But then I notice a bright blue notification at the top of the page.

"A message?" I lean in close to the page as if the proximity will reveal that it's a fake notification or a glitch on the site. But no, it's a real message from someone that I really don't know.

The message is short, but life-changing even in its brevity.

ChannelDel: Your video was good. You should've gotten more views. If you're looking for a way to get a bigger audience, hmu. I recognised the view from the balcony at 5:39. You're in Timm Block, same as me. If you're free around 2pm tomorrow, let's link up at the park on the twenty-fifth floor. I'll be the guy with the pink ponytail and pet rock.—**Del**

I know, as I read the message, that I should pause to question... all of that. From the fact that the person, this 'Del,' figured out where I live from the view outside a balcony, to the whole... pet rock thing, this should be a whole bunch of red flags, and the flags are set on fire. If not for the fact that I *do* want fame and fortune and more than fifty-*freaking*-views, I'd delete the message outright. Because I know better. I've seen the crime shows my parents watch when they think we're all asleep. Even now, things are *bad*. I *know* this isn't smart.

However, desperate times call for desperate measures. And besides, I don't have *that* much time before my siblings decide to break down my door and return to chaos.

I reply to the message with a simple *OK* and then close everything down before I can overthink things and delete my entire account.

Hopefully, I won't regret this.

CHAPTER TWO

Tuesday, January 23, 2057
13:37

THE NEXT DAY, I quickly realise that getting out of the apartment to meet the mysterious Del is going to be a hassle.

Neither of our parents are home, and all of my siblings are in fine, frustrating form. In the end, though, I tell the twins to watch Minnie in between breaks from their Tuesday classes and then strap Tracey's squirmy, solid body into a sling across my chest.

"I'll be back in an hour," I call over my shoulder as I head towards the door. "Don't answer the door for anyone, and if you fight while I'm gone, I'll get Ma to block internet access for you for a week. Do *not* test me."

I smile at the sound of complaining, but when the door shuts behind my back, the soundproofing cuts their complaints off neatly. I take a moment to stand in the empty hallway and just *breathe*. Despite all of our new neighbours, the foot traffic outside of *our* apartment specifically always seems nonexistent. *I've* definitely never run into another person while going back and forth to the different restaurants and stores scattered around our floor.

The moment lasts only as long as it takes Tracey to get tired of us standing still in the hallway, and she starts a frustrated wiggle against my chest, complaining in her own way even though she hasn't learned how to talk yet.

I glance down at my baby sister's grouchy brown face and sigh. "Fine, fine," I say, letting a matching—if fake—scowl settle on my own face. "We'll go, but if you embarrass me when I meet Del, I won't take you to go get ice cream after."

Sure, it isn't as if Tracey even really understands concepts like 'behaving.' She barely understands 'ice cream.' But she grins up at me, eyes scrunched up until their brown is barely visible, and kicks happily within the confines of the sling. So, she gets *something*, I think.

At least in theory.

I take off in the direction of the elevators that will take me up to the park that dominates the centre of the twenty-fifth floor, talking aimlessly as I walk in order to keep Tracey from getting fussy. Meeting Del is anxiety-inducing enough—I do *know* how dangerous meeting a stranger is, never mind meeting one off a ViewTube message—but it won't help to have my baby sister in a bad mood when we might have to run from a predator or something.

As LARGE AS Timm Block is, it still only takes a few minutes to make it to the park. The closer we get to the park, the more people we see. Most of them don't recognise me. With thousands of people already moved into the block and even more waiting to move in once the construction and remodeling are done—as our parents remind us a dozen times a day—only the people from our hall tend to recognise us. The park is largely empty. Lit by solar lights that make the park look like the days outside that I remember from our old neighbourhood. It's one of the best things about this floor, and if not for how I have to find the mysterious *Del*, I'd consider going downstairs and bring my siblings up here so they could tire themselves out in the fake sun. Instead, I take Tracey on a meandering walk around the park, keeping an eye out for pink hair.

I spot Del about fifteen minutes into our walk. Tracey is mostly quiet, soothed into a daze by my gentle pace, and even I was considering finding a bench underneath a lamp and dozing off for a minute when I spot a shock of bright pink hair over the back of a bench facing away from the path.

"Del," I call out, trotting over to the bench at a pace fast enough to gently jostle Tracey from her rest. "It's me—" I pause, unsure how to continue. The name on the ViewTube account is based on mine of course, but I hesitate to tell a stranger my name. But I push through to the end of the sentence anyway. "It's me, Amara. From ViewTube?"

Hesitancy turns the last part of my sentence into a question, the last syllables rising uncertainly. But, just when I'm ready to clutch Tracey tighter to my chest and take off running in the direction of the closest exit, the person on the bench stands up, turning to face us with a smile.

"You're shorter than I thought you'd be," Del says with a once-over that ends with a spreading grin. "Must be all of the little kids in your video. You looked like a giant."

Coming from someone that stands almost a foot taller than me... I snort and shake my head. Del is massive, almost like a tree himself, and he towers over me with a skinny body draped in baggy black clothes. He's *covered* in tattoos, swirls of black designs spotted here and there with neon-bright greens, blues, and pinks. I can't help but eye his tattoos with envy because I've wanted my own ink from the moment I graduated. And yet, despite the fact that Timm Block has its own edgy alternative tattoo and piercing parlour on the thirtieth-floor shopping centre, I still don't have my own ink.

"So you liked my video," I say, putting my hands on my hips and peering up at Del as if that'll chase away the tattoo envy and my anxiety at the same time. "Why?"

Yes, I'd worked hard on the video, and I still think that it deserves more views than it'd gotten, but it's still my first video. Shot in a few rooms of the apartment and in one of the unfinished storefronts that I shouldn't even have access to, it's a simple video with a complicated narrative. Despite trying, I still can't quite figure out what about it would appeal to someone like Del.

"Your camera angles and shooting skills," Del says with a shrug of his angular shoulders. "My friends and I have a ViewTube channel where we do pranks and stuff and it's going well, but no one can shoot for shit." He pauses and then touches the painted tip of his index finger to his chin. "You also seem to know your way around Timm Block and around a camera. We could use someone with your knowledge to help us figure out the best spots to play around. If you're interested, I could introduce you to my crew. See how you feel about each other?"

I bite my lip as I think.

"How big is your following so far?" I ask after a few seconds. After all, it's not like I'd consider linking up with a channel that doesn't have *any* viewers. I'm not *that* desperate.

But Del surprises me.

"Fifty thousand subscribers worldwide," he volunteers instantly. "Most of them are from around here, and they comment regularly too."

I *do* like the sound of that, but—

"What kind of pranks are we talking here? I don't want to get arrested just for some ViewTube hits," I say sharply enough that it makes Tracey jolt against my chest.

Del is quick to shake his head, sending all that pink flying. "It's nothing like that," he insists. "Don't worry. We're all in it to have a good time!"

I sigh and smile warily. "If you're sure..."

Del's own smile widens. "I'm sure. Think you can meet up with us in observatory up at the top floor later tonight?" Del glances down at where Tracey is cuddled up close to my chest. "Maybe just... without the baby?"

I don't need to look in a mirror to know that my cheeks are

burning all the way up to my ears. I look down at my baby sister's scrunched up face and then sigh. "I'll be there, without Tracey," I say, a sullen note in my voice that I can't hide. "Just tell me the time."

"3 a.m.," Del says. "Take the elevator up to the thirty-fifth floor and then the emergency stairs up to the top. Wear something black and try to stay out of the cameras and away from the light strips on the floor."

I can't help pointing out that, "That's a lot of instructions."

Del shrugs again. "We're not supposed to be up there, since it's not done. I'd rather be sneaky than get caught. You get it?"

CHAPTER THREE

Wednesday, January 24, 2057
02:46

I'M NO STRANGER to breaking the rules.

Usually, I'm a small-time rule-breaker at most. Every once in a while, I leave the kids alone to run to the nearest fast-food joint serving up what I'm craving. Sometimes, I go exploring the parts of the building usually reserved for residents with deeper wallets—my parents' access cards work wonders.

This isn't the first time I've bent the rules in order to have my way. It's not even the first time that I've gone through the hassle of sneaking into the observatory at the top of the building.

It's just the first time that I'm doing it to meet other people.

The journey doesn't even take that long. It's easy to sneak out once everyone else is asleep, after all. Dressed in head-to-toe black like a henchman in one of the comics my dad had, passed down from *his* dad, I look like a shadow.

At almost three in the morning, there's definitely no one around on our floor. The elevator that slides open for me with a muted *whoosh* isn't empty, but the old woman with orange streaks in her white hair isn't paying attention to anything beyond the view from her VR headset, bopping her head along to whatever she's watching. Aside from that, the ride up to the floor where I'll be taking the stairs is largely silent. Some people get on, some people get off. The old woman dances her way off two floors before I do, leaving me, for a few moments, alone.

Then the emergency stairs are a straight shot up. It should be easy enough, except—

By the time I make it up those ten flights of stairs, I'm exhausted. I didn't realise that I was *that* out of shape. Chasing my siblings around our apartment apparently does *not* count as exercise. I crash into the observatory with enough noise to wake the dead. Thankfully, there are no dead around, but my loud entrance does make me the centre of attention as seven pairs of eyes zero in on my panting body.

Del, with all of that pink hair, is the only person in the open space that I recognise. I hesitate, rather than joining the crowd of other young adults, but Del takes the decision right out of my hands. He comes up to me swiftly, ground-eating strides closing the distance between us, and slings his right arm over my shoulders, drawing me against his long body.

"Everyone, meet Amara," Del says, voice too loud for the empty space. He keeps talking as he guides me forward. "Amara, meet everyone."

It's like Del's words unlock his friends, sitting around on top of various pieces of covered furniture that still haven't been unpacked and locked into the housing across the open space. All but two of the people around them are taller than me. Del remains the tallest person in the room, but the blonde woman who walks forward and loops her arm through Del's left arm is a close second.

"You must be the camera bug Del found," she says, leaning across Del's body so that she can peer down at me through a lacy fringe of pale eyelashes. "I'm Nova." She smiles then, the expression sweet in a way I'm just not used to. "Del called me his 'little star' when we were in school together and I guess... the name just stuck, once we started dating."

Ah. *Dating*. Gotcha.

I'm not very social, but I manage a smile of my own and duck my head in a shallow nod, stammering a quiet, "I-it's nice to meet you, Nova."

Next to join us is a short, round-faced young woman with smile lines at the corners of her bright gold eyes. "I'm Rebecca Park," she says as she waggles her fingers at me in a quick wave that's easy to reciprocate. "But call me Bex. I handle our audience engagement!"

Next up are Zozo—heavily body-modded with dyed grey-green skin and piercings *everywhere* not covered by their sleek, shimmery black bodysuit—and Pink—a short Black boy with deep brown skin only a little darker than my own. They're also dating—they announce it without saying anything, the shy, shiny smiles as they swing their clasped hands between them all that's necessary to convey that relationship.

"Pink handles make-up," Zozo says with a sly smile that makes me realise that the question written on my face is probably louder than it means to be. "He's who did my dye job! Whenever we don't want to be recognised in a video, he kits us out."

I feel my mouth twist with a frown. *When they don't want to be recognised?* Weird.

Before I can open my mouth and voice that, however, the final two members of Del's little crew join our conspicuous little huddle, and things... change. Del's previously open body language closes off noticeably and he rocks back on his heels hard enough to drag me back slightly with the movement.

The first is almost as tall as Del. Where Del's hair is a blinding pink, this newcomer's hair is a tangle of red curls that sweeps over the pale gold of his forehead and the tops of his eyebrows.

"Are you sure you wanna grab a new camera kid?" he asks Del in a gravelly voice that holds a mocking note. "Is this the kid that did that goofy ass video you wouldn't shut up about? You really think this *kid* will be able to help us?"

"Shut the hell up, KT," Del snarls, before telling me, "Don't listen to him."

It's too late, the damage is already done. It stings more than I'll admit.

I shrug off the suddenly crushing weight of Del's arm and look up at him with narrowed eyes and a hot flush stealing across my cheeks. "You—you thought my video was *goofy?*" I just feel so *dumb*. How could I have thought that *anyone* could've liked that video, after all? How could I have convinced myself that a video that got next to no views would be something that anyone else actually liked. Much less someone like Del?

With tears pricking at the corners of my eyes, I spin on my heel and dart back in the direction of the doors, heading for the central elevator bank because what's the *point* of taking the stairs now? What's the point in being stealthy when people just a little bit older than me wasted their time and got me to sneak out of the apartment for *what—?*

I didn't actually expect anyone in the group to follow me. After all, this is all probably just a game to them. Why would they even bother chasing me down?

Except—

"Hey, hold on, Amara."

The hand that grabs for my shoulder as I skid to a stop in front of the elevator isn't Del's big hand and the voice calling my name isn't one of the ones from before. When I turn around, it's to see the last member of the group, the one that had come up to the group alongside KT.

"What do you want?" I snarl, shrugging off the hand on my shoulder. "Are you gonna make fun of my video too?"

The person in front of me shakes their head hard enough to send their stick-straight black hair flying in a cloud around their narrow pale face.

"No. No," they insist. "KT's just being an ass because our channel is so important to us and normally, Del loops us all in when we're making a big decision like bringing someone new in."

"So they didn't hate my video?" I ask. My voice sounds small, shattered, and the sound of the others comes closer, as if they're waiting for their friend to soften me up. "Oh no, KT *hated* it." The words are said in a breathless rush with a bit of a wince for effect. "But Del wasn't lying about how much he liked it. I promise."

"And why should I believe you about *that?*"

"You can call me Tay," they say with a wide and definitely disarming smile on their face that I have to work not to return on instinct. "I'm Del's best friend. There's no way he'd lie to me. Not about something as important as this since I'm the one who handles putting together targets for our videos." Tay jerks their head in the direction of the room we'd been in just moments before. "Let's go back. We can tell you more about our channel, and you can decide if you want to be famous after all."

And that definitely *is* tempting.

"Fine," I say, "but the next person who calls me a kid is getting dropped. I know none of you can be that much older than me."

"You're what, fifteen? Sixteen?"

I shake my head, frowning the entire time. I'm not *that* short. "I turned eighteen five months ago. So again, I'm *not* a kid."

Tay laughs, the sound too loud for how late at night it is. "I'll try not to forget that."

THE ATMOSPHERE IN the half-finished park once Tay and I return is subdued. Everyone is scattered around the dim room that will eventually be turned into a star-gazing path with mostly natural light during the day, thanks to the glass ceiling. Zozo and Pink are sitting on the ground with their heads pressed together as they scroll through something on the AR display of a pretty expensive-looking tablet. KT is on the far side of the large room, facing away from everyone with his shoulders hunched as if he's received a scolding.

Del, Bex, and Nova are closest to the door, and stop talking the second Tay bursts back into the room with me right on their heels.

"Amara!" Del says, voice loud enough to make me flinch back on instinct before I steady myself. "You're back! I didn't think—"

As much as I want the apology Del *clearly* wants to give, I square my shoulders and make the choice to cut Del off before he can really get going.

"I want to be a part of your channel and I want to have friends," I say, my voice low but fierce. "But I'm not a freaking *kid,* and if you all don't really like my camerawork or my video you need to tell me that up front, because I don't want to waste anymore of my time." The sullen *than I already have tonight* I'd end with if I wasn't a little too shy for that kind of comeback hangs heavy in the room.

Del's mouth opens and then closes without him saying anything further. It's Bex who has to take over the rest of the conversation and she steps forward, drawing my attention.

"We *did* like your camerawork," Bex says. "But we also liked that you clearly know your way around the building. Do you have access to a keycard or something?"

I nod. "Yeah," I admit. "I made a copy of my mom's backup cards. It gives me access to pretty much everywhere in the building, but no one registers it as anything more than a glitch." I'm proud of being able to figure that one out, actually. It'd taken several hours of trial and error and a ViewTube tutorial watched on one of my other cousins' accounts on repeat until I knew the code by heart, but in the end, I had a useful way to get around the apartment block. Sure, I'm not as good at coding as I am at filming, but I can do what had to be done.

Narrowing my eyes, I look at the other people around me. "Is that really why you want me to work with your channel? Because I can get you *access* to parts of the building?"

Sheepishly, Del does this awkward-looking nod-shrug combination.

"*I* liked your video," he insists. "Tay and Bex are who realised that you were filming in one of the locked-up stores on a lower floor. They've been all over the public parts of the building and they recognised the hallway in front of the store, because we filmed there just a few days ago."

I frown. "And what *exactly* do your videos look like?"

Sure, I get it... I'm a little late to the game on that one. I should've asked for Del's ViewTube channel from his first message, but I'd just been so *happy* at the prospect of friends that I'd left *thinking* on pause.

Bex whips out a sleek purple phone that lights up and projects the AR interface in the air above its shiny black screen.

"We do pranks, I think that's what Del says he told you," Bex says as she navigates through the ViewTube interface to their channel and taps on the latest video. "But it's a little more than that."

JUDGE CLAYTON

Sector House 117
Wednesday, January 24, 2057
07:14

JUDGE KIERA CLAYTON is bored.

She's supposed to be filing reports and addressing minor complaints related to the last few cases she and her partner—an older Judge, Samael Reyes, who's been mentoring her since she was assigned to this beat—had closed in the past few days.

Instead of doing any of that, Clayton is on ViewTube.

It's a harmless pastime, that's what she tells herself as she scrolls through the front page, looking for a fun video to sink her time into instead of staring at her desk display and the monotony of filling in forms again.

"Not in the mood for cooking videos," she murmurs absently, flicking the first few videos off to the side and out of her recommendations. Same goes for the latest round of Robodog prototype unboxing. Clayton doesn't want to see a robot dog in a box. If she's *that* desperate, she can just ask her aunt down south to send her a video of her elderly Beagle. "Boring. Boring. Boring."

And then—

The video that catches her eye really shouldn't. Even the thumbnail is blurry and sloppy, with two people with pixellated faces holding cans of paint as they stand to either side of the elevator doors in an elevator bank. It could be any floor in any city block. They all look the same inside and out, for the most part. It shouldn't appeal to Clayton, and she knows that, but... she really does want to see what they're going to do with the paint.

"All right," she says as she taps the play button in the AR interface and flicks it downward so that the video will play at lap level instead of in the air where everyone passing by will see.

In the video, the people behind it—who can't stop laughing as they talk—proceed to fill the audience in on their plans.

"The elevators in this building are looking a little boring," the taller person in the video says. Even with the pixellation obscuring their face, their joy comes through clearly. "So, we've decided to paint the town uh..." They pause for full effect, gesturing at their partner to pick up the train of conversation once they're done speaking. "What colour did our viewers choose last week in the poll?"

A tiny person holding a gallon of paint shouldn't seem very menacing, but the way they shake their can of paint up at the camera before tilting it just enough to show the deep jewel-toned blue makes Clayton feel a brief flash of unease.

"Over 15k of you chose Blue-Ti-Ful in our poll, and we're ready to deliver."

The elevator dings, signaling that the doors are about to open, and the person behind the camera says, "Get ready to run."

The people in the elevator don't even get to get out of the enclosed space. Both cans of paint are splashed in as one, dousing the elevator and its inhabitants with a layer of sticky paint. Chaos reigns for the rest of the video, with the camera dropping down to show a boring beige carpet and sneakers pounding down the hall on the way to a door as outraged screams echo behind them.

Clayton laughs; she kind of has to, actually. She can't believe that anyone would make a decision as careless as that... and for ViewTube clout? If they're not cooling their heels in some kind of detention centre by now, Clayton will eat her helmet.

But before she can check to see when the video was uploaded, the heavy thud of files on her desk jolts her attention away and she looks up, right into the unsmiling face of her partner.

"If you have time to screw around, you have time to finish working," Reyes bites out. "Get this done before we're ready to head out for the day. Or else."

Clayton sighs and drops her phone down to her desk with a clatter. She'll just have to check once she's off the clock. Maybe the channel will keep her entertained in her *actual* downtime.

"I'll get right on that, sir," Clayton promises as she reaches for the first of the files on the precariously positioned tower taking up even more space on her desk. "Don't worry. I'll get all my work done."

Reyes snorts, shaking his head. "We'll see about that. Sector chief's taking this vandalism stuff seriously—these kids damaged a couple of Lawrangers yesterday while their riders were responding to a call. Anything that comes in, I want you to make it a priority."

Clayton makes a face at that, but from behind the protection of an open folder so no one can see her face.

Great. More work for me.

The Mega-City Daily News
January 23, 2057

"Mega-cities" were supposed to be safer. Less violence, less crime.

However, a recent look at publicly available complaints from citizens in the coastal cities—both official reports and social media posts—show that the opposite has happened. In recent months, there has been a startling rise in both petty crime and violence in the self-governing "mega-cities" on both sides of the country, especially in the new high-rise "city blocks."

While experts hesitate to name a specific source for the rise in these crimes, we have pinpointed several weak points causing the system to fracture in these cities. As more and more people move into blocks with limited employment opportunities available, these cities are seeing rising unemployment numbers and uncontrolled population growth. As a result, these cities have seen a growing number of kids and young adults with limited prospects—underemployed, living at home in cramped apartments, etc.—turn to causing trouble in order to have something to do.

The increase in ViewTube search trends for "graffiti" and

"pantsing" is just one of the signs that life in the three "mega-cities" is not going according to plan. The videos range from harmless but annoying pranks to dangerous videos that lead to injury and—in several cases—death. Citizens asking for a response from leaders in both coastal cities have found themselves with unanswered messages and silence from the people in power.

One leader that has stated something about the ongoing crisis in the coastal cities is Texas City Governor Robert Booth. On a recent appearance on *The Very Late Show with James Corbyn*, Booth joked that, "Well, *we* ain't had no problems! Seems to me the coastal cities need to get their homes in order."

CHAPTER FOUR

Timm Block
Wednesday, January 24, 2057
04:21

"Is this... it?"

I look up from the AR display at Bex and her friends, feeling a frown return to my face. "I mean—it's funny and all, but *paint?*" I pause. "Wait. *You're* why my dad had to hire someone to gut an entire elevator in the central bank?"

I actually remember that day. It's been one of the few since moving into the building when both of my parents came home early—and *angry*. Dad was first, just before the kids got out of their virtual classes, complaining about how some 'asshole' had made them take out an entire elevator. Then, my mom came home an hour later, still way earlier than her usual return of nine at night. Her complaint?

"Do you know how many tenants have threatened to break their lease over that *stupid* elevator prank?"

They were standing in the kitchen, not very far away from where me and my siblings were sitting around the table shoveling food into our mouths. The angry note to our mother's voice was notable enough (because she's *never* angry) that I remember *that* even if the hushed conversation afterwards has faded in my memory.

Fixing an accusatory stare at all of them, I shake my head. "*This* is what your channel is about?" I ask, disbelief heavy in my voice. "*This?* I mean, property damage pranks are so... played out. How do you even have so many subscribers on ViewTube?"

Bitterness takes hold of me and I know that part of my frustration is that there's just... so much going on. It's late at night, my video numbers aren't ticking upward, and now... I'm potentially linking myself up with other bored teenagers whose idea of a prank involves... massive property damage. *Really?* Meanwhile, they're drawing in thousands of views for pranks that my little sisters could do. Unfair.

"Coming from the person with one crappy video to their channel's name, *that's* rich."

KT again.

Of course.

He's walked over at some point while we've been watching the video, and it seems as though his decision to be silent has come to an end.

"Zip it, KT," Del snaps. He turns to me and shakes his head. "It's not just pranks. We take our viewers on adventures they wouldn't have on their own. They get to feel like they're actually part of our crew—the way *you're* going to be."

"If I join," I reply.

Nova nods in agreement. "If you join."

"Can I have some time to think about it?"

"We'll send you some more videos and stats for the channel," Bex promises. "And once you watch them, you can send us a message in a few days with your decision. If you can handle running with KT after all, we'd love to have you in our crew. Deal?"

I nod once, sharply. "Deal."

With that, I head off, ducking out of the room to begin the trek down to my family's apartment without running into anyone. I'll think about joining their channel... tomorrow.

* * *

THE MOMENT AMARA leaves to go back downstairs, Del pins his focus on KT.

"Are you *serious?*" Del snarls, anger tightening his features and making his voice tremble. "The kid has access to every part of the building and is pretty decent at camerawork and you wanna scare her off?"

He starts towards KT, menace clear in his posture. Nova darts between them, using herself as an obstacle to keep the two from coming to blows. But her presence doesn't stop the shouting.

"What is *wrong* with you, KT?" Del asks. "Don't you get how this can help us? Sure, Tay and Bex can mess with the cameras, but imagine if we didn't *have* to, because we weren't in the parts of the building with online security systems?"

KT crosses his arms across his chest and pins Del with a *nasty* glare. "I *told* you," he snaps, "We don't need some kid messing up our plans. Just steal her card or pay her to give you access on a new one. You don't need to bring her in."

"Okay, since you're so smart," Zozo says in a flat tone that makes it clear that they don't think KT's all that smart at all. They cuddle in close to Pink, a surprisingly mean look on their face as they peer over the boy's shoulder at the rest of the group. "Tell us how you'd handle Amara deciding to snitch. Tell us how you'd keep her from running to the nearest Judge if she realises what's on our *other* channel before we're ready for the reveal?"

Tay chimes in. "If she's not part of the group, she doesn't have any reason to have our backs," they point out. "If she's one of us—for *real*—she won't turn on us. You know that. You know what happened the last time we tried to let someone in without making sure they had a reason."

They all lapse into silence for several long moments, the memory of their last attempt at connecting with someone that they'd thought would be a perfect fit for their *other* channel keeping them quiet.

It takes a moment before Del speaks again. "She'll join us," he says confidently. "Amara is a desperate, lonely kid, and we're the only people in the building she knows who aren't related to her. She'll do it. We just have to make sure that she comes on board as a fan and not expecting to just do work."

CHAPTER FIVE

Tuesday, January 30, 2057
19:40

IT TAKES ME a week to get back to Del and his friends. In that time, I subscribe to their channel, the one Bex showed me, and watch their latest videos—two more paint-pranks at different parts of the apartment block and a Q&A about body mods with a heavily disguised Zozo.

Aside from that, nothing in my routine changes. I still barely see our parents and I see *too much* of my siblings. I still feel as though I'm largely invisible to them when they don't want something from me. And of course, there's still no one watching my first video, or any of the other ones I try to do when I get free time and privacy to record whatever random ideas pop into my mind. By the end of the week, I was bored out of my mind and ready to message Del or Bex on the ViewTube platform's messaging feature. I still don't understand *how* Del's channel has that many followers for what they put out, but it's a number that I don't see myself reaching anytime soon. So, almost a full week from when I'd met Del and his friends, I send Del a message that will hopefully lead to something big for both of us.

Amaramaramara: I'll do it. What do I need to do next?
ChannelDel: Meet us at the east side elevator bank on the first floor at nine in the morning. We'll take you to where we do most of our work.
Amaramaramara: It's not even in Timm Block?
ChannelDel: It is, but you'll need to go with us the first time since we've got... precautions in place.
Amaramaramara: That's not making me want to show up.
ChannelDel: Trust us.

I HAVE BEEN all over Timm Block in the months since our own move-in day. Partly because, with two parents working in the building itself, I've had to run a *lot* of errands to different parts of the building. But mostly I'm just plain nosy. I like knowing the best places to spend time away from my family, the best restaurants I can afford on my allowance, and the hidden spaces across the building that aren't meant for residents to know.

The unused storage space that Del and the others take me to isn't one of the rooms that I know from my own explorations. I'm dressed casually, something inconspicuous so I don't stand out in the crowd of people doing their own thing around the tower block. I look a lot like I did last week, dressed down in all black and comfortable clothing. At first, I don't even recognise Zozo when they come to get me in front of the elevator bank. *That*'s how different they look from the last time I'd seen them, their skin an inconspicuous shimmery gold instead of the eye-catching blue from before.

"Amara," Zozo says my name at the top of their lungs and everyone in a fifteen-foot radius that isn't on their way to somewhere else turns to track their trajectory towards me. I cringe, shrinking inward as I can feel so many different people looking at me. I want to be famous, noticed. But not like this.

"Keep your voice down," I hiss once Zozo is close enough that I'm not shouting right back at them. "And where *is* everyone else?"

Zozo snorts and starts towing me back in the direction they'd come from, not actually answering my question until we're near a narrow hallway ending in an inconspicuous door.

"Not everyone can have parents who work in the building," Zozo says, their voice cheery. "But there are plenty of rooms that aren't being used and still count as 'public' enough that we won't get in trouble for using them."

With that, they lead me through the door and down another hallway, ushering me past closed doors and empty rooms in a winding maze that makes my head spin trying to keep track of where we are and where we're going. At one point, we even head down a brief flight of stairs that puts us next to the incinerators working at half capacity in the early morning... a massive room that I remembered being on the *other* side of Timm Block from the elevator I got off this morning.

"Where *are* we?" I ask as we finally come to a stop in front of a dark grey door that almost blends in with the wall around it.

Zozo raps on the door with the back of their left hand, knocking out a pattern that I instantly try to file away in my brain. They catch me staring at them, eyes wide, and then grin at me just as the door slides open, revealing the room behind it and all their friends sitting in a huddle together.

"We're where the magic happens."

I BARELY GET a chance to breathe once that door opens. I greet everyone quickly, a rapid wiggle of my fingers, before I'm pushed and pulled to a curtained-off corner of the surprisingly spacious room. Zozo comes with me, but their boyfriend Pink isn't far behind.

"You're going to need to change before I can do your make-up and temp-mods," Pink says, a soft smile on his face as he starts setting up a make-up station. "We won't do too much, not for your first video, but we have a *look* for our channel and you'll want to fit in, right?"

Before I can answer, Zozo hands me a pile of shimmery pale grey fabric and a pair of glasses and shoves me behind the curtain with an order to "Get dressed." From there, Pink plops me in a chair and speeds through a light make-up and mod look that involves tech to protect my identity.

"We all use data disrupters when we record our videos," he tells me as he places the chips at different points across my face. "Without them, your parents would've known exactly who they needed to send a bill to for the elevator." He taps the chip stuck to the tip of my nose and then grins. "It's easier for us because we have piercings and bio-ink to bounce the signal off, but we can't ask that of you. Not yet."

I blink. "I'm not getting a freaking *face tattoo*," I say, my voice inching up louder than I want. "How—What—?"

"Don't worry, tadpole," Bex says while I'm still stammering over the syllables. "We're not doing anything really risky today. We're just playing a little game with some of the people in the block. It'll be *fine*."

"A *game?*" I tilt my head back so that I can look at the other girl's face. "What kind of game?"

Armed with my favourite camera and a pair of too-tight sneakers I borrowed from Pink, I'm bouncing on the tips of my toes by the time we get started. We take two separate elevators up to the twentieth floor food court, the perfect place for a game of what Del and Nova tell me is called the 'What's In Your Pocket?' Challenge. The moment the elevator doors open on the crowd, I activate the camera and trail after Zozo, the main focus of the challenge video.

In the introduction we'd recorded downstairs, Del and Zozo laid out the challenge, for me and for their audience. Zozo won't be 'stealing' from anyone that they don't know, the final part of the video will be a reveal about what weird things people keep in their pockets and of course...

"We're making a point about how easy it is to get away with

stuff in your apartment block," Zozo tells the camera, the wideness of their smile reduced to a brilliant blur of vaguely tooth-shaped pixels on the monitor. "Don't forget to keep your pockets empty and an eye on who's around you or you could wind up living this challenge in real life."

I frown to myself as I follow Zozo through the crowd, aiming the camera discreetly at the narrow spread of their shoulders as they manoeuvre through the crowd. Most of the time, I catch when Zozo snags a wallet or pulls keys or a toy out of someone's pocket. The gold dye, which should make them *less* easy to pay attention to, seems to have an opposite and distracting effect. More people pay attention to Zozo than I'd expect, lots of lingering wide-eyed looks and people trying to talk to them. Sure, there are other people with body mods and dyed skin in the crowd. Some of them have looks so wild that I keep having to remind myself that I'm not here to film *them*. But there's something about Zozo that keeps people looking at their face, not their very busy hands.

I don't quite get it, not until someone doesn't fall for it about an hour into recording.

It's an accident, I think. Someone that's not part of the game thinks he's a target. I'm not sure what's happening at first until it's too late. I see a big white hand gripping the narrow bones of Zozo's wrist in my screen and when I look up, it's to see Zozo face to face with a man *vibrating* with anger.

"And just *what* do you think you're doing?" The man asks, his voice loud and shaking with anger. "You think I wouldn't feel you tryin' ta take the credits right out my pocket?" He's loud about it and rough with Zozo, shaking them as if he can knock the truth out of them with the gesture.

Zozo's eyes widen enough that it registers on my screen despite the pixels and then they jerk away from the man. "It was an accident," they say just as loudly. "Watch where you're walking and maybe you won't have problems like that!"

It's the wrong thing to say, and even I know that. The man lunges at Zozo, and they avoid a collision by inches. He whirls around, looking around the crowd as if trying to figure out what's *really* going on and then—

He notices me and my camera.

My heart leaps in my chest and my fingers fumble with the camera, hastily shutting it down and trying to stuff it in the carrying case I have slung over one shoulder. In the seconds it takes for me to do that, the man pushes towards me with wild eyes, and I know if he reaches me, my parents are going to get involved.

"C'mon," a low voice demands before there's a hand gripping my own and tugging me forcefully in the opposite direction. "Let's get outta here!"

I catch a glimpse of red hair whipping past as we race through the crowd, and if I wasn't so busy trying to *breathe*, I'd wonder why KT of all people has chosen to rescue me. We push past people who blur together, passing people I'm sure I sort of know and strangers alike, and run until we don't hear anything at all. By the time we stop running, we're clear on the other side of the floor and KT... KT is still holding my hand.

"KT, I—"

I don't know what I was going to say, but it's not like I get a chance to say it.

KT shakes his head and then drops my hand as if he'd been holding a hot hard drive. He even wipes his hand off on his own grey shirt.

"We're going back downstairs," he says, his tone clipped. "We've done enough today." When he trudges off in the direction of the poorly marked maintenance door, I follow behind him, my head spinning at everything that's *just* happened.

"Is this normal?" I finally manage to ask when we're halfway down the stairs on our way back to the twentieth floor. My lungs are burning, my legs are cramping, and I can't stop thinking about the fact that we nearly got *caught* on my first time out with them. "That man—he was so *mad* at Zozo. Tell me that doesn't happen all the time."

KT grunts in response, a complete non-answer, and actually speeds up on his way down the stairs, forcing me to pick up my own pace in response until we're practically flying down the stairs. By the time we hit the bottom, I'm thinking about quitting. Quitting ViewTube, quitting Del's channel, quitting *life*. It's so bad that KT has to practically drag me along the winding path back to their headquarters off the main hallways on the first floor. Something neither of us actually enjoys.

LATER, WHEN WE'RE all back in the room together, Del puts my footage up on a portable monitor and plays it all out for everyone to see. Aside from the ending, when Zozo goes one way and KT and I another... it doesn't look half bad.

"You have a real steady hand," Tay says from where they sit going through the pile of credits and wallets from the challenge. "Last time we tried to do this sort of filming, Del's hands shook so much that we had to reshoot the whole thing. Wasted an *entire* afternoon." Tay smiles at me and I can't help the way I duck my head, face warm from the pride in their voice. "With a little editing on Nova's end and the wrap-up recording, this is going to be *perfect*."

"So... does this mean I get to be a part of your channel?" I hate the way my voice sounds, so searching and hesitant. But, I guess that's what I am. "Or do I need to do something else?"

Del shakes his head. "You're in, kid—I mean, Amara," he says, aiming a crooked smile at me over the top of Nova's head. "We'll keep you on the easier channel for now. I don't think you're ready for the tough stuff."

"The tough stuff?"

Shrugging, Del says that, "I know you said you're not a kid, but our other channel is for a specialty audience that likes things a little scarier, a little messier. If this was too much for you, the pranks we do on our other channel might be too much. You might not want to get your hands dirty."

I know when I'm getting played. I *do*. But that doesn't stop me from getting in my feelings and letting frustration edge into my voice. "You have *another* channel," I hear myself saying. "One that you didn't tell me about? *Why?*"

It's Nova who speaks up next. "We're just getting to know you," she points out, so matter-of-fact that it makes my teeth *itch* and I reach up to fiddle with my hair so I'd have something else to focus on rather than the annoyance rising inside of me. "And besides, you were worried about harder pranks, or us wanting access to the different parts of Timm Block and that's... that's kind of what that channel would need from you. Two things you already said you don't want to do, so we just don't want to drag you into it."

I huff, irrationally annoyed that they won't just *tell* me what's going on. "So when will I get to know this big secret about your other channel?"

"Let's just see how we feel in a week," Bex chimes in, her voice annoyingly calm despite the tension crackling to life between us all. "In a week, we'll see if you still want to be a part of our team and if we can trust you with the goods. Deal?"

"Yeah, fine."

CHAPTER SIX

I SPEND THE next week wondering when the other shoe will drop, when Del and the others will decide that they trust me enough to see whatever it is that they're uploading to their 'secret' channel. It could be about anything, I know, but I have a feeling it won't be as simple or as boring as videos of covers or even an edgy cooking channel. In between the usual routine of watching my siblings and the new routine of recording for the channel, spending time in the downstairs room watching the team practise new looks and putting together plans for future videos, my mind somehow still finds (too much) time to spend jumping to the worst possible conclusions.

For the most part, the week goes simply and slowly, but there are several days that stand out to me.

Wednesday, January 31, 2057
10:16

THE CHANNEL NOTIFICATION pings into startling relief over my head in the middle of the morning. I'm supposed to be watching Tracey while our parents take the others to the park on our floor for a day of Family Fun. Our baby sister, as much as she enjoys being carted around in a sling, hadn't made so much as a move towards the door and I'd volunteered to take care of her for a few hours.

So in theory, I'm watching her. In reality? I've been refreshing the main page for Del's channel every few minutes that I can wrestle my phone out of Tracey's sticky, squishy little hands. Today is supposed to be the day when the 'What's In Your Pocket?' Challenge video goes up and I can't wait to see what the numbers look like at first. I'm not hanging out with Del and the others today—my choice—and so there's no one around to see me wrestling my baby sister for the phone before I manage to bring up the video on the display.

"Can you believe it, Tracey?" I say as we watch the channel intro, a bright, fun visual of Nova and Del thanking viewers for clicking. "It's my first video with Del!" I shake my phone at Tracey as if it even matters, but all she does is babble cutely at me and reach her hand up to curl around two of my braids and tug them in celebration.

But it's fine. I know what she means—*obviously,* my baby sister is happy for me. In her own way.

Now, I can't watch the *actual* video, even if it means missing out on seeing how Nova edited my footage into something good. It reminds me too much of racing through the hallways downstairs with KT in front of me, his hair streaming behind him like a banner. That reminds me way too much of the way that man had looked at Zozo, how he'd grabbed them and shouted. How he'd come for *me*—

A soft whine draws my attention away from the screen and down at where I'm half crushing Tracey against my chest. She peers up at me with an accusatory look in her big brown eyes and shoves at my chest with her tiny hands.

"Sorry, sorry," I murmur before shifting her so she can see the display better and I'm not *quite* crushing her. "C'mon, just look at the numbers already. Aren't they great?" In real-time, we sit there and watch the view count climb. At first, it stays in the low hundreds. For ten minutes, I refresh and repeat, already stunned to see numbers higher than I've ever *imagined* on anything I've made. By the time that Tracey gets tired of sitting and staring at what's basically the same screen for twenty minutes in a row, the video has been stuck at just under six thousand views.

So much more than the fifty I'd started with on my own channel.

Friday, February 2, 2057
05:54

I LEAVE THE apartment before my parents even do, leaving them a note on the message board we normally keep for chore assignments and a pile of dishes from breakfast that I don't feel like I can clean before they wake up and start asking questions.

Where are you going?

What are you doing?

Who are your new friends?

And my least favourite question ever:

Why can't you take your siblings with you?

So I leave before their alarm goes off for a change, jamming my feet into my sneakers as I struggle with the massive carrying case for my camera drones. By the time that I make it downstairs, my shoes still aren't on properly, but I can't be bothered to fix that because Tay's grinning face is the first thing I see.

"Is it 'Take Your Drone To Work' Day?" they ask, gesturing at the logo for the drone company that takes up one entire side of the case. "What's the special occasion?"

I shrug, unsure what to say now that I have to actually admit to it. "I want... I want to test out the drones with you guys," I say, my voice low. It's a first for me: not taking the drones out of the apartment, but sharing their existence—with *anyone*. And I'm still dealing with the sting of being kept out of a whole secret channel secret. I almost talked myself out of sharing this with them. "We can take them for a flight, test out the claw attachment I got with them. If you're interested—"

Tay's eyes widen, and then so does their grin. "Tell me you're thinking what I'm thinking," they demand, reaching out and snagging my hand in both of theirs, walking backwards as they walk and towing me in the direction of the hallway that leads to that cramped little room.

"I know you guys like to play with paint a lot," I say, my voice hesitant because I *really* don't want Tay or anyone else to know how much *time* I've spent sitting there and going through every single video that I can on their public channel. "But you've never done a water balloon prank before, and with the drones, no one will know what's happening until it happens."

"Look at you," Tay croons at me aiming a sunny smile over their shoulder. "Already planning to take point on a video of your own. Way to show some initiative! Del's gonna *love* this!"

I find myself grinning back at Tay, and then drop the next part of my plans.

"If you're up for it," I say, drawing the words out almost like a tease. "We can sneak into the fancy park where the *really* rich people in the penthouse suites go. There are enough people who use it to make the test flight a fun one."

Monday, February 5, 2057
18:19

Normally, my parents aren't home early enough to watch the local news bulletins, and even if they are, they don't tend to camp out in the living room to watch them. After a busy day of dealing with other people's problems, the last thing they want to deal with are their own kids and honestly, I don't blame them. Much.

But Monday night, we're all parked in front of the big screen that takes up almost the entire wall in the living room watching different holo reporters talk about what's going on in the world outside of our block—and inside of it. Mostly, it's crime. A lot of different, terrible crimes that could happen or have happened to the people around us.

It's depressing, and Ria says as much when she looks up from the handheld gaming system she's been playing for the past hour.

"How many murders can one city have?" she asks. "Do we have any murders *here?*"

Our mom says, "No," at the same time that our dad says, "Only the one," over our heads. As one, we turn to face our parents, mouths hanging open with shock.

"*Excuse me?*" I don't recognise my own voice at first. "A *murder?* You moved us into a place where people are getting *killed?*"

My mom slaps my dad's shoulder lightly and scowls at him, her pretty face fierce and frightening. "See what you've done," she snaps.

"It really was just the one," my dad says. "And it wasn't even recent. Really, the biggest problem our block has now are all the teenagers running around causing trouble."

I blink up at my dad, unsure if I'm really hearing what he's saying. "You're kidding, right? It was 'just' one murder?"

My dad winces again and shakes his head. "That... didn't come out how I meant it to," he says. "It wasn't... it wasn't really a murder. It was more like a falling out between friends. Judges came by and investigated, took the kid responsible away, and that was the end of the story. It wasn't newsworthy, and it's *over*. Don't worry about it."

Don't worry about it, he says as if we're not all thinking about the fact that someone *died* in the block our parents chose to move us into.

* * *

Tuesday, February 6, 2057
10:52

At first, I don't actually realise that my phone is what's woken me up. I'd gone to sleep late the night before, thinking about the conversation our parents had had over our heads and how casually our dad had been about admitting to a murder in our block. And of course, I hadn't slept well.

So I assume, at first, that I'm awake because of the remnant of another hazy nightmare where *I'm* the unfortunate target of my friends' anger. But then I realise that I have a new ViewTube message notification.

IBEXuBEX: You've been a ton of help this week on the main channel, Amara. I think you could do a good job on the other channel as well. Especially with those drones. If you're still interested, come downstairs after you've finished watching this video.

My heart leaps up into my chest, but, despite the anxiety I feel just from seeing Bex's message, I click the attached video and settle in.

JUDGE CLAYTON

Timm Block
Tuesday, February 6, 2057
11:01

CLAYTON KNOWS BETTER than to be on her phone during patrol.

Obviously.

But she's lucked into the slowest possible beat, following up on a rise in reports from residents in the half-finished Timm Block about annoying teenagers running around and causing chaos. Things have escalated in the two weeks since the vandalised bikes, with damaged security cameras and paint spills around crime scenes that have interfered with the Judges' duties.

Just now, however, Timm Block is quiet. Clayton's spent a few hours rocketing around between floors and chasing subjects for interviews, even managing to briefly sit down with one of the building managers to look at video of the security camera glitches. But after that? There's not much left to do but cool her heels and wait for some of her other leads to be free or for something to happen.

It's almost as if the universe *wants* her to find someplace quiet and go looking for something to watch. And who is she to deny the universe something it wants her to have?

The video that Clayton comes across *this* time isn't on ViewTube. It's hosted somewhere else, links buried within the posts buried within replies on a forum that she won't admit going to on her downtime, or any *other* time. The username of the account that posted the video—and the channel itself on some backwoods bit of Internet greyspace—is a string of letters and numbers that doesn't say anything at all about the channel that runs it or the quality of the video itself. But it quickly becomes clear what kind of channel it is when their 'Greatest Hits Compilation' video appears to be quite literally a compilation of hits.

It's a fifteen-minute-long video, and it opens with a simple black and red title card with the name of the video and a warning to sensitive viewers to *look away if you don't feel like getting messy*. That should have Clayton clicking away, but some morbid sense of curiosity drives her to click 'Play' on the video—but she doesn't let the AR activate a screen in the air in front of her helmet. If she's going to watch this video, it'll be between her and the techs that service her phone next time she has to bring it in because a criminal kicked it into the nearest wall. No one in Timm Block has to know that she's taking this kind of break when she's supposed to be watching over them.

The first clip reminds Clayton of the paint prank she'd watched a few weeks ago. In fact, she notes as she takes in the print of the wallpaper as the doors open, it might actually *be* the same elevator. In this video, right after the vivid blue paint splashes onto the unsuspecting riders, something else gets thrown onto the poor people. Something that makes them shriek with something more than alarm. Even if Clayton wasn't a Judge, she'd recognise the sounds of pain and fear. But the voices from before don't explain what they've thrown or why they're reacting as badly as they did.

The video ends abruptly, cut off as one of the paint-splattered citizens stagger out of the elevator, hands groping as they moan for help.

The next video isn't much better. That one isn't set in one of the samey tower blocks, but outside at a construction zone. Someone walks into the shot in slow motion, ominously swinging a rusty pipe, as they toward an unsuspecting worker settling in for a break with a pair of oversized headphones covering his ears.

Clayton doesn't know if the change of scene makes the anticipation worse or better as she watches the swing of the pipe through the air. She then winces at the crunch of bone preceding a hoarse cry of pain and the following spray of blood that lands on the camera and obscures the view of the construction site. These days, it's so much work to get outside, and few people who don't have to leave their blocks ever do so. That the amateur videographers from before are leaving where they live to do *this?* That makes a chill run down Clayton's spine under the suddenly stifling weight of her uniform.

These days, most of the crimes that she and her mentor have to handle are in-block. They're crimes between people who live under the same roof, who share three walls with twice as many people. It makes clean-up and investigation easy, that's for sure. But these people look like they're *hunting*.

From the construction site and the howling construction worker clutching his destroyed shoulder, the video skips to a clip of an indoor swimming pool where pixellated teenagers test how realistic the fear settings on a robot dog are. Then, it goes to a roof—somewhere old, Clayton notes almost absently; newer buildings these days are two and three times as high. That clip, where the point seems to be startling—or, Clayton suspects, maiming—passersby by dropping increasingly heavy objects off the side of the building, leaves Clayton breathless.

"What—?"

It goes on like this for ten more minutes. Ten more minutes of over-the-top violence and crude, cruel humour. And it has hundreds of thousands of views. For the most part, the violence in these videos *does* look staged. To someone who *wasn't* raised to identify crime at its roots and when it was in progress, this would simply look like an old movie from the 'nineties.

But there's something about it that makes Clayton *think*, and before she even fully realises she's doing it, she's forwarding the link to Reyes.

"Can we get someone on this?" she asks him when he calls her back less than fifteen minutes later. "I think it's worth looking into."

The Mega-City Journal
February 7, 2057:

BREAKING: SOLOMON STEPS DOWN

Citing a desire to return to the "honest work" of street justice, Judge Hollins Solomon has stepped down from his role as Chief Judge effective immediately. Solomon will be succeeded by his deputy Clarence Goodman, as announced in a press conference earlier this afternoon.

The press conference also revealed Goodman's plans for the future of the mega-city. Speaking to an audience of a dozen reporters from around the country, Goodman detailed the first steps he will be taking towards further lowering crime rates in the city and solidifying Judge presence and power in the city.

"In the coming days, I will be creating and working with a new council of senior Judges, who will advise and approve on policy," Goodman said in response to a *Journal* reporter questioning his plans. "This development has been in progress for several months now, and as a result, we will be able to introduce a fairer system for deciding upcoming policy and punishment."

The new Chief Judge also went on to vow that under his tenure, he would increase Judge recruitment in order to build the department up to the strength it needs to have in order to meet the needs and challenges of the future.

First rising to the role in 2051 following Chief Judge Eustace Fargo's death in service, Judge Solomon was felt to be more moderate and politically aware than his predecessor, qualities he demonstrated when he led the negotiation team that hammered out the Autonomy Act with the leaders of the Los Angeles-San Diego and Dallas-San Antonio metropolitan districts. He became more controversial later in his tenure, including the notorious introduction in 2055 of so-called "immigration" quotas into the Boston-New York-Philadelphia district from the mainland United States. Sources close to the Chief Judge's office say this retirement was overdue.

We will provide updates on this story as it develops.

CHAPTER SEVEN

Wednesday, February 7, 2057
11:19

When the compilation video ends, I sit there in my bed staring down at the darkened square of the AR display as if the staticky screen will reveal the truth of what I'd just seen. I've seen worse things, of course—I'm terminally online in the best possible way—but there's a difference between watching old horror movies in the dark and knowing they're fake and *this*... and watching people I almost-know shove people over in hallways or shave off a few years from an elderly woman's life by popping out of a recycling bin covered in fake blood.

This is what Del and my other new friends do on their other channel? In their spare time? *This* is what I wanted so badly to be a part of?

I rewatch the video two more times before I can pull myself away from the screen. I watch the entire thing from start to finish, barely even flinching over the rougher spots or darker moments in the compilation. The video is... a lot. It's a lot and it's upsetting. And yet—

I can't help that there's this awful part in the back of my mind that goes *I wonder how many views this one got...*

It's that thought that does it for me though, the casual cruelty of the thought bouncing around my head like it's *nothing*. I just watched a fifteen-minute-long video of people being hurt in minor or maybe even major ways and I just... I only really cared about the *view count?* No. That's weird and definitely more than a little bit wrong. I toss my phone aside and hop out of bed, rushing through my morning routine—the world's fastest and least helpful shower as well as an all-in-one breakfast bar that leaves my mouth stinging thanks to the artificial sweeteners and all of those vitamins—before deciding to pick my phone back up again. I close the video for good and then tab over to the ViewTube app, fingers hovering over the little line of blue text that shows that Bex is online again.

It takes me a second to find the courage, but I send her a message with trembling fingers.

Amaramaramara: I watched the video. I'll be downstairs in fifteen minutes. I want to talk to all of you.

I know that everyone else has something else they could be doing. Zozo and Pink live and work together, KT works part time in sanitation, and Nova apparently actually has a channel of her own that brings in an income that allows her to go to beauty school online. They're not always available at the same time every day. That I've been able to see them most of the days I've been (somewhat) part of their team is apparently down to luck and lots of it. So there's a chance that they won't be able to meet now, I know *that*. But there's also a stronger chance that they're all going to want to hear what I have to say. Whatever it is. (I haven't thought that far yet.)

Bex's reply comes within the next few seconds:

IBEXuBEX: Okay.

That's it. That's all the response I get.

Hopefully, when I make it downstairs, they'll feel like talking more, because I want answers for what I just saw.

Del is the only person in the room when I get there. Somehow, I'm not surprised. He's sitting on a chair facing the door, his hair a tangled mess around his shoulders and his tattoos gleaming under the very bright overhead light. He greets me with a slight nod and a half-hearted lift of his fingers that's nothing like any previous greetings we've shared. I instantly realise *He thinks something's wrong*. And I mean, he's not wrong, but he's also... not as correct as he thinks he is.

"The fact that you're here, looking like this... I guess that means you watched the video," Del says in a low, rough tone. I nod, and he continues: "And what are your thoughts?"

My mind races a mile a minute because I *genuinely* have no idea where to begin. Except...

"Most of those clips weren't filmed in this building," I say, hesitant at first. "And the camerawork is tighter, better than the paint elevator prank. What changed?"

At first, I don't actually think Del is going to answer me. Actually, I don't think *he* thinks he's going to answer me. He stares off into the distance, silent, his mouth open, for so long that I actually consider simply... leaving.

"We didn't always live in Timm Block," he says eventually. "We were friends before online, had similar interests. We linked up outside back when we were younger. There were more of us back then, and we used to do this all the time."

"What do you mean, 'this'?" I ask.

Del shrugs. "It's easy to have fun if you don't mind hurting people," he says, the casual admission startling because *who just says things like that*? "We had a channel back then too. A little crappy channel on some ViewTube clone that had a loose ToS and no moderation. This was... four or five years ago." He pauses to scrub the back of his hand over his mouth. "Our old camera person, you wouldn't know him, he handled uploads and editing. But we decided we wanted to go in a different direction and well... Here you are."

I don't get it, and I say as much. "Well, what's the 'different direction'?" I say, shaking my phone at Del. "Because the *only* constant across all of these videos is that you're hurting people for views. That's the only thing *I'm* seeing."

Del's thin mouth quirks upward with a smirk. "Do you know how many views our videos on *that* channel get?"

When I shake my head, Del throws his head back and laughs. "We once had a video crack a million views in twenty-four hours," he admits. "Now, I can't tell you what it's about because then you'll *really* run scared, but we have an audience that *loves* what we do and they've been watching us for years." Del's smile, the one he aims at me once he's done laughing like he's just heard the funniest possible joke, is sharp enough to rock me backwards on my heels. "Isn't this what you wanted?"

"Excuse me?" I blurt out, feeling my eyes get wide. "I do *not*—"

"You want attention," Tay's low voice startles me worse than anything else Del could've said in that moment and I flinch, hard. "You're the oldest child and you're lost in a crowd of people who will *never* see you no matter what you do. You know that you deserve better than what you have going on in your life right now, and *that* is what led you right to us."

I hadn't even heard the door open behind me. Tay is *right there*, so close that I can smell the sweetener on their breath from whatever it was that they were eating before sauntering into the room. And they're not alone. Behind Tay is the rest of the gang—and *oh* am I starting to realise that's exactly what this is—and the looks on their faces range from smug (Tay) to suspicious (Bex) to angry (KT, as always).

"Was it even an accident that you found my video?" I ask Del, hurt in my voice and in my heart. "Or is this just a game you're playing? Am I going to be on your other channel next?"

Del bolts up from his chair, palms turned out towards me.

"I didn't lie to you, Amara," he says, his voice soft and sure. "I just... didn't tell you the entire truth." He gestures at our—*his*—friends. "Do you think that you'd actually have started talking to us if you knew what our main way of making money was?"

"You make *money* off of this?" I mean I know in theory that you can make money off of *anything* these days, but even ViewTube has its limits after the LlamaGate Incident of 2036 wiped out dozens of users' savings in five minutes in the name of 'saving the llamas.' There's no way that any of their real videos are actually monetised.

Right?

Just then, Bex edges into the room with a wary look on her face, with Zozo and Pink close on her heels like a pair of bodyguards. "Our videos aren't monetised, true," she admits. "But it's not that hard for us to get funding. Like Del says, we have an *established* audience. There are tens of thousands of people across the world willing to tip us every time we post a new video. Every time *their* strange thing gets shown on screen."

I feel my nose wrinkle. "People are *paying* you to hurt other people? *Why?*"

It's hard to wrap my mind around the concept, although I get it in theory. People pay for what they want to see, and if what they want to see is a group of young adults terrorising the population of an apartment building... they're going to pay plenty for the privilege.

But it's still... so strange.

"And if you're getting paid to make violent videos, why do you all still live *here?*"

That part doesn't make sense to me either. When I'd set up my ViewTube channel, the first thing I'd thought of was how, once I had a big enough audience, I would simply move out. I dreamed of finding a room of my own in Timm Block, somewhere where I'd be close enough to help my parents if they needed it, but far enough that hopefully they *wouldn't*. But faced with seven people *actually* making that kind of money and yet who *choose* not to do anything with it...? "What's the point of making these videos and making money, then?"

There's silence stretching between us all for several moments as everyone in the room looks at one another, like they're using some kind of messed-up telepathy.

I push ahead and keep talking. "Actually, why not just get an auto drone?" I ask. "Why do you need *me* when a high-priced drone can do most of what I can?"

Behind me, I hear KT mutter, "Well, it can't ask useless questions, that's for sure," and I want to whirl around and *finally* let him know how tired I am of being subject to *his* bad attitude, but Del chooses that moment to answer one of my questions.

"You were clearly lonely," he says. The matter-of-fact note to his voice shouldn't wound as much as it does, and yet. "You made an entire movie starring your younger siblings and roaming through the building. You reminded me of... us. The way we were before we started making our videos together and realised that we had something that could be *big* here." He pauses to grin again. "And no matter what KT says, the fact that you can ask questions when a drone *can't* is part of why we have kept you around."

"And the rest of it?"

"We really do want your access to the different spaces around the building," Nova says as she brushes past me on her way to stand at Del's side. "There are so many videos we could make if we only had access to more people, private spaces. If we didn't have to worry about being followed. Our audience could grow even more. On *both* sites."

Nova pauses and the silence that follows isn't very long, but it does feel fragile. "Don't you want to help us grow? Don't you want to be famous?"

CHAPTER EIGHT

Don't you want to be famous?

It's a question I've asked myself several times before. Even just this morning. But there's something different and unsettling about the way that Nova asks it, how they're all looking at me as if they think that *they* are the only people who could make even boring old *me* famous. I don't like it. Even more than the video on that side channel—and the others I haven't seen yet—the way Nova and the others look at me raises the hairs on the back of my neck and leaves goosebumps all over my arms.

"I want... *something*," I say, drawing out the words as long as I can. "But I don't... I just don't get why *this*, why *here*."

Pink, scrubbing a narrow-fingered hand over the bleach-blond fuzz of hair covering his dark scalp, is who answers my questions this round. "At first, I think we started this to try and get back at some assholes in our old building," he says, screwing up his face as if trying to remember the very distant past. "We were... grief, we were really just kids back then. And they were bullies who ran the building and terrorised us for no real reason. Del came up with the idea to film what we did to them."

Zozo cuts in then with a cackle. "We got the ringleader

to meet us in an alley outside of the building and we took a hammer to his hand."

I blink. "Ex*cuse* me?"

They shrug in unison, as if they'd just told me what the weather was like outside rather than how they crippled another human being.

"Yeah," Pink says, eyebrows lifting in question. "It's the only thing we had around, and it didn't take up too much space in the video." He says it like it's normal, to be concerned about the optics of a video where they *smashed someone's hand with a hammer*. "*That* we posted on ViewTube... but it got taken down within a week."

"Of course it did," I say, a little screeching note entering my voice. "You *maimed someone*."

"Someone who deserved it," Del says, his own voice sharp.

I can't help myself.

"So," I say, raising my eyebrows at him and the others. "What about the other people? The ones in the video you showed me? Did they deserve this as much as that bully did?" I cross my arms over my chest and frown, shaking my head. "If you're in it just for the fun, *just say that*, but you can't tell me that this is all out of some weird protective instinct or something."

If I thought the atmosphere in the room was awkward before, it's nothing compared to how tense it is once I finish speaking. Out of all of the people in the room, only KT—for a change—is looking at me like he's not thinking about the best way to shut me up. Everyone else looks like they've already decided I'm the enemy in the room. And considering how they're all standing between me and the door—

I throw my hands up in the air in exasperation and walk *away* from the door towards the bank of monitors that Bex and Nova have been using for edits. I'm closer to Del and Nova when I do that, but moving deeper into the room means that I don't look like I'll make a run for it. (Although I want to.)

"I don't really *care* what you're doing," I say and sadly, it's not entirely a lie. "I just don't want to be friends with people lying to themselves, or to me. If you want me to be a part of this, that's all I want: the truth."

I don't say the rest of it, that I don't want them to maim me either, but I'm sure they've figured that part out.

"We take care of our own," Del says, his voice a little lighter, a little less intense than before. "That's the truth. Don't you want people around you that'll look out for you?"

I know when I'm being 'managed.' But 'managed' is better than the alternative, and I force a smile that hopefully doesn't look as fragile as it feels, and then nod.

"I'm in," I tell Del, managing to hold eye contact for longer than I'd expected. "But I still have some questions." I ignore KT uttering a beyond-annoyed "Of *course* she does" in the background, and keep talking. "I don't know how you've gone so long without having Judges knocking on your door, but that *can't* happen with me."

There's a moment of silence, a shared look between everyone else, before Bex and Tay shift, drawing my attention to them.

"A few of our videos have been taken down over the years," Tay confesses with a shrug and a smile that seems almost... impish. "But we've always made sure to cover our digital tracks well. We use burner accounts, pay for a good VPN service, and scrub every single video of data that'd be able to identify us."

Bex chimes in. "The closest we've come to a Judge sniffing around was a few months ago when that news story came out," she says. "And we made sure another story didn't happen any time soon. So you don't have to worry about having Judges knocking at your door. We're good."

I open my mouth, ready to ask questions about exactly *why* we don't have to worry about any more news stories, but then I realise I don't actually *want* the answer. Instead, I ask. "Okay, so what do I have to do now that I'm a part of... all of this?"

At that, Del brightens up visibly and he gestures for Tay and Bex to come over, closer to the bank of monitors. "Oh, we actually have something in mind for you already," he tells me with a wide, bright smile on his face. He looks so happy, like he's about to loop me in on a new game, not... possibly have me hurt another person. "You said your drones are cleared for indoor flight, right?"

I nod. "They're the biggest size you can use for indoor flight, although some of them I have to swap out the wings and fans. Why?"

"What better way to show that you're really part of the group than by doing something *big*?"

I eye Tay suspiciously. "Big like *what*?"

"The observatory is officially opening soon," Tay says, with a smile on their face that I just don't like. "Remember when you suggested doing water balloon blasts for the other channels? We could crash the official opening ceremony, cause a little chaos. You in?"

"Water balloons," I repeat. "You want me to use my drones to drop *water balloons* on people for your super-secret channel?"

Tay shakes their head. "That's thinking too small," they say with that same unsettling smile on their face. "No one would pay for that. We have *so* many things that we can put in balloons. Gasoline, pellets, a little acid, tacks. We're trying to have *fun*, Amara. Not be *boring*."

I blink. "*Tacks?*"

Tay shrugs. "It's worth a shot."

"It really isn't," I say. "Maybe I could... I could just pilot the drones and we do something... else. Something that doesn't involve someone possibly losing an eye?"

In one moment, the atmosphere in the room shifts and Del narrows his eyes at me as he scrubs his fingers across his scalp.

"But that's the *point*, Amara," he says, the tone of his voice so condescending that I feel my fingers curling into fists in response. "If you don't want to do the stuff that'll make you stand out on *our* channel, maybe you should just stick to your own. Maybe in a few years, people will start to pay attention to you."

The words sting, of course they do. But I shake my head instead of giving in like he expects.

"I'm just saying that I'm not ready to go straight to dropping sharp objects on people," I say. "Just—just give me some time to try to come up with something that's not so... much." It's my turn to shrug, and I try to make the gesture as casual as I can. I want to look uncertain, not like I'm about to make a run for it and flag down the nearest Judge (which I'm *not* going to do... I think). "Why don't you come up with better options for me and we'll uh... revisit it tomorrow? Okay?"

I don't actually give them a chance to argue with me after that. I take off for the door, not *quite* running, but not *that* far from it.

As I make it out the door, I hear KT say, "I'll talk to her."

Hopefully, he won't catch me...

CHAPTER NINE

Of course KT catches me. I'm not very fast, or very tall. With his long legs, it's easy for him.

He catches up with me in the hallway, and for a few minutes, neither of us talk. He follows me back to the main areas of the floor, and then to the elevator. When the doors open, he gets in right behind me, pressing the button for the highest floor that we have access to in the main elevators—the one with the observatory that may not have had its official opening, but is already in use.

"We need to talk," he says, seriously. I feel as if I'm about to get a scolding.

I cross my arms over my chest and glare up at him as the elevator starts to climb rapidly. "You don't like me," I spit out through the panic and anger tightening my throat. "What exactly do we have to talk about? I thought you'd be happy that your friends don't trust me, and they might even get rid of me."

There, I've said it. That's the thing I've had in the back of my mind since talking to Del few minutes ago—that no matter what I do from this moment on, the group won't trust me. They won't let me in on their plans, and they might just decide that it's easier to cut me loose properly than anything else.

My head isn't totally empty.

KT shakes his head, frowning down at me. "That's not what this is," he insists. "That's never been what this is. I don't *hate* you."

"I didn't say that," I say. "But you can't pretend that we're best friends. From the moment I linked up with Del and the others, you have made it very clear that you don't think I belong in your group. You've complained the entire time and you've been rude from day one. What else am I supposed to think?"

KT opens his mouth, and then closes it. Without saying anything. The elevator doors open in a muted whisper of air, and before I can say or do anything, he reaches out, grabs my wrist, and pulls me out of the elevator after him. We walk to the observatory in an anxious silence. I keep trying to pull my hand away, but his grip doesn't loosen at any point.

The observatory isn't empty. Even though, in the middle of the day, it's impossible to use any of the instruments around the massive room to look at the stars, it's still a functional meeting space for people who live in our building. I count about three dozen people walking around. Maybe half of them are people our age. The others are older people or families, some children even. These are the people that Del wants to hurt, for some reason that I can't understand.

"I told them that I was going to talk to you so that you would have a chance at making it to tomorrow," KT says. He keeps hold of my wrist as he half drags me to a relatively secluded area of the observatory overlooking the city around us. I'm too stunned by the realisation that I was right and my 'friends' were probably planning to kill me to stop me talking, and he doesn't break the silence until he has me sitting on a bench facing a massive pane of glass.

"So, what does that mean?"

KT sighs, raking his fingers through his messy red hair. "It *means* that I'm trying to give you a shot at survival you wouldn't have had if I had stayed in that room without following you," he snaps at me, frustration bleeding into his words. "It means that I have to tell you the truth about my friends and why we needed a new camera person in the first place."

I shiver.

I have a bad feeling about this.

"I KNEW FRANKIE from the other building, the one that we all lived in before moving to this block. He was older than all of us except for Del, but we were all just kids when we met. He was one of the best things about living in the old building, and we grew up together terrorising the neighbours—but not like Del and everyone are doing here. We actually started dating in the other building, after he had me star in one of his class projects.

"He got his certification in tech, same as you, and his camerawork was actually award-winning. Real slick shit with high production values because *his* parents had money and they weren't afraid to spend it on him and his work. When we started our first channel, the idea of him doing any of the shoots was pretty laughable, because he was headed for bigger and better things than recording our pranks or getting into fights with other little shits on different floors. At least, that's what I thought.

"So, he didn't film everything, but what he did film was really well done. We had our main channel where we just screwed around, did the kind of pranks we still do on the main channel. But then we started the *second* channel a few months later and well... things escalated."

I interrupt KT's monologue. "Escalated *how?*"

"You know that story they told you about the hammer?" KT asks.

When I nod, he continues speaking.

"That wasn't the first time that they recorded some kind of violence against another person or animal," he tells me. "It was just the first time they could justify it. That *we* could justify it." He shakes his head. "I'm not trying to pretend that I wasn't a part of this, that I didn't join right in on the violence. But I was always honest about what I was doing and why. Del and the others never were, not even to us, or to Frankie."

"Is that why he's no longer with your gang?"

KT's frown deepens. "Something like that," he admits. "Frankie was a lot like you. He asked a lot of questions, and he expected answers. He was okay with some of the violence, but as Tay and Del started putting everything together and amping up how badly they hurt people, he started to ask questions about what we were doing. Especially when we all managed to get spots in this building a few years later. He thought the change of scenery should have marked a change in what we made.

"He used to ask why Del and Tay insisted on actual violence instead of letting him use his skills to add visual effects or to let Nova and the others use make-up or practical effects instead. And then, one day, Nova and Tay attacked an old woman for the channel. And... that was just it, for Frankie. He told us that he wouldn't record for us any more. He told *me* that if I didn't stop working with them, that he would break up with me. I was ready to drop the gang immediately. It wasn't worth it."

I frown at KT and then gesture widely at the building around us as if willing Frankie to pop up out of nowhere. "Okay, but you're still with the gang and I don't see no Frankie. So what happened?"

KT's face just... *falls*. For a second, he looks so broken, so hurt, that I want to retract the question and apologise for even asking it in the first place. His skin pales beyond what I thought was possible even for him, and he covers his face with both of his big hands, uttering a deep sighing exhalation.

"They killed him," KT says into his hands. "Frankie told them that he was out, and they killed him. And every day I have to live with the fact that I didn't save him. Every day I have to live with the fact that I'm still 'friends' with the people who killed my boyfriend, because I'm too much of a damn coward to do what has to be done. Because I'm too afraid of speaking to a Judge and condemning myself in the process."

I don't know what to say. This is... a lot.

"They killed him? Are you sure?"

It's not what I mean to ask, but those are the only words that I managed to choke out. I saw the compilation video, I know that these people that I'm sort of friends with are people who see nothing wrong with hurting others. But, learning that they didn't just kill someone... but one of their friends? *That* leaves me shaking.

KT dips his head in a jerky nodding motion. "I didn't see the video," he says, his voice strangled with emotion. "But I know it exists. They told me it did and that they uploaded it like they did everything else—Bex has always been merciless like that. That's why I didn't want you joining the group. I knew it would be another incident like this. I knew that you wouldn't want to do this. And that they'd hurt you for it."

"But they haven't hurt me—"

"*Yet*," KT bites out. "Trust me. If I hadn't followed after you, you probably wouldn't have made it back to your room." He looks at me, and I'm struck by how haunted he looks. "Someone else would have followed you, and it wouldn't have been to talk."

His words leave me with chills. "But they can't get away with this," I tell him, my voice shaking despite myself. "We have to tell someone—"

"Like who?" KT spits. "The Judges were already here, and they didn't find anything about Frankie's death. Or nothing that made them look at the gang. So, what do you expect *me* to do?"

"I'll talk to them. I'll file a report and try to talk to a Judge." I can hear the frantic note in my own voice, and I hate that for us, but I *am* scared. I'm scared of what Del and the others will do when they realise that KT may have followed me to talk, but not in a way that will help them. I'm scared of getting in trouble. I'm afraid of becoming famous in a way that I really didn't ask for. But it's clear that someone has to do something, and it might as well be me. "Just... can you buy me time? Just a day, maybe a little bit more?"

KT's mouth falls open, dumbfounded. "Are you sure?"

I shrug. "I have to do something," I tell him. "This is a start."

JUDGE CLAYTON

The Grand Hall of Justice
Wednesday, February 7, 2057
15:21

WITHIN HOURS OF Clayton raising the alarm on the videos she stumbled across on her very bored trip across the internet, she has a team in Tek who've pulled up close to a hundred videos from the same group of users. The public still doesn't know about the link between the Berzerker plague in the summer of 2047 and subliminal videos online, and they never will; but the Justice Department has had a dedicated team of online video analysts ever since, and when they go into action, they do it with a speed Clayton finds dizzying.

All of the videos prove to be scrubbed nearly clean of identifying metadata. Aside from visual clues, it's next to impossible to hunt down any information about *who* the gang is or where they're located... but whoever scrubbed the videos made a mistake. They're cocky enough that they've left a little tag behind in the metadata, like a signature.

The arrogance makes Clayton's *teeth* itch, but it works to their benefit. The videos start trickling on the first day, more compilations of excessive violence—some that seem staged and others that are clearly *not*—but other videos as well.

There are vlogs of different lengths, solo videos where different members of the gang enact their preferred types of violence, milder 'Prank Wars'-style videos on an unmonetised ViewTube channel that seems to be updated regularly by the same crew, and even, wildly, a cooking show episode. Every single face on-screen is obscured *except* the victims of violence, censored with high-tech blurring and pixellation or garish make-up that confuses their facial recognition tech, but they can figure out the source later. With dozens of videos, some with clearly repeated visuals when it comes to rooms, hallways, or alleys, they *will* find their targets eventually.

Reyes comes over while Clayton is looming over a Tek going through the latest round of videos they've scraped from the bottom of the internet. His presence makes them *both* straighten their spines, although Clayton can't help unleashing a little bit of her habitual snark.

"Can we help you?" Clayton says, turning to face her supervising officer with a sunny but sharp smile. "You're interrupting the energy here, Reyes."

Clayton realises she's pushing it as Reyes's thin-lipped mouth tightens. She figures he's reconsidering agreeing to be her mentor for the next few years.

It doesn't last. It never does.

Reyes clears his throat and declines to engage with Clayton's mild needling. "Your report, Clayton, leaves out where *you* were when you saw these videos."

Clayton blinks. "M-*me?*"

"Yes, you," Reyes says. "ViewTube's algorithm recommends videos based on where you're located or where you've been. So do other sites online. So, we can figure out where *some* of those videos were recorded based on where *you* were when you first saw them."

Clayton hesitates. If she comes clean about where she was, she *might* provide a necessary break in the case. But then Reyes will know that she's been taking time off from her rounds and handling reports... to comb the internet for weird videos.

"Clayton," Reyes says, a familiar impatience edging into his raspy voice. It's a tone that brooks no sass or argument. "Where were you when you saw these videos?"

"I was... I was in the office the first time, with the ViewTube one," Clayton says on a wince. She tries to offer Reyes a smile, but he's not playing with her. (He never is.)

"And the second?" Reyes asks, his tone neutral enough that a newer Judge might find reassuring. "Where were you for that one?"

"Timm Block," Clayton confesses. "I was there a few days ago; we'd had a bunch of reports from the building about different teenagers causing chaos. I did a quick patrol and then paused to take a quick break."

That manages to shock Reyes. He goggles at Clayton for a second before snapping his fingers at the nearest unoccupied Tek-Judge. "Pull up all recent reports from Timm Block," he orders. "Cross-reference the reports with the videos. See if any details match up. Get as many eyes on this as you can."

Clayton perks up. "What about more recent reports, the ones that might *not* have a video attached to them, because the video isn't out yet?"

Reyes's mouth quirks in a smile that send a chill up Clayton's spine. "*That* is a very good question," he says decisively. At first, she thinks that's the end of it and that she's got away without getting chewed out, but then Reyes's gaze sharpens. "Come with me for a moment, Clayton. We have some things to... clarify before I set you loose on the Tek-Judges."

The nervous gulp that Clayton lets out is loud enough that she knows he can hear it. "Yes, sir."

Reyes leads Clayton to a small room off to one side of the lab. It's a cramped room, a cross between a storage closet and a supervisor's office. It's also, mercifully, empty, so that no one can see Clayton flinch when Reyes whirls around on her with his eyebrows drawn down in a scowl.

"I understand that I've given you a lot of leeway because you *are* good at what you do," Reyes bites out through a jaw clenched so tight that Clayton can see a muscle jumping in his cheek. "That does not excuse your continued lack of professionalism and discipline. Especially here in front of Tek-Judges who expect certain standards of behaviour from people like us."

Clayton dips her head in a jerky nod. "I understand, sir," she says, her voice barely louder than a whisper. "I'm sorry, sir." But she can't help herself, impulse control out the nearest window, because she follows up her apology with a defence. "But at least I was helpful. The videos I've been watching are going to help us find the vandals."

Reyes grunts at Clayton. It isn't a very nice grunt. "And—"

"And sometimes, new crimes or problems just need new minds with new solutions," she says, with growing confidence. "You had no idea where to start with the vandals. Because of me—"

Reyes cuts her off. "Because of your *slacking*."

Clayton continues speaking. "Because of my 'slacking,' we have a better chance of finding the vandals and putting a stop to them before they escalate even further." She manages a cocky grin for Reyes despite the panic turning her knees into jelly, and then says, "We wouldn't be here without me."

Reyes's glare is fierce, but it only lasts a few moments before he inclines his head in a shallow nod. "You make a good point," he begrudgingly admits. "But that doesn't excuse the fact that you were slacking off during your shifts."

"I *do* understand that, sir," Clayton is quick to say. "It won't happen again."

"I'm sure you *think* it won't," Reyes says. "But to make the message stick, you'll be working in the labs with the Tek-Judges and going through reports." It doesn't sound like a lot in terms of punishment and Clayton opens her mouth to say as much before Reyes beats her to it. "*And* you'll be handling shifts in traffic and transportation for two weeks after the end of this case, followed by another two weeks of report duty."

It's boring, busy work that Clayton has *never* liked... and that's why Reyes has chosen it as a punishment detail.

"I understand, sir," Clayton says again. "Thank you, sir."

IT TAKES CLAYTON four hours, but she eventually finds something. It's a new report, actually; it comes in just as she's about to call it quits and take her lumps from Reyes. It's new to the database: a short message, with sparse details, from a clearly marked resident in Timm Block.

Amara Dawson: I know my new friends are hurting people. They've even hurt their own friends. I want this to stop before it gets too dangerous. I'll tell you everything I know if you send a Judge to meet me at the twelfth-floor cafeteria in Timm Block tomorrow at 2pm. I'll be wearing a pink hat. You can't be wearing your uniform.

It's too good to be true.

That's the first thing Clayton thinks when she reads the message. The second is that even if this is a trap, it'll probably be worth it. She taps the nearest Tek-Judge—a mousy little thing with a swirl of bright yellow hair swooping over their pale forehead—on the shoulder and then asks, "Can you pull up this person's information for me? Reyes and I need to know everything about this Amara Dawson in the next hour."

"Are you sure?" she says, scanning the message dubiously.

Clayton nods once, decisively. "The way I look at it," she says, "If this is a trap, it's from the people who made those videos. If it's *not* a trap and this person knows who's behind the videos? This is the biggest break we could ask for."

"When someone sends in a report like this, it's *easy* to find out more about them," the Tek says with a shrug. "The report function sends in documentation of the user's system, where they're at, and all personal information that the system thinks is relevant."

Clayton nods to show that she understands. "So, what does 'relevant' look like?"

The Tek-Judge types a few characters into the keyboard and brings up a display of digital files.

It includes a photo of a young woman—little more than a girl, Clayton thinks—taken during registration for Timm Block's facial recognition and biometric security services. She's staring at the camera with a willful, mulish look on her face. Bright blue hair sweeps over the brown skin of her forehead, flaring over the top of her thick-framed glasses. She looks like she's trying to be tough, in the picture, but Clayton sees right through her. This child has to be several years younger than Clayton is. Practically an *infant.*

"How old is she?"

A little more typing, a little more scrolling. "She just turned eighteen," the Tek says. "She graduated from a hybrid school with certifications in tech and coding. Her family moved from farther out into Timm Block just a few months ago. Her internet history and behaviour in the building have been pretty normal, except..."

"Except what?"

"Well," the Tek says, hesitantly at first. "She started a ViewTube channel recently and, like the people we've been tracking, she likes to tag her videos in the metadata to keep track of things. She doesn't always scrub the rest of her data very well—it's clear that she's recording and posting from her room in Timm Block and other places in the building—but even when she does a data scrub, she keeps her sig embedded." The Tek-Judge pauses as if to draw out the suspense and then, when Clayton doesn't do more than raise her eyebrows expectantly, slumps and continues more sulkily. "The data tag *also* shows up in a few of the more recent videos from the users you had us searching for."

That Clayton wasn't expecting, and she whirls around fast enough she hears her neck crack. "It's *what?*"

The Tek pulls up another row of files and gestures at the videos that come up. "Some of her videos were flagged in the search we did earlier and one of the others went back to see what other videos came up. A reverse search just now pulled up videos on her personal channel, and the common element the system found—"

"Was her tag."

The Tek nods. "Yes," she says. "Which means she's a direct connection to the group you're looking for."

"I need you to get all of this information together in a format Reyes won't yell at us for," Clayton says as she pushes herself up to her feet. "I'll need something *good* to get Reyes to sign off on a team for this. I'll be back in twenty minutes with the big guy."

She leaves without waiting for a response from the Tek. Either she'll get it done—

Or they'll *both* get yelled at.

CHAPTER TEN

Timm Block
Thursday, February 8, 2057
13:54

As I sit in one of the lesser-used cafeterias in Timm Block, I start to wonder if anything I've done so far has been a good idea. From starting my ViewTube channel to linking up with Del and his gang, have I made a single good choice in the past few weeks?

I rest my elbows on the table and then drop my face into my cupped palms, sighing as I think of the latest bad call I've managed to make. Filing a report with the Judges, *requesting a meeting with one*. I don't know what I was thinking... meeting with a Judge at a time like this? I might as well hand over my passes, my camera, and my drones to Del and the others. I might as well just... let them hurt me, the way KT told me they hurt Frankie. Because they sure as hell will after they find out about this. Hopefully, the Judge that comes won't look *too* much like one. I hope they have enough sense to realise that they'd be putting me in danger if they show up in full uniform.

The cafeteria area isn't super busy ever, but at the time I scheduled our meeting, it's basically empty aside from the people who work here. I'd been able to grab a drink—an over-priced green smoothie that makes my lips pucker every time I take a sip—and a table overlooking the entrance to the cafeteria. Sitting alone for twenty minutes was more than enough time to wallow in my thoughts, and I'm getting tired of it.

A shadow falls on my hand, distracting me from my thoughts, and I jump, almost knocking over my drink.

A gloved hand darts out to steady it.

I look up, up, *up* into the super reflective surface of a pair of shades. "Th-thanks for saving my drink," I stammer, reaching out to settle the cup. "But you didn't have to. It tastes like crap." I tug the cup across the table towards me, stopping just short of pulling it into my half-zipped jacket. I glance back up, taking a good look at the person in front of me. They're taller than me—but *everyone* is, outside of my younger siblings—with black and white braids held back from their narrow face under a headband. I clock the lighter brown skin exposed at the wrists between their sleeves and their gloves, and I realise—

"If this is how Judges go 'undercover,' then I'm surprised you've never been caught before," I say without thinking, narrowing my eyes as I take in the woman before me. The glasses should've given up the game earlier, I realise. The woman in front of me could look like someone that lives in the block if not for the mirrored lenses obscuring her eyes from view—too much like the helmets Judges wear.

"Sit down," I hiss, flapping my hands furiously at the seat in front of me. "Sit down and take the glasses *off*. You could only be more obvious if you'd driven one of those bikes through the doors." The Judge doesn't drop into the seat in front of me, so I slap the palm of my hand against the top of the table. Not *that* hard, but the Judge still jumps a little before sitting. "So, *you're* the one that's going to help me out? You don't look much older than me."

The Judge scowls as she takes her glasses off, revealing dark eyes, narrowed beneath very thick eyebrows. "You're literally a child," she snaps, eyeing me as if she's considering getting up and just leaving me to the consequences of my own actions. "But keep talking... I'm sure that if you bother me hard enough, I'll absolutely help you out with what you need."

The sarcasm in her voice makes me flinch in return, and I stare down at the table, at my drink. I hate how small I feel in this moment. How weak asking for help makes me feel. But I asked this Judge here for a reason, and I will see it through no matter how embarrassed I feel about it. So, I raise my cup to my lips and take a deep sip of the still disgusting drink, using the moment to re-stabilise myself and rethink my approach. We got off to the wrong foot for sure, but that doesn't mean I have to keep wobbling on it.

"I'm Amara," I tell her, managing a smile that quickly falls flat. "You?"

The Judge's mouth purses with a tight frown, and for a second I think she's not going to answer at all. But then she shakes her head and says, "You can call me Clayton."

"Judge Clayton," I test it out loud. "Thank you so much for agreeing to meet with me. I know I didn't give you a lot to work on, and I'm sure it would have been easy to write this off as a prank or even a trap, but this is serious."

"I know," Clayton says in a serious murmur that chills me. "I've seen the videos that your 'friends' have been putting out. I've read the reports of what happened in the other building. I was on your case for a week or so before even *you* knew you had a problem."

That is unexpected. I know that Judges are everywhere and that they see everything, but Del and the others had been so proud of their routines and their ability to hide in plain sight that I had just assumed that Judges were not on their scent yet. I thought I was really doing something by reaching out to the Judges and setting up this meeting.

"So you'll help me?" I ask. "You'll help stop them before they make me hurt someone, right? Before they hurt someone else?" I pause before saying. "They killed—they killed one of their friends for just saying he didn't want to be a part of this. Do you know what they'll do to me for talking to *you?*"

Clayton grimaces at the thought and scrubs one gloved hand over her braids. "We won't let that happen," she promises. "Just tell me where to find them and my team and I'll take care of things."

As I open my mouth to agree, my phone vibrates in my pocket.

Twice.

One is from Bex, and the sight of her username makes me nauseous. The other is from KT.

IBEXuBEX: Come up to the observatory ASAP. We're going through with our plan and we need help with the drones. Don't let us down.

OKayTee: I couldn't hold them off any longer. Good luck. Be careful.

I—

I *freeze.* I stare down at my phone with my mouth half-open and I just can't move. I can't breathe. I can't *think.*

"What's wrong?" Clayton asks, worry clear in her low voice. When I don't answer, she reaches for my phone and reads both messages. "Are these—?"

I nod. "It's them," I mutter. "It's the gang. I don't know if they know about *you*, but they definitely know I'm not interested in being their kind of famous." I want to drop my head down to the tabletop between us, but both my cup and phone are in the way. "They're going to *kill* me."

Clayton winces, but tries to soften the situation. "You don't know that for sure..."

"I promise you," I grit out through clenched teeth, "that they don't actually need my help with the drones, but they're *my* drones and they know I don't want them *broken.* If I don't come, they're gonna know I'm up to *something.*" I squeeze my eyes shut until they sting. "Please. You *have* to help me."

Except she doesn't. We both know that. She can just... leave, and go file a report about our conversation. There's nothing stopping her from simply taking down my information, copying the details on my phone, and going back to wherever Judges go when they don't need to bust some heads. Maybe someone at the Justice Department tails me on the building cameras, maybe a squad turns up later and busts Bex and the rest partway through whatever they're about to do. But if she does that, then I don't know what will happen to *me*.

But Clayton surprises me. Instead of brushing me off or telling me that I don't need to go to the observatory, or that I'll be fine if I do, she looks at me for a moment, and then pulls out her own phone from one of the deep pockets in her jacket. She taps a complicated pattern on the touch screen and then raises it to her face.

"We're going to need backup," she tells whoever picks up on the other side of the line. "And bring my uniform. I think this is going to get messy."

CHAPTER ELEVEN

THE THING IS, I still have to go up to the observatory on my own.

Clayton and her backup—Judges that she knows and has worked with—can't come with me without warning the gang what's coming. So, I have to take the elevator by myself.

It's not technically 'by myself,' because in Timm Block, there are rarely any empty elevators no matter what time it is. I get into the elevator with about a dozen people I don't know. They all live here, obviously. If they didn't, the elevators simply wouldn't let them go above a certain point in the building. They're normal people, boring people, and so they don't look at me, just as hard as I'm not looking at them. By the time we make it to the top floor, the elevator is down by half. Six of us get off the elevator, and I am one of three people that turn to walk towards the observatory.

Every step I take towards the entryway leaves me breathless, anxious, my mind churning through what-ifs. What if Clayton and the other Judges don't come as backup? What if Del and the others launch straight into an attack? What if KT has turned on me and told them about the Judge?

I realise, as I get closer to the observatory, that more and more people are coming back into the corridor from the darkness. Feet away from the entrance, the crowd leaving the observatory becomes a crush. People are running and screaming and shouting as they try to push past each other on the way to the elevators. I hear the hum and whine of my drones' wings, and I realise that whatever Del and the others have planned, they've already started.

I don't bother with excuse-mes as I push my way through the crowd. There's no point. All of my focus, my energy goes to keeping myself upright as the small crowd shove against me in their panic. There's no *time* for politeness. Some of the people running by me have bruises, others have cuts. There's a strange scent in the air that I can't quite place, but it seems as though whatever they did with the drones didn't involve water at all. I frown, hoping that they didn't go with some of their worst options.

By the time I make my way through the doors, the rush has dropped from a relative flood to a trickle. I'm able to press my back flat against the wall next to the door and that's where I stand for the first few minutes, trying to get a look at what's going on around me. I hear that whine again and tilt my head back to see my drones hovering overhead.

Del and the others are not immediately in sight, but I hear a shout coming from my left and look to see KT and Pink struggling over the controls for the big drone.

"That's not how they're supposed to work," KT snarls, his hands gripping the outside of the remote control. "You keep dipping the drones before it's time and raising them way too high up in the air. You're going to get them caught in wires or hit the ceiling. Be *careful.*" I can see them struggle, but Pink doesn't seem angry the way that they would be if they were dealing with me. I hesitate, torn between marching forward and slipping back outside before anyone can see me, so of course that's when I'm noticed.

Bex calls my name. "Amara," she says in a voice louder

than I've heard her use at any point. "You sure took your time getting up here."

I shrug. "Not my fault," I tell her, trying to sound casual and not as if my heart is about to fling itself out of my chest from how hard it's beating. "It was pretty busy downstairs."

There's a sense of discomfort in the air. Gone is the fragile sense of potential friendship between us that had been there just a week ago. In just a day or so, I've gone from a potential friend to a definite enemy and it shows in the way they're all watching me. How they monitor me as I pick my way across the wide empty space separating us.

"I know you've been busy," Zozo spits out, bleached eyebrows drawing together as they grimace at me. It's a judgemental look, a mean look. I don't like it. "How was your talk with your new... *Friend?*"

Oh.

"So, do you think you are the only people in this building that I know?" I ask, before remembering that *yes*, they do know that. I shake my head hard, sending my bangs flying. "She's just someone I met downstairs. It's not a big deal."

Del steps forward, his arms crossed over his chest as he glares at me. "It's a *pretty* big deal if you're out there talking to reporters and telling them our business."

That is not what I expect to hear.

"Excuse me?"

Nova takes point, stomping forward in her super high heels and gesturing at me with the wicked points of her fingernails. "Don't lie to us!" she says, almost shrieking. "We know you were talking to that reporter woman downstairs. We know you have no intention of joining us properly or of actually earning your place in our group." She looks sullen, like my little sisters when someone tells them they can't have an extra treat after dinner. "I backed Del up when it came to you, you know," she says. "I helped get you into this group. And this is how you repay us? By talking to a *reporter?*"

I don't know what's worse in their books: talking to

a reporter, which I didn't do, or talking to a Judge who is currently on her way upstairs with backup. But I'm not going to volunteer any information to them. I shrug my shoulders and then tell the group: "I wasn't talking to anyone that you need to be concerned about." I use a snotty tone on purpose, the kind of voice that annoys both my parents and siblings in one easy move.

It works just like I want it to.

Del's face gets all pink and splotchy with his anger and he actually takes a step forward towards me, uncrossing his arms as his fingers clench into fists. "Were you talking to a reporter or not?" he says in a low deadly voice. "And *think* about how you want to respond to us."

I snort, because... really? "You know that you're not my parent, right?" I spit the words out through a grin that feels painful, manic on my cheeks. I should be afraid, and I am, but I can't get over Del talking to me like he's twice my age. I can't get over the fact that he's *scolding me*. "I'll talk to you how I want. You're literally not the boss of me." I see him opening his mouth as if to yell at me some more, and I cut him off. "She wasn't a reporter. Are you happy?"

Overhead, the drones dip and buzz as KT and Pink continue to bicker over the remote control. I glance upward and spot the red 'live' lights on both drones.

"A-are you *streaming* this?"

Tay scoffs at me, so condescendingly obnoxious it makes my *teeth* itch. "Of course we are," they say. "Unlike you, we have a job to do, and we like to make sure our audience is satisfied." They gesture at the observatory with a wide, nearly unhinged smile. "Sure, it's not what we'd planned to do, to introduce you on our channel properly. But... you did say you wanted to be famous."

"*This* isn't what I want," I tell the group, waving my arms around wildly. "*This* isn't real fame. No one knows your name. They just know the bad things that you do."

"And all they're going to know about you is what you look

like when you die, live on their screens," Tay says, still smiling. "You were a loser when Del came across your channel, and you're going to die a loser. How does *that* feel?"

"Honestly?" I launch myself forward without thinking about what I'm even doing, slamming my fist into Tay's smug face with every single ounce of strength in my body. It's not the smartest choice I can make, but... it's a satisfying one. I keep hitting Tay as I ride their body down to the artificial grass underneath our feet. They grab at me, trying to fight back, but I have one thing on my side that they don't: a lifetime of fighting with my little siblings.

The scrape of nails against my forearms stings and when I glance down at them, there are raised red lines across my brown skin, but nothing can dampen the satisfaction of watching Tay's eyes (one blackening around the edges) widen with fear as I pummel them.

It takes two people to drag me off Tay: Bex and Zozo. Zozo loops their long, dark blue arms around my waist and hauls me backwards. The dye must be fresh, because my struggles smear the colour over my skin, and Zozo curses in my ear as I claw at them.

"St-stop fighting us, *grife*," Bex snaps as she grabs at my hands and wrenches them away from the blood and dye. Bex is stronger than she looks, and, with her help, she and Zozo manage to fling me to the ground a few feet away from the rest of the group.

The rough landing makes me cough and pain jolts up from my hip where I'd hit it.

"I thought you wanted to put on a show for the cameras," I snap, mind racing as I scramble to my feet so I'm not flat on my back in front of the gang. I have no idea where Clayton and her backup is, but I know I don't have much time before they realise that there are seven of them—six, if KT hasn't betrayed me—and only one of *me*.

We're so busy staring at each other, that I almost miss when Pink tries to take a step forward to join the cluster of people surrounding me... but KT stops them with a firm shake of the head and one big hand held to the shorter boy's chest. None of the others see it, they're looking in the wrong direction for *that*, but... now it's five against one.

"I don't believe you about the reporter," Del says in a loud voice that rings through the too-tense silence. "Maybe I'll take it easy on you if you tell me what you told her." He gestures at me with his palms turned outward as if trying to gently urge me to confessing the sins I've committed. "Is this really how you want to go out?"

Shaking my head, I say, "I don't want any of this. And I didn't talk to a reporter." I take a small step backwards, mentally trying to judge the distance between where I am and the still-open doors to the hallway outside. I contemplate running for a second, but where would I even run *to?* They know who my parents are, where we live, *that I have little siblings*. Running would do more damage to them than anyone else.

I'm gonna have to stand my ground.

"If you want to know what I told my friend—if I told her anything about *you*," I say through gritted teeth. "You're going to have to beat it out of me." I want to take the words back the second they're out of my mouth, especially when Tay gets to their feet and pulls a blade out of their back pocket, but the look in their eyes tells me that was never an option.

"If that's how it has to be, Amara," Del says, shrugging. He waves at the rest of the gang around him, urging them on as the drones, on an auto routine, circle us overhead. "Make her talk."

It's chaos from that moment on. We go down in a tangle of arms and legs. I manage to hit Tay in their other eye, before Bex grabs my arm and wrestles it down to the ground. I'm fighting and clawing at every inch of skin that I can because I refuse to go out without a fight. I also refuse to talk. I keep my mouth closed unless I'm biting someone and that works, until I am reminded of the knife and Tay's hand.

The pain slides into my *chest,* and it's so deep that I can't breathe, I can't move. All I can do is flop backwards on the ground, my mouth open, my eyes wide. Pain short-circuits my senses and my vision starts to go black around the edges before it fades out—

Entirely.

CHAPTER TWELVE

The strangest part of waking up, I think, is the fact that I didn't expect I'd ever open my eyes again. I jerk upward, sucking in deep gasps of air that burn my lungs. My hands scrabble across grass and across fabric until I feel another hand grip mine. This hand is gloved, and strong, and I know without tilting my head backwards that the person holding it has to be a Judge.

"I see I got here just in time," Clayton says with a smile on her face. It's the only visible part of her face, her pleased smile, thanks to her helmet. She's dressed in the full Judge uniform, and where she should look unapproachable and even menacing, all I can think of is *finally, I don't have to do this any more*. Because if the Judges are here, that means I don't need to be.

Struggling to sit up despite the pain in my chest and the way that I can feel blood tacky and warm along my side leaves me breathless. I look around the room, unsure what I was expecting... or what I'm seeing. The observatory is a mess.

The gang, or what's left of it, is fighting a squad of Judges, and losing. It's messy, violent, like they're fighting for their lives, which I guess they may be. I don't know how long I've been unconscious, beyond the way that the blood is sticky on my skin, but I can't imagine too much time has passed because I'm still alive and so is everyone else.

I watch, mouth dropping open in awe as a tall, broad-shouldered Judge wrestles Del to the ground and cuffs his long arms behind his back. Nova is already out of the running, laying down on her side with her hands cuffed in front of her. Her face is a mess, make-up streaming everywhere, and her eyes are red. "Let me go," she shouts, trying to jerk her wrists free of the cuffs. "I didn't *do* anything *wrong*."

Everyone ignores her, their attention fixed on the actual *pile* of Judges on top of Tay and Bex. I recognise the shade of the flailing limbs and the sound of the swearing ("Let me fucking *go*" in Tay's unfortunately familiar voice overlaying Bex's panicked cries). They're fighting the Judges trying to cuff them, something that I don't recommend, and it's clear that they managed to do *some* damage while I was unconscious. At least one of the Judges has lost his helmet, and I see a bruise streaking its way across one sharp cheek.

"Clayton," the man shouts at the top of his lungs. "How's the kid?"

Before I can retort that I'm *not* a kid, Clayton shouts over me. "I got the bleeding to stop and she's conscious. She should be fine, don't worry about us!"

Personally, I think it's still a good time to worry about *us*, because not all of the gang is cuffed. I suck in a deep anxious breath when Pink actually manages to kick a Judge off him and make a run for it, but he's tackled again pretty quickly. I then wince at the pain jolting through my body, clutching at my side in response.

"What—when did you *get here?*" I say, the words forced out through the ache in my chest. It hurts so much. Every single breath I drag in is a chore and a punishment at the same time. "Because it sure feels like you took your time."

Clayton laughs. "We were almost too late," she tells me. "We'd hacked your drones easily—and you should really fix that—and were monitoring the situation when that one"—she pauses to gesture at where Tay is *still fighting*—"when they stabbed you. We actually thought you were dead when we stormed the room. Judge Reyes had me peel off from the chaos and check on you and I skin-sprayed you before you could bleed out. You're not out of the woods yet, kid, the Med-Judges are on their way."

"Oh," I say, feeling my head spin. "I-I almost *died?*"

Clayton nods once and then catches herself, shaking her head. "You were fine," she says, backpedaling like she didn't just scare me. "You'll *be* fine. It wasn't major blood loss and you're *clearly* talking to us." I can't see her eyes to judge her expression properly, but the shape of her smile is clearly a grimace. "Which is good. Considering some of the videos your friends made… We're glad we got to you in time."

Out of everything I've been through, *this* is what breaks me: Clayton's gentle voice, the weight of her hand on mine. I start crying before I even realise the tears are coming from me. Sucking in great big painful gasps of air despite myself, despite the pain. And I can't stop blubbering, no matter how hard I try and no matter how much it hurts.

"I didn't want this," I tell Clayton, willing her to believe me. "I didn't want to hurt people. I didn't want to help them hurt people.

"I just wanted to be famous. Why is that so bad?"

EPILOGUE

KT DOESN'T KNOW what to expect when Judge Reyes ushers him into a computer lab dimly lit by banks of monitors after picking him up from the holding cube he'd been in for the better part of a month. There's an analyst in front of each one, hunched over their keyboards with their gaze fixed on the different files flitting across their screens. None of them look up as Reyes leads him through the maze of computers to a small room at the very back and pushes him through the door.

The small room is a mess. There are computer parts everywhere and monitors bolted into the walls behind a cramped desk. Each monitor shows something different. Some show crimes in progress, others show files cycling across a screen. A few show video footage of citizens just... minding their business in their homes, or in the public areas of different blocks. The weak light from the monitor bank shines down on a tiny woman with warm gold skin and a sleek dark purple bob with bangs that brush the top of her thick-rimmed glasses.

"KT, let me introduce you to Judge Miller, Interim Head of Tek-Div's Public Surveillance Unit," Reyes says. "Judge Miller, let me introduce you to your newest grunt."

"*What?*" KT spits out, staring at Reyes with his eyes opened almost painfully wide. "I'm her *what?*"

Reyes crosses his arms over his broad chest, looking unbothered. "It's either this or a ten-stretch in a cube like the rest of your little friends," he says. "Out of your group, you're the best fit for this kind of rehabilitation, and besides... Recently, it's been suggested to me that the Department needs young minds and fresh perspectives."

KT *is* young, but—

"But what about Amara?" KT asks. "*She* was the one who wanted this recognition. She's the one who wanted all of *this*."

Reyes's nose wrinkles with a faint frown. "We asked *her* nicely, but she said she had other plans."

THE VIEWTUBE VIDEO is titled *Justice Department FASCISTS crack down on kids playing pranks*. It's a shaky video recorded on a phone from behind a plastic bush that shows a chaotic scene where Judges tackle and arrest a group of teenagers that seem to be fighting for their lives.

Its summary reads, *Judges shouldn't be allowed to go overboard on residents. If there's a better way to stop crime, they haven't found it yet*, and at last check, it has over twenty thousand views.

In the sea of comments, one back-and-forth stands out:

Anonymous: This is a good video, but if you're going to post stuff like this you need to cover your tracks a *lot* better - I can show you how.

unc1v1Lfru1t: Screw you, I don't need your help!!

Anonymous: *sighs* I see kids like you all the time, Aaron Johnson of 2253 Timm Block. You *all* need help. The Judges can find you easy as breathing.

unc1v1Lfru1t: WTF delete that! Who the hell are you?

Anonymous: Me? I'm no one. Just someone who used to want to be famous like you.

The Mega-City Times
March 15, 2057

Brazilian president Francisco Oliveira has become the latest leader of the global south to speak out against the growing power of the Judges in the United States. He follows Indian Prime Minster Kiara Kapoor, who published a scathing criticism of recent choices made both in the Justice Department and across the United States government. Headlines around the world, in countries both hostile and friendly to the US, are calling the movement an "Anti-American Alliance," and President Chambers is facing bipartisan pressure to respond to the growing crisis.

In a statement provided to the *Times*, President Chambers announces that she will be reaching out to the other heads of state who have criticised policy decisions in recent months. Sources in the White House suggest she's discussing a possible peace summit later this year or in early 2058.

Senator Harvisson (I-OK) added his own fuel to the flames stoked against President Chambers. "If the President isn't confident that she can get the job done, she should just get out of the way," Harvisson said to an audience of supporters earlier this week. He went on to add that, "The developing crisis is symptomatic of the failures of both major parties. Someone has to step up to the plate and take control of the crisis before it blows up." The speech will add further weight to speculation that Harvisson is planning a run for the White House in 2060.

With Harvisson's comments, all eyes are fixed firmly on President Chambers as we await her responses to both President Olivera and Senator Harvisson.

This article will be updated when we receive a response from the President's team.

ABOUT THE AUTHOR

Back when they were a child, **Zina Hutton** once jumped out of a window to escape dance class in the Virgin Islands. Now they're an author who tends to leap headfirst into new stories and topics the second that inspiration strikes. Zina lives in hot and humid South Florida where they're never far away from a notebook and/or an iguana. Zina currently works as a freelance editor and writer with publication credits in *Teen Vogue*, *Fireside Fiction*, *The Mary Sue*, *Strange Horizons*, *ComicsAlliance*, *Polygon* and *The Verge*. You can find the majority of their work at their digital arts and culture publication *Stitch's Media Mix* and on Twitter as @stitchmediamix.

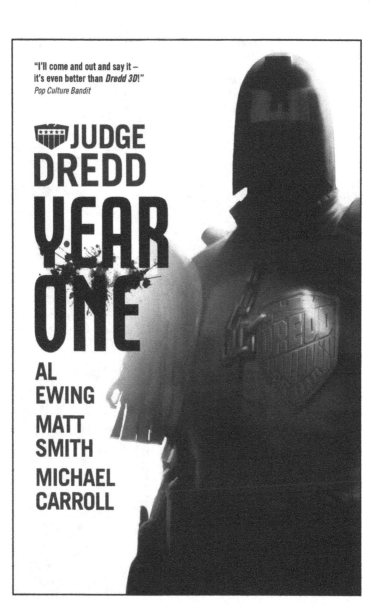

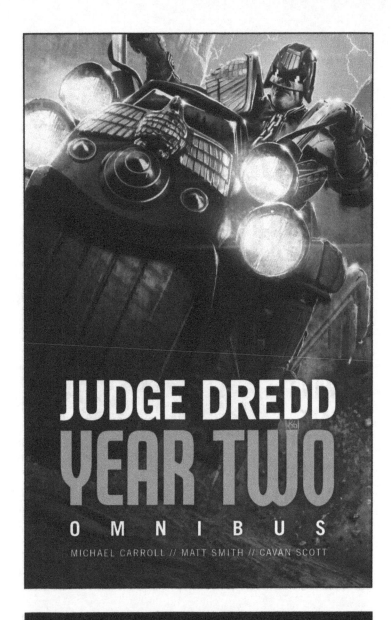

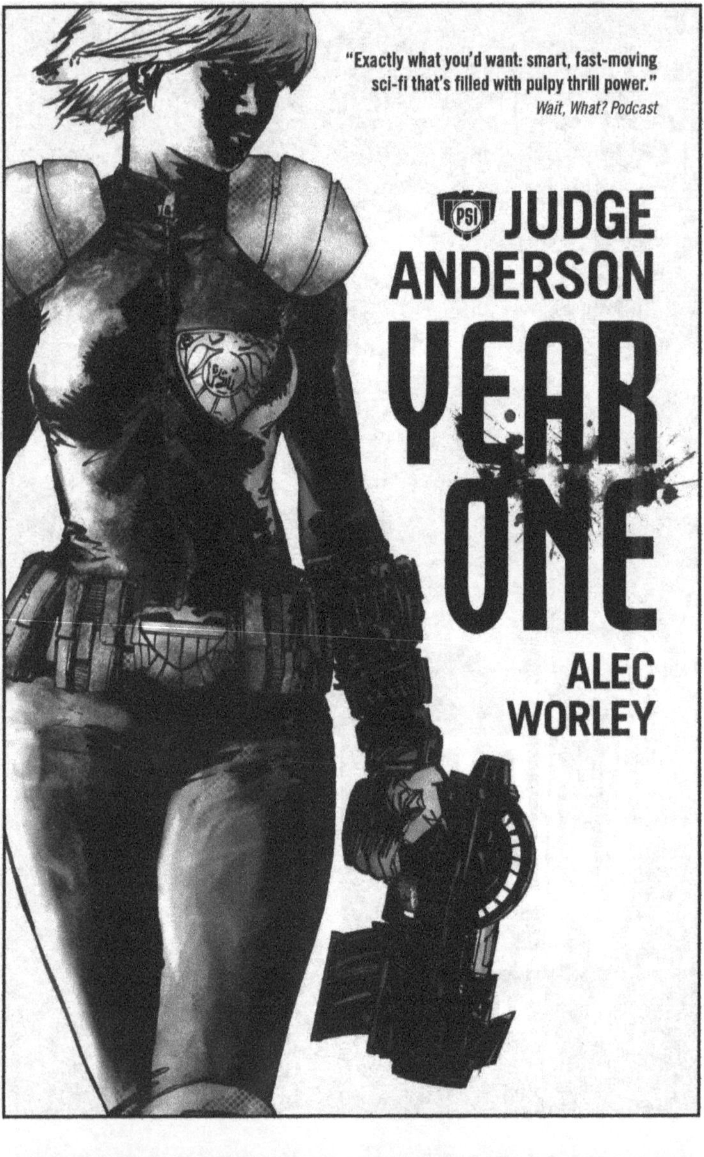

"Exactly what you'd want: smart, fast-moving sci-fi that's filled with pulpy thrill power."
Wait, What? Podcast
PSI
JUDGE ANDERSON
YEAR ONE
ALEC WORLEY

JUDGE FEAR'S
BIG DAY
OUT
AND OTHER
STORIES
FEATURING
STORIES BY
ALAN GRANT
CAVAN SCOTT
GORDON RENNIE
SIMON SPURRIER
AND MANY OTHERS
EDITED BY MICHAEL CARROLL

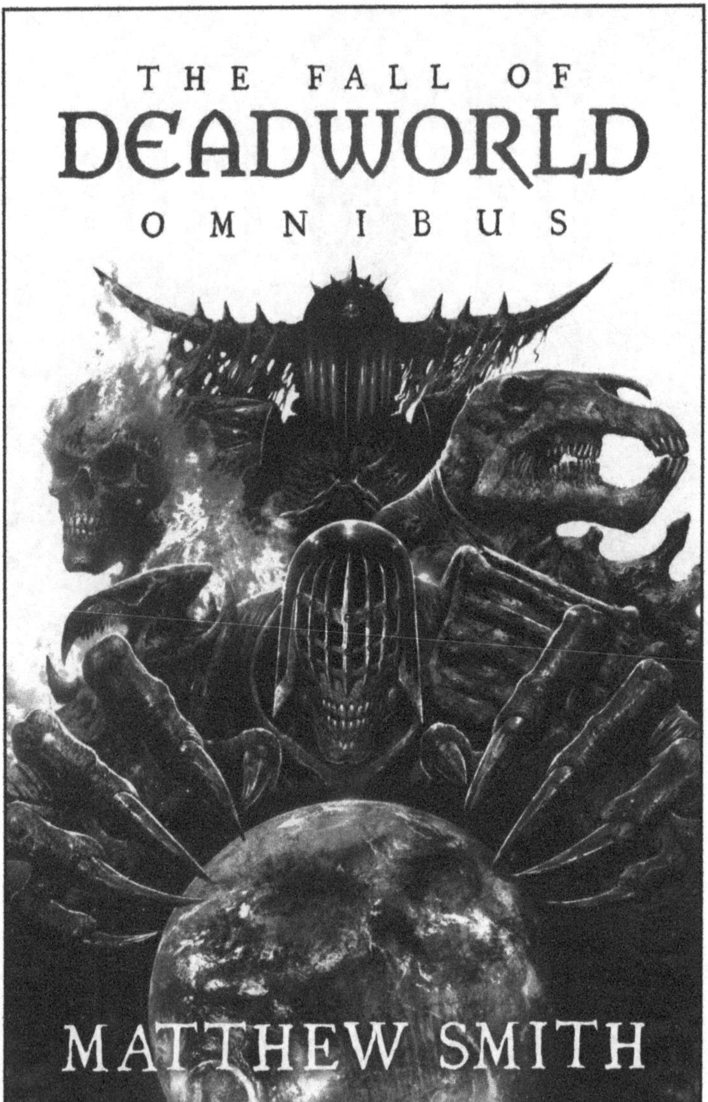
THE FALL OF
DEADWORLD
OMNIBUS
MATTHEW SMITH